TESLA AND THE PYRAMID

TESLA
AND THE
PYRAMID
A TECHNO-THRILLER NOVEL

JENNER BROWN

monolith

This book is a work of fiction. Any references to historical events, real organizations, real places, or real people, living or dead, are used fictitiously. Other names, characters, places, and events are products of the author's imagination and are used fictitiously. Any resemblance to actual events, places, organizations, or persons, living or dead, is entirely coincidental.

Copyright © 2024 by Jenner Brown. All rights reserved.
First Edition: 2024. Published by Monolith.

Cover image: Cassiopeia A by NASA, ESA, CSA, STScI, Danny Milisavljevic (Purdue University), Ilse De Looze (UGent), Tea Temim (Princeton University)

No part of this book may be reproduced in any form or by any electronic or mechanical means, including information storage and retrieval systems, without written permission from the author, except for the use of brief quotations in a book review.

Trade Paperback ISBN: 979-8-9913744-3-9
Hardcover ISBN: 979-8-9913744-4-6
eBook ISBN: 979-8-9913744-2-2
Library of Congress Cataloging-in-Publication Data has been applied for.
0 2 4 6 8 1 3 5 7 9

Sir Isaac Newton observes light's spectrum of energy, frequency, and electromagnetic vibration.

When Einstein was asked how it felt
to be the smartest man alive, he replied,
"I don't know, you'll have to ask Nikola Tesla."

FACT:

When Nikola Tesla died, US intelligence agents seized two truckloads of controversial research from his New York City residence.

John G. Trump—an MIT physicist and uncle of the president—led the review of Tesla's discoveries. All the government disclosed was that Tesla's last works were esoteric and speculative. What they saw remains heavily classified.

Tesla reportedly kept a black notebook containing his final invention—his Ninth Symphony.

It has never been found.

FACT:

All locations, archaeology, mythology, symbols, and speculative scalar physics are accurate and real.

All organizations depicted exist and are based on real groups, although some names and circumstances have been changed.

PART I
TESLA

1

Times Square, New York
Professor Tony Koviak

"WHAT DO you know about Nikola Tesla?"

Is this some prank?

I don't know a thing about Nikola Tesla, only something vague about electricity and cars. Why would analysts at the CIA need to speak with a professor of ancient anthropology about an inventor from the Gilded Age?

It's like asking a chef about string theory.

Times Square is a zoo this morning. I usually avoid it at all costs. But here I am, weaving and dodging through mangy Elmos and breakdancing Minions, trying not to get swallowed by packs of tourists.

I swear, this place is designed to induce sensory overload. Hawkers are out in force. I wriggle through them with matador spins because—get this—I'm meeting with the CIA *in five minutes*.

About Nikola Tesla.

The rain has left the sidewalks shiny, and flashing billboards reflect off them like a cyberpunk fever dream. I glance up at a psychedelic ad—

Aaand I almost slam into a half-naked cowgirl playing guitar.

Ah, Times Square, never change. Actually, please do.

Meeting with the CIA is bad enough, but the most important flight of my life leaves JFK airport in four hours. I need to hustle.

"Professor Tony Koviak? What do you know about Nikola Tesla?"

The bizarre call came twenty minutes ago out of nowhere. I'm not exactly the go-to guy for science questions. Sure, ask me about the Eleusinian Mysteries of Ancient Greece or Predynastic Egypt.

History dorks like me don't have secret brunches with spy agencies. At thirty-two, I'm just a lowly associate professor of anthropology at Columbia University, a few blocks up Broadway. There must be dozens of Ivy Leaguers better qualified. *So, why me?*

I check the time and start to jog.

March winds are picking up, so I flip up the collar of my expedition jacket and shove my hands into warm pockets.

I'm leaving New York for good today. I'll miss it. I'll miss the earnest students, the lecture halls, and Joe's Pizza—come on. A French grad student once told me that "in the New York, anything is the possible."

Infinite possibilities, except when the CIA summons you on your way to catch a flight to Istanbul.

Yeah, I'm swapping bagels for baklava because I've been selected to do excavations at the most important archaeological site in the world, a little charmer in Turkey called Göbekli Tepe.

My former headmaster at Cambridge recommended me for the prestigious gig. I think he wants to see if an American will screw it up. Spoiler: I'm not planning to. It's a huge break for my career.

If I make my flight.

Gotta move faster.

I tried telling the CIA guy I didn't have time, but he was … persuasive.

"Professor Koviak, you'll wanna see this," the Mafia voice said—definitely a smoker. Probably Italian.

His thirty-second explanation implied my career was over. It spooked me, okay? Do I have a choice? It's the CIA, for crying out loud.

"Café Un Deux Trois, Theater District, you know it?" he had asked.

And like an idiot, I'm curious.

Now, crossing the glittering technothrob of America's Square, I picture my packed bags sitting in my empty apartment. I pull up my mobile boarding pass, doing the departure math again. I can make this.

Alright, Tesla. This better be quick.

2

NSA Utah Data Center
Director of Operations

ALL HELL HAS BROKEN loose at the NSA.

The director of operations stands in the firestorm, his prickly demeanor ratcheting up as his eyes sweep the control room.

"Lock down all external access points," he orders. "I don't care who's requesting clearance, shut it down."

What is going on at the damn CIA? he thinks, resisting the urge to start beating people.

To privacy advocates, the Utah Data Center is the scariest building on Earth. Built in 2014 at a cost of billions, it handles zettabytes of information—surveillance on every phone call, text, and internet search worldwide. The equivalent of one Library of Congress processed every ten seconds.

Its data archive is mythic.

The director leans over a technician's screen, and his face tightens. He moves to another station, lashing out at bewildered staffers.

"Incoming transmission ... from Prague!" a comms tech shouts.

"Prague?" the director wrinkles his nose. "On-screen."

A video feed fills the central monitor, showing a dim palace stateroom. A shadowy female figure is set back from the camera.

He mutters under his breath, "Who the hell is this?" His voice rises. "We're in the middle of a crisis here—"

"Status report." A stern American woman demands, whispering to someone in the darkness off-screen.

I don't have time for opportunistic politicians, he thinks.

He squints at her silhouette. "And you are?"

She steps into the light. Her tone is that of a monarch about to roll heads. "Your commander in chief. Report."

A hush falls over the data center. The only sound is chirping technology.

Perfect. The president is involved.

A flustered security specialist with a ruddy complexion steps forward. "Madam President, at 0146 hours, our IDS flagged an anomaly. The attack originated within the CIA. They bypassed all cybersecurity protocols and accessed sensitive compartmented information. The breach was surgical, cutting multiple firewalls."

"What were they after?"

"Highly classified files in Deep Sector Alpha-Six, ma'am. Among our oldest and highest-security archives, including an array of archaeogeologic projects. No one here seems aware this sector even existed. It's a ghost archive."

The president's eyes flick to someone off-screen. She asks softly, almost rattled, "Surveillance footage?"

"Erased, ma'am," the security chief replies, lifting his wounded chin defiantly. "We've been on the horn with Langley all morning. Whoever did this knew our systems inside and out."

"You did say archaeogeologic?" She's almost breathless.

"Yes, ma'am."

Analysts look on uneasily as the president leans on the desk, sinking into thought.

The director steps forward. "I'll contact FBI, give them—"

"No," she interrupts sharply, straightening up. "Standby for further instruction." She makes a throat-slashing motion to her aide to kill the stream.

There's urgent conversation in the shadows in the brief delay before her feed cuts out. The president is agitated, yelling orders to someone. "Clear my schedule. No, I don't want NASA. Get me the Smithsonian—"

3

Café Un Deux Trois, Times Square
Tony Koviak

THE CAFÉ IS BUSTLING. I scan the crowd, but no one fits my image of a CIA agent. I settle by the window and watch the door.

The aroma of cappuccinos and baked goods fills the air, and the hiss of espresso machines blends with muted conversations. It's usually soothing, but my fingers tap anxiously. I don't know why it's *Flight of the Bumblebee*.

At least my apartment near Bryant Park is a quick cab ride away. I chose it because of its proximity to the New York Public Library, which is much cozier than Columbia's reading room.

Oh, crap ... did I lose my passport? My heart does a jig. I pat my jacket pocket. Phew, there it is. I glance at the mug shot: hazel eyes, square jaw, dimpled chin, gentleman's haircut. Same old me. Maybe a bit less idealistic these days.

Wallet? Check. I slide out a photo of my dad, a prominent Egyptologist. He gave it to me shortly before he died. It shows him in his office, rugged like Hemingway, a picture of an Egyptian site on the wall behind him.

He would've loved my new job.

I flip over the photo to the message he scribbled on the back: a hand-drawn model of the solar system with the number 33:27. It's a timestamp referencing his favorite classical music section from *The Planets* suite by Gustav Holst.

A solar system ... because we were two academics who shared a love of ancient cosmology.

"Can't go wrong with the music of the spheres, son," he told me, referring to the ideas of Pythagoras and Plato.

I tuck it away and check the time. Words can't express how much I don't want to miss my flight. Big team meeting tomorrow—not great to be the guy who fought for grants for two years and then flakes out.

I weigh my options. The CIA wouldn't track me down if it weren't important. But can I risk missing my flight? No. That's it, I've waited long enough. I stand to leave.

"Professor Tony Koviak?" A gravelly smoker's voice is behind me.

I turn and see an odd pair.

The man's Jersey accent is real Sopranos tier. "I'm Agent Frank Vergazza; this is Agent Andromeda Dey, with the CIA. You're not in any trouble. There's been an unfortunate incident, and we're hoping you can help us locate something."

My nerves jangle. These two don't look like any spies I've seen in movies.

Agent Vergazza looks like an aging mafioso with a shock of jet-black hair slicked back, graying wing tips, a gold chain under an unbuttoned shirt, and pleated slacks. His tired eyes are bambino-brown. He's like a crime boss dressed for a road trip to see Dean Martin play in Vegas. I wonder if there's a Cadillac outside.

Then there's Agent Andromeda Dey. Late twenties, a storm of reddish hair, tall, disinterested. She's all freckled cheekbones and cat-like blue eyes that watch me like she'd rather be anywhere else. She looks ... well, not like a fed. Boots, old army/navy store military jacket. No Scully-pantsuit business here. She's more grad-student-on-a-hiking-trip than secret service.

A crystal gemstone necklace hangs around her neck, and I'm getting major hippie vibes.

I compose myself. "What can I do for you, Agent Vergazza?"

"Call me Frank. We know you're leaving for Göbekli Tepe. Why's it so special?"

It's odd being asked a question they could've looked up on Wikipedia. I give them the quick and dirty.

"Well, it's seven thousand years *older* than Stonehenge, pushing civilization back to the Ice Age. Historians are annoyed because it shouldn't exist."

"Why?" Frank asks.

"Because we thought only hunter-gatherers existed then. Turns out they were building massive celestial calendars when they weren't riding around on saber-tooths. Only five percent is excavated. Lots of mysteries." I glance at my watch. "How can I help you?"

"Yeah, we know your flight leaves soon." Frank is scanning the crowded café. "Let's chat somewhere more private."

My calm exterior cracks. "I don't have time to—"

"There's more to Göbekli Tepe than you can imagine, Professor," Frank says. "You wanna know what it really is?"

Well, shoot. I didn't see that coming. Now I'm intrigued. Curse my insatiable curiosity; it's what got me into anthropology in the first place.

4

Times Square is a current of electricity as we step into the morning flow. I don't have time for this, but now I kind of want to hear what they have to say. We walk fast, moving through snippets of a thousand conversations. A military helicopter hovers high above, its rotors thumping like a distant drumbeat.

"Why do you need *me*?" I say, my voice barely a ripple in the crush.

Agent Frank Vergazza's eyes flick between me and our surroundings. He's hunting.

I follow the two agents down Forty-fifth Street. The neon glare of Times Square fades behind us, giving way to a gritty stretch of bodegas and worn-out storefronts. I'm starting to think this might've been a huge mistake.

What the hell am I doing?

Frank scans each doorway, but they're all locked or packed with people. Finally, he stops in front of a grand building adorned with Greek columns—the Lyceum Theatre—Broadway's oldest-running theater. Its classical elegance stands in stark contrast to the urban decay around it.

Lyceum—the name conjures Ancient Greece. I know the history well; I teach about it at Columbia. In 335BC, after Plato died, Aristotle renamed Plato's Academy the Lyceum. It was the center of all knowledge in Athens.

"This'll have to do." Frank sounds irritated.

He gestures for me to step into the empty lobby of the Lyceum. The interior is adorned with Beaux Arts flourishes and winding staircases. Big wooden doors lead to the auditorium, crowned with a grand *L* as if leading to Versailles.

A young woman with a shaved head sits in a box office window. She looks up and then returns to her phone.

Am I about to get whacked? I'm pretty sure I don't owe money to any underworld bosses.

"All right," I mutter. "Why are we in a Broadway theater?"

The agents glance at each other, and I catch a hint of uncertainty.

"You familiar with this?" Frank reaches into his leather satchel and pulls out a thick binder labeled PROJECT NEPHILIM.

A dark jolt sweeps through me. The Nephilim are the primordial beings of myth from the Book of Genesis, the most mysterious figures in the Bible.

"Can't say that I am," I reply.

Frank's eyes seem disappointed. "This is highly classified research done by United States intelligence agencies, above top secret. They've been working on this for over a century."

"The CIA is doing ancient research?" I ask, glancing at the exit. It's best to be polite with mob boss spies holding classified binders. "Let me guess ... you've got a warehouse full of Ark of the Covenant crates."

Frank grunts appreciation for the joke and pats his satchel. "Better. We got a dozen hard drives, kid. This binder's just a taste."

"How do I fit into this?"

He flashes a sly smile. "Your lucky day. We need an academic chaperone, and you're our guy." He coughs into his fist, pounding his chest.

Wait, are the top secret hard drives in his man bag? Here? Totally normal. "I don't understand. Are you saying the US government has been researching human origins?"

Frank turns to his junior partner. "Is he even listening? History is a lie, Professor. *Capisce?*"

"History is a lie?" *Oh. Wow.*

"Yeah. It ain't right, kid."

"*History?*" I chuckle.

"What Vergazza means," Agent Andromeda Dey drawls hoarsely, "is the history *you* know is wrong."

I let out a skeptical laugh. "The history *I* know? Well, there goes my tenure."

Impatience flashes across Frank's face. He's tapping his foot, eyes darting to the box office girl, then around the lobby. Did he just check for cameras?

"You said this was about Nikola Tesla," I remind them.

"Tesla's at the core of Project Nephilim," Frank replies. "Old-timers at the agency think he was the whole point." He narrows his eyes. "What do you know about Atlantis?"

Oh no. You've gotta be kidding.

I can't help the incredulous smile. "Just an allegory Plato made up in Athens to warn about societal decay. It's philosophy, Agent Vergazza—a bedtime story."

His face is smug, like Robert De Niro's. He looks at Andromeda. "Bedtime story."

"I prefer 'creative myth-making.' What do *you* know about Atlantis?" I counter, wondering if this is some influencer publicity stunt. Social media is swarming with crazy history uncles. Next, he'll claim pyramids are interdimensional portals.

Why does the tall one with excellent bone structure keep checking the entrance? She's practically strangling the strap of the little embroidered flower pouch slung over her shoulder. Something's off.

My phone buzzes. A text alert. Flight's on schedule. I need to wrap this up.

"Look, I have to go." I step to leave, and Frank grabs my arm. His grip digs into my biceps.

I meet his intense stare. "I don't know what you're playing at, but if you want to intimidate me, you should've sent Navy SEALs."

"Is everything all right?" The girl calls from the box office, eyes now fixed on us.

Frank replies to her, never breaking eye contact. "We're fine. Just checking showtimes." He releases my arm, his tone reassuring. "Please. We don't got much time."

Good—*neither do I!*

I smooth my jacket, weighing my options. I could make a run for it, but now I'm curious again.

"You really wanna see this," the female 007 says with a lazy smile.

I half turn to her. I've forgotten her name. "Agent ...?"

"Dey." Her big sapphire eyes are amused. "Andromeda works."

"Andromeda." I take a breath. Hell of a name. Yeah, she's definitely a New Age type. "Okay, I'll bite. What Earth-shattering revelations does the CIA have about Atlantis? Did you find it on Google Maps?"

She's unfazed. "You wanna see this because what's on those hard drives will make your career obsolete, and those people at Cambridge didn't tell you everything about this world."

I'm unprepared for that.

What's going on here? Atlantis ... Nephilim ... Tesla ... secret research—what is this? If it's a prank, someone's done their homework.

"Show him the Tesla doc," Frank mumbles like the Godfather. "We don't have time for academy bozos."

Andromeda sweeps her folk-rock mane behind both ears, and now she's going into her jacket with a wry grin that makes her freckled cheekbones pop so big they almost look swollen. She's enjoying my torment.

"This is the last known work of Nikola Tesla," she says, unfolding a worn piece of paper. "Dated the day before he died in 1943."

She hands me the fragile document. I check to see if she's serious, then peer down in the soft light. My breath catches.

"Tesla made *this*?"

5

Café Un Deux Trois, Times Square

"Yeah, I saw them," the upbeat barista says, pointing to the café's front windows.

She squints at the photographs. "Those two were talking with a cute academic guy. They seemed in a rush—left without ordering." She wipes her hands on her apron. "Can I get you gentlemen something? We have a fantastic Crêpe Normande."

The CIA agent leans forward with an unpleasant scowl, badge raised, voice cold and monotone. "Did they say where they were going?"

The barista's nose wrinkles with an impish smile as the milk steamer hisses over her words. "Why would they tell me where they're going? I make cappuccinos!" She twirls away from the grumpy agents, grabs a tray of omelettes au choix, heads for a table, and calls back, "They're good!"

The agent bites his teeth at her as his partner speaks into a hidden earpiece, "Confirmed sighting in Times Square twenty minutes ago."

6

Lyceum Theatre, Broadway
Tony Koviak

I HOLD the fragile Tesla page in my hand, my mind crackling with wonder at the symbols scattered across it. They look like random, ancient daydreams.

"You're holding one of the most disruptive documents in US history," Frank says.

Oh, great. No pressure.

Now I see why they came to an anthropologist and not an electrician. It's covered with archaic iconography.

Frank continues. "Nikola Tesla laid out his final invention in a small black notebook before he died. It's said to be a real banger—his Ninth Symphony—some superweapon. Tesla hid his notebook, and it's never been found. It's the holy grail in intelligence circles."

Andromeda watches me closely. "The government would hand back the Louisiana Purchase to get what's in that notebook," she says.

Frank lowers his voice, fingers brushing under his chin. "This document is the key to its location. Uncle Sam hasn't cracked it in eighty years. We're hoping you can."

So I'm supposed to decode an esoteric daydream that's stumped the entire government since World War Two?

A striking diagram in the center of the page makes my blood flow. Years ago, a mentor at Cambridge showed me something similar—a sketch of Planet Earth with the Great Pyramid of Egypt superimposed.

"This is interesting," I say, trying to keep my voice steady. "This diagram shows a peculiar fact about the Great Pyramid of Giza. Its dimensions are a scale model of Earth."

"How so?" Andromeda leans in, her eyes scrutinizing the page. "Any object is a scale model of Earth at some ratio. A basketball, this theater ... my ex-boyfriend."

A hippie with a shrewd mind.

"Yes, but unlike your ex, the pyramid does something rather ingenious. Its ratio to Earth is precisely 1 to 43,200."

She looks blank.

I sigh. "Precession of the equinoxes—" I begin and immediately regret it. It's like explaining quantum physics to my childhood cat, Cleocatra.

I baby step to the exit, deciding to simplify. "It's a precessional number. The pyramid encodes the number of years it takes Earth's wobble to complete one full revolution."

Frank clears his meaty throat. "Wobble?"

"Okay," I say, checking the time with mild panic. "Earth's axis is tipped over and wobbles like a spinning top, causing the precession of the equinoxes."

I covered precession in my thesis at Cambridge. Plato's great "Platonic Year" is when celestial bodies return to their original positions in a cosmic cycle. Fun fact: Polaris wasn't always the North Star. It was Vega in the Ice Age, during the Age of Leo.

"The pyramid builders knew Earth's size?" Frank asks, scratching his stubble.

"Yes. And how long it takes to wobble on its axis. The wobble also explains the zodiacal ages, how the sun moves through a ring of constellations, spending 2,160 years in each 'age.' We're now entering the Age of Aquarius, you know, like the song says."

The Great Pyramid also solves the tricky math of "squaring the circle" by projecting the geometry into three dimensions. I'm not sailing down that rabbit hole in a Broadway theater with my flight departing.

It's surreal, though—why would Nikola Tesla doodle obscure pyramid facts in his final message?

Andromeda is delighted, like I just shared her horoscope. "You're talking about astrology," she says.

"No, I'm talking about very ancient cosmology."

Frank looks unimpressed. "What about the doodles?"

I study the doodles. "Three well-known gods." I point to crude depictions: Zeus holding a thunderbolt, Thor with his hammer ringed with lightning, and the Hindu god Indra wielding a staff emitting rays of energy. Tesla scribbled their names beneath like chicken scratch.

Below this trio of lightning gods is a row of ancient megalithic sites on a timeline, like a string of pearls.

"Everyone knows these," I say. "Easter Island, Machu Picchu, Giza, Babylon, Angkor Wat in Cambodia."

I shake my head. "Why would Tesla draw all this?"

Frank's hopeful expression fades. "Think hard. You sure you haven't seen *any* of this before?"

"Why would I have seen this?"

"Tesla had a fascination with the esoteric." He's pressing me now like mafia, stepping into my space. "How do they connect? You must've missed something. Did your father tell you anything about this doc?"

Whoa. This just took a turn for the cryptic and bizarre. Why would my *dad* know about this? "Agent Vergazza, I have no idea why Tesla made this. These sketches are random and unrelated."

I've humored them long enough. My tone sharpens. "You've got the wrong guy."

Frank throws up his hands. "No problem, no problem ... eh— uh, any of this ring a bell?" He flips the document over, revealing a large electrical circuit Tesla drew on the back.

The rectangular diagram is broken on one edge by a switch gap. In the center is a hand-drawn model of the solar system. The sun sits in the middle like a transistor, its filaments reaching out to the inner planets like components on a motherboard. Earth is on the edge, opposite the switch gap.

I scoff. "Guys. I'm not an electrician."

Agent Dey explains. "Tesla had thousands of patented ideas

sitting in boxes. The CIA believes this circuit represents whatever's in his lost notebook, his final masterpiece."

Frank rubs his snub nose. "They brought in the best electrical engineers and physicists. No one has a clue what this is. Knuckleheads. His ancient doodles connect to it somehow."

Truly fascinating. But I'm not interested in electrical circuits. I shrug at the solar system in the center and opt for the simplest interpretation.

"The sun was worshipped in many civilizations," I say. "It symbolized light, the cosmic ocean, the gods—is that the Empire State Building?" I make a puzzled face at the famous skyscraper sketched in the margin.

"Yep." Frank sighs. "He scribbled the Chrysler Building, too. Kooky stuff."

"Maybe his notebook is there?"

"Nope." Frank's frustration seeps through. "Because of this doc, the feds shook both buildings upside down. Nada. Zilch."

"Why does the CIA want the notebook so badly?"

Andromeda is getting antsy, chewing a nail. They're definitely in a hurry, too. "He was working on advanced weapons tech," she replies. "His final invention is said to make the atom bomb look like a firecracker—a planet killer. Bigger than his earlier weapon, 'teleforce'—Tesla's death ray."

"Cool name." I edge closer to the exit. "Guys, I really gotta—"

Frank blocks my path. "Tesla's protégé knew what this circuit was and how this document reveals the notebook's location where Tesla explains the science."

Andromeda cuts in. "But the CIA intercepted this document before his protégé ever got it. They grilled the poor kid, but he never talked."

"How do you know the government didn't find Tesla's notebook?" I ask.

She taps the document. "We work in the CIA data archives. I've combed through all eighty research trunks they took from Tesla's place. No black notebook. They're still searching."

"Why would Tesla go to such trouble?" I wave at the puzzling document. "Why not just give the notebook to his protégé?"

"Tesla spent his last fifteen years in isolation," she says. "He was a broken man ... penniless, alone, totally forgotten. He was pushing ninety and frail. Maybe he couldn't get the notebook to anyone he trusted."

Frank nods. "He was trying to pass it to the only person he still had a relationship with: his protégé. He knew the government was desperate for this tech. They spied on him for years, especially during the war."

The two agents look at each other, and Frank nods reluctantly, like some decision was just silently made.

Andromeda pulls a photo from her worn-out army jacket and holds it up to me. "Recognize this guy?"

My chest constricts. It's my dad. Shaking hands with a man I don't know. "Why do you have a picture of my dad—"

"Your father was *deeply* involved with Project Nephilim," she says. "He was one of the core researchers. He deciphered this ancient circuit thing." She holds the page up at me.

I shake my head in disbelief. At a loss for words. *Why would my—*

The solar system.

A memory sparkles.

"My dad couldn't have been ..." I trail off in a stupor of thought. *Oh shit.*

Frank steps in. "You remember something?"

My eyes go to each of them. I'm disoriented as a cold sweat ripples over me. I suddenly don't feel so hot.

"Professor?" Andromeda says, taking my arm.

I slowly pull out my wallet and remove the photo of my dad.

Impossible.

I flip it over to my dad's drawing of the solar system. It's *identical* to Tesla's sketch. In the center of the sun is the number 33:27—Gustav Holst's music time stamp—the coolest part of the composition.

She glances down, practically tearing it from my hand.

"My dad gave me this ... just before he died," I say.

"Numbers?" Frank exclaims, on the verge of a coronary.

Her eyes go cold and planetary as she studies it.

Then she jolts. "I don't believe it. I've seen this number. A *lot*. It's all over the Tesla files."

"For the love of da pope, spill it, girl."

"3327 ... Tesla's room number at the New Yorker Hotel. Where he lived alone for over a decade. Where he died." She turns to me. "Your dad was sending you a code."

"No," I protest. "It's a music thing—"

"Tesla's room!" She cries.

Frank rolls his eyes. "That geek memory's gonna get you whacked. They went in and took everything when he died."

"What if he hid it?" She holds up the document. "What if it's still there?"

Frank blinks for a long moment.

"Guys." His voice is low, like the grave. "I grew up in the city. The New Yorker's just down the street."

7

I'VE HAD the most sought-after document in US history ... *in my wallet?*

"Tesla's room at the New Yorker Hotel!" Andromeda repeats in the dim theater lobby. "3327."

My dad was involved in this. Why?

I lean on the staircase for support. Nothing makes sense.

I have to catch my flight!

Blinding daylight floods the lobby. A man in a suit strides through the doorway. His gaze locks onto us, and he pulls a gun.

Wait, what?

Frank walks toward him, clutching the Project Nephilim binder. "Hey, take it easy—"

The gun roars. Frank staggers, eyes wide, crimson blooming on his chest. Pages from the binder scatter like startled birds.

I lurch upright, frozen.

Crack! Crack! Crack!

Loud gunshots erupt beside me. Andromeda's firing back. Her shots hit the intruder's torso, jerking him down in the doorway. He slumps with a gasp as another agent peeks in from the sidewalk.

"Shots fired! Shots fired!" he shouts into his comms. Andromeda fires again. A bullet slams into his femur. He tumbles out of sight, his pistol peppering Midtown.

She lunges at Frank, dropping to her knees. Blood is getting everywhere. "Frank! Frank, stay with me!" Her voice is frantic.

I apply pressure to his chest. It's soaked. No good. I don't know what I'm doing.

He's looking up at her, blue lips trembling, eyes ghostly. *"The veil ..."* His body slackens. Frank's gone.

"The hard drives!" she shrieks, clawing at the satchel strapped around his heavy body. The latches are locked. She grabs at Project Nephilim pages scattered on the floor, stuffing crumpled sheets into her pocket.

Bullets whiz past, splintering the wood behind us. The agent outside is crawling back. Andromeda fires, and he goes limp.

Three people dead at my feet. Is this some mafia thing?

Two more men appear at the entrance. She shoves me toward the auditorium doors, emptying her magazine at them until her gun clicks empty.

"Go! Go! Go!"

We burst into the theater, racing down aisles of purple chairs. Epic Broadway music fills the space. Actors rehearse on the stage; a flamboyant director paces them through their moves.

"Five, six, seven, eight!" he shouts as dancers twirl in Tudor costumes.

Reaching the stage, I hoist Andromeda up by the waist. We scramble through the stunned cast. We need an exit—now.

"Help us!" Andromeda is screaming, Frank's blood smeared on her face.

The director's palms are out wide. "Excuse me, this is a live rehearsal!"

"We need help!" I shout, pointing back, hands coated in Frank's blood.

I turn to a pack of bewildered women; their astonished faces are powder white with red eye shadow. They just stare.

I whirl to the director.

Crack! Crack! Crack!

Gunshots ring out. People scream and scatter. Chaos erupts. The music stops. Bullets pelt the stage, splintering plywood and shattering foam sets. More shooters are running down the aisles, guns blazing.

They're trying to kill us. Why are they trying to kill us!

"Why are they shooting at us?" I yell.

Andromeda throws me into the void behind the curtains.

We plunge into a backstage labyrinth—racks of costumes, makeup tables, glowing mirrors. The air is thick with the scent of old wood and greasepaint. My panic rises; it's a maze back here.

I grab her arm. "Why are CIA shooting at *CIA?*"

"Long story." She tries to pull away.

"What's that supposed to mean?"

"It means we're dead. Now come on—"

"Not good enough." I block her path. "You're not CIA, are you?"

"Yes. We're CIA." Her eyes are daggers.

I release her arm like hot coals. "What did you drag me into?"

"We gotta *move*, Professor!"

A bullet zings overhead, and she Wrestlemania-kicks me down a narrow corridor where a stagehand is pushing a rack of wigs. It topples as we bolt past.

"Watch it!" The stagehand curses as another bullet shatters a light.

"Exit!" I sprint toward a metal door marked with a glowing sign. We run down a black hallway lined with famous signatures.

I crash into harsh daylight. Andromeda smacks into me. We're out on the steaming pavement of Forty-sixth Street. The misty sky is sprinkling.

What now?

"Up there!" Andromeda dashes toward a cross street, away from Times Square.

I bolt after her because I believe these guys will execute me. And because she has info about my dad. We round the corner, sprinting at full speed, then barrel down two more alleys covered in a sea of fire escapes.

"Wait!" I gasp, struggling to keep up.

"We need to get off the streets," she says between breaths.

What's going on!

My mind reels. My legs are Jell-O. We run two more short blocks and into a secluded alley. I finally catch her arm and forcefully throw the data analyst against a brick wall beside a dumpster.

"Stop." I pant, clutching my side. "Just. *Stop.*"

Andromeda is wincing from exhaustion. Her tangled strawberry hair is swept over her feral eyes. "You're gonna get us killed," she says.

"What the hell is going on?" I'm searching her face for clues. "What aren't you telling me? Who are you?"

Her eyes dart in confusion, her voice raw. "This isn't right. CIA doesn't shoot on sight. They bring people in." Fear is brewing across her face.

"We need to call the police." I pull out my phone.

"The *police*? I don't have time for this." She rips it from my hand and hurls it onto a nearby rooftop.

"What in the actual—" My teeth grit hard. "I bought that *yesterday*."

"Oh no, not the phone!" She mocks. "How will you survive, Professor? It's not like we have trained killers on our ass or anything."

I glare at her, my shock morphing into a simmering resolve. "You know what? Screw you. And screw your super-secret spy thing. I didn't sign up for this. I'm going to the police."

She grabs my arm. "Well, tough luck. I didn't want to come up here, but Frank said we needed you. New York was a *big* mistake."

Her freckles scrunch up, and she brings both fists to her forehead. "Stupid!" She slaps the brick wall. "Frank had everything. It's all back there." She closes her eyes. "They have all of it. My life is over."

Chills rake me. I start to question her sanity. Had I just seen people gunned down? My voice catches in my throat, strangled. "What are you talking about?"

She looks defeated. "It all went to hell last night. Now they know who *you* are."

I give a sidelong glance and huff with disbelief. "I had nothing to do with this. He was … I was just … *Tell them, Agent Dey*."

"You don't get it." She's adamant. "You're in immense danger."

"Why would you say that?" I kind of believe her.

"We're so in over our heads."

I glare with disgust. "What do you mean it all went to hell? You're CIA—"

"We're whistleblowers. *Rats*." She throws her hands up. "We stole from the NSA archives. We had a plan, but it all went south."

"*What?*" I shouldn't have had that bagel.

"I'm sorry. You weren't meant to be involved."

"You dragged me into this!" I stab a finger. "I'm gonna miss my flight—"

"Your *flight?*" She's incredulous. "Oh, I'm sorry, did we interrupt your busy schedule of digging up rocks? My bad."

My nostrils flare. "Those rocks are my livelihood."

"Well, guess what, Lara Croft? The only livelihood you should worry about is the literal one. Because the guys chasing us don't give a damn about your little archaeology project."

"Why should I trust *you?* You just *shot* two people! Maybe you're the one I should be running from."

"They've seen your face. You're marked." She shakes her head. "You think *I* wanted this? I had a life, too. Then Frank showed me the Nephilim files. Your dad discovered something." She hesitates, looking me in the eye. "Then he disappeared."

Pain and horror blur my vision. "No. That's not true. Now I know you're lying. My dad died in a—"

"You think it's an accident we came up here just for *you?* There are a hundred better-qualified experts. The world's best historians have scrutinized the symbols on this document for decades. Your father was murdered because he discovered where the notebook is —and what's in it. Did he ever talk about it?"

"No—never."

"He was protecting you."

I think my heart's gonna explode.

"Tony." Her expression softens. A tear slips down her cheek. "I am *so* sorry to be the one—" She looks away and tucks her wild hair behind her ears. "If we find Tesla's notebook, we may find answers about your dad. He uncovered something terrifying."

I flinch at the words.

Am I angry or anguished? Or just dead inside? Hard to tell. All of the above? My stomach is sick.

I toss my head at her. "What did you steal?" I ask, then realize. *Oh …* They stole Project Nephilim. That's not good. "What's on those hard drives?"

"The true story of human history," she says. "Things that will make you question reality. We were gonna blow it so wide-open."

"What did Frank mean about Göbekli Tepe?"

"It's not what you think. It holds a warning from the time of Atlantis—about what happened twelve thousand years ago. They don't want it revealed."

"Who's they?"

"No time to explain. Frank said a global power structure has infiltrated governments, academia, and media. He said they use veil symbolism. I don't know. If you go to the cops, you'll disappear. I swear it. We have to move." She grabs my hand, pulling me along in a daze.

Veil symbolism?

She thinks aloud. "If we find Tesla's notebook, we can negotiate immunity. It's a huge bargaining chip. You don't understand how important it is to them. Whatever Tesla discovered is profoundly connected to Project Nephilim."

Okay, then.

The drizzle continues as we pass a food cart vendor. Andromeda calls out, "Which way to the New Yorker Hotel?"

"The New Yorker?" the vendor replies in a Bronx accent. "Over on Eighth."

We're running again, dodging taxis on Eighth Avenue. I'm still hurling questions, but she doesn't answer.

I'm definitely not going to Turkey today.

"Don't you have spy contacts or something?"

She snorts a humorless chuckle. "I'm an underpaid civil servant. A data geek."

She's out of breath as we jog. "Frank had it all figured out. He'd been researching Nephilim solo for years. He came to me a few weeks ago—yeah, I had a normal life, too. We were going public, but Frank thought we could find Tesla's notebook by talking to you. He was sure your dad told you something."

My adrenaline surges. "Look, I don't want any part of your conspiracy theory, okay?"

She gives me an annoyed glance. "There's no going back now, Professor. You saw what they do—look!"

Up ahead, an imposing Art Deco building rises skyward, tapering in steps like a Babylonian ziggurat. Enormous red letters are emblazoned across the top: NEW YORKER.

8

I FOLLOW Andromeda through the golden revolving door of the New Yorker Hotel. It's odd that Tesla lived in a hotel. The Art Deco lobby sparkles with golden second-story railings and a massive chandelier straight out of the Gatsby era.

I can't be involved in this. I'm a respected academic!

I've never doubted our institutions. How is going to the police a bad idea? The concierge desk is right there. I could get help, set the record straight, explain my situation to the authorities. But Andromeda's disturbing warning is leaving me full of doubts. I saw Frank shot in cold blood. I've been shot at repeatedly! We're not safe, that much I know. And her integrity rings true in a way I can't explain. Teaching gives you that kind of discernment.

I have to trust her for now because, you know, *people are trying to murder me*. But I also need to know what's really going on.

The late-morning rush fills the hotel lobby with an energetic buzz. Travelers glide through on their morning outings. Some stand at the front desk; others lounge in leather armchairs with lattes and laptops. A scent of jasmine and tobacco clings to the historic interior from the Grand Old Days.

"Agent Dey—"

"Andromeda works."

Great, first-name basis with my captor. Just like Stockholm syndrome. Cool. "There's blood on your jacket," I say.

She twirls, dismayed by the giant red stains running up the side of her vintage military jacket. With a shudder, she slips it off.

Underneath is a crisp, sleeveless white blouse buttoned to the collar. She slings the strap of her small, embroidered pouch onto a shoulder, and I catch sight of a tattoo on her bare arm: seven dots forming the Pleiades constellation. Below, it reads PER ASPERA AD ASTRA.

Through hardship to the stars.

I smirk at her granola pretensions. The pairing is peculiar, and considering her name, the mythology lover in me wants to know her story. I take her grisly jacket and discreetly stuff it into a nearby trash bin. "Come on."

We cross the grand lobby and find a bank of golden 1920s elevators. Andromeda presses the call button.

"Room 3327," she says. "Tesla had an obsession with the numbers three, six, and nine. His room number is math: three plus three is *six*—two plus seven is *nine* ..."

"Why three, six, and nine?" I ask.

"He claimed they were the key to the universe." Her lower register is husky. "He got a bit ... eccentric with it. He'd circle a building three times before entering. He slept three hours each night. Bought things in packs of three. Everything had to be multiples of three."

"Strange guy," I mutter.

A vintage bell dings, the doors open, and we enter. "Floor thirty-three," I say, pushing the metallic button.

A young couple rushes in, catching the doors before they close.

"Going up?" The man grins.

Andromeda nods, angling her bloody cheek away from them. The woman's eyes are on her, taking in her disheveled appearance.

"Long night?" the woman asks in a judgy tone.

Andromeda forces a smile. "You could say that."

The man nudges his partner, oblivious. "Told you this place is haunted. Probably saw a ghost, right?" He snorts.

I'm watching Andromeda. Is she unraveling? I'd take the ghosts over this ordeal.

The woman presses a button, and the elevator lurches upward. I hold my breath, hiding the blood on my hands. The bell dings, and the couple exits on floor ten. The doors begin to close, but Andromeda forces them back open.

I give her a puzzled look.

"Stay here. Hold the door," she says.

With my finger hovering over the DOOR OPEN button, I watch her tall frame float down the hallway. She stops at a housekeeping cart and rummages through bins of mini shampoo bottles and lotions.

Really? Pilfering freebies at a time like this?

She fishes around in a stack of towels, then darts back, holding up a maid's master key card.

Up on floor thirty-three, the hallway is empty. We hurry down the plain corridor adorned with vintage sconces and find a passage leading to a single door: room 3327. A brass plaque with a portrait of the hotel's famous resident reads THE NIKOLA TESLA ROOM.

Andromeda taps the key card, and we slip inside.

"What are we looking for?" I ask, scanning the sterile space. It's like any modern hotel room.

"Something the CIA missed." She moves to the closet and opens the door with one quick motion.

The beds are neatly made, and a window is drawn open. Two vintage posters framed on opposite walls are the only hint that the room is remarkable. One is an image of Tesla sitting inside a Tesla coil in his lab, surrounded by vast arcs of lightning. The other is a vintage New Yorker Hotel poster signed by Tesla himself.

"You take the bathroom," she says over her shoulder. "I'll start here."

I head to the small adjoining room. I pause in the doorway, glancing back at her with concern. She's kneeling by the bed, reaching under the mattress.

In the mirror, I see a bedraggled mess—disheveled brown hair and shell-shocked eyes. Agent Vergazza's dried blood covers my hands like a Stephen King novel. It's smeared on my jawline. Repulsed, I scrub myself until the soap bar is covered in red bubbles.

"Any luck?" she calls from the closet where she's standing on the luggage rack, examining the dark recesses for clues. "When

Tesla died in here, his nephew broke in and opened his safe before the CIA arrived. Tesla's notebook wasn't here."

I raise an eyebrow. "And you think he, what, hid it under the floorboards?"

"It could buy our freedom, Professor." She kneels, feeling the carpet for irregularities. "Hotel staff said Tesla's behavior became erratic. He developed odd rituals. Some said he lost his mind." She looks under the bed again. I stifle a chuckle.

"That was eighty years ago. It's all remodeled. If the notebook was ever here, it's long gone."

"Trust the vibes," she says, eyes closed like she's some Jedi.

"The *vibes?*" My fingers rake my scalp, dread spiking.

"I have a good feeling it's here. Hard to explain." She rummages through the desk drawers, shakes a Gideons Bible upside down, and peers out the window to street level. "Hey," she whispers. "They're here."

I rush over. Thirty-three stories down, a black SUV is swerving to a stop in front of the hotel. Dark suits are spilling out, movements urgent and purposeful.

Without warning, there's a plastic tapping at the door. "Housekeeping."

We wrench upright in a panic, and now we're fumbling into the tiny closet, closing the door as someone enters. Mercy—it's not even big enough for *one* person. We're a human Jenga tower. I reach up and silence a hanger.

"Hello? Housekeeping."

Oh no. We left Tesla's document on the bed!

The closet is dark and suffocating. I'm wearing Andromeda like a tactical vest, two heartbeats thumping. *The hell am I doing?* Her hot breath is on my neck. Panic wells in her eyes. I put a hand over her mouth and shake my head slowly as her eyes squeeze shut. Now she has to sneeze. Hell no. I clamp her face harder, and she knees my groin.

Stop it!

A second set of footsteps enters. More assertive.

Andromeda raises her pistol by my ear, arm bent awkwardly. She's inserting a new magazine with a soft click; the motion crushes my ribs. I scowl in pain, shaking my head, imploring her not to shoot anyone else.

Muffled voices are approaching the closet. Hotel staff. The handle turns, and the door opens a sliver. Light slashes Andromeda's gemstone eye, a sparkling blue ocean of terror.

I hold my breath, hands instinctively squeezing her shoulders. *Get me out of here!*

A stern, older woman's voice is right outside the closet. "They've checked out. You may prep the Tesla suite anytime."

More shuffling, then a loud sigh. "Housekeeping has *really* fallen off lately. Stains in the sink, doodles left on the duvet. I mean, *really*." A paper crumples into the wastebasket.

"Tomorrow, during the tech conference, this suite is to be open from ten until noon for registered attendees *only*."

"Yes, ma'am," a younger woman says meekly. "I'll have the room prepped within the hour."

"And have them change this wrinkled bedding, for godsakes."

Both footsteps are leaving, and the door slams.

I tumble from the closet, and Andromeda crashes to the carpet on her hands and knees, gasping with beads of sweat on her forehead. She's staring at Frank's dried blood on her wrist.

"You okay?" I crouch with a hand on her back.

"Give me a sec," she forces out.

I sit on the bed in a daze. This is nuts.

Andromeda slumps, then crawls to retrieve the crumpled Tesla document from the trash. "There's nothing here. It won't take the CIA long to search the hotel. I'm sorry." She looks down with a lump in her throat. "I'm sorry I dragged you into this. Frank and I thought we had it all figured out."

Her eyes are vacant, and her shoulders droop. We'll be captured. What happens now?

She stares out the open window, her face strangely focused. I follow her gaze to the curtains swaying under the air vent.

She steps to the window, full of concentration.

"What is it?" I ask softly, moving behind her.

Just a few blocks east, the Empire State Building dominates the view like a modern-day obelisk, elegant and magnificent. How many times had Tesla stood here gazing at it?

A white pigeon lands on a nearby ledge, watching us with a knowing red eye. In the distance, storm clouds gather over Brooklyn. The weather's coming in again.

A glimmering object catches my attention off to the left—the silver Art Deco arches crowning the Chrysler Building, glinting in a patch of morning sunlight.

"Wait." She's holding up the wrinkled page and walking backward across the room. Her face is ethereal, head tilted, eyes fixed on the baseboards. She stares down at Tesla's strange electrical diagram, her gaze moving from it to the floor and back.

"It's not a circuit," she whispers. "It's a map of this room."

9

ANDROMEDA DEY HOLDS up the Tesla schematic, working out its geometry as a possible map of the inventor's floor plan. "Look," she says, pointing out each landmark like a tour guide. "Window—that's this switch gap here in the circuit. Empire State and Chrysler Buildings—orientation markers." She rotates the page.

Her eyes flummox at the solar system in the center of the page. "The sun ..." She surveys the room's bland carpet. "Tesla drew the sun in the center. Something must've been right here."

"It's under the floor," I say, dropping to the baseboards and feeling the carpet's edge. "Help me pull it up!" Great, now I'm committing property damage. Next thing you know, I'll be stealing hotel bathrobes.

Andromeda's eyes drift upward to the vintage ceiling lamp, a circular light with pointed sunrays, just like on the map. "Hold on." She flicks the light switch. A cozy yellow glow fills the room.

"Sun," she says, pointing up with two fingers.

I grab a chair and position it under the lamp. Climbing up, I press my face close to the ceiling. There's something beneath the paint. I reach out. "Oh wow. There are ridges under here."

She's craning her neck. "Filaments."

"I'll be damned," I say. Tesla drew his solar system up here like Michelangelo. It's been painted over.

Andromeda rotates the document ninety degrees. Now, Earth is on the wall with the poster. Tesla's map is three-dimensional!

"Earth," she says, moving to the wall. But there's nothing—just a picture of Tesla inside a gigantic Tesla coil, engulfed by arcs of plasma lightning.

I run a finger over the velvety wallpaper. Our eyes meet. *It's in the wall.*

Andromeda is yanking the picture from its screws. She grabs a hanger from the closet and begins slashing the wallpaper into ribbons. "Grab that key card and scrape."

"Yeah." I chisel at the wall with the plastic card like a deer hunter skinning a kill, peeling back layers of old wallpaper: 1970s ... 1950s ... It's like archaeological strata. The oldest layer is a vibrant green pattern from the 1920s. "Look at these layers—"

"No time for archaeology, Professor." She tears away a large flap.

"I know. But that's not how you excavate. We can't afford to miss—*ah, screw it*." I slash at the wall, and plaster dust coats my hands. Then I see it—thick pencil strokes, the unmistakable outline of a small Planet Earth.

Tesla papered over it!

She gasps as I claw away more wallpaper. A one-foot-square joinery scar frames the planet—a secret compartment.

Also, I'm starting to really like Nikola Tesla.

"Move back," I say, grabbing the brass lamp from the bedside table. I tear off the shade and flip it over, wielding it like a sledgehammer. I bash it into the Earth drawing. The plaster cracks, dust raining down. After a few strikes, the lamp breaks through.

I wipe dust from my eyes and peer into the hole. Reaching in, my fingers touch something cool and smooth. I pull out a perfect sphere of polished steel, the size of a billiard ball, and surprisingly heavy. Glad I'm not the only one who hides metal Easter eggs in hotel walls.

"What on Earth?" Andromeda marvels.

"Literally." But this isn't a notebook.

Something else is inside the wall. I reach back in and grasp a long, slender object—an antique tuning fork. The tarnished steel is cool to the touch, the tines humming faintly as I hold it up. Along one prong is a Victorian script: *369 Hz / F#.*

"Interesting artifacts," I slip into archaeo-speak.

Andromeda rolls her eyes. "Artifacts? It's about as useful as a paperweight."

Tesla had scrawled a message on a scrap of paper.

10

I STARE at the strange objects in Andromeda's hands: a perfect steel ball and an antique tuning fork.

"Was Tesla moonlighting as a piano technician?" she quips, examining the fork etched with *369 Hz / F#*. She taps it against the steel sphere, and a hypnotic tone reverberates through the room.

I raise an eyebrow. "He really should've stuck to his day job of inventing ... I don't know—*everything?*"

"Three, six, nine." She notes the tuning. "Been seeing those numbers around."

I squint at the scrap of paper tucked with the relics, reading it aloud, "Remember our conversation last Sunday regarding my secret lab." I flip it over. "If this is the government, you shall not proceed."

"Secret lab!" She's floored.

Great. No notebook. And the CIA is probably reviewing lobby footage as we speak. We're toast.

"He must've been spooked," she says, studying the shattered wall, "to go to such lengths to hide his work. If Tesla was hiding it from the government—"

"Then he left clues for someone he trusted to find it." I finish, noticing how in sync we are.

"You ever see *Lord of the Rings?*" she asks.

"Yeah." It's been a while.

She turns to me. "If you were Gandalf and had the One Ring, what would you do?"

"Hide it in the Shire to keep it from Sauron?" I reply. "Nerd alert." I was going to say hide it in Elrond's bathroom, not a day for jokes.

"Tesla had no hobbits." Her gaze softens. Maybe she has a soft spot for eccentric, lonely geniuses. "When he died in here, it took two days before anyone even found him. He had every reason to be paranoid—under surveillance. Years before, just as his inventions were about to blow away the competition, there was a suspicious fire in his lab. He knew it was sabotage."

Makes sense. Throughout history, people have hidden dangerous ideas for safekeeping.

"Why would the government seize his work and bury it?" I wonder aloud. "It's like they erased Tesla for some reason." I look at the bed, envisioning Tesla alone and forgotten.

"There are waves on this note," Andromeda says. "Look."

Sure enough, three faint wavy lines are penciled in the corner.

She bolts the door. "We need to hurry."

"These wavy lines look technological," I say, "like a symbol—"

"Radio waves!" she exclaims. "Tesla had a massive beef over—"

"The invention of the radio! He claimed Marconi stole his patents."

Wait ... how do I know that? Oh, right. I read about it a few minutes ago by the *other* poster. I fly to the opposite wall. A vintage print shows the New Yorker Hotel from the 1930s.

"Maybe there's a connection between the document and—" Andromeda starts.

"The radio tower on top of the hotel. Check out this poster."

Tesla had scrawled in pencil across the hotel's tall radio tower: *It was my idea, Marconi!*

A plaque beside the poster summarizes the drama with the Italian inventor Guglielmo Marconi. Marconi was hailed as the Father of Radio, but Tesla said he was using seventeen of his patents. Courts ruled for Marconi, and the reputational damage was done. Marconi got filthy rich while Tesla languished in poverty. Only after his death did the Supreme Court recognize Tesla as the true inventor.

I once saw a memorial at Columbia University. Tesla gave a speech on campus in the 1890s on the future of radio. The school was "Columbia College" then.

"Radio waves! Look!" She taps the radio tower in the poster. Three wavy lines are up there in faded pencil.

Oh man, does that mean ...?

Something about the hotel's architecture nags at me. It's oddly familiar, but I can't put my finger on—

Holy crap.

It hits me like a lightning bolt. I stumble back, visions of ancient Sumer and Mesoamerica whirling in my mind. The hotel is a—

"I think I know why Tesla chose to live here," I whisper.

11

Prague, Czech Republic
The Demiurge

IN THE HEART OF PRAGUE, the Kinský Palace stands as a rococo masterpiece on the medieval Old Town Square. In an upper stateroom, an antique phone rings on a wooden desk.

By the light of an eighteenth-century window, a well-dressed older man—known only by his code name, Demiurge—takes a hissing drag from a cigarette. Wisps of smoke curl around his face. His wrinkled eyes stare at the bustling square below. He squints, deep lines creasing his paper-thin visage.

The phone continues to ring behind him.

He taps ashes into a tray before a framed photograph of a young Franz Kafka, who once attended school in the palace. In a cloud of brightleaf tobacco, he turns and lifts the receiver.

"Demiurge," he says.

"We have a development … at the CIA." The woman's voice is authoritative—one recognizable to millions.

He listens silently as she debriefs him, taking another pull from his glowing cigarette. Across the square, Prague's medieval Astronomical Clock Tower revolves, its dials tracking the sun, moon, and zodiac. The clock strikes the hour, and a skeletal figure representing Death turns an hourglass over in his hand.

The clock's creator, Master Hanuš, was blinded with hot pokers, and his tongue was cut out in 1490 to keep its secrets hidden.

Secrecy, above all, the Demiurge thinks. *Especially here at the endgame.*

"We need a contingency," the woman says.

He takes a final drag before stubbing out the cigarette. His voice is a bland American monotone—featureless, like a banal corporate accountant.

"Our power relies on the illusion of stability. It's all a puppet show, and fragile. We just have to run the clock out, just a little longer. People need to stay unaware of what's about to happen. We don't want to wake the sleeping giant."

"Our agencies will—"

"Your agencies have failed to contain this threat. This is now everyone's problem." His voice darkens. "We're taking over."

A pause. "Understood."

"Madam President."

"Demiurge."

He hangs up and then dials a number from memory. It rings only once before it's answered. Outside, tourists gather as Death's hourglass empties beside the zodiacal clock. "Mobilize Targeting Division. Rules of engagement tier-one, capture/kill—kinetic solution is authorized."

12

New Yorker Hotel
Tony Koviak

The vintage poster in Tesla's room at the New Yorker Hotel shows a pyramid-shaped skyscraper stepping up like a ziggurat against the New York skyline. Art Deco meets Babylon.

I nod to the radio tower. "Secret lab?"

A solar flash ignites behind her eyes. "Is it crazy to think Tesla was using the hotel as a …?" she trails off, electrified.

Moments later, we're sprinting down the hallway on floor 33 toward the fire stairs. We're near the top, just a few flights up to a door marked Roof Access–Authorized Personnel Only. Andromeda pushes it open. We're on a rooftop terrace. The sun's vanished behind heavy clouds.

I step to the edge. Wow. New York City stretches out, a sprawling world of steel and glass. The Empire State and Chrysler Buildings stand majestic, and the streets below are a pulsing grid. The rusty railing feels like the deck of an old steamer ship.

A gust of wind cuts across the rickety walkway, nearly pushing Andromeda over the brink. She backs away, clutching the crumbling wall behind us, blood supply leaving her cheeks.

"Afraid of heights?" I ask.

She gulps, lifting her big eyes to peek at the frightening overlook. "More like an aversion to the laws of gravity."

Above us, there's another roof deck—the hotel's top—with a radio antenna reaching heavenward. She points at the pole with a metal sphere on top, telling me it's just like Tesla's old lab in Colorado, where he first sent wireless power.

The clever CIA analyst shares a startling thought. Had the destitute inventor continued his energy experiments using the *hotel* as a gigantic transmission tower? The scale is astronomical. The idea is exhilarating, but there's no time to ponder.

"Up there." She's heading for the stairs to the top deck, where the radio tower stands, and up we go.

I survey the dizzying view in all directions. The vast dome of sky doesn't look real.

"It's gotta be up here," Andromeda says, starting to search.

I look around, archaeologist mode fully engaged. The base of the tower is made of limestone blocks. I crouch to inspect and see a rudimentary carving on one of the stones, like a manufacturing stamp.

It's an elongated letter Y.

I trace the eroded edges of the Y. The stone is pitted and scarred from decades of weathering. The mark is crude—not a maker's mark. Old, desperate hands scratched this.

"Over here," I shout.

Andromeda rushes over and kneels beside me. The breeze lifts strands of her hair. "What is it?"

"Aftermarket tag."

A siren wails in the distance. She tenses. A hand instinctively goes to her gun. "We need to hurry."

"I wonder …" I study the mark. "Give me the tuning fork." She hands it over.

I hold up the musical relic, its aged patina gleaming. "Give me your gun."

"What? No."

"I'm not gonna shoot you."

"And I thought you were a serious scholar."

"Hold up that steel ball, then."

She glances around, then obliges, eyeing the fork skeptically. "Not exactly standard archaeological procedure, Professor."

"Standard is boring." I hold up the fork, which now looks an awful lot like the elongated Y.

With a swift motion, I strike the tuning fork on the sphere. A piercing tone rings out, powerful and haunting.

F sharp, I presume.

I hold the vibrating instrument near the limestone, an inch from the strange marking. Several long seconds pass, and I feel kind of stupid now. I silence the tines to think of a new plan.

Then I hear it.

Another block is ringing to my left.

A haunting F sharp tone emanates from the stone. It makes the hairs on the back of my neck stand up. It's as if the wall is moaning, like a voice from the crypt.

The mortar around this block is different than the rest—a different texture and shade. Almost invisible.

I press my ear to the limestone. "It's in the stone."

Andromeda is already going for the fire ax mounted nearby. I move back as she runs up like a berserker and chops into the masonry with a war cry. It obliterates. The singing block is only a thin veneer, a brittle false front. Behind it is a hollow chamber.

Tesla, you sly fox.

The ax clatters to the ground. Andromeda, hair everywhere, kneels, peering into the hole. She reaches in, silences a second vibrating tuning fork, and pulls out a vintage cigar box. Inside is a small black notebook covered in eighty years of dust.

Another scrap of paper reads *the future is the past*—N.T.

"Why the theatrics?" I ask, equal parts delighted and annoyed.

"Tesla was a showman," she says. "He loved demonstrating science with flair. Illustrative setups were kind of his thing. He had to be sure."

"Next time, maybe just an email?"

I lean over her shoulder as she opens the notebook. The leather cover cracks. The pages are yellowed; the pencil strokes are crisp. Tesla scribbled a phrase on page one: PROTO-WORLD ENERGY VIA THE NATURAL MEDIUM.

I've never heard the term "proto-world" before. Something about it feels primordial and otherworldly.

"What's this?" I point to a symbol in the center: a triangle inside a circle. The numbers one through nine wrap around it like a clock, nine at the top. The numbers three, six, and nine are circled, sitting like orbs in a perfect triangle formation.

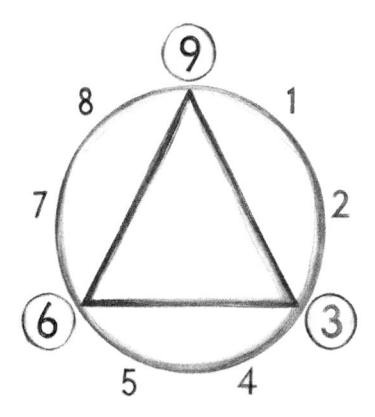

Three, six, and nine—Tesla's obsession.

I've seen a similar symbol, a rather famous one—in alchemy, a triangle inside a circle represents the philosopher's stone.

Was Tesla an alchemist?

She flips through pages filled with science and technology way over my head—technical schematics, diagrams, math, raw designs—like patents or blueprints. Equations and sketches are everywhere.

"It's real. It exists," Andromeda says, laughing. She reads a scribble: "The universe is electric.... What does that even mean?" Her eyes are teary.

She reads more: "He claims here that he discovered an infinite energy source, some cosmic force." Her exposed arms have goosebumps from the March chill.

"It's above my pay grade," I say.

She shakes her head. "Earth is part of some cosmic circuit, like on his diagram. What are 'fundamental forms?'"

Fundamental forms ... that's Plato. His Platonic solids are the foundation of all creation. That's the third time Plato's come up since I met this CIA agent.

"So, Tesla found some new type of power?" I ask.

She considers it. "What happens when the greatest genius of all time goes full monk mode for a decade? I think I'm holding the result."

Whoa. Something catches my eye. I grab the notebook.

"Hey," she protests. "We don't have time for this. Let's *go*."

"Hold on," I say. It was near the back. Why are *these* in here?

A section is full of ancient references: the Great Pyramid of Giza, Mexico's Pyramid of the Sun, Incan walls, Easter Island heads—page after page of obscure mythology. Tesla was obsessed with antiquity.

Did he stuff these in by mistake? Mix up two hobbies in his old age? Use the notebook for both? The classical world can't possibly be connected to Tesla's final masterwork—the man whose work led to ninety-five percent of all inventions.

Why is Nikola Tesla's Ninth Symphony filled with ancient allusions?

I flip back to the title page. *Proto-world.*

"This is no weapon," I say quietly.

Andromeda's cheek pulls up in a half smile, making her look like an awestruck Pippi Longstocking as she speaks, "We need someone who knows Tesla."

13

From the rooftop of the New Yorker Hotel, I look over at the pulsing billboards of Times Square. Did I just survive a shootout over there?

The military helicopter is still hovering, but now it's drifting toward us.

Forty stories below, New York City is a muted hum. Without warning, scraping metal screeches from the lower terrace. Someone's forcing open the rooftop access door, our only way down.

I throw up a hand to Andromeda and shove the notebook into my jacket pocket. Terrible options swirl in my mind. An iron service ladder clings to the parapet. I run to it. Andromeda follows, but in her panic, she leaves Tesla's steel ball on the ground.

Peering over the edge, my head spins. The ladder descends to a lower terrace, ending mere inches from a sheer drop to street level. One slip, and we're sidewalk pizza on Eighth Avenue. No cage, just a ladder. Pedestrians look like colorful ants below. Madison Square Garden looms across the street.

Great. This ladder is about as stable as the Bronze Age chronology.

Okay, Tony, remember your rock-climbing days at Cambridge. Except now it's a forty-story drop on a 1930s death ladder. *No pressure.*

Andromeda takes one look at the rusted ladder and freezes, eyes wide with terror. "I'm not going down *that*!"

I'm already over the ledge. "They're going to *kill* us."

She glances back. We only have seconds.

"I'm going to die," she whispers, her eyes like moons.

Over the parapet she goes, knuckles white and bloodless. As her weight settles, the antique bolts creak and pull two inches from the concrete. The ladder tilts outward, and she gasps like a banshee.

"If you fall, fall to the *left*," I yell.

"You shut your mouth, teacher!"

"I thought agents were trained, like James Bond."

"I work in a *cubicle*!"

The ladder shimmies with every move. She's clutching the tuning fork wrapped in Tesla's map. March winds lash her hair into her eyes.

Her breaths come in panicked gasps. She inches down above me, eyes glued to the wall.

An archaic rung rolls under her foot, and both legs fly off. Hanging by her arms, she screams, feet kicking. The tuning fork tumbles away, vanishing into the streets below. Tesla's map is swept up high into the wind and twirls away toward Midtown.

"Tony!" She's kicking my head, scrambling for a foothold.

Oww.

She finds a rung and continues down. Probably more afraid of being shot now.

On the terrace, she collapses onto me, legs buckling as color returns to her face. "Tony! I lost the document and the tuning fork!"

"We don't need them." I pat the notebook in my pocket. "We have this."

We find a service elevator and burst from the loading dock onto the street, racing down Thirty-fifth against the crowd. "We gotta get off the grid," she says, "somewhere they won't be looking."

I hurry alongside her, my mind spinning. "This is insane. I can't just run off with you."

She pulls her hair over her face. "Don't look now." She nods toward two men in dark suits, a hundred yards behind. Even at this distance, their purposeful stride gives them away.

"Head down, keep moving," she says. "Blend in."
"Do they see us?"
"No."
I steal a glance. One agent is looking directly at me.
"Yeah," she groans. "*Run!*"
We weave through the morning crowd and fly down a side street lined with cheap shops, then around a corner. We press against the bricks and hold our breath as heavy footsteps thunder past.
"*In there,*" I mouth.
We dart into a small electronics shop with flickering green fluorescents. Shelves are piled high with outdated components and tangled cords. It smells like hot plastic and ozone. We head to the back through a door marked EMPLOYEES ONLY. An elderly Sri Lankan woman is counting inventory. We ignore her protests and push through a metal door into another filthy alley.
Racing down narrow streets, we dodge dumpsters and startled cats. The stench of rotting food assaults my nostrils. Graffiti-covered walls close in; neon signs glow from basement windows like gateways to illicit underworlds.
"Where are we going?" I shout over another blaring siren.
"Out of Manhattan," she says. "I know someone who can help." She glances around. "This way!"
A bullet whizzes past my ear, shattering bricks beside me. They're on us! I push her forward. Instead of running down the avenue, Andromeda just hurtled into a subway entrance.
"Not down there," I yell. "We'll be trapped!"
She's already on the grimy tile floor. I follow, knowing we're dead. We vault over the turnstiles. A train sits with doors open. *Maybe—just maybe.*
"Freeze!" Two agents are clattering down the stairs, guns drawn.
I shove Andromeda into the car as one agent grabs my arm. The doors start to close. I struggle, but his grip is an iron vice.
Andromeda pulls her sidearm and fires two shots. The agent staggers back as a loud synth tone blares, and the doors slide shut. The other agent unleashes bullets that shatter the window beside us. She screams and hits the floor. Two passengers cower under the seats.
The train lurches forward with a whine, leaving the agents

slapping the car in anger. The driver at the far end never even noticed.

I collapse into a plastic mustard-yellow seat—one of those '70s trains—legs shaking, adrenaline still coursing through my veins as the roaring wind rushes into the broken window. I glance at Andromeda as she studies the subway map.

"You know," I say, "when I agreed to help the CIA, I thought it would be more 'academic consultation.'"

"Didn't read the fine print?" She leans against the door marked NO LEANING, eyes closed, as the train rattles through the humid labyrinth. "Me neither."

"Where to?"

"A little place called Wardenclyffe. Tesla's former lab."

14

THE RAIN RETURNS as Andromeda hails a cab in Queens. She swipes her credit card, prepaying for a trip to White Plains, but we don't get in. Decoy. Moments later, we're in another cab, speeding across Long Island. She really wants to get to a place called Wardenclyffe.

I have the urge to alert friends and family. *Patience, Tony.*

We don't speak. Her mood has darkened. She's pale, almost ghostly, still as a statue. The shock of Frank's death must be sinking in.

Guess I'm running off with a rogue CIA agent. Truth is, I haven't maintained personal relationships all that well. In all my studies, I haven't had much time for friendships. It's ... isolating. There's a strange comfort in having her here.

"Tell me you have a backup plan," I say.

"It's not great." Her voice is a smoky rasp. Is she meditating? "Someone on the inside alerted the CIA last night. We weren't ready. We scrambled to upload the Project Nephilim data to an encrypted digital vault—barely succeeded—but the passcode was in Frank's bag."

"Can you hack into the vault?"

She laughs dismissively. "CIA uses post-quantum encryption. A brute-force entry would take five ... roughly five—"

"Five hours?"

"—five billion years."

"Then let's use the notebook to barter amnesty."

"No need." She gives a melancholy smile. "I set up a dead man's switch. If we don't access the Project Nephilim cache in forty-eight hours, it'll be emailed to me—and a hundred independent media outlets, influencers, and academics worldwide."

A fiendish hippie. "How did you have time to set that up?"

"The drive up from Langley was a few hours. Vergazza had a satellite laptop."

"So, all we have to do is not get caught for two days? Why do we need this Tesla expert when we have the notebook?"

"Insurance," she replies. "Going public may backfire without proof of authenticity. The moment we leak it, we lose leverage over the government; it's over. And if we try to cut a deal, they'll seize it and discredit us. We're in a bad spot. If anything goes wrong with the dead man's switch, it's all we have."

I start to understand. We need an affidavit … and a potential ally.

"But that's not all. Tesla is deeply connected to Project Nephilim. I need someone to help me understand why."

Maybe this guy can shed light on what my dad was into.

Tesla's esoteric fascinations whirl in my mind—his sketches, the notebook's cryptic pages. Is this what my dad learned before he was killed?

"Frank had a list of contacts," she continues. "There was a scientist, a Tesla expert. If we ever found the notebook, Frank planned to go straight to him."

"What's so special about him?"

"Dr. Cassian Wilder," she says, gazing out the window. "Probably the most brilliant geophysicist alive. A Caltech prodigy who left academia for the private sector. He's obsessed with Nikola Tesla. He's pioneering new tech based on Tesla's radical ideas."

"Why didn't Frank just go to him?" Frustration slips into my voice. "Why drag me into this Tesla business?"

She glances at me. "Tony, isn't it obvious? Frank was convinced your father told you everything. Going to you was his big gamble."

A knot tightens in my stomach. Did I get Frank killed? "So where is this Wilder guy?"

"Running an energy start-up at Wardenclyffe, Tesla's old lab.

Right here on Long Island." She nods toward the horizon. "We'll be there soon."

Our taxi glides down the highway. Decaying houses give way to trees, bringing a merciful sense of seclusion.

Andromeda pulls the crystal necklace from her blouse and begins fiddling with it. It's pearly-white with a bluish iridescence that shifts as it turns. New Age suspicions confirmed.

"How'd you get that name, anyway?" I ask, hoping to lighten the mood.

"Parents were hippies," she says, eyes peacefully closed. "They had seven of us—all girls. We lived in a commune in the high desert. I fared better than my sister, Amethyst River."

"You're kidding." I stare. She isn't kidding. "What's ... *your* middle name?"

She fidgets, and the eyes open. "I don't have one."

"You're a rotten liar."

She huffs, running a finger over the hand-stitched flower on her pouch. "Wildflower."

I chuckle softly. "And the tattoo?"

She rubs the arm with a wince. "All seven sisters got the same Pleiades tattoo." Her eyes grow sad. "Well, six of us did, anyway."

"The Seven Sisters from Greek mythology. Nice. I like the name, by the way. Ancient Greece is my field, so I kind of have to."

"Don't get all bookish on me, Professor." She looks away, her wild mane obscuring her face.

"What made you want to be a whistleblower when you grew up?"

A smile flutters, then her face loses all expression. "When I was twelve, heavily armed federal agents raided our commune. They claimed the community was engaging in illegal, antigovernment activities. In the chaos, my little sister, Luna, was accidentally shot and killed by an FBI agent."

Her voice catches, chin quivering. "Sometimes I forget what she looked like."

She swallows hard. "The government just ... they just covered it up, like it never happened. No one was held accountable. My father was arrested on bogus charges, spent years in federal prison. Our mama couldn't handle it. She ... well, it left me and my sisters to fend for ourselves. The commune took us in—they did right by us—but the IRS deliberately targeted them. Took everything. Our land, our dreams."

I have no idea what to say. Good Lord.

"It's a strange thing," she whispers. "To be sixteen and know your life is already over."

She watches the passing woods. "I had a knack for computers in community college. Joined the agency at a job fair. I don't know why. I wanted to believe in something again—can you understand? I was lucky to find a mentor. Evelyn. She took me under her wing, fast-tracked me for leadership. Until I stumbled onto her involvement in illegal domestic surveillance. She turned on me, got me reassigned to a dead-end data analyst position in a forgotten dungeon. That's where I met Frank."

She tucks the crystal back into her blouse, buttoning it to the top.

"Birthstone?" I ask, nodding at the necklace, hoping to shift the subject.

She shakes her head. "Moonstone. It was Luna's."

Damn. "I'm sorry."

"It was another life."

"And you're, what, hoping to bring down the whole system?"

"We have to bring them down," she says, like the world depends on it. "There are things I haven't told you, Tony. Dark things."

Who's them? I'm not here to topple some intelligence cabal. I just want the truth about my dad. Salvaging my life would be a plus.

I open the black notebook, eyes scanning Tesla's mind-bending schematics. Most people would need a lifetime to grasp this. I flip to the back pages with the ancient musings. That's more interesting. Cryptic geography and Egyptian symbols? I'm practically giddy.

What did Nikola Tesla know about the classical world?

An entire spread is dedicated to the Great Pyramid of Giza. A 1940s newspaper clipping shows its internal chambers.

Andromeda watches me. "Project Nephilim is about a lost, advanced civilization in remote prehistory. Real Jules Verne stuff."

I stiffen, looking up. *That subject again.* Still, part of me wonders if there's some truth buried in the crazy.

She leans closer, intrigued. "What if Nikola Tesla stumbled onto something about—"

"A long-forgotten past." That idea has been gnawing at me. "Don't love the idea of secret government projects—"

She cuts me off with a giggle. "Oh honey, they've done this for decades. They're suppressing the tech. I swear, confiscated exotic energy patents are half the files in that NSA Data Center."

"Why?"

"Oh, you know, the usual." She ticks off on her fingers. "Power, resource control, social engineering, preventing mass psychological collapse. Just another Tuesday in the Rose Garden. And … something else …" She runs a hand through her hair, scanning the driver to make sure his earbuds are still in before speaking.

"What else?"

"It's just …" She shakes her head, looking like she might throw up. "There's something else big they're hiding. It's bad."

"*What?*"

"Not here. That rabbit hole's too deep for me right now."

I lean in closer. "Tell me."

"I said no." Her eyes cut to the notebook. "What matters is this. They don't have *this*. Tesla's discovery is what they're really after."

15

"HISTORY IS A LIE, KID."

Frank's words won't stop rattling in my head. If my dad was involved with Project Nephilim, I need to see those files.

We're on our way to have the notebook authenticated by the Tesla guy. Then we wait for Andromeda's dead man's switch to trigger and release the Kraken.

After that—

"We didn't lose everything, Tony." She digs into her wildflower hippie pouch and pulls out two mangled pages, edges stained with dried blood. "I almost forgot. I grabbed these from Frank's binder before we nearly got aerated."

I unfold the pages. A faded red stamp reads TOP SECRET—PROJECT NEPHILIM. Date: January 13, 1975.

It's a report by Jean Vendôme, a renowned postwar French archaeologist doing clandestine research for the CIA, typed on an old-fashioned typewriter. The title stops my heart: PLATO'S HERMOCRATES AND THE ANTEDILUVIAN HALL OF RECORDS.

"This can't be real," I say. "Is this some prank?"

Wait ... A sinking feeling hits me. I glare at her. "Seriously, am I being pranked?" I think for a moment this whole morning may be some elaborate gag.

She gives me *The Look*—that one.

Not a prank.

I scan the document. "This says a completed version of Plato's lost Atlantis trilogy exists at a location in Europe associated with—finance." I scrunch my nose at the last word. How is *finance* related to an ancient Plato text?

"I don't follow," Andromeda says, rubbing her eyes.

"The lost trilogy is Plato's account of Atlantis," I explain. "His final work, left half-finished, mysteriously cutting off midsentence, as if he died pen in hand."

Plato was my focus at Cambridge. People have speculated for ages that the missing final book in the trilogy once existed, perhaps in the Library of Alexandria. We only have the first two books.

Scrolls faced the perils of conquests, fires, and human error. They passed from Egypt to Rome to Byzantium and, finally, to Europe. Not everything survived, but Plato intended to complete his account of Atlantis. He even named the third book: *Hermocrates*.

Now Jean Vendôme is confirming that Plato finished it!

Plato's Hermocrates exists? Book Three of the Atlantis trilogy! I'm like a kid who's found a hidden level in his favorite video game.

Vendôme was a renowned scholar. I studied his work as an undergrad. Every freshman has a Vendôme fifth edition. The late Frenchman was not the speculative type.

"Andromeda, this is incredible!" My pulse races. "Plato's Lost Dialogue!"

She seems uninterested. She's somewhere else. I temper my enthusiasm and try to explain. "The Atlantis trilogy is three books: Timaeus, Critias, and Hermocrates."

The taxi air is stuffy. I crack the window and let sharp March air hit my face.

"Vendôme never found the lost book," I say, tapping his conclusion: Hermocrates location unknown.

"What does antediluvian mean?" she asks.

"Before the flood—as in Noah's flood. That's what the second page here is about." I turn to page two. "Vendôme claims that *Hermocrates* reveals the location of the Hall of Records."

"What records?"

"All of them. The Hall of Records is the mythical library of Atlantis."

Vendôme lists two tantalizing clues to its location:

```
1. An overworld marks the location.
2. An underworld lies at its feet.

Sadly, all trails have gone cold.
—Jean Vendôme, 1975
```

I'm electrified. It's the most thrilling thing I've ever seen. What was Jean Vendôme trying to say? That it's *real*? No one believes in the halls. The idea of Vendôme hunting Atlantis is absurd, like discovering that Mozart's favorite band was ABBA. I suddenly wish I had Frank's binders.

"Jean Vendôme was searching for the fabled Hall of Records! The library of Atlantis!" I'm almost shouting. The driver glares at me in his mirror.

"Oh yeah," Andromeda says dryly, "the Hall of Records thing. There was a whole section on that."

"Good Lord, *Wildflower*, what did it say!"

She shrugs, looking miserable. "I dunno. Something about the underworld. Libraries. Atlantis. Disney shit. There were cats."

Cats? My mouth hangs open.

She sniffles. "I wish Frank were here. He'd know what to do. He researched this for decades, Tony. The wrong agent died."

A loud text alert startles us. She pulls out a buzzing flip phone from her pouch.

"Oh, so you get a phone?" I sigh.

"Burner." Her face goes ashen as she reads the message: *You have 24 hours to return what you stole. After that, there will be no place on Earth you can hide.*

She huffs a grunt and chucks the phone out the window into the howling wind. Her face is horrified. "If we're caught, they'll show no mercy. No courts, no trial, no rights. We'll vanish." She pauses. "Like your dad."

My stomach churns. Nausea creeps back. My life is falling apart, and I can do nothing. I drum on my knees. "We should leave the country. Run the clock out. Maybe we should just go now."

"We're almost to Wilder's place. Let's grab the affidavit and hightail it."

She takes a deep breath. "We weren't supposed to find it. Project

Nephilim is ultranational—not part of CIA systems. Frank found it compartmentalized in the NSA's Utah Data Center. Sections were in Ukraine, some in the Philippines. It's run out of Europe. America's just the muscle."

That's unsettling.

I bite my lip, thinking of a myth.

"What?" She looks ill.

"You're like Prometheus. You've stolen the forbidden fire from the gods—their secret knowledge—and you're giving it to the masses."

She looks hopeful. "What happens to him?"

I regret mentioning it. "Well ... uh. In the myth, Prometheus is punished for his defiance, chained to a rock, and his liver is pecked out by an eagle every day, only to regenerate and suffer the same fate again and again—forever."

"You're a real jerk." She turns away. "Prometheus had it good compared to what they'll do to us."

Jean Vendôme fills my thoughts. Do I have this straight? Plato's lost Atlantis trilogy exists somewhere in Europe known for *money*, and the text reveals the location of the Atlantean Hall of Records—a place with both an overworld and an underworld.

Got it.

I groan. "My life's work is in my apartment. Years of research."

"The CIA already has it," she says. "It needs a firmware update anyway. You'll learn more from Nephilim in one hour than you've learned your whole life."

I watch the drizzle, uncomfortable with the suggestion. A jetliner is rising over the expressway. I wonder if it's my outbound for Istanbul. I imagine my team waking up to the news that Professor Tony Koviak is MIA.

Our taxi turns down a gravel drive. A dilapidated sign reads WARDENCLYFFE.

Tesla's former lab.

16

THE WOODS ENCIRCLING Wardenclyffe are dense, and a rusted chain-link fence wraps around the site.

"Let's not tell Dr. Wilder about our situation," Andromeda warns. "This is a billion-dollar, space-age start-up. There will be important people on site. Let's get in, grab the authentication, and get out."

The taxi pulls up, and the driver removes his earbuds. Loud music leaks from them. She pays him with a credit card. I frown. "Can't they track that?"

She flashes a stack of prepaid VISA gift cards from her pouch. Must be about five grand. "Getaway insurance; bought with cash."

I nod at the pouch. "You should've put the tuning fork in there."

"Like I had time to think on the death ladder!"

We step out and look at Tesla's lab. It's a wreck. Weeds choke the grounds; fire damage and shattered glass glint beneath boarded-up arched windows. A faded DANGER sign hangs on the crumbling wall.

She squints at the spooky ruins of Wardenclyffe. "This can't be right."

The rain has made the grounds smell damp and earthy. I shiver as we wriggle through a gap in the fence and cross the gravel yard.

She's hugging her bare arms, probably wishing she'd kept the blood-soaked army jacket. "What a dump," she mutters.

"Still trusting those vibes?" I ask, eyeing the graffiti-covered brickwork. A tower topped with a wrought-iron globe rises like a chimney on a Wonka factory. I don't think anyone's been here in years.

"Come on." She's pointing to two cars parked on the gravel and heading for the entrance.

The door creaks open to a shadowy hallway. A pungent mildew assaults me, and I cover my nose with my shirt. Floorboards groan underfoot. The peeling paint flakes off at my touch. Not gonna lie; it's a creepy place.

Parts of the ceiling are blackened and collapsed from a recent blaze, exposing pipes and ducts. Eerie brick arches lead to dark corridors lit by blinking LEDs with a greenish glow. Graffiti and ... other substances are everywhere. The stench is unbearable.

So much for a billion-dollar start-up.

"Tesla built an enormous tower out back," Andromeda says as we step over broken glass and mouse droppings. "He was trying to transmit electricity wirelessly."

"I didn't see a tower."

"They tore it down," she explains. "It was financed by J. P. Morgan, who thought Tesla was building him an electrical empire. When he found out Tesla was secretly experimenting with wireless power, well, Morgan had one question: 'How do we meter it?' He built his wealth on oil and gas and the rail infrastructure needed to transport it. Morgan was furious. He rug-pulled the entire operation, and Tesla never recovered."

"You know a lot about Tesla."

"I scoured his files, looking for clues to the notebook. He was close when he lost everything. Must've sucked."

We pass a crooked picture in a broken frame. A photo from 1904 shows the lab in its heyday. Behind it, a gigantic triangular tower rises, topped by a bulbous cap—Tesla's Wardenclyffe Tower.

Our footsteps echo on the concrete floor. Big chunks of the wall are missing, revealing empty rooms. I can't shake the feeling we're being watched. *Great*, the only thing worse than a decrepit lab is a horror movie creeper.

I turn down a dim hallway with a bulb going haywire. The word *death* is spray-painted with anatomical graffiti. Did we just glitch into the Backrooms?

What is this place? I shudder. The layout is a maze.

Muffled voices drift in through the broken windows. Someone is out back.

17

WE FIND a back door that opens onto a large grassy field. There's a metallic tang in the air. The field is overgrown. In the center stands a twenty-foot metal tower with a bulbous steel ball on top.

"Jimmy don't touch it," a man bellows. "It's toxic!"

"Sorry, Cassian!" Jimmy yells back.

Cassian Wilder is mid-thirties, lean with deep-set eyes. He has an unruly mop of hair and big retro glasses that—no joke—make him look like Jeffrey Dahmer.

He's having a meltdown. "The other plate, Jimmy!" he hisses.

"Dr. Cassian Wilder?" Andromeda calls, moving toward him.

He turns, mouth puckered in confusion. "Who's asking?"

"We'd like to ask you some questions."

He smirks. "Not today."

Jimmy, his assistant near the tower, shouts, "Cassian! The mercury's spinning up fast, man!"

Without warning, a blinding arc of plasma lightning erupts from the top of the tower. Jagged bolts shoot over our heads and punch the grass with a punishing *crack*.

"Down!" Cassian tackles us to the ground.

We're trapped under the wild lightning as the air sizzles above. Heat scorches my back.

Cassian is army-crawling between thunderous bolts. One strikes a foot from his face. He lunges for a control panel and shuts off the main breaker.

In an instant, the terrifying show is over. The metal sphere atop the janky tower smokes badly.

"Sorry about that," Cassian brushes himself off as we stand. "You really shouldn't be back here. Whatever you're selling, I'm not interested."

"Professor Tony Koviak, Columbia University," I say, extending a hand but internally doubting if he's the handshake type. "This is my colleague, Agent Andromeda Dey." She winces at the real names. Yeah, that was a bonehead move. I'm not used to super-secret-spy stuff, okay?

"Right," Cassian nods skeptically. "And what brings a professor and a ..." He eyes Andromeda. "What exactly are you an agent of? State Farm, was it?"

"I work in ... special collections," she says vaguely.

"Collections?" His eyes narrow. "Wait ... is this about the bank loan? Look, we're almost—"

"We're not here about your debts, Dr. Wilder," she interrupts.

He sizes us up. "I'm kinda busy with this tower melting down, if you don't mind."

He's moving to a control panel at the tower's base and shouting to his assistant. "Jimmy! Get me the duct tape and a box cutter!"

Jimmy, a thick guy with a small face, waddles off and disappears into a small outbuilding.

"Is this a Tesla tower?" Andromeda gazes up in fascination. She motions to the lab. "It's smaller than the one in the photo."

Cassian raises an eyebrow. "Oh, you're one of those?"

"We need a professional evaluation of a rare Tesla document," she says. I've heard *that* line before, like when I agreed to meet Frank. We're putting this guy in danger just being here.

"How many electricians said no before you got to me?" Cassian sighs.

She beams. "You're top of our list, Dr. Wilder."

He surveys his derelict startup. "Call me Cassian. You must be desperate, lady. But I'm done dealing with academia—too precious. More dough in the private sector."

Andromeda studies the hissing wreckage. "How does it work?"

He halts, gauging if we're for real. "It was Tesla's vision, the thing he worked on his entire life."

Cassian squats to examine the foundations. "He filed a patent in 1905 called 'The Art of Transmitting Electrical Energy Through the Natural Medium.' People thought he was nuts, and now his idea has ruined *my* life, too."

"What was the patent for?" I ask.

"Transmitting electricity via the natural medium—Earth and sky. No wires, just standing wave currents that could be tapped anywhere on the planet."

"Did he succeed?" I ask. The idea seems ridiculous.

Cassian snorts, pushing up his retro frames. "What do you think?"

"Then, why haven't we developed this tech?"

He half-grins. "Well, that's the trick, Mr. Chips." He wrenches at a latch on the tower's base. "Tesla said Earth was like a small steel ball. Attach an electrode on one side and pass a current to the other. The geology checks out."

"Energy transmission *through* the Earth?" Andromeda marvels. "So cool."

Cassian points up at her. "It is cool."

I whisper to Andromeda, "The steel ball in Tesla's wall …" She shakes her head, warning me.

"How can electricity travel through Earth?" she asks.

"Well, the entire planet is one big circuit," Cassian explains. "Earth conducts. The upper atmosphere conducts. But the space between doesn't, forming an insulating layer. Tesla's tower bridges the conductive layers, forming a loop."

Andromeda seems to consider it. "So then, lightning is the circuit connecting naturally for a moment?"

"Look at you, all science-y." He turns to me, adjusting his glasses. "Isn't she lovely? Exactly correct. The ionosphere above and the Earth below can be bridged. It's the key to Tesla's idea."

He knocks the rusting tower frame. "This cranky energy vampire is a Tesla coil. Designed to pulse power into the global circuit—old Nicky's magical *natural medium*."

He pauses, assessing us through his oversized lenses. Are they slightly tinted? "Why are you two here again?"

Andromeda tucks her wild hair behind her ears, which makes them flare like Dumbo's. "We have a little problem."

"Well, you've come to the right place for problems," Cassian replies. "They're shutting us down. Bastards pulled our funding this morning." He smirks ironically. "Just like Tesla."

He turns to the smoking tower. "My business partner drove off an hour ago, declaring the whole project dead."

Andromeda's lips tighten with condolences, and then her face brightens. "We bring glad tidings." She's holding out Tesla's notebook to him, eyes ablaze, as if it's his own personal tarot card. "This belonged to Nikola Tesla. He kind of worked it out."

Cassian grins. "He kinda worked it out?"

"Yes. He did."

"Worked what out, sweetheart?"

"The natural medium ... thing—it's all in here." She presses the book at him. "We found his lost notebook."

Cassian laughs in staccato. "Tesla's lost notebook is a myth."

"It's not," she insists. "We found it in his room at the New Yorker Hotel two hours ago."

His face screws up dismissively.

Andromeda holds the notebook out further. Cassian swipes it skeptically. With an amused shake of his head, he opens to a random page and reads the header to one of Tesla's equations. "We see how the numbers three, six, and nine represent the mathematical vector governing how scalar waves propagate through vortices in the lattice of higher-dimensional space *mother of fuck*—"

"Easy, cowboy." She snatches the notebook back as his eyes bug out behind the big lenses. "It's a lot to take in."

Cassian rips it back, and she growls, "Hey!"

He flips to the first page and reads the title: PROTO-WORLD ENERGY VIA THE NATURAL MEDIUM. He squints. "Why are the words from his patent changed?"

"Not our field," she says. "The CIA expected it to be some kind of weapon. Will you provide a statement of authenticity—"

"Weapon?" Cassian's eyes light up. "Nah. This is his design to transmit power wirelessly. Only ..." He turns over a few pages. "A whole lot *more*."

I snatch it from his hand—it's a notebook snatch-fest. I show him the title page with its baffling number diagram: a triangle inside a circle. "What's *proto-world*?" I demand. "Was Tesla interested in the ancient world?"

I'm pressing Cassian the way Frank pressed me a couple of hours ago. Yeah, it's been a weird day. He stares at me like I'm cuckoo, then says, "I've never heard it phrased that way."

I flip to a back page. "Why did he draw this Egyptian ankh?"

He blinks. "What the hell is an *ankh*? That's Tesla's electric oscillator. One of his greatest achievements."

I go to protest, but he rakes his floppy hair and says, "He was notoriously interested in the esoteric. Tesla burst onto the scene and revolutionized everything—bam, he's famous and celebrated. Then he starts getting kooky ideas. They turn on him. Now he's an outcast, a pariah. But his genius never left, and he *never* stopped working in private." Cassian glances at the notebook. "Looks like he made some upgrades. *Hey, can I see that?*"

"Cassian!" Jimmy yells. "The mercury, man!"

"Ah, shit." Cassian spins toward a large mechanical box with bubbling liquid inside. Wires snake out in all directions. I swear if I see the word *Acme* anywhere, I'm out. The box is topped by two metal plates that face each other like electrodes with a spark gap.

"Too hot, Jimmy!" Cassian shouts. "Bring that mercury temp down, or you're gonna blow the whole place."

Against my better judgment, I step closer, staring into the hypnotic vat of swirling silver liquid. It ripples in strange, reflective patterns, like a futuristic lava lamp.

"What is that?" Andromeda is mesmerized.

"Don't touch," he warns. She pulls her hand back. "It's hot, liquid mercury. It's electrified."

"Is that part of Tesla's design?" she asks.

"Nah, that's my own little witchcraft. Mercury is highly conductive. This box is the tower's capacitor."

I have no idea what a capacitor is.

Cassian eyes the dangerous mercury, removes a hissing cable, and the sloshing liquid calms. "This little dreamcrusher sits atop the tower and gathers energy like a battery. Only capacitors release *all* their stored energy at once in a massive pulse. Imagine the full battery of an electric car slapping out in *one second*."

"That's a heck of a slap," I say.

"Now, imagine a tower pulsing out such a slap every second and voilà—*Nick-oh-lah's* magnifying pulse transmitter—Earth energy, baby."

"So that's Tesla's vision," Andromeda says.

"Simplified version ... for idiots." Cassian grits his teeth as he cranks a wheel on his mercury-filled capacitor. "If Tesla had been allowed to fulfill his vision, we'd have colonies on Mars by now."

He turns to Andromeda with a sigh, brushing off his hands. "Can I, uh ... see that notebook?"

18

Andromeda hands Cassian the makeshift document, scribbled in her meandering longhand. It's a hasty word salad of terms like "veracity," "indisputable," "most truthful," and "authenticity." *Is this gonna hold up? Do courts still matter?* I get the feeling Andromeda Dey knows as much about expert legal discovery as my aunt Florence.

She thrusts the pen at Cassian, chin up, defiant. He signs with a disinterested sigh. "I don't think this is a real—"

"It's very real," she insists.

Real like Bigfoot.

Cassian eyes Tesla's notebook. "Can I at least make photocopies?"

"No."

He holds out the signed form, then pulls it back when she reaches for it. "I'm not just gonna let you walk outta here with that science, sweetheart."

"Is that a threat?"

He adjusts his oversized glasses. "Do I look like the violent type?"

"Forget about it," she replies, grabbing for the document.

He lifts it away. "I can't do that," he says, pretending to tear it, making tutting sounds.

"All right, listen." She faces him impatiently. Her nerves look shot. "You really don't want to be involved in this."

"Ohhh." His brows lift. "So, what ... you two are in some kinda trouble? No offense, Agent Dharma, but I don't trust you not to lose it—or sell it on Etsy."

"A word?" I say, pulling Andromeda aside as she protests. She looks miserable again.

I wonder if it's not too late to turn around, call the police, and face the music. But a crazy idea has been percolating. Out of earshot, I say, "We need to lie low. Preferably out of the country, right?"

"Yeah."

"I know a place."

"Where?" She's nibbling her thumb.

"Third World. No prying eyes. Off the grid. I know someone."

She snorts. "You underestimate the CIA."

"Someone who will be very interested. Atlantis is kind of his thing."

"I'm listening."

"Fabian Faust."

I explain that Professor Faust was my mentor at Cambridge. His recommendation got me the faculty position at Columbia. His reputation was legendary—a brilliant Danish archaeologist known for unorthodox theories and groundbreaking research. He had an undeniable mystique; students from all over packed into his overcrowded classes, sitting in the aisles.

But Faust flew too close to the sun. One fantastical claim ended his career overnight.

He published a radical paper claiming Atlantis was real. He came to believe it passionately. The academic community mocked him; they turned on him savagely. So, he doubled down.

A month later, he was stripped of his positions and expelled. He was an instant pariah; anyone associated with him became toxic. Everyone distanced themselves.

Even me.

His spectacular fall from grace was excruciating. We'd been close during my time in England. I had to denounce him. I went on record, branding his work as pseudo-archaeology. I couldn't understand how someone of his caliber fell for fairy tales. The wounds are still raw. We haven't spoken since.

Professor Fabian Faust turned his back on academia with a devil's trill, happily choosing exile.

He could afford to.

Rumors at Cambridge whispered about his net worth. I never asked, but his family is Danish aristocracy. After World War One, they plowed their ancestral fortune into Europe's blossoming aerospace industry. Faust is obscenely wealthy.

And there's another reason to go. Faust might already know much of what's in Frank's Project Nephilim files, making him a natural ally. Once we recover the lost data from the dead man's switch, we'll show him, and he'll want to help.

"Do you trust him?" Andromeda hugs herself as we stand in the cold breeze. "Sounds like you pissed him off."

"Unequivocally. He has no love for institutions or authority. He detests government and claims it hinders his work."

"Where is this dreamboat? Is he single?"

"He's doing excavations at Machu Picchu in Peru."

She's considering it.

"I doubt you're getting through TSA," I say.

She pulls a fake Latvian passport from her pouch. "I know all the cool kids at the CIA. It's you I'm worried about."

"Me?"

She cocks her head. "You think you're getting on a flight, Professor?"

Right. I'm a fugitive. Definitely flagged. Big Brother has me nailed.

Her eyes darken with thought. There's a devilish grin. "Wait a sec." She pulls out a *second* Latvian passport. "This is so crazy it just might work."

It's Frank's fake passport.

She tells me her plan—talk about risky.

"Jimmy!" Cassian calls from the tower. "We're not the Long Island Power Company, bro. Why is this thing still hooked to the grid?"

"Generator's out of gas!" Jimmy replies.

"I need a grant." Cassian huffs, kicking the metal frame.

I watch him muttering to himself like a crazy person, running a hand through his tousled hair—the leather jacket, those vintage glasses—trying to take him seriously as a renowned scientist.

I rub my neck. "What about him?"

"What *about* him?"

"It's his life's work. I don't think he's gonna let us waltz out of here with Tesla's Ninth Symphony."

She stares at Dr. Wilder, jaw set hard in thought, more like irritation at this new liability. "Tesla's breakthrough is at the core of Project Nephilim," she says quietly. "I need to know why."

"What are you saying?"

She has difficulty even uttering the words. "We need him."

"What?" I didn't expect her to say that. But who am I kidding? After learning the truth about my dad, I need to know, too. If anyone can crack this mystery, it's this Tesla guy.

She holds up the notebook with a wry smile. "He needs a grant."

I see where she's going with this. "I don't love dragging an unwitting person into a manhunt. We'll have to tell him. It has to be his choice." I throw up my hands. "I'm staying out of it."

Andromeda strides over to Cassian. "Dr. Wilder?" Her tone is urgent. "Okay, you're on. We're going to meet someone who might even fund your project. But we have to leave for Peru—today."

Cassian idles with laughter. "Peru? *Today?* Ever heard of FaceTime? What is he, some expat, tech-bro crypto millionaire?"

"Billionaire," I say. "And he's a true believer in spending for the cause."

"Whose cause?"

"He throws out grant money like candy at the Rose Parade to projects that align with his … aesthetic." I glance away. "I can put in a good word."

"Let me get this straight," Cassian says. "You two just stumbled on the holy grail of physics, and your first thought is, 'Hey, let's take it to Peru!' You're both a little bonkers."

"Says the man who's been chasing Tesla's daydreams," Andromeda says.

"Touché. But there is a science to my madness." Cassian pauses. "*Billionaire?*"

I nod.

"Today?"

We both nod.

He squints up at his smoking tower, sighs deeply, then looks over at the crumbling facade and shattered windows of Tesla's Wardenclyffe lab, where his bumbling assistant is knocking over boxes of coupling bands.

The birdsong has stopped; only the March wind whistles through the bare trees. I know what he's thinking. His project is dead. There's nothing left for him here.

"All right." Cassian sighs in defeat, flipping the main breaker with a loud pop. "I'm gonna regret this, aren't I?"

Andromeda hesitates and glances at me. "Cassian, before you decide, there's something you should know."

PART II
ATLANTIS

19

The Chicago World's Fair, 1893

IT'S night in the White City and the lights of the Columbian Exposition glitter in the distance. The fair dazzles with a hundred thousand incandescent bulbs—a triumphant showcase for Westinghouse Electric and its young genius, Nikola Tesla, whose alternating current has bested Edison's in the war of the currents.

"What's happening?" a young boy asks, perched on his father's shoulders.

"Just watch," his father whispers. "You're about to see something you'll never forget."

In a dark, mist-shrouded field, a crowd of wealthy socialites is gathering for a mysterious demonstration. Mr. Tesla himself stands before them, his shoes hidden by swirling fog. He holds a clear lightbulb the size of a watermelon.

"Why is that man holding a glass ball?" the boy asks. "Is he going to break it?"

Tesla smiles playfully in the starlight, lifting the bulb to his side with a magician's flair. The crowd holds its breath—no wires or fixtures—just a gaunt man holding a globe in an open field.

Suddenly, the sphere glows in his hand. Gasps ripple through the audience as ethereal light illuminates their astonished faces. Tesla waves the bulb, walking among them. Murmurs spread as they grapple with the impossible sight.

"Magic!" a man says.

"Witchcraft," an old woman whispers, crossing herself.

"*Ouch!*" The father winces as his son grips his scalp in wonder.

Tesla's blue eyes shine softly as he approaches the boy, the wireless light casting a halo around them. His expression is gentle and kind.

"The future is free."

20

Cusco, Peru
Tony Koviak

How the hell *am I in Peru?*

It's the morning after our escape from New York. Let's just say that disguising myself as Frank Vergazza wasn't my proudest moment—Yankees hat, scarf, eyeglasses that made me look like Eugene Levy—the works.

Andromeda told me it's common knowledge in intelligence circles that TSA is security theater, an illusion of safety. She instructed me to ask the TSA agent at the podium if they still allow duty-free liquids on international flights. Cognitive jamming, a common CIA tactic.

It worked.

He barely glanced at Frank's photo before giving me an enthusiastic rundown of the rules. I walked right through.

The hair color mostly washed out. I have a newfound respect for *Mission Impossible* masks, I lived it!

The Sacred Valley in Peru is nestled in the Andes like a lost fairy-tale kingdom. Predawn clouds hang low, swirling over everything, adding to the mystical vibe.

Andromeda and Cassian are with me on the Ollantaytambo train platform. Cassian has a backpack slung over one shoulder, stuffed with his laptop and other gear. He's wearing the Dahmers—yeah, I've named his big retro glasses.

Andromeda sports a bohemian field jacket. Her ragged mane, tucked under a dark beanie, makes her look like Folk-Rock Barbie. At least she's embracing the criminal chic. She picked up both items at JFK.

"Perfect," Cassian grumbles, pacing like a rain cloud. "A lovely time of year to sightsee in the Andes ... with Jason Bourne hunting us."

The high-altitude air smells of woodsmoke and moss, but Cassian doesn't notice the scenery. Another wave of existential ranting bubbles up. I think he regrets coming.

"Federal fugitives," he exclaims. "That is *wonderful*."

"She kinda got me, too." I offer in solidarity. He shoots me a glare. "Look, I once spent three months living in a tent in the Sahara, tracking down a rumor about a lost temple. Trust me, I understand the doubts."

Watching his mental tug-of-war back in New York was a masterclass in psychology. He wanted that notebook so badly. After glancing at just two more pages—*two!*—he decided, CIA or not, he'd follow it to the ends of the Earth. His choice.

"Dammit, Tesla. Son of a ...," Cassian had cursed under his breath. He said he'd learned more from those pages than in all his years at Caltech and Wardenclyffe *combined*. He mumbled like a madman on the flight, "He did it. He did it." Over and over.

I remind him we're going to see a billionaire who can offer a grant. It's like trying to pep up the Scarecrow on the Yellow Brick Road—the Wizard can fix us! Truth is, not even Faust can salvage this train wreck. No one can. Revealing Project Nephilim and whatever allies it brings is our only hope.

Twenty-four hours until Andromeda's dead man's switch emails us Frank's classified CIA files—a century of government research on deep human origins—stuff she swears will rewrite history. Oh man, I'm *dying* to read it.

Faust will be blown away and become a powerful ally. That's the plan, anyway.

Or he could turn us in.

A cluster of eager tourists gathers for the train, decked out in hiking gear. Languages float around us ... bits of German, a line of Korean, a Brazilian laugh. A group argues in Turkish about directions. I suppress a smile, resisting the urge to tell them in Turkish that their map is upside down.

The whistle blows, and we join the crush of outerwear into a blue passenger car labeled *Machu Picchu–Cusco* in yellow letters. The journey provides unparalleled views of the Sacred Valley as it snakes along the Urubamba River.

Andromeda leans close. "Once we reach Machu Picchu, we need to lie low. The CIA's reach gets shaky out in the sticks. We should be okay."

I contemplate all the ways this surprise reunion with my controversial mentor could go wrong. We have unfinished business.

"It's best we don't tell Professor Faust anything until we have the Project Nephilim data," Andromeda says, her brows knitted.

"Faust has some quirks," I warn. "Best to let me do the talking."

21

"*Ahí abajo!*" The security guard points. *Down there.*

I follow his gaze to a group of students digging in the grass below a massive stone wall.

The view leaves me speechless, just like it did when I first came here as a newbie undergrad. Machu Picchu is something else.

Along a towering ancient wall of megalithic stones, a team of young people carefully clears overgrown grass and dirt from the foundations. Probably archaeology students from a local university. Judging by the residue, they've removed about two feet of Earth.

Figures. Faust must have bought his way into this sensitive UNESCO Heritage site. I wonder how much he's paying the authorities and their foot-soldier guards. For Fabian Faust, price doesn't exist.

I cover this site in my lectures at Columbia. The cyclopean wall he's unearthing is the outer face of the Temple of the Three Windows—Machu Picchu's most mysterious feature.

Three beautiful trapezoidal windows, each about three feet tall, are precisely carved into the wall, an engineering marvel.

But why is the world's most infamous researcher of lost civilizations digging here?

There's a large canvas field tent, one side rolled up.

A tall figure in wool pants and hiking boots oversees the excavations. He's wearing a rugged Scandinavian jacket with lots of pockets. In his hands are a trowel and a brush. Even from a distance, I'd recognize that preternatural silhouette anywhere.

Dr. Fabian Faust. The portrait of Nordic sophistication. Pale and drawn, chiseled features, prominent angular nose. Despite being fifty-nine, he has a vibrant energy, deep-set gray eyes, and dark blond hair swept back over the tips of his ears, giving him the look of a Victorian vampire.

We cross into his work site. Faust kneels beside a student, clearing debris from the foundations. The student whispers that he has visitors, but Faust keeps working, ignoring us, until a familiar voice stops his hand.

"Is this the face that launched a thousand condemnations?" I say, invoking the famous line from the 1592 play about Helen of Troy: *Doctor Faustus*.

Slowly, he looks up as if seeing a phantom. His mouth opens slightly, but his expression doesn't change. "Tony Koviak," he whispers, his Danish accent lending a soft Germanic lilt. "You are the last person I expected to see down here." He rises, eyeing my companions.

I squint up at the iconic landmark. "Whose campaign did you bankroll to get access here?"

He turns back to his work, features sharp with concentration. "Have you come to save me from my folly?"

Hey, at least he doesn't seem to know I'm *wanted by the CIA*. His remote exile works in our favor. I debate how much to divulge about Andromeda's identity and decide to be honest. We're going to tell him everything when we get the Nephilim files, and I don't want to damage his trust.

"May I present Andromeda Dey, a data analyst at the CIA," I say. "And Dr. Cassian Wilder, a Caltech geophysicist."

Faust extends a cautious hand, only mildly intrigued. His piercing eyes never leave me as he shakes hands. The hurt of my betrayal is still there. He nods to his assistant. "Paulo, continue along the foundations. Keep to the Paleolithic layer."

Paleolithic layer? That's impossible—that's older than Göbekli Tepe!

Faust's theories on prehistoric, advanced civilizations cost him everything: tenure, reputation, and career. Yet here he is, still chasing the dream.

"Tea?" He turns and walks toward the spacious field tent.

Inside is an intellectual sanctuary: Persian rugs, antique desks, a World War One cot with wool blankets—a wilderness man cave worthy of Caesar. The scent of aged canvas mingles with cold mountain air. Brass lanterns hang from tent poles like a Byzantine library. Ancient Roman busts sit atop bookcases. It's like he brought his study into the wild.

The canvas flaps gently in the breeze as Faust moves to a wooden table with a camp stove. A ceramic kettle is simmering on a low flame. He prepares four mugs of Earl Gray like a priest offering a benediction. He adds steamed heavy cream and butterscotch, then dusts with pink sea salt and hands them to us. "As long as there is tea, there is hope."

Classic Faust, embracing every drop of *hygge*, the uniquely Danish art of creating cozy environments and luxuriating in life's simple pleasures.

I notice the canister of Earl Grey is a local blend infused with Peruvian coca leaf, the same plant used to make hard cocaine when processed.

No wonder he's so prolific.

"Now." Faust settles against the creaking desk, eyes glinting with dark curiosity. "Why have an anthropologist, a geophysicist, and a data analyst come to my humble outpost?"

I hold the hot mug, watching the fog roll over the steep terraces. "What can you tell us about advanced civilizations in the Ice Age?"

22

"WAS THERE a high civilization in remote prehistory?" I ask Faust point-blank. He's undoubtedly questioning my motives after my very public denouncement.

Faust draws up like a dark swan. "Proceed carefully, Professor. Those who eat of the forbidden fruit of knowledge shall surely die."

"You can say that again," Andromeda says under her breath.

He sharpens his gaze on her, eyebrow raised. I should've warned them about his razor-sharp analytical mind. "Oh, I know all about the CIA's interest in the ancient world," Faust says.

He does? I glance at Andromeda, then Cassian. My poker face blows.

"Do you want to know what the CIA has found?" he asks, blindsiding us into silence. "I know what they've found," he says sardonically.

He turns to Cassian. "Dr. Wilder, what is your area of expertise?"

Cassian adjusts the Dahmers, uncomfortable with the sudden spotlight. "Geophysics and electromagnetic field theory. Specifically, I've been researching Nikola Tesla's ideas on wireless energy transmission."

Faust's forehead lifts. "Tesla? How intriguing. And how, pray tell, does that relate to an archaeological excavation in the Andes?"

Cassian shoots me a look. "Still wondering that myself, Professor."

When we told Cassian that Tesla's lost notebook was the centerpiece of Project Nephilim—that the CIA's been hunting it since 1943—he glitched out. Now, he's determined to uncover why the government's so obsessed and how it all connects. I still can't fathom how Tesla relates to history. I'm wrestling with the idea that Atlantis was even real. Cassian's digging into the science; no one is more qualified. Having Faust involved is a huge plus. I won't spill everything until we have Andromeda's data safely in hand, but I suspect his research overlaps with Project Nephilim.

"We came across something extraordinary, Faust," I say, feeling a thrill. "Something remarkable."

Faust is riveted.

I decide not to reveal too much yet. "Perhaps you could bring my colleagues up to speed on your … work."

Truth is, I have *no idea* what he's been up to. I skimmed his wild theories years ago, like a driver who can't look away from a wreckage. I need a crash course myself.

Faust half-smiles, almost wistful. Yeah, he's still wounded. "If you insist upon self-immolation, you're in luck. You've come to the perfect place to see it firsthand." He sips his tea.

"Machu Picchu?" I ask. "What does the Sacred Mountain have to do with your—" I sidestep the more offensive term. "—research?"

"That's *not* what the Inca called it," Faust snaps. "How is your Quechua, Professor?" he rasps, referring to the Incan language.

I hesitate, unsure where he's leading. American studies aren't my forte. Many academics secretly believe there's not much to see in the Americas compared to other parts of the world.

Faust continues. "Machu Picchu means *ancient mountain*. The Inca called it that. The foundations were here when they found it. They claimed it was built by *giants*." He hisses the word for effect.

"Here we go," I exhale.

"Not actual giants," Faust chuckles. "Giants of intellect and civilization. A sophisticated people who lived long before."

The Inca didn't establish Machu Picchu?

"Show me," I say.

He tips his head like a gentleman. "Though you may feel a little like Alice, eating a dangerous tart. One side makes you larger." He picks up a folder. "I'll show you something stranger than Wonderland. History is a lie."

Andromeda's eyes flick to me. Those were Frank's exact words. I flinch at the memory. Faust has stumbled onto what the CIA is hiding. Now I'm the one riveted. I've always thought of his mind like a great steel trap, set under tension and ready to turn you on your head with a snap of wild genius.

As we leave Faust's tent, crisp mountain air fills my lungs. The thin atmosphere at this altitude makes each breath feel like a sip of icy water.

Faust leads us down to the site with the dignified air of Obi-Wan Kenobi leaving his exiled cave—if Obi-Wan swapped his lightsaber for Ray-Bans.

"The past does not explain itself; it is written like the mystery of lines etched on a man's face, only hinting at its story." He guides us to an imposing megalithic wall.

"What do you know about our past, Professor?" Andromeda asks, walking behind him.

He stops and grows still, his voice echoing from the wall. "Have you ever felt homesick for a place you've never been? A vague sense of something lost—to time? A longing for a home that never was?"

He turns to face her. "What if that loss you feel is a memory? An echo of something real?"

He pauses, gazing up. "Tell me, Agent Dey, what do you see?"

She stares up at the massive architecture, seemingly impressed he remembered her name. "An Inca wall."

"No." Faust points to the highest part. "Those are Inca walls."

Along the top is a layer of stonework made of small, crude fieldstones, like the stacked stones of an English sheep field.

"Look closer," Faust says. "Can you spot the three building styles?"

My trained eye catches it instantly. Three styles, and the oldest is the most advanced.

"To be clear," he adds, "the Inca built most of what you see here, atop older megaliths. The terraces, the houses, all are Inca. They were master builders."

"How old are these foundations, then?" Andromeda asks, glancing up at the towering megaliths.

Faust smiles. "The Incan culture lasted three hundred years, contemporary with Tudor England. These megaliths are much older. Worldwide, we see technology regressing, from advanced to crude."

It's true.

I once lectured at Columbia on Egypt's mystifying architecture. People assume human advancement is linear, from primitive to advanced.

The Great Pyramid—among the oldest structures—was the most precise building in the world until the Paris Observatory in 1667. It contrasts sharply with the crumbling mud-brick pyramids of later dynasties.

Egypt started out driving Ferraris and ended up with wagons.

And don't even get me started on Göbekli Tepe in Turkey, my new job site. That megalithic stunner appeared fully formed at the end of the Ice Age, with no earlier culture in sight. Around the planet, the earliest constructions are the most impressive, as if part of our story is missing.

On the mist-shrouded terraces of Machu Picchu, I shove my hands into warm pockets, staring up at Faust's ancient mountain. Lebanon, Malta, Peru—*why is the* oldest *archaeology always the finest?* I've been a researcher long enough to know that coincidences aren't as common as people think.

"Interesting, ya?" Faust says. "Newer cultures repurpose the old. But what came before?"

He gestures to enormous megaliths rising from the ground like abstract art. "Some grow out of the Earth, like forgotten dreamscapes, almost science fiction, as if they've been here for eons."

Cassian crouches, examining the stones. "The weathering certainly predates Tudor England. I'd say contemporary with the Avebury stone circles."

"Caltech geophysicist, did you say?" Faust remarks smugly. "Wait until he sees the enclosure of the Great Sphinx of Egypt."

I let his odd comment slide.

"Is there no way to date the stonework?" Andromeda asks.

"Can't carbon-date stone, no organic material," Cassian replies.

I nod. "These walls could be five hundred or fifty thousand years old, no way of knowing."

Faust points higher. "Those terraces climb above the tree line, vanishing under permanent ice sheets, as if the climate were once different."

"Spooky," Cassian says.

Faust nods. "Ya, nothing here fits the standard model of history."

23

Inside Faust's canvas man cave at the Temple of the Three Windows, the cloud cover brightens. Machu Picchu glows as if God set up a celestial softbox for a heavenly photo shoot.

Cassian sips his second cocaine brew. "Who built it?"

Faust lowers his voice. "You've certainly heard of them."

"Don't believe the rantings of an old dreamer," I quip. "He's been watching too many alien shows."

"It's not *aliens*." Faust's wolf-gray eyes are hurt. "The story of our species is fantastic enough."

The Danish academic walks to a box of field tools and pulls out a coiled rope. Is he gonna do rodeo? Wrangle up some Atlanteans?

"Modern humans have walked Earth for at least three hundred thousand years, possibly eight hundred thousand—things keep getting older." Faust hands one end of the rope to Andromeda and walks thirty paces out into the swirling fog.

"This rope represents our timeline." His voice rings out as he lays it on the grass. He trots back and pinches off one inch of rope from her hand. "This single inch is all of recorded history. The rest is shrouded in the mists of time. Forgotten."

It's a powerful visual. A timeline that deep is well outside my field. But it's a lot of rope disappearing into the fog. It would mean humanity's history is far more complex and ancient than we imagine.

Faust is in full flow now, eyes blazing with fervor. He's always had a magnetic intensity, a way of making you want to believe. "Fully modern humans, with the same capacity for reason, intellect, and creativity, existed for nearly a million years, and they say we wandered around with clubs."

"'What a piece of work is a man.'" Andromeda quotes Shakespeare out of the blue. "'How noble in reason, how infinite in faculty. In action, how like an angel—'"

"'In apprehension, how like a god.'" Faust stands tall, Herculean. "The beauty of the world. The paragon of animals." He winks at her. "Hamlet is Danish."

"The record is clear," I object, feeling like I need to push back on these outlandish claims. *I'm a Columbia professor!* "Civilization began in Sumer in 4500 BC. We're talking about hunter-gatherers —cavemen."

Faust looks amused. "You've been sorely missed, Tony. But you must consider the facts. I have much to show you."

I point at the rope. "Are you suggesting human civilization stretches back that far?"

Cassian shrugs. "Absence of evidence isn't evidence of absence. Just because we haven't found proof doesn't mean it didn't exist."

I frown at the geophysicist. "You're on *his* side now?"

"Faust is kinda right," Andromeda says wearily, like an actor off-screen.

Faust steamrolls over her. "We are a people with amnesia! We've forgotten our own story!"

"Please, don't say the A-word." My anti-A-word conditioning runs deep. I can feel my Tweed Club card being revoked. I'm becoming one of them! I know I shouldn't provoke him, and I know the US government itself is now confirming that it's real, but we're talking about my life's work here, my core beliefs.

"Dismiss Plato at your peril," Faust warns. "Atlantis was real, not some underwater fantasy with magic crystals."

Well, *hallelujah*.

He gestures at his rope. "There was another before it and another before that. The idea resonates in our hearts because it's our collective memory."

"Atlantis?" Cassian laughs. "I don't believe in mystical cities and crackpot conspiracies, Professor. You're chasing a myth." He glances at me with concern.

"Precisely correct." There's lightning in Faust's gray eyes. "The everlasting constellation of myth—the key to our past. Today's settled science is yesterday's heresy, Dr. Wilder. You, of all people, should know that. Our track record is abysmal. I'm afraid it's those who cling to an outdated model of history who are guilty of irrationality. They are blind men groping through the dark."

I sigh. "I hope you have more than ropes and walls to prove this."

Faust turns to his desk. "My boy, you have no idea."

24

Renaissance paintings stare down at me from the khaki canvas glowing in the sunlight. It smells like camping gear and old leather inside Faust's field tent.

Andromeda leans in my ear and whispers, "Everything Faust is saying is in Project Nephilim. So maybe don't be a belligerent ass about it."

Best behavior. Scout's honor.

Atlantis is real … Atlantis is real … Atlantis is real …

"Plato's account of Atlantis was a morality tale," I argue anyway. "A warning about hubris. Many fables are just that: legends. Like the Labyrinth of Egypt, which later inspired the labyrinth in Crete with its Minotaur."

Faust laughs, breaking his calm Nordic demeanor for the first time. "Yet Knossos—the mythical city in Crete—was found, Tony! An underground labyrinth filled with bull iconography. Even Troy was thought to be a fable, ya? Made up by Homer in the Iliad until Heinrich Schliemann discovered the ruins."

Excellent points. Ugh, I hate it when he makes sense. I remember Project Nephilim and hold my tongue.

Faust sweeps his hair behind his ears, studying me like a falcon. "When inventing a morality tale, you don't detail the city's exact dimensions. Plato went to great lengths to place Atlantis geographically. That's unnecessary."

He gestures to Andromeda. "Like the Andromeda of myth, you're chained to the standard model, Tony Koviak."

"Does that make you Perseus then, here to unchain me?"

He scowls. "You came to me seeking the truth, ya? You can leave anytime. I don't want to fight, for goodness' sake."

"Where do you believe Atlantis was, Professor Faust?" Andromeda asks.

He is resolute. "North America was the homeland of Atlantis."

"You're shitting me," Cassian blurts out.

"Plato was explicit. Atlantis was beyond the Straits of Gibraltar, on the opposite continent across the *true* ocean—the Atlantic."

"Plato said that?" Cassian's eyebrows shoot up.

"Ya."

Wait. Does Plato have Atlantis in North America? My head spins. I've read that text endlessly and never registered the explicit mapping. How could Plato know about the Americas?

"Most miss it. We see what we want to see," Faust says, unfurling a map across the table. "The Piri Reis map," he announces.

"A remarkable copy," I say, picking it up.

"It's the original."

I pull my hand back with a gasp, suddenly aware of the ancient gazelle skin under my fingers.

"Created by a Turkish navigator in 1513," Faust explains. "Compiled from ancient sources, which puts it on the same footing as the Alexandria documents."

We lean over the yellowed parchment, tracing the radiant navigation charts and jagged coastlines.

"What are we looking at?" Cassian asks.

"A smoking gun," Faust replies. "This is a world map. Portugal, Africa, and Brazil are all here." He points to a section. "And this is Antarctica, centuries before its discovery."

"Only not as we know it," Andromeda adds, "It shows the coastline *without ice*, matching NASA's ground-penetrating satellite images. So, the cartography is from when Antarctica had a temperate climate."

We all turn to stare at her. She shrugs.

"How do you know that?" the Scandinavian whispers, eyes trembling.

I watch the color drain from his face. I've never seen him so rattled. *Antarctica without ice!* What's in her encrypted CIA files?

"Please, Professor, proceed," I urge. My own curiosity just hit hyperspeed.

A strand of hair falls into Faust's eyes as he straightens. He looks like he wants to grill Andromeda, but holds back.

"And all this proves Atlantis was real?" Cassian asks, knitting his brow.

"Allow the mosaic to form a picture," Faust replies. "Stay with me. We'll get you out of Plato's cave yet." It's a jab at academia, suggesting they trap people in a cave of falsehoods.

"Atlantis wasn't a city. It was a global seafaring civilization."

25

"WE'VE BEEN FOOLISHLY SEARCHING for a lost city," Faust says, leaning against his desk. "Atlantis had colonies and outposts around the world."

Cassian frowns. "I thought oceans were barriers to movement."

Faust dismisses him with a wave. "Oceans weren't barriers—they were superhighways. Especially during the last Ice Age when sea levels were four hundred feet lower."

"So, you're saying Atlantis is the root of all cultures?" Cassian asks.

"*Præcis,*" Faust exhales. *Precisely.*

"We see Atlantis reflected in a mirror shattered into a million myths," he says, turning to me. He hands me a familiar encyclopedia. "Professor Koviak, no one is more qualified."

At Columbia, I give a mean lecture on comparative mythology. It's so popular that the anthropology department opened it to all students and moved us to an auditorium.

I skim through the colorful pages. "It's true, all cultures echo the same motif," I say. "Every creation myth follows a great cataclysm of flood and fire. A civilizing hero shows up and restores the gifts of agriculture, language, laws, architecture—you get the idea."

"One tale could be a myth," Faust says darkly. "But when nearly all cultures tell the same tale, perhaps it's history."

"In Greece, they're the Titans, existing in the time before

Olympus," I say, then flip to a page showing the massive Edfu Temple in Egypt, covered in hieroglyphs. "The Egyptians called their lost homeland *Atlen*. It wasn't Egypt. It was far away in the west. They called that time *Zep Tepi*—the First Time. The time of the gods, before Dynastic Egypt began."

"Dynastic is the time of the pharaohs," Faust clarifies, leaning in. "Zep Tepi was 'the place where the things of Earth were filled with *power*.'"

The way he emphasized the word *power* makes me think of Tesla's notebook with its mysterious "proto-world energy" and pyramid daydreams. I make a mental note to explore that later.

I turn the page. "In India, the Hindu Vedas call their homeland *Atala*, the Shining Island."

"Note the similarity to the word *Atlantis*," Faust says.

I turn to a spread of the Pyramid of the Sun outside Mexico City. "The Aztecs called it *Aztlan*. In Israel, the Book of Enoch says their founders hailed from across a western ocean. And let's not forget mighty King Atlas." I stop on an image of a Greek god bearing a sphere on his back.

Faust leans in. "No doubt you've seen him carrying the weight of the world on his shoulders, the perfect symbol for preserving the flame of civilization after the end of all things. What do we call a map of the world?"

"An atlas," Cassian mutters, still processing the torrent of information. "How do we know they didn't arrive at these ideas independently?" Cassian cleans his foggy lenses.

"My thoughts exactly." I gesture to Cassian, clinging to my precious worldview. "Professor Faust suffers from parallelomania. He sees connections everywhere."

"Better than parallelophobia," Faust fires, "and not seeing connections anywhere. Let's meet the Atlanteans, shall we? Allow me to introduce the civilization bringers."

Civilization bringers. Oh boy, I know where this is headed.

Faust narrows his aristocratic eyes. His voice is low and mythic. "There are always seven."

"In Mesopotamia," I say, "they're the Seven Sages. The Phoenicians called their founding seven kings 'Alateans.'"

With the heaters churning, it's warm inside Faust's study.

Andromeda removes her jacket, revealing the sleeveless white blouse, still buttoned to the neck. The morning dew has given her hair extra body; it's wild around her.

Faust notices the Pleiades tattoo on her arm. His eyebrows lift. "An interesting mark. Rather ironic—a CIA skeptic with a Pleiades tattoo?"

"Oh, I'm not the skeptic," she drawls.

Faust looks at her again, calculating like a fox.

"Ironic, how?" I ask. "The Pleiades are well-known in mythology."

"Ya," Faust says, eyes on her tattoo. "The Pleiades are indeed the Seven Sisters of Greek myth—there's that number again. But do you know what else they were called?" He baits me with a vampiric gaze.

"They were called ..." I hesitate. "The Atlantides."

Atlantis is on her goddamn arm.

Faust turns back to the desk, eyes deep-set and shadowed. He whirls like a sorcerer. "It's a mythological echo of the seven primordial civilization bringers! They survived an apocalypse and tried to rebuild their world!"

Faust's assistant, Paulo, enters the tent, bringing a gust of cool air. "Forgive the intrusion." Paulo has the poise of a bullfighter. He sounds more Seville than Cusco. Late forties, thick stubble. His boots are caked with mud and grass, his suntanned face glistening like he just wrestled an anaconda. Outside, the archaeological dig buzzes with activity.

"Come, come." Faust waves him in. "Perfect timing, Paulo. Everyone, meet my inimitable Number One, Mexico's finest archaeologist. We were just discussing the civilization bringers. Paulo, would you tell our guests about Viracocha?"

Paulo's eyes burn. "Ah, *the founder*. Here in Cusco, we have Viracocha. Local myth says he raised a special tool, or technology, out of Lake Titicaca. It was the key to everything they achieved."

"There's that water again," Faust interjects. "Even in the Bible, God moves upon the face of the waters in the beginning. Water, because Atlantean refugees arrived from the sea. In Polynesia, Maui even uses his hook—a technology—to pull up his sunken homeland from the sea."

He strokes his chin. "A powerful item thrust up from a lake? Now, where have we heard that tale?" He feigns intrigue. "Oh, right … the Lady of the Lake!"

Arthurian legend. Knowledge arriving from water.

Is Faust implying Excalibur is a technology myth? I'll be damned. *Excalibur*—the sword Arthur used to restore a lost utopia. Holy balls, Camelot is an archetype of Atlantis!

"Yeah," Andromeda says nonchalantly. "Excalibur is the Sword in the Stone, the tech in the stone. It symbolizes how the lost technology of Atlantis is locked in their megaliths. Legend says the sword can only be pulled from the stone by one worthy—in this case, scientifically advanced people—because the lost tech lies dormant in their stone constructions, waiting for civilization to understand the science again."

Faust and I stare at her, mouths unhinged.

She shrugs. "CIA research."

Excalibur is a symbol of lost science! Okay. I don't care what camp you're in; that's just cool.

Faust is struck mute. His eyes glow like embers. He's starting to understand why a CIA analyst is here, and he'll want more. We're playing our hand too soon. Best to slow down until the dead man's switch triggers the release of the full cache of Project Nephilim files.

"Merlin, of course." Faust composes himself. "He must be a civilization bringer, a survivor from Atlantis. Echoes of echoes of echoes."

Paulo's been waiting patiently. "Professor, we have a problem." He holds up a walkie-talkie.

Faust's eyes narrow. "What kind of problem?"

26

CIA Headquarters, Langley, Virginia
Director of National Intelligence

INSIDE THE CIA COMMAND CENTER, tension has been steadily ratcheting up all day. A rare Code Black has summoned every analyst from their homes, and unhappy faces now hover over glowing screens.

"Don't plan on going home tonight," the director of national intelligence declares.

A scrawny, moon-faced analyst with a skinny tie stands at his terminal. "Sir, priority update from Homeland Security."

"Spit it out," the director snaps, not bothering to mask his irritation.

"Agent Andromeda Dey boarded a flight to South America with two accomplices."

"You're not serious." The director's voice drops to a low growl, barely containing his fury.

They were allowed to flee the country?

He curses under his breath, seething at the ineptitude of the FBI and local authorities tasked with apprehending the fugitives. *Segmented bureaucracy will be our downfall.* Things just got a whole lot more complicated.

"Where are they now?"

"Cusco, Peru, sir."

The director sighs heavily. "Get me in touch with our Lima field office and dig up any South American connections with these wild cards," he says, his eyes scanning over the data streams cascading across the screens.

He signals to the CIA director while leaning over the ops table without looking up. "Sandy, open the gray line to Targeting Division. The clock just flipped gamma in Prague."

The word *gamma*—code for imminent kinetic engagement—sucks the oxygen out of the room. Seasoned analysts trade nervous looks; they've heard the war stories: Targeting Division arrives, and someone's world ends before dawn. Invoking the secretive task force in daylight feels like summoning a storm god, or vocalizing "Bloody Mary" three times in a bathroom mirror.

"Listen up." The intelligence chief lets his voice carry the length of the bullpen. "Priority Echo, eyes-only DNI. Kill it all."

Keyboards freeze. The order means this isn't happening: no logs, no transcripts, no traceable metadata. Monitors dim as technicians pull power from the recording rack, and the big-board feed resets to hard black.

This is spinning out of control. If we don't handle this, the Demiurge will step in. That's not going to happen on my watch.

27

Machu Picchu
Tony Koviak

FAUST'S ASSISTANT, Paulo, stands at the tent entrance, his voice purring like Puss in Boots. "We have a problem. The authorities are questioning our permit to excavate the interior walls. They threaten to shut us down."

Faust's jaw tightens. "Tell them we simply *must* have access to the interior."

Paulo spreads his hands. "It is one of the biggest tourist areas."

"Give them American cash," Faust snaps, rising from his desk. "Tell them their children will have full rides to Harvard if you must —give me the radio." He gestures impatiently. Paulo hands over the walkie-talkie.

"Diego? Diego, are you there?" Faust barks into the radio.

A crackle. "*Sí.*"

"Listen here, Diego," Faust says coldly. "Don't make me call your boss. If you don't allow our team access to the interior walls at once, you'll be found in violation of section twenty point six of the World Antiquities Act. Your position will be replaced, and you'll spend the next two years in prison for obstructing international treaties. Is that clear?"

Silence. More static. "*Sí.* Of course, *Señor Faust.*"

Faust thrusts the radio back to Paulo. "Make it happen."

"Will do." Paulo wipes his brow and slips out.

"What's the World Antiquities Act?" Andromeda asks, puzzled.

"Damned if I know." Faust grins.

"Okay. I'm starting to get it," Cassian says. "Myths worldwide encode the same tale of Atlantis. They were wiped out and tried to reboot."

Faust retakes his spot by the desk. "You're ahead of most historians, Dr. Wilder. Even India has the Seven Rishis, who survive a flood and reboot civilization."

"Greece has Deucalion and Pyrrha," I add. "They ride out the flood in a box. But Egypt has the greatest ones," I say. "They're called—you guessed it—the Seven Sages. They brought their knowledge from distant western shores."

"The leader in the Egyptian myth was Thoth," Faust says. "He has many names: Thoth, Hermes, Mercury—all the same individual. For Egypt, Greece, and Rome, he restored lost civilization."

"What were they escaping?" Cassian asks.

"Disaster!" Faust slams his fist down. "The end of the last Ice Age ripped Atlantis apart. It was sudden. Catastrophic. They tried to reboot, and they *failed*."

Silence fills the tent. Outside, the busy dig continues with shovels, student voices, and birdsong.

"What would you do"—Faust's voice cracks, eyes haunted—"if you knew everything would vanish? Art, science, culture—they must have suffered unimaginably."

"You've missed the most famous one of all," Andromeda says.

"Oh?" Faust sits up, genuinely stumped.

She laughs. "Noah."

"Ah, ya." Faust chuckles. "Legend says he landed on Mt. Ararat in Turkey, not far from Göbekli Tepe, our oldest site."

I have to push back. "Wouldn't we find evidence of their cities?"

Cassian shakes his head. "Leave the Statue of Liberty outside for twelve thousand years and there wouldn't even be a stain on the dirt."

"*Planet of the Apes* got it wrong?" Andromeda feigns horror.

"But what about underground structures?" Cassian asks. "Wouldn't they have built bunkers?"

Faust's eyes gleam. "Bang-on, Dr. Wilder. That's precisely what we're searching for here at Machu Picchu."

I must have heard that wrong.

Faust is still hunting for the Atlantean Hall of Records! The passion that consumed him for years. I think of the documents in my jacket—Jean Vendôme's research with new clues about the fabled library's location. The late archaeologist claims it's marked by an "overworld" marker, with an "underworld" at its feet. I'll wait to tell him. Faust is going to flip out.

"Mr. geophysicist," Faust spins to Cassian. "When did the Ice Age end?"

Cassian is flustered, then replies, "Twelve thousand five hundred years ago?"

"Mr. anthropologist, what is Plato's date for the sinking of Atlantis?"

I scan my memory. "Twelve thousand five hundred years ago."

"An oddly exact number," Faust purrs.

Yeah. That's ... *weird*.

"Sea levels rose four hundred feet," Cassian says. "Profound climate change. The start of the Holocene."

Andromeda's face blanches, and she shudders audibly at the word. Something about his mention of the Holocene rattles her.

"Does the CIA know something about the Holocene?" I ask her.

"I don't want to talk about it," she says, turning away.

"Why not?"

She hugs herself, shifting uncomfortably. "I just don't, okay? It's upsetting."

"Now you have to tell us," Cassian crows.

"No—I don't." Her face is annoyed.

Cassian lifts a hand at me. "You're gonna let her cop out like that?"

Faust watches her intently. What does she know about the dawn of the Holocene? Something bad must've happened twelve thousand years ago.

"Fair enough." Faust lowers his voice to a conspiratorial whisper. "Let's turn to the *true* hallmark of Atlantis—their pyramids."

28

Wardenclyffe, New York
Jimmy

COLD MIST BLANKETS the field behind Nikola Tesla's former lab at Wardenclyffe on Long Island. In the fog, a crumbling replica of Tesla's tower looms half-disassembled. Jimmy, the former assistant to Dr. Cassian Wilder, stands beside it. His usual exuberance has faded, replaced by creeping dread.

Without warning, rough hands shove him to his knees in the wet grass. His heart hammers in his chest. The scene unfolding is like a twisted dream.

What the hell is this? Jimmy wonders. Are they government agents? That's what they look like, secret service or something. "What do you want?" he shouts at his captors, upset by the sudden detention.

They don't speak.

To his right, a line of young men in dark, tailored suits stands in the drizzle. Chins raised, chests out. A lean man with a pale face is at their head, like a drill sergeant, raven hair artfully tousled to his shoulders. Pitch-black aviators hide his eyes, and he wears a black, tailored blazer. There's a menacing elegance to his cool exterior.

The agents remain expressionless as their commander walks among them, scrutinizing his ranks. Even from a distance, Jimmy senses the man's fury. He watches, waiting for someone to speak. But no one does.

Are they mute?

One agent trembles as the leader turns on him. It appears he's made some mistake. His head bows low, hands shaking. He gestures desperately toward the lab, pleading without words.

But still, no one speaks, just occasional hand motions. The miming chills Jimmy to the bone.

The agent's lip quivers. He's begging now, eyes big with fear. The commander strikes him. Jimmy flinches at the sudden violence.

The agent collapses to a knee, finally shattering the silence with a wail. He's pleading, his voice full of dread, tears streaming down his cheeks. Jimmy can't quite make out his hysterical shouting—something about 'not wanting to go.' The other agents stiffen, eyes fixed ahead as if his vocal outburst violates some vow of silence.

Without a word, the leader reaches behind the man's ear and yanks out a device. Blood slicks the hardware in his hand. Its LEDs flicker wildly. The agent convulses, face slackening. He topples over, twitching, staring blankly at the gray sky like a lobotomized man.

What in the—

The commander turns his aviators to Jimmy. A primal terror grips the lab tech. The man approaches and crouches to eye level. Beneath his blazer, an armored vest bears a three-dimensional black cube.

"Hey, screw you, pal," Jimmy snarls in his South Boston. "I want my lawyer."

Soft electronic chirping pulses from behind his ear as the man produces a sleek, matte-black circlet from his jacket bristling with polished electrodes and strange electromagnetic projectors, like crown jewels. He looms over Jimmy like an archbishop and places the technological ring on his head.

Jimmy's mind explodes with sensation. His mouth drops open as waves of fear and despair crash over him. Agony rises into ecstasy, then plunges into crushing dread. His hands feel miles from his body. Dimension distorts around him as the horror of some derealization stretches space infinitely.

A loving whisper roars in his mind—more of a feeling than sound—as if the blast of a Saturn-V rocket was an emotion:

Where did they go?

The question overwhelms Jimmy. Images of Cassian and his two visitors flash before him. He can feel their faces imprinted on his subconscious. The urge to answer overpowers him.

"I... I don't know," he whimpers, tears streaming. "Please, I don't know!"

The circlet pulses, intensifying dread. Jimmy screams, and his body shakes. "Peru!" he gasps. "They talked about Peruuu!" Panic consumes him, but he's paralyzed. His mind spills open, and the memories tumble out.

In his agony, a gentle thought bubbles up like an angel's whisper.

You are free—you will never need to worry again, Jimmy.

The man in the black blazer removes the ring. Jimmy's face goes slack, one eye pulling unnaturally to the side. His wrists hinge, and he slumps to the ground, gaze vacant, his mind wiped, grunting incoherently.

Inside, Jimmy feels calm. He doesn't need thought now. He's free.

29

Machu Picchu
Tony Koviak

"Knock yourself out," I say, dropping a satellite laptop onto Andromeda's lap. "Told Faust our luggage was lost."

She exhales with relief. "You sure know the way to a data analyst's heart."

Andromeda nestles into the leather chair inside Faust's rustic tent, a wool blanket draped over her legs. The others have trekked up to a bluff to get a better view of Machu Picchu. She's logging in to an email account.

"How long until the dead man's switch triggers?" I ask.

"Later today," she replies, fixated on the screen. "I'll stay here and keep an eye on it."

I nod, pulling out two rugged hard drives and placing them on her blanket. "Back up everything onto these."

She plugs them in, scrolls through the folders, then furrows her brow. "They're filled with Faust's research."

Shoot. This tears at my academic soul, but we need the data: "We may have to delete it." I wince at my own words. She glares at me. I hesitate at the tent's entrance. "He must have backups somewhere, right?"

She eyes me disapprovingly. "Tony—"

"Look," I say, lowering my voice. "Considering what's in Project

Nephilim, he'll probably thank us, right? Might even cut us in on his fortune if we play our cards right."

"I'm *not* deleting his work, Tony," she bites out.

I tap my fingers on the edge of the table, thinking quickly. An idea sparks. "How much space does the laptop have?"

She looks up, eyebrows raised. "The internal drive?"

"Yeah," I say, leaning over to peer at the screen.

She navigates to the system info, eyes scanning rapidly. A smile spreads across her face. "Good call. Faust's laptop is *maxed out* with memory."

I grin. "Spares no expense. Copy his research onto the laptop, free up the hard drives, and back up everything we need without deleting a thing."

She nods, mangling her thumbnail. "I'll start the transfer now."

30

I CATCH up to Cassian on the winding trail to Machu Picchu's overlook. He's got his nose buried in Tesla's notebook. Andromeda finally let him borrow it—provided it never leaves our sight. I guess we've got trust issues.

"What's got you so enthralled?" I ask between breaths.

He doesn't even glance up. "Tesla's universe is electric."

"Well, yeah. He's the electricity guy."

"No, you don't get it. *Everything* is electric. It's a radical shift. We're not talking alternating current anymore. This is a whole new vision of the universe."

Okay.

Cassian's eyes practically glow. "The 1943 Tesla is light-years ahead of the 1905 Tesla I based my work on," he gushes. "It's like he sat back, watched the physics debates of the twentieth century, and said, 'Hold my brandy.'"

"Sounds dramatic."

"He didn't stop at lights and motors. He went into scalar physics—stuff that defies everything we know." He flips pages, muttering about *plasmoids, zero-point energy, scalar waves,* and *aether.*

Okaaaay.

He's rambling like a mad scientist. Which, to be fair, he kind of is. "Didn't the whole 'aether' thing get debunked?" I ask.

His face animates. "Yes! Then physicists discovered it's real and snuck it back in under a new name: the quantum vacuum. We've been using the wrong electrical equations! My entire education is a lie." He breathes the words in distress.

"Tell me about it," I grumble. Ever since Andromeda Dey burst into our lives, it's been one long episode of 'Everything You Know Is Wrong.'

"Tesla never accepted Einstein's relativity," Cassian continues. "It can't reconcile the cosmic and the quantum—the big and the small. Gravity and mass don't account for plasma, which is ninety-nine percent of matter in the universe!"

I hike alongside him, letting him work through his thoughts.

"A dude named James Maxwell worked out the equations for electromagnetism, including scalar potentials. Then Oliver Heaviside simplified them by zeroing out the scalar component because he couldn't measure it. Poof, gone! According to Tesla, relativity—built on Heaviside's lazy equations—is a house of cards built on sand."

"So, Einstein was wrong?"

"No. Einstein's work is bang-on. But we've barreled down a dead-end road, ignoring scalar physics and the aether. It's set us back a century." He looks genuinely distraught.

Part of me wants to geek out; it's fascinating stuff. But I'm kind of preoccupied with, you know, *staying alive*.

"What is the aether?" I ask.

"It's the base code of the matrix. Our reality is projected from it."

Nice. I can sorta grasp that analogy.

"*TRON* is a better analogy," he says. "Its world is electric."

He fiddles with his signature '80s glasses as if adjusting the frequency of his thoughts. "The aether is the crystalline lattice structure that exists everywhere, penetrating everything. It's made of pure energy potentials, not physical stuff, a hidden ocean all around us."

Interesting. The Egyptians believed in a cosmic ocean. Is that the aether? Is that heaven?

He gives me a sideways look. "The aether is *beyond* our familiar three dimensions, in the fifth dimension. Our physical world—everything we see, touch, and measure—is like the surface of that ocean. The aether's energy condenses into matter, like whirlpools in water. Atoms are vortices—knots of aether manifesting in our spacetime. Scalar waves, like the ones Tesla worked with in Colorado, can travel anywhere through the aether *instantly*. Which is bonkers."

"Instantly? Doesn't that break the speed of light thing?"

He grins wider. "The speed of light is a limit in *our* spacetime. In the aether, it doesn't apply. Tesla's science could send information across the universe instantaneously. Imagine the universe is a piece of paper folded so two distant points touch. In the aether, every place and time can be accessed on demand."

Every *time*? Cool. Maybe I can go back and not answer Frank's phone call.

"Tesla believed in the aether to his dying day," Cassian says. "Modern physicists canceled him over such Victorian ideas."

My legs ache as we climb. Cassian is still describing his electric universe. "Space isn't empty. Turns out structures are connected by vast electric currents flowing from the aether. That's why the cosmic web looks the way it does: immense filaments of matter forming a web of galaxies across billions of light-years. It mirrors electrical discharge patterns, like neurons in a brain.

"Oh, and stars?" He's flapping the notebook. "Yeah, they're massive transdimensional power converters, sitting at nodes of vibrating frequency in the aether lattice. They suck in zero-point energy from higher dimensions and convert it into the electromagnetic stuff we see as a star. They're insane."

"Uh-huh," I nod, eyeing the ancient mountain through the mist, feeling like a dummy.

Cassian turns to me, totally serious. "Tesla cracked a true theory of everything."

Then, out of nowhere, he hits me with whiplash. "Oh, by the way... Faust signed on."

Wait, what? I stop in confusion.

"I pitched him for funding. For my new project. Got the green light!"

"That's great!" I fist-bump him. "Told you he's a believer in spending for the cause."

Cassian accidentally drops the notebook in the dust, yelps,

scoops it up, and dashes ahead to catch up with Faust. He's itching to incorporate Tesla's revelations into his designs ASAP. Here we are, about to rewrite history, and I bet he'd leave right now to update his damn tower.

31

CIA Headquarters, Langley, Virginia
Director of National Intelligence

THE FLUORESCENT LIGHTING in the Command Center is unnerving. The national intelligence director massages the bridge of his nose, breathing deeply. One of the perks of his position is not having to work in rooms like this.

His secure phone vibrates—Tehran station chief calling. He lets it ring. No time for that. The director shouldn't be down here. He oversees sixteen intelligence agencies with a budget of $65 million, but today he's playing cat-and-mouse with a rogue agent and a bumbling college professor.

This should've been a routine containment operation.

Screens update overhead, casting blue light on analysts at their stations. Red markers blink ominously over a map of South America.

"Explain to me," the director growls to no one, "how three high-priority fugitives managed to slip through our net and land in Peru."

A disguise & identity specialized-skills officer from the Office of Technical Service is already at his side, ready to deliver the bad news. "Sir, they used forged documents and avoided standard protocols. They flew out of JFK under aliases we've just now uncovered."

"Just *now*?" His gaze could freeze lava. "They left hours ago. What the hell have you been doing?"

The analyst shifts, and his voice drops to an embarrassed whisper. "Sir, their forgeries were top tier, our guys made them, sir. They didn't trigger any flags in the system."

The director's blood pressure rises, and he suppresses the urge to start firing people.

Just then, his CIA chief approaches with a tablet in hand. Her face is a mask of irritation. "We've received a communication from Targeting Division."

His stomach turns. "Give me some good news, Sandy."

"They're taking over the operation."

"Like hell they are," he bellows. "This is our jurisdiction."

She lowers her voice. "Sir, they have a directive." She hesitates, leaning closer. "From Prague."

"Of course they do."

The Demiurge is overreaching this time, waltzing in and hijacking our mission like this.

It means they're afraid of something.

The director of national intelligence knows the real purpose of Targeting Division, the so-called "angels"—the world's most elite hunting force. They're ultranational, a disembodied ghost division that reports directly to Prague. They don't take orders from Langley or the Pentagon. The mystery surrounding them is by design. The director is the only person at the CIA who knows the true nature of power in this world.

He considers defying the directive. *Bad idea.*

"Sir," she cautions, "the division is en route to Cusco. We're instructed to hand over all intel and stand down."

32

Machu Picchu
Tony Koviak

I climb up to the bluff overlooking Professor Faust's dig site. Machu Picchu sprawls beyond, bathed in sunlight. Clouds cling to the mountainside, making the ruins float. It's magnificent, and for a second, I almost forget the craziness I'm caught up in—almost.

Faust's Mexican assistant, Paulo, stands at an easel, working on an oil painting. He's skillfully captured the landscape.

Cassian is laughing with Faust about something as I arrive, out of breath.

"Atlantis was a pyramid culture!" Faust claps Cassian on the shoulder. His eyes blaze with fervor. "Ah, Koviak, just in time. I'll need your help. Dr. Wilder wants to talk pyramids."

I haven't heard Faust's latest heresy on ancient triangles. This should be good.

The ever-stylish Cambridge professor pulls a folder from under his arm. He has that legendary teaching flair, and I sense an epic demonstration brewing. He pulls out a page showing pyramids from around the world.

"Pyramids are on every continent," Faust says. "They encircle the globe." He swipes Paulo's sketch pad and draws a familiar constellation.

"Orion," Cassian notes.

"A disciple of the hunter?" Faust says, referencing the Greek myth. "Then, you'll be delighted to learn the Giza Pyramids are laid out to mirror his belt stars." He holds up a close-up of the three belt stars, then adds a satellite photo of the Giza Plateau, showing all three pyramids.

"Coincidence," I dismiss.

"I might agree with you, Dr. Koviak, but for one problem." Faust introduces another photo of three pyramids in the same layout. "This arrangement is seen at *another* site, on the other side of the world."

The Pyramid of the Sun.

The photo is of Teotihuacan, the Aztec stunner outside Mexico City. Same layout as Orion's belt, mirroring the Giza pyramids.

Okay. That's bizarre. And kinda freaky. I've never been to Mexico's famous pyramids.

"That's not all." Faust holds up another image.

"You've already shown us Giza," I say.

He smirks. "This is China. A pyramid complex outside Xi'an. Also aligned to the belt stars."

[figure: four panels labeled Orion, Egypt, Mexico, China]

"China has pyramids?" Cassian asks.

"Dozens," Faust coos. "They're blurred on satellite maps and hidden by trees. I believe the Smithsonian has had a hand in this treachery."

"The Smithsonian?" I wrinkle my brow. I've dealt with the Smithsonian many times. It's nothing but delightful old curators at their wonderful museums.

Faust is adamant. "The Smithsonian is actively suppressing ancient discoveries that do not fit the accepted narrative, Tony."

He sounds conspiratorial, like Andromeda. I wonder what she knows about the Smithsonian. I'll have to ask.

"Why aren't China pyramids big news?" Cassian presses.

"No one's allowed to examine them," I reply. I'm aware of the China pyramids.

Faust adds, "The pyramids in China predate the Chinese dynasties by *thousands* of years."

"We don't have empirical proof," I argue.

"Because no one is permitted to dig!" Faust explodes.

Cassian lifts a finger. "Hold up. If these pyramids are worldwide and all aligned to Orion's belt stars, that suggests global coordination. How could they have done that over such vast distances?"

"I like your new friends very much, Tony," Faust says. "Historians tell us pyramids are tombs—monuments for kings. They say a pyramid is a natural shape for primitive peoples to build. I disagree. It's complex geometry. They conform to the mathematics of pi and the golden ratio."

I recall Tesla's diagram of the Great Pyramid Frank showed me—the one showing how it's a scale model of Earth—an odd thing for a tomb. I study the photos, trying to make sense of the Orion phenomenon. "Then what are they?" I ask.

Faust's eyes shine, his voice like Nordic ice. "These are not tombs. They are machines."

33

Faust can't possibly believe the Great Pyramid is a machine.

Cassian fidgets. "What kind of machines are we talking about, Professor?"

"Gigantic ones!" Faust shimmers.

I scoff. "I can't believe I'm listening to this conversation."

"You must consider the evidence." Faust is solemn as a vicar.

My students sometimes turn up wild pyramid theories. Social media is a breeding ground for outlandish conspiracies. Now, here's my mentor—objectively the best in our field—outdoing them all.

"Oh, *Professor*." I fold my arms. "Are you referring to Khufu's Pyramid?"

"I don't call it Khufu's Pyramid anymore." His words are sharp. "I prefer *Great Pyramid*. They are not tombs, Tony. Egypt was a colony of Atlantis."

"You're not just saying that because you're banned from Egypt, are you?"

Cassian jumps in. "How are they machines?"

Faust hesitates, eyeing me nervously.

"Fabian …" My tone borders on scolding parent. He's never shown trepidation like this.

"The pyramids were energy devices."

My hand flies to my forehead with a groan. "Absurd! I grew up on the Giza Plateau. My dad led excavations at Saqqara. The pyramids are symbols of ascension—royal tombs—a path to the afterlife!"

"Ya, the *after*-life," Faust says. "Life after the end of the world. After the floods, the apocalypse. The mythology is the way back, the road map for rebirth, don't you see? They encoded everything, Tony." His eyes plead, a coy smile tugging at his lips. "You must admit it's an ingenious method—one that would endure—impervious to the ravages of time."

"There's a literal sarcophagus in the King's Chamber of the Great Pyramid," I counter. "A rectangular granite coffer."

"No man can fit inside that box. Something functional was in there."

"Functional?" Cassian's Dahmers are engaged.

"Ugh." My teeth gnash.

Atlantis isn't real, gang! I can't come to grips with it. I want to protest, but words fail me. Faust is challenging my life's work. Really? Myths are designed to encode lost knowledge? Pyramids are machines? Madness.

Then again ... Frank, Andromeda, Project Nephilim, my dad—they're all real. Can history be a lie?

"Think about it, Tony." Faust's voice is seductive. "No burials were ever found in a pyramid—no hieroglyphs—nothing dynastic. In the Queen's Chamber shafts, they found strange copper terminals and schematics resembling electrical diagrams. Those awkward passages aren't meant for people to traverse."

"They were meant to keep people out!" I have to push.

"The Valley of the Kings." Faust lifts his chin. "Now, *that* is a proper Egyptian tomb. *That* is how pharaohs were buried."

I'm gut-punched. Faust is relentless.

He's right. The Valley of the Kings is a magnificent, subterranean cathedral of the New Kingdom, where King Tut was discovered. Its sloping, spacious hallways draw you in with reverence as you descend to ornate chambers—every inch covered in colorful hieroglyphs—a space designed for people.

The contrast is appalling. The Great Pyramid—the oldest structure—is something else entirely.

"Karnak, Luxor ..." Faust twists the knife. "Dynastic temples lack the megalithic signature. Their columns are small disks of soft sandstone stacked up, an easier method later adopted by Greece. The Great Pyramid has granite blocks, hundreds of tons each, hoisted high into the sky."

He turns to Paulo. "May I commandeer your sketch pad, my Mexican compadre?"

"Always stealing my things, Professor," Paulo sighs.

Faust hands me a charcoal pencil. "Show us the alchemical symbol for *fire*." He breathes the word like a dragon.

With a quizzical look, I press the pencil to the paper, drawing a perfect triangle.

△

A triangle. I think of Tesla's circle diagram with triangle points at three, six, and nine—the alchemy symbol of the philosopher's stone.

"*Præcis,*" Faust whispers.

He writes a single word next to my triangle: *pyramid*. "Please explain the root etymology."

I narrow my eyes. "You have the prefix *pyr*—from the Greek for fire—as in pyro." I write it out.

"And the suffix?"

I write out *amid*. "*Amid*—Old English from the Greek μέσος, *mesos*, meaning middle."

Fire in the middle.

"What, what?" Faust feigns shock. "Are you certain it doesn't say 'tomb in the middle'? Perhaps '*pharaoh* in the middle'?" He tugs at an imaginary beard. "But we have the wrong language, ya? Show us the *Egyptian* word for Great Pyramid."

I dive into my internal library. My lips move silently. I raise the marker: *Ikhet*. "Great Pyramid."

"No. The *literal* translation, Tony."

"The Glorious Light."

"*Præcis,*" he breathes.

I'm dumbfounded. Pyramids are ancient tech. Tech for *what*? I realize I'm crushing the pencil, knuckles white. I massage them until they tingle.

"We see what we want to see," Faust says softly. "Find what you love and let it kill you." He smiles warmly, shifting gears. "Your father —Flinders Koviak—was the greatest archaeologist I ever knew."

This is … astonishing. Who am I, anyway? I'm of no consequence, just a lowly associate professor. I have no real achievements. I have yet to publish anything. I'll likely end up as just another academic footnote. I've never tried to pretend I'm some renowned trailblazer like my father was.

But maybe there's something bigger than all that. Something of real consequence. Maybe I could try to crack the greatest mystery of all time. One the CIA has been covering up.

Here on this grassy overlook at Machu Picchu, with the ancient world stretched before me, my marble worldview cracks like a bolt from the gods. Faust is right. Andromeda is right. Dad was right. I need to update my firmware. It's all a legacy of something before— something lost.

Something they're deliberately hiding.

In his final years, my dad spoke less about his work. The reason becomes clear and leaves me anguished. He found something. *You were protecting me, weren't you, Dad?*

An overwhelming urge hits me to tell Faust everything, to make him an ally. Bad idea. I overcome that impulse.

"So much misunderstanding." Faust faces Machu Picchu, hands clasped behind him. "It's hard when you've invested your entire career into a worldview. There's a lot at stake. I should know. I had more invested than you can imagine. Academics are trapped in their little silos. How can they ever hope to see the full picture?"

I think for a moment, recalling an old legend. "Have you heard the story of the British inventor Sir William Siemens when he climbed the Great Pyramid?" I ask.

"Can't say that I have." Faust is demure.

"An Egyptian guide told me. Siemens was on top of the Great Pyramid. He felt an odd tingling. He sipped from a wine bottle, and it gave him a painful shock. Intrigued, he turned the bottle into a crude Leyden jar, wrapping it with damp paper to collect a charge.

Sparks flew when he raised it. His guide, frightened, tried to snatch the bottle but was thrown back unconscious."

Faust laughs. "Egyptian authorities don't permit anyone to climb the pyramids. For conservation, no doubt."

I instinctively push back. "There's nothing inside the Great Pyramid that could generate electricity. Just empty chambers. Thousands of tourists flow through every day."

"Whatever was in there," Faust says, "was looted away long ago."

"Not *every* chamber," I say, feeling a shiver.

"What do you mean?" Cassian says, noticing the shift in my demeanor.

"The Void," I say quietly.

Cassian's eyebrows rise. "The *void?*"

"In 2017, an international team did muon detection scans of the Great Pyramid."

"Muon detection?" Cassian thinks. "Brilliant." He explains how muon particles from space pass through solid rock. You can see cavities when they hit empty spaces, like an X-ray.

I nod. "Their sensors triangulated a massive void above the Grand Gallery—a hundred feet long. The archaeology community was stunned."

"A hundred feet!" Cassian's eyes bug out. "You're telling me there's an unopened chamber inside the Great Pyramid the length of an NBA basketball court?"

"Some dispute the findings," I say. "It's only one scan."

Faust tsks me with a finger wag. "*Two* independent scans have now confirmed the Void."

"There was *another* one?" I listen as Faust tells us about a 2022 scan confirming the Void. I'm an ancient anthropologist—yeah, the idea of an unopened chamber is more magical than Christmas Eve.

"Stop messing with me." Cassian's face is a mix of awe and doubt. "Good Lord, why haven't they gone in?"

Faust's face darkens. "Egyptian authorities say there is nothing there."

"Or they're afraid of what they'll find," I say.

34

"Tony! Tony!" Andromeda is rushing toward me in a wild panic as we arrive back at the dig site. Her face is white as chalk. Something's very wrong.

She grabs my arm, pulling me away from the others with surprising strength. "It's gone." She gasps, hyperventilating. "It's all ... *gone*."

"*What?* What's gone?"

"It's ..." Her frantic blue eyes lock onto mine. "It's wiped—erased."

"What are you talking about?" But I already know.

"The files don't exist anymore!" she explodes.

"The switch didn't trigger?"

"There's nothing to trigger, Tony!" She spits the words.

"Okay." I hold up her limp frame. "Okay, just ..." Oh boy.

I guide her to a low stone wall and help her sit. "Just—start at the beginning. What happened?"

"There is no *what happened!*" she cries. "They found it somehow. They have Frank's hard drives. Maybe they—" Her eyes search to make sense of it.

"It's *gone?*" I grit out through my teeth, my own panic rising. "How could it be gone?"

"They're the CIA!"

"There are no other copies? Backups?"

"No time!" she wails.

We sit there, breathing like idiots, gripped by that particular kind of stupor that shuts you down when the shock and horror of something are too great to form coherent thoughts. Three times, I go to speak, but I can't.

The Project Nephilim files are wiped.

"We have nothing," she finally says. "We're finished."

"No," I say firmly. "We have the notebook. And we have Faust."

35

THE PROJECT NEPHILIM files are gone.
A million thoughts slash at me. I can't focus. Faust's field tent feels suffocating as the implications set in. I try to camouflage my panic.
I'm going to live out my life in prison.
Under the canvas, Faust's chef serves a luxurious brunch. The aroma of coca tea mingles with crispy bacon and buttery pastries. Sunlight filters through the open flap, glowing on fine china and gleaming silverware.
This should be wonderful. Instead, I'm too sick to speak.
Cassian is lapping it up, fruit skewer in hand, laughing with Professor Faust. He doesn't know about the deleted files. He's ready to sail into the sunset with Faust's grant money.
Andromeda's earlier panic has evolved into a blank stare. She pushes away her sánguche de chicharrón, unease evident.
Faust laughs heartily, telling Cassian about the time a Portuguese researcher hit on him in the agora of Aphrodisias—Aphrodite's city. "I've read the myths; it was a hard *no!*" he roars.
I force a weak smile, trying to shake off the dread. We can't let Faust know our situation. Not now. I cradle my fourth cup of cocaine tea like a jittery addict.
Conversation is a good distraction. I throw out a thought troubling me on an ethical level. "Doesn't this deep history idea rob cultures like the Inca of their achievements?"

Faust leans back, serious now. "Oh, I don't see it that way. We're all products of the former world. What came before shapes us all." His eyes glint with conviction. "The Inca share that legacy. They did mighty things. Hell, most of the stonework here at Machu Picchu is Inca. We're all building on the ruins of Atlantis. No culture is exempt. In that sense, we're all robbed. It's an equal-opportunity robbery, ya!" He chuckles. "No culture sprang from the grasses in a vacuum. If anything, this draws us together under a common heritage. It brings humanity closer, erasing divisions."

"Everything is a remix," Cassian says.

"Præcis."

Andromeda is staring at the Persian rug like an asylum patient, arms clutching her torso.

"We see history through a glass darkly," Faust muses.

Paulo flashes a pirate grin straight from the Spanish Main. His deep voice lilts, "It's like we've been looking at one page of a book, thinking it's the whole story. But there are chapters upon chapters we've never even glimpsed."

We eat in silence. I nibble my Peruvian sandwich. I'm starving, but I can't swallow. Sounds from the bustling dig site drift in, and the wind flaps the canvas. The foggy morning has given way to a patchy blue sky.

Jean Vendôme's report weighs heavy in my pocket. With the Nephilim files wiped, I can't resist—

"Fabian," I say, breaking the silence.

"Ya?"

I look at Andromeda for a moment, wavering on a precipice. Her eyes meet mine, questioning.

The loss of the files changes everything. Faust's knowledge and resources might be our last chance. I can't shake the feeling that my old mentor is meant to be part of this journey.

Screw it.

I set down my plate and pull out the crumpled Vendôme documents.

Andromeda's eyes are black holes. Her lips form a silent protest.

"What are you really searching for?" I ask Faust.

Years ago, at Cambridge, he told me something that's haunted me. I glance at the CIA documents. "Are you still looking for the Hall of Records?"

Faust stops eating. A shadow crosses his face. "Tony, it's a fool's journey. I'm not certain anymore that it even—"

"Jean Vendôme found it." My words hang in the air.

His eyes widen, and his fork clatters to his plate. "Vendôme? He disappeared in the '70s." Skepticism laces his voice.

"He found the markers, Fabian." I hold out the top secret report with a fluttering grin. "Confirmation of an antediluvian Hall of Records. Vendôme believed it was real. He was working for the CIA. I … I can't decipher the clues."

Andromeda shifts in her seat like a volcano about to erupt. I feel the heat of her glare as Faust leans forward, running a hand through his hair and taking the bloodstained pages.

"What records?" Cassian asks through a mouthful.

"The Library of Alexandria," Faust says coolly, "was but a pathetic copy of the original Hall of Records, the complete repository of Atlantis. Legend says they buried everything to survive the cataclysm."

Cassian is amused behind the Dahmers. "You think that's real?" But after our earlier conversations, I see doubt in his eyes.

I squirm. Yesterday, I didn't believe any of this. "I always thought the Hall of Records was a fairy tale. A spooky bedtime story for little Roman children in the age of Caesar."

If anyone can decipher Vendôme's puzzle, it's Fabian Faust.

36

Faust is rummaging through his cabinets and chests like a warlock packing for a long holiday.

I wait outside on the grassy expanse beyond his tent, taking in Machu Picchu's sweeping terraces, now filled with tourists. His private excavation site is cordoned off so his team can work undisturbed. The rope from his earlier demonstration—representing humanity's timeline—is still at my feet: eight hundred thousand years of missing civilization.

What a mind-bender.

"You." Andromeda is striding toward me, a level of anger I haven't seen. "We need to talk." She grabs my collar and drags me behind a stone wall. Yeah, she's pissed. Rightfully so.

I didn't see the slap coming.

Slap!

I deserve it. She's trembling, and I can feel the fury radiating off her.

"How *dare* you show Faust those documents without consulting me?" Her hands are on her hips. "What do you think this is? We shouldn't even be down here." She turns away, muttering, "I need to start making decisions for myself."

"Hey." I rub my stinging cheek, reaching for her arm. "I know. You're right. I'm just trying to balance caution and strategy. We need help. I'm trying to get us help."

"Well, you deserve a sticker." She burns. "Trying to get us help or chasing after your antediluvian Xanadu? Faust could be on the phone with the police right now. Next time, you talk to *me*."

I nod—next time. I'm relieved, she's not leaving. It hits me how much I depend on this stranger now. I wonder if she feels the same. Yeah, I'm pretty sure we need each other.

My tribunal is cut short when Faust approaches. The Danish professor looks deranged, his usual icy demeanor replaced by nervous energy. His voice quakes. "Andromeda, Tony, I must speak with you urgently."

We follow him into the tent. He paces by his desk, eyes wide. His hands shake slightly. "I've analyzed the Vendôme document."

I step forward. "You found something."

Faust holds out a page I haven't seen before.

It's an old document, a photocopy of a grainy carving. It's slightly crooked and distorted like it was made on a 1960s Xerox. It's research by Jean Vendôme from the 1970s. Only this one is *not* stamped by the US government.

The carving shows a profile view of an ancient underground labyrinth with multiple levels. Vendôme had scrawled a cryptic subtitle: THE UNDERWORLD LOCATION IS GUARDED BY AN OVERWORLD MARKER.

It mirrors the mysterious quote on Jean Vendôme's Project Nephilim research. "Vendôme made this?" I ask.

"I acquired it at an estate sale in Venice some years back." Faust's eyes hold a new mania. "I had no idea what it was until I saw your document. They're connected."

"What am I looking at, Faust? A labyrinth?"

"The missing half of Vendôme's puzzle." He's glowing. "Overworld. Underworld. And now a labyrinth! All markers for—"

"The Hall of Records," I finish.

"I know where it is, Tony." His voice is sanctified.

My mind reels. I have to remind myself we're talking about the legendary library of Atlantis—the holy grail of archaeology. The library that makes Alexandria look like a pawn shop.

Faust knows where the Hall of Records is!

"Where?" I ask, gulping air.

He launches into a frantic explanation, pointing out key passages and symbols. I listen intently as he lays it all out.

When he's done, his face turns grave. "We must act quickly. If we can decipher this, others can too." He storms out of the tent, calling for Paulo to start packing.

Andromeda and I are left alone. She's shaking her head, and the wild hippie hair is a lion's mane swallowing her ruddy cheeks. She's been crying.

"No—no way. Sorry," she rasps in defiance. "Clearly, something anthropological and bewitching just happened. But we need to disappear."

I step closer, adamant. "No, no … if we find this place, we won't even need Project Nephilim. This is the obvious play, the ultimate disclosure."

She exhales in annoyance, looking away. But now she's considering it.

"We have nothing to lose. Come on," I urge. "Faust is our best shot. Let's break this thing wide open!"

Slowly, by degrees, she nods with a sniffle. "Yeah—okay."

37

THE LAND ROVER hurtles down the winding mountain road, tires spitting dirt as we cling to the incline. We're jostling in the back like paratroopers heading for a drop.

Are we really going to the Hall of Records?

I envision my team in the Fertile Crescent—the world's finest archaeologists. I've traded them for a band of vagabonds and discarded renegades on a ridiculous quest for Atlantis. Yet, it's an impressive crew.

Part of me believes in Greek oracles. The Romans called it *amor fati*—love of fate. So be it, universe.

Paulo is driving like a rally car racer, a Mexican cigarette dangling from his lips. Tangy smoke wafts back to us.

"When Atlantis was destroyed"—Faust is saying—"the survivors planned to reboot civilization. They knew the world would descend into darkness. So, they hid the records of their lost civilization, libraries of knowledge waiting to be reborn from the ashes."

He pauses, eyeing us as we bounce around. "I know where they hid these records in the Americas, in the heart of their Mesoamerican colony."

Andromeda is bobbing like a rag doll. That's a carsick face if I've ever seen one. She asks, "The missing book in Plato's Atlantis trilogy was the *Hermocrates*, right? The third book? Doesn't Vendôme say it reveals the location of the Hall of Records?"

"You're well-versed in classics, Ms. Dey," Faust says. "There's more to you than meets the eye, I think."

"I've seen a few things." She swallows down her nausea.

"We don't have the full trilogy?" Cassian asks.

I shake my head. "In Critias—Book Two—Plato was getting to the juicy stuff about Atlantis when it cuts off abruptly. It's a scene with Zeus about to dish something epic."

I quote the last passage: "'And when Zeus had called them together, he spoke as follows …'"

"What did Zeus say?" Cassian needs to know.

"That's just it," I shout over the rumble. "That's how it ends, cutting off mid-sentence. We don't even know if he finished the trilogy."

"Plato *did* finish it," Faust snaps, his voice rising over the off-road tires.

Andromeda palms a window as we skid around a hairpin curve. "Is there proof of that?"

"Certainly!" Faust says. "Historical records are clear. Ancient accounts attest to the trilogy's completion. Proclus—a disciple of Plato—saw it. It was likely lost in the flames of Alexandria."

Faust is right. Proclus claimed the Atlantis trilogy *was* finished.

"Electric gods!" Cassian yells out of the blue. He holds up Tesla's notebook, showing sketches of three gods—Zeus, Thor, and Indra. The same ones I saw on Tesla's map document.

"Speaking of Zeus, he shows up in Tesla's notebook," Cassian says. "That's what these are, electric gods." He traces the lightning Tesla emphasized.

Faust squints at the sketches, eyebrow arched. "Nikola Tesla drew that? I must insist; you three are up to something rather unbearable."

My adrenaline spikes. Do we tell Faust about Tesla? I glance at Andromeda—a slap-worthy offense, for sure.

"Electric gods." Faust chuckles. "I hadn't considered them that way. Wielders of lost technology, perhaps?"

"Avatars of a former elite," I suggest.

Cassian nods. "Thor summons lightning with his hammer. Zeus hurls thunderbolts. I don't know the third guy."

"Indra," I say. "The Hindu lightning god. His vajra shoots bolts. Maybe symbols of a lost science, like Excalibur."

Faust smiles. "Don't forget Aztec Tlaloc, Japanese Susanoo, and Chinese Lei Shen. All electric gods, as you say."

I nod, a connection forming. "Horus, too. Known for controlling lightning in Egypt."

Cassian grows thoughtful. "What if Atlantis was rooted in some technology they discovered?"

"*Præcis*," Faust says.

"Why suppress all this?" Cassian asks, forgetting we're undercover.

Faust frowns. "Suppress?"

Andromeda gives Cassian *The Look*, and then she gazes out the window. An internal debate is playing on her face. Finally, she speaks. "Professor Faust, the US government has researched ancient history extensively. They know about Atlantis. Everything you've discovered—they already know. I've seen the classified research." She pauses. "That's why I'm here with Professor Koviak."

I watch Faust's steel-trap mind at work. He's piecing together our true agenda. "Interesting," he says. "As I said, I know all about the CIA. They approached me to do their dirty work."

"You're joking," I say. "Fabian, my dad was working with them."

"I told them to piss off."

"Again, why classify it?" Cassian presses.

"Some ideas are too powerful," Andromeda answers. "Think of our system. Debt-based finance and social control depend upon a certain ... order."

I think of Orwell's *1984*. The Party rewrites history, so the people rely on it for the truth.

"He who controls the past controls the future," Andromeda says.

"Ya. The winners write the history." Faust agrees.

"And erase it." Andromeda's eyes meet mine. "Some powerful people believe they're ushering in a greater good, preparing for a better world."

Paulo yells from the driver's seat, enveloped in tobacco smoke, "Airport!"

38

Cusco International Airport, Peru
Captain of the Cusco Police

THIS BETTER NOT BE TRICKSTERS. *If I miss kickoff because of our bumbling mayor, there will be hell to pay.*

The police captain waits beside a SWAT vehicle flanked by flashing cruisers. He checks his watch and scowls.

White UN military trucks roar onto the airport tarmac, screeching to a halt mid-runway. Men in dark suits flood out, led by a pale figure in a black blazer and aviator sunglasses. He surveys the bustling taxiway as his ranks fan out, taking intercept positions.

Foreigners.

The captain frowns as a junior agent approaches him—*he's so young*—a blinking device is softly chirping behind his ear. His eyes are a penetrating blue, almost otherworldly.

"Ground all aircraft. No one leaves," the agent says in crisp Spanish.

The captain raises an eyebrow. A gringo flawlessly speaking the difficult Cusco dialect?

What's going on here? We don't take orders from outsiders.

"No." The irritated captain refuses. "You shut down the airport, you shut down Cusco. We have this covered."

The young intelligence agent doesn't blink. *"Covered?"*

He tilts his head ever so slightly—more electronic clicking from his scalp. "Your officers are inept, Captain. I've mapped the vulnerabilities. They're exposed at Terminals Two and Four. Service entrances around baggage are blind; two cameras are down, neither flagged in logs. And your officer at South Gate?" The chirping intensifies as the agent pauses with a distant stare. "He's texting his girlfriend about empanadas."

The captain can feel his blood begin to boil. He's always had a short fuse. His fists clench.

I didn't survive the Shining Path Maoist guerrillas back in the '80s just to take orders from foreign intelligence goons like this.

The hardened police veteran inhales. "Whoever you are, you don't know *my* city. Don't tell *me* how this works. I've negotiated men into giving up their mothers—"

"Yes, you're a negotiator." The agent interrupts amid more clicks. "Two thousand nine. Hostage case in Lima. You saved one of them. But the shooter still killed an officer. You hesitated just long enough to give him the opportunity."

The words slam the captain in the chest. That file is sealed. Completely classified. No one—*no one*—outside his tightest circle knows those details.

"You also missed irregular flight plan submissions from four private charters this morning," the foreigner continues.

The captain stares, astonished.

"Shut it down," the agent repeats.

The captain holds his gaze, then relents. "*Sí, señor,*" he grumbles. *Wonderful. More paperwork.*

The unnerving youth turns and walks away toward the terminals.

Up in the tower, air traffic controllers sip coca tea. A message snaps them to attention: "Cease all operations out of Cusco airport immediately—terrorist threat." Silence blankets the room. They exchange tense glances, then spring into action.

39

Campamento Regional Airport, Peru
Tony Koviak

OUR LAND ROVER pulls up to a tiny airstrip outside Machu Picchu. Faust's private jet waits on the crumbling tarmac, turbines already humming.

"I never fly into Cusco," Faust says as we step out of the vehicle. "Last time, an airliner lost its landing gear on the runway. We were grounded for days and had to drive to Puma Punku for a flight out of Bolivia."

"My passport was stolen with my luggage in Cusco," I lie. "Not looking forward to dealing with the embassy."

Faust pauses; there's a suspicious hurt in his eyes. He's not buying it. *Damn, I'm a terrible liar.* I may have just blown his trust. He waves it off with a sad look—he knows I'm lying. "You won't be needing it," he says.

We follow Faust and Paulo up the jet's stairs into a sleek, luxurious cabin. He gestures expansively. "There's a fully equipped water closet in the back if you'd like to freshen up. Kitchen's over there. Make yourselves at home."

So, this is how billionaire aristocratic archaeologists travel.

I head straight to the bathroom. One look in the mirror, and I barely recognize the haggard face staring back. *What am I doing?* Running off with an exiled scholar and a fugitive CIA agent to find the fabled Hall of Records? How did my life get so... cinematic?

But hey, there's a walk-in shower and fresh razors. *I'm so using those.*

After freshening up, I settle into a plush leather chair across from Andromeda. A small table separates us. Exhaustion hits me like a wave. I've been running on adrenaline since New York, but now it's drained, leaving a bone-deep weariness.

We're at cruising altitude when Faust strides into the cabin with Paulo. Tension radiates from them.

"Andromeda?" Faust says gravely. "One of your colleagues is trying to reach you."

Her body stiffens.

Paulo, usually stoic, looks concerned. He holds up a tablet with security footage from the Machu Picchu dig site.

That can't be good.

Three men in dark suits are on screen. There's no audio, but one is questioning a student at the dig. They look like agents. The one in charge has dark hair loosely tousled to his shoulders, giving him a witchy vibe. He wears stylish aviator sunglasses and a fitted black blazer, not your typical federal agent look.

But something's off. His movements are ... unsettling. His head tilts in sync with the talking agent, like a ventriloquist. Probably just a video glitch, but it gives me the heebie-jeebies.

Paulo pauses the video. "They were asking for your whereabouts."

Andromeda forces a smile. "Oh, that's one of my local contacts. We were supposed to have lunch. I'll let him know our plans changed when we land."

Faust raises an eyebrow, his expression uncertain.

Something catches my eye. "Paulo, may I borrow your tablet?"

He hesitates. "Of course." Handing it over, he adds, "But please, be careful. Seriously. It contains much sensitive information."

"Absolutely." I zoom in on the paused image as Paulo and Faust retreat to the cockpit. A design on the agent's tactical vest is peeking out from under his blazer—a symbol of sacred geometry.

"Why does he have Metatron's Cube on his chest?" I ask.

Andromeda goes ashen. "What did you say?"

"The symbol of Metatron," I repeat. "The cube on his vest."

She's rigid. Her anxiety is contagious. I'm instantly unnerved.

"What?" I ask. "You know what that is?"

"Are you sure?"

"Yeah. Who is he?"

She's devouring her thumbnail. "Metatron is a code name. The old-timers in the agency won't even speak it." Her eyes dart. "I've heard creepy rumors of MK-Ultra-style CRISPR gene editing. They've pioneered brain-machine interface programs with military AIs—real DARPA stuff."

Oh, wonderful.

Her voice drops to a whisper. "Metatron leads Targeting Division. One of the blackest ops. A ghost in the machine." Her big eyes drift with confusion. "I always thought Metatron was some Transformers cape shit, an agency urban legend. You're telling me this guy's real?"

I don't know what to say. Metatron is certainly a real person from mythology. "He's an apocryphal figure," I reply.

"Tell me something good."

"It's not great." I shudder at the thought of an inverted, corrupted version of Metatron, the most powerful angel in myth.

She covers her mouth, like telling a secret. "At the CIA, he's nicknamed the Voice of God."

"That's correct," I say. "Metatron is called the Voice of God. Some say he was Enoch—one of Faust's antediluvian sages—transformed into an angel to protect the cosmic order. Given three sets of wings, called the Lesser Yahweh. Other angels bowed to him. In Islamic lore, he's Mīṭaṭrūn, the Angel of the Veil, the only angel who knows what lies beyond."

She grips the armrest tightly. "The veil?"

"Yeah, why?"

She exhales shakily. "They're not CIA, Tony. We're talking about an ultranational shadow government—the government's government. Secret societies and Illuminati stuff. They use veil symbolism. It's somehow significant to them."

"The government has a government?"

Perfect—now there's a secret society pulling strings behind the scenes, obsessed with veils. Can the crazy train let me off on its way to the Twilight Zone? Rod Serling, let me off!

I think of possible connections. "Metatron was given a special crown."

"The crown," she says. "That's the technology Metatron is said to have." She's staring at the image. "What does the cube signify?"

"Metatron's Cube encodes the Platonic solids, the building blocks of creation." Plato again. He's everywhere lately. My stomach churns with equal parts fascination and dread. "I get the feeling this guy's name is intentional."

She nods. "They project their intentions, like some compulsive ritual, like they have to show their agenda, hidden in plain sight—karma or something."

"The Voice of God?"

"Or the devil. He reports to a man called the Demiurge."

My skin crawls. "Can we stop with the creepy monikers? It's weirding me out."

"Code names have always been a part of intelligence operations. As I said, they love to project their agenda with symbols."

"That's odd. Plato mentions the Demiurge in his Timaeus dialogue, Book One of the Atlantis trilogy."

"You're kidding. What does it say?"

I dig deep. "Plato says the Demiurge creates a new order using *intelligence* to usher in a utopian world. It's generally positive. In gnostic tradition, the Demiurge is malevolent."

Wait. Have intelligence agencies been wrapped up in some higher agenda from the beginning? I can't let myself go there.

"Artificial intelligence is the core of Targeting Division," she says. "This shadow government founded all the major AI companies. Today's most advanced AI models are decades behind what Metatron uses."

Fantastic—now they're hunting us.

She lowers her seat back and closes her eyes with a sigh. I stare out the window as the jet soars through cloud canyons. Myth and reality are blurring faster than I can handle. Another thought comes to me.

I think she's already asleep when I say, "You only take flak when you're over the target, Andromeda. They're afraid."

40

THE BOAT POWERS upriver like the *African Queen,* its engine struggling like a chain-smoking asthmatic. The wake is a silky mix of mud and debris. Jungle presses in from the riverbanks, and vines drape like snakes. Howler monkeys shriek from the foliage.

It gives you the feeling of being watched.

Professor Faust is convinced the Atlantean records are hidden out here in the Yucatán wilderness. So, we're headed to the ancient Mayan ruins of Yaxchilan.

Andromeda sits beside me, zipping Tesla's notebook securely into her jacket. Can't risk losing our only bargaining chip overboard. She swiped it from Cassian after we lost the Nephilim files, and he's not happy about it.

He's been badgering her for it nonstop. "What, don't you trust me?"

"No," she answers flatly.

"I was just starting to crack it," he complains.

"We won't need it after this," I say, hoping to ease the tension, or maybe just convince myself.

There are no roads out here. It's an hour up the Usumacinta River to access the mysterious Yaxchilan.

Paulo chartered this dilapidated boat—called a *lancha*—by handing over wads of cash to a Ch'ol boatman in the village of Frontera Corozal. That was after we landed on the so-called airstrip —more of a red dirt line scratched into the wilderness for bush planes. The jet stopped yards from an impenetrable wall of trees. My heart's still racing from that sketchy landing.

"My friends," Faust says, clasping his hands together. "You are all part of history now. It's in Yaxchilan!" he thunders, his voice booming over the sputtering boat engine.

I lean back on the lacquered bench, grateful for the breeze cutting through the jungle heat. Faust sits across from me, cool as ever in his Ray-Ban Wayfarers, linen shirt, and slacks, a touch of mid-century flair in the middle of nowhere. Our conversation has been, well, lively.

"Professor Faust," I say, "Mesoamerica isn't exactly my wheelhouse. Are you sure this particular corner of Hades holds the library of Atlantis?"

His eyes gleam with a fervor that's borderline obsessive. "America is the true cradle of civilization," he says, his Danish accent giving the words a melodic lilt. "The New World is, in fact, the Old World."

He lets that sink in.

"I've identified dozens of potential sites for the Hall of Records on the American side of the Atlantean Empire," he continues. "Jean Vendôme's report narrows it down ... to one."

His confidence is infectious. Can this be it? An Ice Age hall of records predating Göbekli Tepe?

"What does the Frenchman tell us?" Faust asks. "First, the completed version of Plato's infamous Atlantis trilogy exists in Europe at a place known for finance, and it reveals the location of the halls." He pauses, adjusting his sunglasses. "But we haven't found the trilogy, so that's no help, I'm afraid."

"Maybe we should track down Plato's lost trilogy," Cassian pipes up. "If he spells it out ... can't be that many places in Europe known for finance."

"London was the seat of global finance for centuries," I offer.

Faust shrugs. "In ancient times, it was Babylon, then Rome, then Constantinople. Could be anywhere. Vendôme's markers are a safer bet. And what are those markers?"

I think back to Vendôme's 1975 CIA report. The title's a mouthful: *Plato's Hermocrates and the Antediluvian Hall of Records*. "The clues are an overworld marker with an underworld labyrinth at its feet," I recall.

"Run it by us again, Professor Faust," Andromeda says. "Why do you think it's in the Yucatán?"

"Yaxchilan is a perfect match," Faust replies, excitement creeping into his voice. "There's an overworld above—an imposing temple known as Structure 19."

"Imaginative name," Cassian mutters.

"Below it is a winding labyrinth, an underworld the Maya call the House of Darkness, descending multiple stories underground, just as Vendôme specifies. It's Yaxchilan, I say!"

This site ticks all of Vendôme's boxes. My excitement is rising.

"Surely, this place has been explored," Cassian says skeptically.

"I don't believe it has, Dr. Wilder." Faust counters, gesturing to the dense jungle flanking the river. "Few people come out here. There's not even cell service."

I glance at Andromeda. She seems equally relieved by our remote location. Faust kept this mission under wraps; no one knows why he and Paulo abruptly left.

"We must remember," Faust continues, "the Library of Alexandria shows us such collections were a feature of the past."

"Plato also mentions a Hall of Records," I say. "In Egypt, in the city of Sais."

"Ya," Faust adds. "Jesus spent his childhood in Egypt. Legend says it was Sais where Jesus was educated before returning to the Holy Land."

"Maybe you should search there," Cassian suggests.

"No longer exists," I point out.

"There could be *many* halls," Faust says. "Atlantis wasn't merely a city; it was a global, seafaring civilization. Facing annihilation, they'd establish multiple archives across their outposts to preserve knowledge." His eyes darken. "We're culminating their efforts in this hemisphere twelve thousand years ago."

Cassian chuckles. "So, myths from all cultures are a riff on the same theme: a civilizational reboot courtesy of some wandering wizard LARPing about the good old days with a swag bag of lost tech?"

"In a nutshell," I reply.

"And we're headed to an Atlantis prepper bunker?"

"You could say that."

"Fantastic," Cassian drawls to Andromeda. "Always wanted to be a sidekick in a Lucasfilm fever dream."

Faust tucks his dark blond hair behind his ear tips, crosses his legs, and pushes the Ray-Bans up his sharp nose, the picture of nonchalant cool. "There's another reason it's at Yaxchilan—a civilization bringer we haven't mentioned."

"Votan," I say.

"*Præcis.*"

The boatman glances nervously at me, his weathered hands tightening on the rudder. Votan—the supreme Mayan deity.

Paulo picks up the tale. "Votan arrived in the Yucatán from an island kingdom across the sea called Valum Votan. He brought civilization to the Maya and built a House of Darkness where he buried the records of his homeland on the Usumacinta River." He points to the water. "*This* river."

"Once again," Faust says, "myth shows the way."

So many signs point here. It really is Yaxchilan.

Paulo continues, "A British-American explorer, Augustus Le Plongeon, discovered the Popol Vuh—the history of the Maya. They claim to descend from a lost continent that sank beneath the waves."

"Yaxchilan, *adelante!*" The boatman calls. *Yaxchilan, up ahead!*

The ruins rise from the jungle, eerie and imposing.

The site is vacant. We haven't seen a soul since the village. There's no official presence out here—too remote and no tourist cash to justify the effort.

Faust tells us thousands of buried pyramids are scattered from the United States to the Amazon. The Americas, he insists, are the true home of pyramid culture, his Western Atlantean Empire.

Andromeda steps off the boat onto coarse grass as giant ants scurry. The deep jungle here hangs wetly over us as we approach the ruins. It's getting dark.

Atlantis will have to wait until morning.

41

THE BOATMAN STARTS a campfire as twilight fades, woodsmoke curling into the thick jungle air. Faust and Paulo hover over a camp stove, flipping quesadillas in blazing hot cast-iron pans, and the aroma of sizzling cheese wafts into the trees. Our tents look like they'll collapse if someone sneezes. If it rains, we're screwed.

"Where's Andromeda?" I ask, realizing she's missing.

Faust points with a spatula toward Structure 19.

I squint into the gathering darkness and spot her silhouette perched atop the ancient temple, like an ethereal guardian against the dusky sky.

Cassian looks up and grins. "Doing her Zen thing?"

Probably right. Her granola tendencies run deep. She keeps saying there's a "sacred geometry" to our lives, that energy is in everything. She has this habit of pressing her palms against megaliths and going completely quiet. First time, I thought it was just hippie theatrics. Then she started describing details about the site that weren't in any of the published research. That's ... that's probably a coincidence, right?

And look, I know how that sounds, but after all I've experienced, let's just say my worldview is having technical difficulties.

I decide to join her. Climbing the steep steps is brutal; the Maya certainly didn't believe in handrails. Cassian huffs up behind me.

At the top, Andromeda sits cross-legged, eyes closed, palms

upturned on her knees. The moonstone around her neck catches the last glint of light. She's barefoot, her boots and socks neatly set aside. We settle beside her silently. She opens one eye, smiles faintly, then resumes her meditation.

The view from up here is breathtaking … and eerie. We're incredibly remote, and the western sky blazes with oranges and purples.

Andromeda unwraps a linen cloth holding black Yucatán soil and slender green herbs. "Paulo and the boatman say these are sacred to the Maya," she whispers. "They're used for healing and cleansing."

She crushes them together, releasing a potent herbal aroma that cuts through the humid air. We watch as she smears the earthy paste over her brow, closes her eyes, and breathes deeply, arching her back slightly. She's whispering a mantra—can't quite catch the words.

She offers the mixture to us. Cassian and I exchange glances like immature schoolboys but follow suit, dutifully dabbing the paste on our foreheads. It feels primal up here atop a ruined temple.

Andromeda resumes her deep, rhythmic breathing. I match it, letting the tension of the past few days seep out of my body. *This is nice.*

After a while, she pulls Tesla's notebook from her jacket and hands it to Cassian. "Just keep it safe," she says softly. She plants her bare feet on the stone, pulling her knees up and flexing her toes.

"Sore feet?" I ask.

"Grounding," she replies. "Drawing energy from Earth."

I nod toward the notebook. "There's a clipping about Antaeus pulling energy from Earth in the back."

"I saw that," Cassian says. "From a 1930 article Tesla wrote in the *New York American*."

"Who's Antaeus?" Andromeda asks, eyes still closed.

"Greek mythology," I explain. "Antaeus was invincible when in contact with the ground. Hercules cleverly beat him by lifting him off the Earth. Interesting that Tesla mentioned him."

"Tesla and I would've been pals," she murmurs, wiggling her

grounded toes. "Funny how he's not taught in schools. You ever think about that?"

"His legacy was killed," Cassian says, cleaning his glasses. "Erased from the curriculum. By the '80s, no one knew who Tesla was. People only know him now because of the cars. They even robbed him of a Nobel Prize. He beat Edison in the war of the currents, and AC power is our greatest invention. Einstein got one for showing light is both a particle *and* a wave. Niels Bohr got one for saying an atom is a little solar system. Both were Tesla's ideas. Oppenheimer just happened to make a nuclear bomb *one year* after the government stole eighty boxes of energy research from Tesla's hotel room—cool how that worked out for Oppy."

He pauses, closing the notebook, brow clouded. "Einstein was wrong," Cassian says softly. "Light *isn't* a particle. According to this notebook, photons don't exist. It's all waves. Everything is light."

Andromeda stands, now pulled from her Zen flow. "It's almost like someone doesn't want us to know about Tesla," she says, stretching her lanky limbs.

Cassian gets up. "When are you gonna tell us what you know about the geologic transition from the Ice Age to the Holocene?" he asks her. "What had you so spooked?"

She looks queasy, turning to head down with a head shake. "I have enough to worry about."

42

It's a new moon, and I've never seen so many stars—stars like jewels. The campfire is dying, hissing and spitting sparks up toward Orion. Orange flames dance vividly across the ancient ruins, our own psychedelic light show right here in the Yucatán jungle.

I slap another mosquito dead. The night has swallowed our camp, darkness pressing in. I shift on this torture device of a camp chair digging into my ass as Faust pours chamomile tea into chipped enamel mugs.

Andromeda grimaces beside me on her own chair of pain. Firelight flickers over her wild hair, making her look like some kind of jungle witch. Faust, Paulo, and the boatman join us around the fire—the whole gang's here.

A blood-curdling shriek cuts through the night. A howler monkey is watching curiously from atop Structure 19, where we had meditated earlier. Kinda cute for such a death cry. This jungle is seriously creepy after dark.

I forgot how much I love camping. You don't get out much when you're stuck in the lecture halls of Cambridgeshire and Morningside Heights. I'd been looking forward to that at Göbekli Tepe: open space.

Andromeda and Paulo have started singing 1970s easy listening. Random but okay. Her voice is a dead ringer for Karen Carpenter's. A whistleblower with a voice. *Who knew?*

Cassian breaks the tranquility. "How old do you think the Egyptian pyramids are?"

"Officially?" I ask. "Four thousand six hundred twenty-four years old."

"Rubbish," Faust grumbles.

I shrug. "History gets fuzzy that far back. Fun fact: Cleopatra lived closer to the moon landing than to the pyramids' construction."

"What makes you think they're older?" Cassian asks Faust.

"A great many things, Dr. Wilder."

Andromeda sips her herbal tea. She tilts her head, thinking it over. "What's the strangest thing you've heard about the Great Pyramid?"

"Napoleon," I reply without hesitation. "He spent the night inside alone."

Cassian perks up. "Is this a ghost story, Koviak?"

"Yes." I stare into the flames. "Napoleon wanted to sleep in the King's Chamber. At dawn, he emerged, face drained of all color. When his men asked what happened, he refused to talk about it. Years later, on his deathbed—exiled on the island of St. Helena—Napoleon almost revealed the secret, but only whispered, 'No, you'd never believe me.'"

Andromeda shivers, eyes gleaming. "We need to visit the pyramid, *right now*! Professor Faust, get the jet ready!"

The boatman watches us, not understanding a word but sensing the mood. He tosses more logs on the fire, and a plume of red soars into the black.

"There are other tales," Faust says softly. "Allied pilots in World War Two wouldn't fly over the pyramids. Instruments went haywire every time. Animals won't approach them; guides keep their camels away."

His voice drops. "And then there are the sounds."

A chill rakes my spine. I know exactly what he's talking about.

The sounds.

Andromeda glances at me. "You've heard these sounds, Tony?"

I nod slowly. "Inside the pyramid, walls sometimes hum with strange overtones. Whenever tourists chant, you feel the vibration in your soul. There are reports of people hearing their name whispered over their shoulder, only to turn and find no one is there —real *Tomb Raider* stuff."

My voice is almost a whisper. "I never go into the pyramid alone."

A howler monkey screams, and we all jump with roars of laughter.

Cassian wipes his teary eyes, still convulsing. "So, these halls ... they just ... uh ... stashed everything into a bunker before the cataclysm?"

"Makes sense," Andromeda says. "If the world were ending, you'd bury knowledge—physics manuals, medical books, Shakespeare, instructions for the internet."

"No internet," I say.

"Ugh," she retracts. "I miss my pre-social-media brain."

Cassian points at her. "But an electrician's handbook would be nice."

Faust leans back, eyes burning like a prophet. "In ten thousand years, you think they'll remember us accurately? iPhones will become sacred myth: 'Behold, the gods of old who gazed into dark mirrors and spoke to invisible beings!' The Apple logo will morph into a symbol for a new religion."

He chuckles. "Historians might argue whether the 'United States' even existed. Suggest it did, and they'll call you crazy."

"Why doesn't modern archaeology explore this angle?" Cassian asks.

Faust lifts a finger like he's dropping wisdom from the mountaintop. "Because orthodoxy is a club, and anyone who questions it is thrown out."

He's not wrong. But Faust isn't doing himself any favors by making enemies of the entire academic establishment.

"How long has this been happening?" Faust says, voice rising. "Has civilization been advancing and getting wiped out for millions of years? Like Sisyphus, rolling his boulder up the mountain time and again?"

"All right, you ol' ray of sunshine." I stand, stretching my stiff limbs.

The gods are watching. Tomorrow, the survivors of Atlantis get their long-awaited victory.

43

Göbekli Tepe, Turkey
The Demiurge

IT'S THE WITCHING HOUR, and the night sky is a field of constellations over the Fertile Crescent. March winds howl over the primal terrain, gusts swirling into the circular Ice Age enclosures of Göbekli Tepe—the world's oldest archaeological site.

The Demiurge ascends a rocky path winding up the prehistoric mound. Brass lanterns line the way, red embers blowing from them. A cigarette flares between his lips, smoke rolling over the shoulders of his tailored overcoat as he follows the haunting call of a woman's voice echoing from the ruins.

A tall, rectangular curtain has been erected over the pathway, like a surreal, otherworldly portal against the stony landscape. Its dark, symbolic fabric quietly waves and flaps in the wind.

Two slender women face each other like sentinels at the grand partition, clad in black dresses stitched with arcane symbols. Black veils shroud their faces like statuesque brides. As the Demiurge nears, their heads turn in unison.

He flicks his cigarette and lifts a hand, revealing a ring etched with a symbol from a lost age. "I serve the mothers," he says, bowing to them.

Silently, they part the veil, allowing him entry beyond.

He steps down into a time capsule.

Above him, the infamous Pillar Forty-three looms with its solar and zodiacal carvings—a celestial date stamp of the last end of the world. The end of Atlantis. It shows constellations as they were twelve thousand years ago, a dark time in the solar system. The Age of Leo, opposite our Age of Aquarius on the great arc. When humanity last passed through the cosmic veil of cataclysm.

One eternal round.

Inside, rings of megalithic pillars shimmer with a thousand points of candlelight. A flaming brazier stands in the center of the hulking towers, bathing the stones in an orange glow.

Around this astronomical masterpiece, hundreds of elites from around the world have gathered, eyes fixed on the proceedings. Well-dressed and radiant, they line the shadowed high places around the rim of the site like sculptures, peering down into the enclosure, faces lit from the firelight below.

The Demiurge moves among them. *If the world knew who was here, they wouldn't believe their eyes.*

The ritual begins, a sacred tradition stretching back millennia.

We are the keepers of the truth—the saviors of humanity.

A woman enters the stone enclosure adorned in Ice Age jewelry and stands before Pillar Forty-three. She's wearing a black dress stitched with symbols of prehistory, her hair slicked back, and a white veil of cords hangs to her lips like a shimmering fringe, covering her face.

She holds an exquisite papier-mâché globe representing Earth.

The stars look down as she gracefully walks the circular path of the pillars, through the constellations, her veil rippling in the wind. She stops at a symbol on the far side. Her clarion voice rings out, heralding the Age of Aquarius—the water bearer. "The age of flood and of fire! The time of the veil is at hand!"

A taller mother joins her—her face veiled entirely in black—and sets an iron grate over the flaming brazier. A curtain of sparks spins up into the night, the wind scattering the embers into the stones. The Demiurge feels the heat.

The mother holding the globe places it on the fire, and the outer crust blisters and peels away, revealing a bright golden sphere. She reaches into the charred pile with gloved hands and lifts the hot sphere high, speaking the forbidden words in archaic Sumerian.

The assembly shouts the ancient words jubilantly.

THE PRIMORDIAL CEREMONY HAS ENDED. Ambitious figures whisper in the windswept pillar enclosures, forging alliances for the apocalyptic years ahead. The gathering offers them a chance to strategically position themselves for the coming age.

The Demiurge observes them—billionaires, politicians, tech moguls—most of their faces are plastered on newsstands: filmmakers, hedge-fund managers, media barons ... history's *real* players.

The president of the United States stands among a small group in an adjacent stone enclosure. Her hair is pulled back in a bun, and she wears austere high fashion. Candles glow around them, giving the megaliths a primitive color.

"The coup attempt within the CIA has been crushed," she reports, as casually as one might announce the winner of a school board election.

A Korean woman turns. "Oh? I hadn't heard of a coup."

"You wouldn't have. That's the point of a coup," the president replies. She hesitates. "And no, we haven't found Andromeda Dey." Frustration edges her voice, revealing how much of a thorn this rogue agent has become.

The Demiurge listens.

The president continues as others step in to hear the dramatic news. "Vergazza and Dey acted alone. However, their amateur heist triggered a coup attempt."

She lets it hang in the air. "The *real* coup."

The Korean woman folds her arms. "Another faction in the CIA? I thought we had full control."

"So did we," the president admits. "They'd been plotting for years. Vergazza and Dey unknowingly pulled the pin on that grenade. The insurrectionists acted prematurely. Now"—she allows herself a hint of satisfaction—"they're all in custody."

"Sounds like a victory," a man says.

"A coup within the CIA, and we weren't informed?" a European banker asks, candlelight dancing on his face.

"I'm informing you now." She turns to a British MP, her voice sharp. "And London? What news of that fiasco?"

"It's true." The English MP replies. "A sister coup was attempted in England. The two groups have been secretly allied on opposite sides of the Atlantic for some time."

"And?" the US president presses.

"The British coup remains ... unresolved."

A collective murmur follows. "Intolerable," someone mumbles.

"Why weren't we told?" another asks.

The Demiurge interjects, his tone reassuring, "The king himself is handling the English insurrection. There's no cause for concern."

"King Edward saw beyond the veil before his passing last year," someone says. "But his heir has not."

"The blackmail we have on the young king is life-ending," the Demiurge says. "He won't betray us."

Silence settles as his words sink in.

"And Andromeda Dey?" the secretary of the treasury asks, her voice smooth but cold. "As long as she's free, we're at risk."

"Dey no longer has the stolen data ... we believe," the president replies.

"You *believe*?" a Russian oligarch growls.

An Argentine man shifts uneasily. "Should they succeed—if this information gets out—what then?"

The Demiurge fixes him with a steady gaze. "Humanity slips into darkness. We return to the Garden of Eden—a reset none of us would survive. We are humanity's only hope. Without us, civilization vanishes."

"Global markets must remain stable," the American president says. "Public confidence cannot waver in the run-up to what's coming."

"And the media?" a mogul inquires.

"Already managed," the Demiurge assures. "Narratives are in place."

The US president exhales slowly. "We proceed as planned. NASA assures us the geomagnetic excursion is at least a decade away. We have time to prepare. We stick to the timeline." She steps closer to the Demiurge, her voice low. "Just so we're clear. If they *do* succeed in disclosure—"

"Run your little kingdom," the Demiurge cuts her off with a rasp, his tone firm. "Fear doesn't suit you."

She meets his gaze unflinchingly. "I prefer caution over arrogance."

"Metatron will handle it." His eyes drift to the tall, veiled mothers in black standing beside the golden Earth atop the flaming brazier. "What we have set in motion cannot be undone."

44

Yaxchilan, Mexico
Tony Koviak

DAWN IS BARELY a sliver of aqua in the eastern sky when Faust and I start rattling the other tents like kids waking up their grumpy parents on Christmas morning.

"Rise and shine!" I shout.

Cassian is crawling from his collapsed tent. He's drenched in dew.

As the first sunrays filter through the jungle, mist rises, casting a warm glow on the Mayan stones. The howler monkeys have gone. The air feels electric.

With everyone gathered and clutching steaming cups of coffee, Paulo leads us across the central acropolis. We pass a temple adorned with a beautiful stone lattice, called a roof comb. A massive, winged jaguar is carved in the center.

"Winged jaguars," Faust says.

"The Maya call them *Balam*. Feline guardians of the underworld," Paulo says, gesturing grandly. "The Maya built everything you see. Master architects."

Paulo—a former professor of archaeology at the prestigious National Autonomous University of Mexico—was utterly won over by Faust's worldview. He's a true believer in Atlantis, but I'm sure there's also a financial upside in the picture.

We reach Structure 19. The overworld marker.

"Lights on," Paulo says, igniting a flashlight. He slings the high-powered beam up to the pinnacle of the architecture. The constellation of Leo is barely visible in the early sky. The air is dewy, saturated with the thick smell of jungle foliage.

I've seen countless ancient sites, but Yaxchilan hits differently. There's a foreboding in the air that's hard to shake in the Mayan and Aztec world. Andromeda tugs at my arm. "Look," she whispers.

Across the acropolis, a figure watches us from the foggy trees. He turns and disappears into the jungle. Hopefully just a wandering local. Still, it's unsettling.

We enter a doorway into a Mayan hallway with corbeled walls.

"I can handle jaguars," Cassian says. "Better than, like … the Mummy or something." He makes animal claws at Andromeda.

She swats him away. "Oh, I wouldn't be so sure. The House of Darkness sounds like an '80s horror flick."

"I'd watch that," Cassian grins.

We explore the ground level—nothing yet. Andromeda stumbles on a loose stone, nearly losing her footing. I grab her elbow. "Easy there."

"Over here!" Paulo's voice echoes from down the dark corridor.

Faust strides ahead, his flashlight beam bouncing off stone walls. I quicken my pace to keep up, turning corner after corner. "Faust?" My voice echoes as I'm lost for a moment. A beat of silence.

Then, "Over here! You've got to see this!"

I retrace my steps and find him at the lip of an ominous stone staircase plunging into darkness. "The labyrinth," he says, voice tinged with reverence. "In myth, labyrinths were paths to enlightenment but also traps for the unworthy." He glances back with a half-smile. "Let's hope we fall into the former category."

Vendôme's underworld marker.

We descend single file. The maze below Structure 19 twists and turns, connected by stairways. Each level feels like we're dropping deeper into Dante's Inferno. It would be easy to get lost in here. Bats and whip spiders are everywhere.

The air is cool and damp at the lowest level, smelling archaic, like the Mediterranean sites I know so well.

Andromeda runs a hand along the stone walls. "There's nothing here," she says.

"Wait." Paulo takes a few heavy steps, his eyes shut in concentration. "Do you feel that? The floor …"

"Hollow," Faust says.

Cassian taps his foot experimentally. "Could just be an acoustic anomaly. Let's not jump to conclusions."

"Good idea, Cass!" Andromeda jumps and slams her feet down. The stones ring like a bell.

"There's something below us," I say. Another level? Faust and I share excited glances. "Check the walls!"

I search a branching passage, shining my flashlight onto the walls and examining the stonework.

"Something's off," I murmur, stepping closer. "Give me some light." Andromeda swings her beam up. "These wall stones are mismatched. See how they extend behind this side wall? This isn't the original construction."

Someone has walled up this alcove.

For a moment, I worry it's a modern repair, like when I excitedly dated a "prehistoric" layer at the Epidaurus Theater in the Peloponnese, then found a buried can of New Coke from 1985. A Harvard colleague still sends me a can of Coke every year on my birthday.

No. This masonry is ancient.

I run a hand along the seam of the stones. "The Maya were protecting something," I say.

I wonder if the world's ready for what's behind this wall.

45

I DRIVE HOME the final blow with the sledgehammer, and the stone wall beneath the labyrinth collapses into a black hole of billowing dust. We've been hammering for twenty minutes, taking turns. Exhausted, I lean against the stones, coughing as the stench of damp stagnation wafts from the breach.

Within the void, another staircase drops precipitously into darkness. The walls down there are different, like a textured weave. Is it fabric? Some kind of ornamentation? My eyes must be playing tricks.

The material is ... breathing.

Light beams swing down into the underworld. The stairwell is covered in a sea of—*spiders*. Big-ass, glossy spiders.

It's a nightmare hole.

The monsters coat every inch of the walls, from ceiling to steps, waiting in their webs. It's a doom funnel of twitching black abdomens. The skittering of a thousand agitated legs rushes up with a dry, rasping noise.

"Oh, hell no," I say.

Faust raises an eyebrow. "Arachnophobe?"

I wobble my palm uneasily.

"Baby," Andromeda purrs.

I knit my eyebrows up at her, wounded.

Cassian steadies himself against the wall, blowing out a shaky breath. "You sure you want to go down ... *there?*"

Faust and Paulo stare like he's blasphemed the Madonna.

"*Vamos.*" Paulo steps over the broken wall with a muchacho's grin, finding footing on the first stair as two enormous spiders scuttle away.

"Those bright colors look poisonous," Cassian says weakly. We do sound like babies. But … they have the shape of black widows—the worst shape—only bigger.

"Shh," Paulo says. "Do not disturb them. These are harmless. But if you see a little one …" He grimaces in pain.

"Those must be six inches." Cassian swallows the words like a fist.

"Man-babies first." Andromeda gestures to the hole of death. She's enjoying this.

"Nah, ladies first," Cassian says.

I climb into the infested lair after the CIA analyst. Her bravado evaporates when she squints at the rippling ceiling with a million reflective eyes. She's silently screaming.

As we step into the suffocating darkness, I keep a hand near her shoulder, delicately nudging spiders from our path. They're fast little buggers. Light beams swing from point to point, revealing the nest growing thicker as we descend. Large abdomens ripple nervously above when the lights blind them.

"Keep the lights on the steps," Paulo hisses.

The air grows colder as we enter the underworld, taking on a distinct spider scent. Who knew spider lairs had a *smell*? The clammy darkness presses in around us.

A spider the size of a hand threads down right in front of me, hovering over Andromeda's neck. I go to warn her, and it swings into *my* face with a featherlight touch of pure horror.

I flip out—a wild flailing that sends a cascade of spiders raining down on everyone.

Panic erupts.

We writhe and spasm down the living staircase, covered in agitated spiders. Flashlights clatter away. Screams echo in the darkness. Our footing slips. Hands thrust into dark web nests for balance.

Faust and Cassian gasp—their eyes covered by glossy legs—as

they stumble and roll down the remaining steps, crushing dozens of juicy abdomens. Frantic spiders are hopping everywhere.

Andromeda shrieks, her face and hands tangled in webs. She goes down head over heels, dragging me into a barrel roll.

At the bottom, we're a pile of quivering spider meals. We drag ourselves down a long hallway free of the demons. At a safe distance, we stop, clawing at our infested, web-strewn bodies with rough grunts.

"I'll. Never. Sleep. Again," I exhale, brushing myself violently.

Andromeda gasps for air, glaring daggers at me. "Professor Koviak is *not* coming with us on the way back out."

I glower back, catatonic.

"This doesn't resemble the Mayan structures above," Paulo says, eyeing the smooth granite walls. The workmanship is minimal and ultraprecise. He squishes a juicy spider under his boot. "The Maya never built this way."

Andromeda shudders, pulling a massive spider from her strawberry hair with an existential groan.

"Remind you of anything?" Faust asks, standing up.

My voice wavers. "The Grand Gallery in the Great Pyramid. The Osirion."

"We're in the former world," Faust says. A colorful spider crests his shoulder; he brushes it off and leads us down the dark passage.

Paulo holds a small video camera, documenting the discovery. With webs on his ear, Faust turns to the lens. His voice fills with gravity. "Today is March the sixteenth, at 7:36 ante meridiem, and we have entered the American Hall of Records."

"Stop," Andromeda calls from behind.

We turn. She stands frozen, her beam angled at the wall. I join her, adding my light. The only marking anywhere in the otherworldly space is on the wall. We walked right past it.

"Impossible," Faust whispers.

Uh … I'm pretty sure that symbol can't be here.

46

I PEER up at the strange symbol on the wall. It looks just like a—
"What's a Norse rune doing in Mexico?" Andromeda asks.

ᛉ

Professor Faust stands like a classical statue, his voice resonant. "This is from the Elder Futhark alphabet. Proto-Germanic. A guardian symbol for protection of the homeland, common across my native Scandinavia."

Wait. The lost homeland—Atlantis.

The mark is stamped into the stone with astonishing precision; its beveled edges are crisp as if machined by modern tools.

I run through my limited knowledge of Iron Age Norse symbols. It is indeed a protection rune.

"The Algiz," Faust confirms. "Interesting that it should appear here, protecting Atlantis. Protection of the homeland knowledge from a cataclysm, perhaps? In Norse mythology, the Algiz is also associated with learning. For Vikings, it signified a direct download from the gods."

He's right. The Algiz rune symbolizes the connection between our world and Asgard, the world of the Æsir, the Norse gods. Asgard is the former world.

Asgard. Camelot. Egyptian Zep Tepi. Aztec Aztlan. Hindu Atala—all the same lost homeland: Atlantis.

"Well, I guess we can cancel that research trip to Norway," Andromeda quips.

But this doesn't make sense. "This hallway predates Germanic civilization by thousands of years," I say, perplexed.

"Unless ..." Faust tracks in on the symbol. "Unless it's not a Nordic rune." His eyes widen, a smile curling his lips. "Oh, you will love this, my Philhellenic friend." He turns to me. "It's way upstream from the Norse. This is no rune. It's *another* symbol—do you see it?"

I gaze at the three upward-pointed tips, tilting my head. I hear my father's voice from our digs in Egypt: "What do you see, son? Don't just look at the mark—look at the world around it. That's where the true story hides."

The tips stem from a single long trunk, like a devil's pitchfork—Recognition strikes.

"A trident," I whisper. Symbol of Atlantis. "Poseidon's trident."

Faust laughs heartily, clapping my shoulder. He draws a hand over his hair. "A primordial version. Perhaps the Germanic rune descends from high antiquity. Who knows where these symbols originate?"

I rummage through a database of symbols. "The Valknut—a prominent symbol in ancient Scandinavia—is three pyramids intertwined. These symbols could be a deep human memory."

"Poseidon?" Cassian touches the carving. "Like the Jason Momoa water guy?"

"The founder of Atlantis," I explain. "Plato tells the tale. Poseidon, oceanic wielder of the trident, another electric god. He was the father of King Atlas, the guy carrying the world. The Romans called him Neptune."

We approach the end of the passage. The air is deathly still; a silence envelops us. I exchange a glance with Faust; his eyes are calm but intense.

We step into a pristine chamber, no bigger than a master bedroom.

Aaand ... it's empty.

My heart sinks.

Faust rakes his beam around frantically, desperate for some hidden door or secret compartment. But there's nothing, just one big room of polished, megalithic blocks.

We spread out, combing for clues. *Anything.*

Something is in the far corner. I rush over to a stone tablet fragment shaped like a triangle—the only item here.

"It's empty." Faust breathes it like he's being stabbed. The flashlight slips from his grasp, hitting the floor. His voice is hollow. "It's all gone."

The broken triangle shard has four characters from a language I've never seen.

One character is similar to the letter *V* from the Latin alphabet, though I know that's unlikely. Latin stems from the Phoenician alphabet, the first phonetic writing system, where each symbol represents a sound.

The other characters are totally abstract. One features a circle with a horizontal line through its center, like a planet with an equator.

Something about these characters is wonderfully space-age yet archaic, like a logo for the Roman Empire Space Program. They seem oddly familiar. Have I seen them before? Somehow, it reminds me of Dad's work in Egypt.

We're going to need a new Rosetta Stone.

"Look at this!" I call out.

"It's gone." Faust crumples to the floor, crushed. "It's all gone." His voice leaks bitterness, face half in shadow.

"There's a carving here," Paulo yells. "On the wall."

I move to it. It depicts two felines sitting back-to-back over an underground labyrinth. Cat paws outstretched, tails intertwined.

I think instantly of the Egyptian god Ruti, a double feline god, always shown as two cats seated back-to-back. Ruti is the guardian of the underworld, exactly like the winged jaguar cats above us here at Yaxchilan. Ruti symbolizes what's beyond the horizon, representing yesterday and tomorrow.

One of the cat carvings is gazing at the constellation Leo.

"They were here!" I rush to my mentor and shove the stone triangle toward him. "Faust, they were here. *Look!*" He doesn't seem to notice.

For a long moment, no one says anything.

Faust pushes himself back up slowly, but something's off. His hands tremble. His breath comes in labored, ragged pulls. He paces the room, gripped by some rising mania. The man who once lectured on Søren Kierkegaard's serenity now braces against the stone wall, muttering Danish curses.

Then, out of nowhere, he pins his gaze on Andromeda. "Where is it?" His tone is unhinged. He stumbles toward her like a drunken bull. "You know where it is."

"Oh, come on," Andromeda shoots back, eyes darting to me with alarm.

"*Where is it?*" Faust rasps. "I've heard your whisperings ... your scheming. You're keeping secrets."

He's ranting, losing himself completely now. "You speak of Nikola Tesla—of the antediluvian world. You bring me classified documents. Your government knows *everything*. I know they do."

"Easy," I say sharply.

His tone turns vitriolic, and he advances on her with a feral intensity. "You arrive at my door with talk of the Ice Age. Your laptops and luggage are conveniently missing. Passports lost. Do you think I'm a *fool?*" His face contorts, and he clamps onto her shoulders, eyes moving rapidly between us. "I know you're running. I know you're hiding something very dark from me."

Andromeda's jaw tightens. "Get your hands off me." She knocks his grip away, and he stumbles back.

"She's lying, Tony!" Faust closes the distance to her.

"Whoa, whoa." I step between them, pushing the professor back. "She doesn't know anything, come on."

Andromeda balks, tone elevated. "Newsflash, *Professor*, I *quit* the government! My life was the collateral damage on your stupid jungle quest."

That gives him pause; he's breathing heavily, and then he leers at us, accusatory. "I haven't believed you since the moment you arrived."

Andromeda flinches as Faust comes at her again, his body coiled. She shoves him back, eyes flashing. "Back off, old man," she growls.

"What else are you hiding?" he demands, inches from her face, clearly distraught at this painful turn of events.

"You have no idea the shitshow this expedition has caused us," Andromeda fires. "If you've got something to say, say it. Otherwise, get out of my face."

"This doesn't solve anything." I wedge myself between them, pressing a palm against Faust's heaving chest. *Where did this come from?*

Faust locks his frenzied gaze on her. I hold him at bay until his wild fit begins to ebb. Andromeda's fist is cocked, ready to strike. His manic eyes sweep to her, then away again. His hands unclench, and he staggers back one step. Then another.

"You don't understand," he murmurs, defeated. "None of you understand."

No one moves as he stalks out of the chamber, leaving the shard discarded on the dusty floor like trash. Paulo swallows hard, bends to pick it up, then silently follows Faust out.

"That guy's got issues," she mumbles after a moment.

Well, that sucked.

Status? Federal fugitives. Project Nephilim data? Vaporized. American Hall of Records? Cleaned out. And Faust? Somewhere between midlife crisis and Viking funeral pyre. Game over.

I'll never know why they killed my dad.

Can I spend the rest of my life in hiding? *Knowing that I let them silence him?*

Because they win if I quit.

After his death, I read his field journals every night for a year. It wasn't the coffee-stained sections on Haplogroup X anomalies, or the Amazon LIDAR scans that captivated me. It was his last entry I couldn't let go of:

"One day you'll change the world, Tony."

Change it *how*, dad? My life's a wreck.

Andromeda's kicking pebbles by the cat carving, traumatized and angry, about to go volcanic. That wasn't cool, how Faust ambushed her like that. Cassian looks on like a man watching his future vanish in real time.

My hands are restless. Not fear. *That* feeling. That electric itch when your trowel grazes a buried tomb slab. Whole body telling you to *dig deeper*.

I've got nothing left to lose.

The government doesn't fear Atlantis because it's fiction. They're terrified of humanity learning civilization is a reboot. Mass disclosure would topple their whole empire.

Atlantis was global. So there must be other halls, bigger ones. Jean Vendôme said Plato's Atlantis trilogy reveals where. It's as good a lead as any.

Having such hopeful thoughts right now is absurd. But there's no *life* to go back to. What else am I gonna do? I don't know why I think I can do this, but I've never had a clearer objective. I'm going to find Plato's lost Atlantis trilogy.

And I'm going to convince Faust to join me.

Yeah, this vendetta is gonna get me killed.

47

Mexico City, Mexico
Tony Koviak

UP HERE ON the hacienda patio, the pyramids of Teotihuacan dominate the landscape, three massive, dark triangles silhouetted against the sunset. Not a bad view.

Owls hoot and coyotes yip from the mesquites. This luxurious hilltop hacienda outside Mexico City gives me real déjà vu of the view of Giza from the Mena House Hotel in Cairo: different continents, same vibe.

The mansion—a colonial Spanish jewel worthy of Zorro—belongs to the family of Paulo's girlfriend. They're out of town. The family is Mexican elite, though Paulo says illicit influences are in the picture. Power in Latin America seems to come with a price.

I can't help but notice the slums clinging to the pyramids' edges, another similarity with Giza. So many wonders are cradled in poverty and corruption. I regret never having visited here before. These pyramids have a brutal, imposing presence, like a fortress city from some sci-fi desert world.

And they're gigantic.

We've come to Mexico City at Faust's urging because he and Paulo are taking care of some business in town. We told them it's our best jumping-off point to catch a flight. Truth is, we have no escape plan.

Andromeda stands by the balcony, eyes closed, tapping her sternum rhythmically in some kind of energy-cleansing ritual. She's still fuming from her run-in with Faust at Yaxchilan. She's doing her best to Zen it out. They're playing nice for now, but there's tension. I have a new role: camp counselor!

Her hippie skill set is keeping her sane. I'm coming around to it. She's got a real feisty side. But there's this other side ...

She keeps telling me to "trust the vibes."

Where I see Imperial Inca settlements, she sees sacred vortexes. Ripples in her coffee, cracks in the sidewalk, fluffy clouds ... to her, they're messages in some hidden medium. I'll catch myself watching how she interacts with, well, *everything*. She'll pause midsentence to smile at a bird like they're sharing some cosmic inside joke. Starting to wonder if they are.

Faust invited us to visit Teotihuacan in the morning. He wants to see the site with fresh eyes before heading back to Machu Picchu, but it's an unnecessary risk.

We're in deep trouble. It's not looking good. Once again, Tesla's notebook is our only asset. We're debating whether to take it public or try leveraging it for amnesty.

Cassian strolls in wearing only a bathrobe, his mop of hair wrangled into a wet rat tail. "You weren't kidding about that water pressure," he says, leaning over Andromeda and sniffing dramatically. "You don't smell anymore, Scully. How will we ward off the evil spirits without your jungle funk?"

Her eyes fly open. The mantra she's been humming shifts to something about choosing better friends, and her sternum tapping intensifies.

"What's next for you, Cassian?" I ask.

He flops onto the outdoor sofa, pulling the robe over himself. He surveys the opulent balcony. "Think I'll stay here, change my identity. Just have to steal Paulo's cartel girl."

"This isn't a game," Andromeda says, moving to a chair. Worry is etched on her face.

He sighs. "I don't know. Find a good lawyer. Show Tesla's notebook to some buddies at MIT, see if we can make a go of it."

"Make a go of it?" she says, sarcasm dripping. I know what she's thinking. Like the rest of us, Cassian will never have a normal life again.

"Come with us," I urge. "Let's find Plato's trilogy, crack the Tesla puzzle. Faust will be all over this. The Hall of Records may even have info on pyramids. I know you're dying to know."

He grins. "Hate to break it to you, but I'm only in this for the notebook and the funding. Kamikaze quests for Atlantis? Yeah, good luck with that."

"Cassian"—Andromeda is solemn—"if you return to the States, you'll vanish."

He falls quiet, shifting his jaw at his uncomfortable new reality.

She shoots me a look, still simmering over Faust. I see the reprimand coming. "I get that you're eager to dash off with your bestie and hunt for treasures, but we're not sightseeing with him tomorrow."

Faust asked me to join his hunt for other halls of records. I'm torn between chasing Vendôme's mysteries with the world's most dangerous anthropologist and, well, saving my bacon. "We can win Faust to our side," I say.

"Win him to our side?" Her laughter holds traces of panic. "Read the room, Tony. The man's obsessed with his own delusions. He'd throw us to the wolves if it meant finding his Disney Kingdom. You heard him in that spidery hellhole."

"Watch it. Faust is genuine. He's not the enemy here."

"Oh, cut it out."

"What?"

"Yeah, he's a real hero," Andromeda says. "Wake up—this isn't some academic exercise. We're probably going to be killed, and trust me, the CIA doesn't give a damn about your tenure track. They disappear problems like us."

Ouch. That was a low blow. "You think I'm doing this for my career? They killed my dad. I'm out for blood. Besides, I doubt Metatron is even after us; we're not that important. We're no longer a threat."

"He is." Her tone sharpens. "We have the notebook—the one thing they want. We're *not* lollygagging at the pyramids, and that's final." She's trembling. "I didn't join the agency to end up on the wrong side of a manhunt. We need to finish what Frank started. No more chasing legends, Professor."

"And how do we do that?" I ask.

"No one's gonna believe you, hon," Cassian chimes in. "Go public, and at best, you'll end up on the fringe podcast circuit, wedged between Tartarian mud floods and Vatican UFO cover-ups."

She lifts an eyebrow. "Says the guy who thinks Tesla's kindergarten sketches are the key to free space energy. We're all hopeless losers here, Cass. The difference is I'm trying to keep us alive."

Cassian is right, though. Without evidence, we're cooked. The notebook alone may not be enough. We found one hall of records; we can find others. She may not see it, but we need Fabian Faust.

So, I'm going with him to see the Mexican pyramids.

48

Frontera Corozal, Mexico
Agent Vexity, Archon Class
Artificial Synapse Signature: SYN-Δ13F6
Targeting Division

THE YOUNG ARCHON Class targeting agent has only been with the division for two years. For Agent Vexity, it's a lifetime commitment, requiring a fake death.

Technically, he doesn't exist.

What he'll receive in return, after the reset, is worth a thousand lives.

He studies the coordinated finesse of the veteran Archangel Class agents as they grip the boatman's shoulders, forcing him to his knees. The higher Archangels—having proven their minds can handle a godlike influx of AIs—have a second neural implant linked to their brains.

The sweltering heat of Frontera Corozal smothers the young Archon, but he feels only a cool sensation as his biohacked body adjusts. His own AI chip bleeps softly, directing his hypothalamus to dissipate heat by dilating blood vessels.

A military helicopter is cycling up for departure, rotors beginning to swirl. Villagers lurk at the edges of the clearing, eyes wide with fear.

Metatron, the head angel, towers over the trembling boatman, his ivory face expressionless.

This won't take long, the young agent thinks, as the AIs instruct his body to release serotonin and endorphins. Discomfort and stress melt away, leaving only a sharp focus.

The boatman looks up in confusion. "Please ... I don't understand," he whispers in Spanish.

Agent Vexity doesn't speak the language, but his mind translates like a native.

Metatron produces a smooth ring of matte-black metal bristling with technological sensors.

The man is about to truly live. To experience exaltation—the full potential of his brain.

Metatron places the crown on the boatman's head, the neural nodes pressing against his scalp. His body scorpions as the link snaps into place, forming a technopathic bond. Emotions—euphoria, awe, pleasure—flow from Metatron's mind.

A gasp escapes the boatman's lips, turning into a sob of pure ecstasy.

The young Archon watches in fascination. *I still can't believe this technology exists.* All the disclosure junkies fixate on black project propulsion and energy technology. It hasn't dawned on them that AI biotech has developed in parallel for decades. In secret labs, the neural tech was perfected, allowing powerful AIs to interface with human biology.

Public neural-implant startups are to Targeting Division's wetware what American Airlines is to a gravitic warp drive.

Metatron's interrogation is full of warmth. The boatman hears the statement in his mind: *"You are loved. Let go. Tell me everything."*

The boatman's eyes roll back as theta waves plunge him into a trance. His mouth moves, words tumbling out in a slurred whisper. Metatron delves into his psyche, ransacking his gray matter. The man's elation shifts to horror as his deepest secrets are pillaged. His face contorts in a silent scream.

Metatron removes the crown with an electrostatic jolt. The boatman collapses lifeless, eyes drifting apart, mind erased.

Only the elect shall pass the veil of fire and flood.

49

Mexico City, Mexico
Tony Koviak

"THE WORLD ENDS *every twelve thousand years—like clockwork.*"

That wasn't on my ruined-life bingo card, but here we are. I now know why Andromeda got squeamish back in Peru when we discussed the Holocene, our current time period on Earth.

Turns out the CIA knows how the world ends.

We're up on the hacienda's rooftop around a dining table, night sky draped over us. The three great pyramids of Mexico glow in the distance, bathed in artificial floodlight. Faust called in a chef from the city's best restaurant: tacos al pastor, mole negro, chiles rellenos, Mexican street corn. I'm famished. *It's so good.* Colorful dishes clink as we dig in.

Andromeda nurses a mug of peppermint tea, her hair gathered over her sleeveless white blouse like a sheaf of wild wheat. She's making efforts to bury the hatchet with Faust. Sometimes, you just have to pretend something never happened.

Cassian leans forward. "Explain to me how a global civilization like Atlantis just vanishes." He snaps his fingers.

Faust wipes his mouth. "The cataclysm. The abrupt end of the Ice Age."

"Sure, but *erased*?" Cassian scoops beans onto his plate. "So, there was flooding—move to higher ground—adapt, rebuild."

It's a good question.

"It was more than floods," Andromeda says softly, and a hush falls over the table. Faust is now watching her like a bird of prey.

Cassian smirks. "You finally gonna tell us what the CIA knows about the cataclysms that ended the Ice Age? Don't think I forgot about that, missy."

She hesitates, eyes on the pyramids. "All the tinfoil hat people think the big coverup is aliens or 9/11," she says, glancing at me. "The real cover-up is Project Nephilim." She takes a steadying breath. "And its sister—Project Holocene."

Hold on. *Project Holocene?* I thought we weren't keeping secrets.

"I didn't think it was relevant," she pleads with me, voice wavering. "It's technically a subsection *within* Nephilim. People at the CIA—and Congress, for that matter—are scared to mention it, but those at the top know. I thought it was a prank until Frank showed me archives he'd been piecing together for *years.*"

"Project Nephilim?" Faust's eyes dart to me. He's coiled like a spring.

Paulo lights a cigar and refills his mezcal, lids half-closed. His end of the table is quickly engulfed in tangy smoke. I really don't want another bar brawl. *Tread lightly, Wildflower.*

"Tell him, Professor Koviak," Andromeda goads me, a storm brewing in her eyes. "Tell him how we almost died in Nikola Tesla's hotel room. Tell him about Metatron."

"Metatron?" Faust says, aggrieved. "The apocryphal archangel?"

Yikes. She's letting it all spill out. She's breaking, and I can see she doesn't care anymore. Didn't see this coming.

Faust leans forward, waiting for the juicy deluge.

"Nephilim wasn't the one that got me," Andromeda continues. "Atlantis? Cool, whatever. Yay—humans have been around a while. Okay. But Project *Holocene?* That one shook my soul. I couldn't sleep for days."

Everyone has stopped eating. Cassian's fork clatters.

"What's Project Holocene?" I ask gently.

"It's the government's Earth-science research—pole shifts and solar events."

Cassian leans into the candlelight. "Pole shifts? Those take hundreds of thousands of years."

She shakes her head tersely. "It happens in a single day and night. The world ends every twelve thousand years, like clockwork. It's in the geological record. NASA and USGS know. Atlantis was the *last* end of the world. That human timeline rope Professor Faust laid out? It's strung with countless civilizations, all reset by a recurring apocalypse. This has all happened before, and it will all happen again."

I swallow. Can't say I like the sound of that.

"I knew it," Faust whispers, then louder, "I *knew* it."

"How?" Cassian presses.

Her eyes fix on the horizon. "Earth's mantle floats on deep molten layers. It's normally all locked together. During a pole flip, a weakened magnetic field allows cosmic energy to liquefy it, causing the core to decouple from the mantle. Earth isn't a perfect sphere; there are imbalances in its mass. The planet essentially tips over."

Cassian chuckles nervously. "You're talking about Charles Hapgood's research, the Harvard scientist."

"Hapgood was moonlighting for the CIA."

"Sure, tectonic plates move," Cassian says. "But continental drift takes millions of years."

"Normally, yes," Andromeda says. "But the pole flip triggers a free spin. Due to centrifugal force, the heavy ice caps swing out to the equator.

"Sounds like the Dzhanibekov Effect," Cassian notes. "In space, rotating objects periodically flip their axis for no reason. It's a favorite trick among astronauts."

"The government's known since the 1940s."

Cassian listens grimly. "Go on."

"The end of the Ice Age wasn't random climate change," she explains. "It's part of the cycle. The North American ice sheets were the polar ice caps of the former North Pole in Hudson Bay."

I nearly spit my cola. "Hudson Bay was the North Pole?"

"Those American ice sheets were offset toward America. They didn't exist in Asia. They should expand uniformly from the poles." She gestures toward the pyramids. "During the Ice Age, these pyramids were at Virginia's latitude."

Her voice becomes hushed as if she's sharing a dangerous secret. "Frank had classified photos of pyramids poking out of the ice in Antarctica, which was in the tropics. The Sahara was green back then."

"Egypt wasn't always a desert?" I ask, astonished.

Cassian grins at me. "You don't believe her ghost stories, do you?"

"Einstein did," Andromeda says with a hint of defiance. "He wrote the foreword to Hapgood's book. A Russian scientist named Velikovsky continued his work. Einstein told his secretary to give Velikovsky anything he wanted. Fourteen days later, Einstein was found dead in his office—Velikovsky's book was open on his desk."

"Come on," I protest. "That can't be true."

"It's verified in a December 1975 *Reader's Digest* report." Her eyes meet mine. "Whatever was in Velikovsky's book was so troubling that Einstein may have died reading it. According to Project Holocene, our planet wobbling like a drunkard isn't even the worst part."

50

CIA Headquarters, Langley, Virginia
Director of National Intelligence

DEEP within the CIA Command Center, the director of national intelligence glares at a wall of glowing screens with satellite images, surveillance photos, and streaming data. Phones trill incessantly. Analysts are hunched over keyboards as they compile profiles on their highest-priority targets: rogue agent Andromeda Dey, Tony Koviak of Columbia University, geophysicist Cassian Wilder, and estranged billionaire archaeologist Fabian Faust.

Dossiers are prepared on each individual.

"Profiles!" the lead analyst barks, snapping his fingers. Sweat beads on his brow. "I needed them yesterday!" He rubs his burning eyes, fighting fatigue.

Too damn slow, the director thinks. He slams his hand on the desk. A young analyst jumps. "State and Homeland Security are breathing down my neck. And the president won't stop texting me for chrissakes!"

Dealing with the Andromeda Dey fiasco was bad enough. Now, with chaos unfolding in the United Kingdom, everything is going off the rails. The British government is facing a full-scale revolt, and the MI6 coup is causing bedlam.

What's happening in London is going to trigger Armageddon.

"Yes, sir." The flustered analyst is eighteen hours into her shift and surrounded by empty coffee cups. She hits SEND. The classified files are transmitted to Mexico City's Centro de Investigación y Seguridad Nacional—CISEN—Mexico's CIA. Mexican intelligence is now alerted to the imminent threat on their soil.

> CLASSIFICATION: TOP SECRET // REL TO MEX.
> DISSEMINATION: COMPARTMENTED TO MEXICAN FEDERAL SECURITY FORCES.
>
> This dossier contains profiles of four HIGH-VALUE TARGETS wanted in connection with terrorist attacks against the United States. Intelligence indicates these individuals have fled US jurisdiction and are currently AT LARGE in Mexican territory.
>
> Subjects are confirmed to have masterminded and participated in the planning and execution of terror attacks against US government facilities and personnel.
>
> These individuals should be considered ARMED AND DANGEROUS—approach with extreme caution.

"Gotcha," the director exhales, eyes scanning the profiles on the big screen. False-flag operations are never easy, especially not on this scale. Fabricating a terrorist attack is a dangerous gamble; the media frenzy will be a circus. He can't fathom why three ragtag fugitives are worth all this trouble.

They're losing their damn minds over in Prague.

He's never seen the Demiurge overreact this way. Whatever this threat is, it's shaken those within the veil.

51

Mexico City, Mexico
Tony Koviak

The Great Line!

A wild thought hits me as Andromeda spills the CIA's darkest secrets like gossip at a yoga class. I slam down my sangria, splashing some on the table. "Tesla's map—the one with the string of ancient sites!"

I leap from my chair and dash into the hacienda.

"Is he coming back?" Andromeda jokes behind me.

Moments later, I return, carrying an antique globe from the parlor. It looks like it sailed over on the *Niña* itself.

"Planning a voyage, Magellan?" Andromeda quips.

I wave a red marker at Paulo. "Mind if I scribble?"

Paulo puffs a cloud of indifference and gives a careless shrug.

I mark Tesla's sites: Easter Island, Machu Picchu, Giza, Sumer, and Angkor Wat. Then, I draw a red line connecting them—a perfect ring around Earth.

"Check this out." I set the globe on the table. "If Hudson Bay was the North Pole before, could this line be the old equator?" I tilt the globe, but the line doesn't match the equator at all. I feel kinda stupid now.

"I don't follow, Tony," Faust says, frustration mounting.

"Never mind." I sigh. "Sorry about the globe, Paulo. I thought maybe—"

"Wait," Andromeda interrupts, leaning forward. "Where's the North Pole when that line is the equator?"

I rotate the globe so the red ring sits level. "Alaska."

Her eyes widen. "Oh, it's a former equator all right ... from *four* pole shifts ago."

"Four shifts ago?" This is getting obscene.

"Project Holocene identified four previous poles," she explains. "They measured thousands of ancient sites. Turns out, most align to one of these former poles."

Faust nods vigorously. "Yes! Many old foundations have exquisite precision, yet the cardinal orientation is wrong. It's maddening."

"The Smithsonian is ahead of you, Professor," Andromeda says. "The Temple Mount in Jerusalem aligns with a pole over Greenland. Your Peru sites? They point to this pole near Alaska, the oldest one."

I tap the globe. "Machu Picchu is on this Great Line, along with Giza."

Faust stares at the globe with wolfish eyes. "You said the pole shift isn't the worst part."

Her expression darkens. "In the '60s, the CIA classified a report called *The Adam and Eve Story*. It was so disturbing that they locked it away. A sanitized version was released on the CIA's website in 2013."

"What does it say?" Cassian asks, almost whispering.

"During a pole shift, Earth tips over, but the oceans and atmosphere keep moving, like hitting the brakes without seatbelts. Waves wash over continents. Winds rake the surface. Stars would appear to fall across the night sky. It happens in a day and night—real end-of-the-world stuff."

"For fanden," Faust curses in Danish. "That explains the genetic bottlenecks. Maybe Plato wasn't exaggerating."

"New fear unlocked," Cassian mutters, adjusting his glasses. "I've been contemplating Faust's idea that Atlantis was based in North America. One oddity sticks out: our megafauna—like saber-tooths and mammoths—went extinct overnight, while Africa's survived. Maybe North America was ground zero for something terrible."

"Yeah." Andromeda goes paper-white. "You've just hit on the worst part: the sun."

52

The end of the world?

Maybe we could have some happy thoughts for once?

Agent Sunshine just dropped an apocalyptic nuke, as if I didn't have enough problems this week. This CIA rabbit hole has no bottom. I curse Frank and Andromeda for not securing their explosive intel.

"Those who survive the floods face something worse," Andromeda continues, going full-dystopian. "Cassian, what do you know about the galactic current sheet thing—"

Cassian looks down, poking his rice and beans. "Tesla was right. The universe is electric. The galactic current sheet ripples out from the Milky Way's center like a ballerina's skirt. The peaks and troughs reverse polarity because the top and bottom of our galaxy's magnetic field rotate opposite each other, like a toroidal vortex. The way a battery has a positive and negative."

"Do you know how long each ripple wave takes to hit us?" she asks.

"No."

She sounds almost reverent. "Twelve thousand years. Like passing through an electric veil—"

"And so"—Cassian's eyes widen—"our entire solar system flips polarity when it passes *throughholyshit*—" He goes rigid.

I think I missed something big.

She nods. "All the planets pole flip together."

His mind is crunching science. "That explains why other planets are also experiencing warming."

"NASA noticed," Andromeda says. "In 2023, the InSight Mars Lander found Mars had begun rotating faster, too."

"That's … that's not good." Cassian is flustered. "While our magnetic field flips, it's almost gone—like in *Star Trek* when the ship's shields go down. We'll get bombarded with plasma arc discharges, cosmic thunderbolts, real wild magic."

"One horseman at a time, please," I sigh.

"Project Holocene has elderly people on videotape," Andromeda adds. "Saying how the sun appears white today, but they remember it being yellow in their childhoods—a sort of pole flip Mandela Effect due to the weakening magnetic field. This is what killed the Neanderthals. Hell, they probably built the Great Line."

Whoa. That's a mind-bender. Rival hominids have entered the chat. They did have bigger craniums.

She's almost pleading. "Don't you see? Frank said governments know. They're prepping. It's why they're spending like there's no tomorrow. They've stopped caring if people notice. Every political action is just a diversion to buy time."

"How does something this big fly under the radar?" I ask. "My cousin in the FBI is a decent guy, a model citizen."

"Information silos," Andromeda replies, sipping her limeade. "Worker bees don't see the big picture. Information is fragmented. Interagency cooperation is discouraged. They control universities. Agenda-driven research becomes the cornerstone source for new studies, defining 'truth.' Those who piece things together are discredited and removed."

That's appalling. I hate the notion.

Cassian leans back, waxing poetic. "On some level, everyone's waiting for the end of the world."

Faust and Paulo have been listening, stunned into silence, content to let us divulge this exotic worldview.

"Wait," I say, feeling a little queasy. "You're saying the next cataclysm is … *now?*"

Andromeda hugs her torso. "NASA projects we'll pass through the next galactic reversal point in the 2040s. People as far south as Cuba will begin seeing auroras until …" she trails off.

"Atlantis 2.0 will happen in our lifetimes?" Cassian deadpans.

The table falls silent. Everyone has pushed back from their food. A coyote howls in the desert night.

A chilling thought strikes me. "You said it's like a veil?"

Cassian nods. "Yeah, the galactic current sheet is like a wavy electric curtain."

I rub my chin. "In myth, Metatron is the Angel of the Veil, the only angel who knows what lies beyond."

Andromeda looks disturbed. "Frank said they use veil symbolism, Tony. Their goal is to create a new global order. What if this shadow government is preparing for the next reset?"

Oh God. Perfect. Now we're dealing with a doomsday cult.

"What shadow government?" Faust is going to blow a gasket.

"Bad news, gang," Cassian groans. "Our magnetic pole began racing ten years ago. It's halfway to Russia—not good."

Paulo cuts in with a Spaniard's chuckle. "Is that why all the billionaires are building bunkers?"

Andromeda points at the Mexican. "You're damn right. They're even constructing a ten-thousand-year clock in the Texas desert —the *Clock of the Long Now*. Ticks once a year, and the long hand ticks every century. Project Holocene says it even has a cuckoo that appears every millennium."

Whoa. These people plan in millennia.

"Plato said the sea swallowed Atlantis in a single day," I say, a knot forming in my stomach. "The Egyptians mocked the poor Greeks for remembering only *one* flood when there were many."

"Cataclysmic pole shifts," Faust says after a long silence. "Herodotus noted the sun shifted four times, rising where it now sets and setting where it rises. A curious turn of phrase for a Greek historian."

He turns to me. "Do you recall the tale of Phaëthon?"

I sure do. "He's the son of Helios, the sun god. He took his father's chariot, lost control, and scorched the Earth."

"Ya," Faust sweeps his hair over the tips of his ears. "Curious that it's from the Atlantis trilogy. Do you recall what Plato says?"

I dig deeper. "He insists the story is *not* a myth. That it describes bodies moving in the heavens and a great cataclysm that repeats after long intervals. Humanity starts over like children, forgetting the past."

Passing through a veil—into a new Earth.

Plato is describing orbital physics and galactic electromagnetism.

Paulo joins our apocalyptic freakshow: "Mayan codices say the world is purged by fire at the end of each *Sun Age*," he adds.

"Reminds me of the Bible," Faust purrs. "'Fire came down from God out of heaven and devoured them. Earth wobbled like a drunkard. The stars fell'—"

I finish the verse. "'The heavens opened like a scroll. Every mountain and island moved from its place. The elites hid themselves in caves and said to the mountains, fall on us and hide us'."

I look at Andromeda. "Book of Revelation."

"Enough!" Faust stands abruptly, commanding attention. His voice rings out as he strikes the table. "I will help you." His jaw sets firm. "It's clear you're not on officially sanctioned business."

His gray eyes glitter. "Tell me what you need—anything."

53

ONE, two, three ... One, two, three ... One, two, three ...

Plato and Tesla—they're connected.

I jolt awake. Again. Seriously?

The hacienda is silent as a tomb at—what is it now? Midnight? Oh, the witching hour. Perfect.

The numbers keep looping in my head. *One, two, three.* Over and over. What's your deal, brain? All I can think about is Plato's Atlantis trilogy. The first words of Timaeus, Book One: "One, Two, Three"—as if those numbers hold some importance.

Tesla was nuts about the number three.

Jean Vendôme's research has forced its way back into my thoughts. I can't shake his riddle:

Plato's completed trilogy ... is in Europe, at a place having to do with finance. It reveals the location of the Hall of Records.

Finance? Hall of Records? I'm missing something here.

But I know someone who can help.

It's a terrible idea.

I creep down the hallway, white drapes billowing from open windows, moonlight painting everything like a black-and-white movie. I pass conquistador armor and Goya paintings and end up hovering over a vintage telephone in the old Spanish parlor. The antique globe stands beside the table, ringed with red marker, Tesla's Great Line.

I lift the receiver and dial Cambridge University's switchboard.

54

Cambridge University, England
Professor Orson Pellinor

ENGLISH RAIN HAS POUNDED the school all morning, drenching the vaulted Tudor chambers of the Classics Department. In his austere office, Professor Orson Pellinor, head of Classics, sips his second cup of tea an hour early, warding off the chill. The architecture feels like a medieval abbey in the gloom. Mid-sip, his telephone rings, causing his teacup to slosh.

"Professor Pellinor speaking," he answers, his voice weary with a crisp English edge.

"Pellinor?" The caller's hard, rolling 'R' marks him as American—yet vaguely familiar.

A slight hesitation. "Uh—*Yes?*"

"It's Tony Koviak, sir."

A ghost from the past. Pellinor straightens, owl-like eyebrows lifting as he sets down his teacup. Koviak had studied in the Department of Anthropology but often sought Pellinor's mentorship on Plato and classical texts. Hearing his voice warms the professor's heart. He'd even recently nominated Tony for a position at Göbekli Tepe.

"Koviak!" Pellinor exclaims. "Great heavens, man! Aren't you supposed to be in Turkey? Your team's been knocking on about your absence. Is everything all right?"

"I—I don't have much time to explain."

Papers rustle over the line. His former student asks, "Do you remember your work on finance in the classical world?"

"Well, of course, I do, my boy." Pellinor turns his baggy eyes to his wall of dusty volumes, aggrieved at the mystery of the inquiry. He's a leading authority on trade history from antiquity through the Renaissance.

"Can you tell me, sir, the principal centers of finance from the beginning up to the Enlightenment?"

"Well," he sputters, "numerous hubs over the ages—Babylon, Constantinople, Venice, London—even New York, as you well know."

A long pause. The transoceanic line softly pops and clicks.

"Finance? My dear Tony, I hope you're not in some monetary predicament."

"Do any of those places connect to the works of Plato?"

Now it's Pellinor who hangs on the line, flabbergasted, his bushy eyebrows dancing. "Certainly not, I should say!"

"Professor ... one more thing."

"Yes?"

The voice on the other end of the line sighs. "If you had to guess where Plato's missing Hermocrates is hidden—if you only had *one* guess, where would you say it's located?"

"The lost *Hermocrates*?" he blusters. "Mr. Koviak, that is highly speculative. I'm sure I haven't the *foggiest* where—"

"Please, Professor."

He chokes back his bewilderment. "There's no proof it ever even existed," he stammers. "But ... I suppose one might start with Proclus. In antiquity, Proclus insisted the Hermocrates was completed. Claimed he'd seen it himself."

Silence. Then Tony asks, "You said Venice was a center of finance?"

Pellinor chuckles. "My boy, from the late Middle Ages into the High Renaissance, Venice was the epicenter of it *all*." He waits, puzzled. "Tony ... what are you on about?"

"Thank you, Professor. I owe you everything." Tony's voice wavers. "You may hear some things. None of it is true. Can you keep this our secret?"

"Koviak! ..." Pellinor rises from his chair. "Where *are* you, man?"

But the line goes dead with a soft click. The only sound is the rain pelting the diamond-latticed Elizabethan windows.

55

Mexico City, Mexico
Tony Koviak

OUT ON THE hacienda's dark patio, the sky is full of stars. A techno-blue line on the eastern horizon heralds the coming dawn over Mexico City. I stand here staring at the enormous black triangles—Mexico's pyramids—in the same Orion layout as Giza. A million scraps of history whirl through my mind.
    Lost manuscripts.
    Renaissance finance.
    Proclus—a devoted disciple of Plato.
    Venice.
    My heart beats wildly, and my breath hitches. The Pleiades hang above Orion.
    Wait a damn minute.
    Boom! In a blinding flash of insight, the jigsaw falls into place.
    Yeah. I know where Plato's lost Atlantis trilogy is.

56

It's morning in Mexico City.

Faust is eccentric, but his presence brings a security I've missed since this whole ordeal began. We've won him to our cause—to expose the cover-up—and that's a game-changer.

After our grim dinner last night, Andromeda and Faust cozied up by the fireplace for a heart-to-heart. She laid it all out—the CIA, the cover-ups, our struggle to expose the truth. Everything. And, well ... the gods must be high. By bedtime, they were laughing like old war buddies.

Faust is bewitched. He's ready to risk it all. And when Fabian Faust goes all in, he does it with Zeus's righteous fury ... blank checks, a private jet, and the one thing we desperately need: sanctuary.

We're leaving for Eastern Europe this afternoon. Some location he assures us doesn't require passports or flight plans. He knows people. A place no Western power can reach, our new base of operations. As if that wasn't enough, he's offered each of us *twenty grand* a day to be advisors on this new quest. I protested—the pay is obscene—but he insisted. And let's be honest, we're broke.

Faust has leads on where the other halls of records might be. The theory is that Atlantis, being a global civilization, hid its knowledge worldwide when the end came.

I haven't told a soul about my call with Pellinor. Once we're somewhere safe, I'll tell Faust and the others that I know where Plato's manuscript is hidden. That's right, I know where the lost Atlantis trilogy is! And let's not forget, it supposedly reveals the location of the *big* Hall of Records.

Ground crews are prepping Faust's jet at a small regional airport for the long haul. Someone mentioned they're loading filet mignon for dinner. Things are looking up. With two hours to kill, Faust wants to visit the Mexican pyramids. Works for me, because I do too.

We're jostling in the back of a taxi van. The mood is optimistic. We're approaching the Pyramid of the Sun.

Minutes later, we're walking up a gravel path to Teotihuacan. The morning sun casts an iridescent glow over the vast ruins. This place is enormous. As we near the gates, I remind Faust and Paulo to avoid eye contact with a platoon of watchful Mexican policemen.

They're Team Baddies now.

The sign reads UNESCO WORLD HERITAGE SITE.

"UNESCO," Andromeda scoffs as we approach the entrance sign. "Of course they'd be involved."

"What's wrong with UNESCO?" Faust asks. "They protect ancient sites."

"Exactly," she smirks. "They control what gets revealed. Machu Picchu, Egypt ... it's all gatekeeping."

"What are you talking about?" I ask.

She fixes me with a look. "The UN in UNESCO is for United Nations—peculiar niche for a geopolitical entity. Ever heard of Göbekli Tepe, Professor?"

I chuckle. "Japanese fast-food chain, right?"

"Yeah, well, your dig is a *big* deal to these veil guys. It's a time capsule from Atlantis. It tells the real story."

I raise an eyebrow. "As the world's leading authority on Göbekli Tepe, I'd say that's a stretch."

She rolls her eyes. "Oh, pardon me, Professor. Who do you think funds your little sandbox?"

Wait. What?

"The UN and the World Economic Forum wield significant influence over your site," she continues. "They won't excavate it fully and are building orchards over it."

I start to protest, but hesitate. She's … not wrong. Göbekli Tepe—the world's oldest site—has been partially buried under concrete walkways and viewing platforms. Only a fraction has been excavated, and administrators are now talking about keeping it buried. It'd be like knowing a hundred Stonehenges are underground and building over them.

And it's UNESCO.

They don't want it opened.

———

Teotihuacan is a real stunner. I take in the scene. My gaze lingers on the Pyramid of the Sun, its silhouette sharp against the Aztec sky. The scale and geometry remind me of Giza. That's becoming a theme.

Daybreak slashes a golden streak across the pyramid's dark face like a painter's stroke. Below lies the Avenue of the Dead, a long plaza connecting all three pyramids like a runway. Stone risers line the avenue, giving it the feel of a Roman chariot racetrack. Tourists are already milling about. A few brave souls ascend the steep steps of the Pyramid of the Moon at the far end.

"Remarkable, isn't it?" Paulo's eyes gleam with pride as we step onto the avenue.

"Truly," I say. "Hard to believe I've never been here."

"The Aztecs called it the Place of the Gods," Paulo says, spreading his arms wide. "Like Machu Picchu, it was ancient when they found it. No one has deciphered its original name from the oldest sources."

"Lemme guess," Cassian says. "Aztecs have a civilizing hero."

"Quetzalcoatl." Paulo snaps a finger at him, walking backward. "Seven sages survived a cataclysm, led by Quetzalcoatl from Aztlán—Atlantis. He taught them civilization and promised to return."

Quetzalcoatl—*another* civilization bringer. Seven sages. It really is a global memory.

"The evidence is getting embarrassing," Andromeda says. "Why don't historians connect these mythological dots?"

"Egypt folks don't talk to America folks," Faust says sardonically. "Siloed academics can't see the forest from the trees."

"Have a look around," Paulo says. "We need caffeine. I'll be over at that darling café just off the plaza." He points to a small outdoor bistro on the edge of the grass and darts off.

Faust, Andromeda, Cassian, and I head for the massive Pyramid of the Sun. A broad staircase leads up from the avenue to a large courtyard at its base.

"Do you recall the dimensions of the Great Pyramid of Giza?" Faust asks, face buried in a brochure map. His eyes shift to me, sparkling with curiosity. "Specifically, the width of its base?"

I've modeled Giza extensively; the dimensions are burned in my brain. "The Great Pyramid's width is 230 meters," I reply.

Faust hands me the brochure. "An oddly specific number—they're the same size."

I give him a wary side-eye. "Didn't take you for a jokester, Professor."

"I'm not joking, Tony." He hands me the brochure.

The width is 230 meters.

Holy—

This can't be real. I squint at the Mexican pyramid, my disbelief mounting. A surge of cosmic wonder washes over me. Can this be? The pyramids now seem wildly significant. It's global.

Faust draws back an aristocratic smile. "Not only are both complexes aligned to Orion's belt stars, but they share the same footprint."

This can't be possible.

Cassian chuckles slowly; the Dahmers tremble. "What are the odds of that happening by chance?"

"Zero," Faust says. "It's almost as if—"

"They had a common blueprint," Andromeda finishes.

"*Præcis,*" Faust breathes. "A standard they took to colonies around the world."

The Mexican pyramid isn't as tall. Same footprint, gentler angle. My eyes trail up the central staircase, watching tourists climb. It's flatter than its Egyptian twin, like a godlike palm squished it down.

"That's not all." Andromeda peers over my shoulder at the site map. "The Avenue of the Dead … its orientation is odd."

"What do you mean?" I ask.

"According to this rose compass, true north is that way." She points due north with one hand and down the avenue with the other. "These pyramids are aligned to Hudson Bay," she concludes.

"The former pole," I say.

Faust cranes up at the pyramid. "That means these pyramids are at least twelve thousand years old."

57

WE'VE MADE our way down the Avenue of the Dead to the Pyramid of the Moon. "Lemme see that." Cassian rips the glossy brochure from my hand and flips it over. "Check this out. In 2014, a team from Mexico's National Institute of Anthropology discovered pools of liquid mercury deep inside these pyramids. Why are there pools of liquid mercury?"

Strange. Cassian was tinkering with that exotic silver stuff back at Wardenclyffe. I remember seeing it swirl in his capacitor contraption.

"Mercury has remarkable conductive properties," he continues.

Our resident Caltech prodigy tells us how he first learned about mercury's electrical potential from a Dutch physicist named Heike Onnes. The guy achieved superconductivity using—of all things—liquid mercury.

"Superconductivity is the holy grail of electrical distribution," Cassian says. "Modern power lines bleed energy. Even Tesla wrestled with this during the war of the currents. Edison's direct current could only go a few miles. Tesla's alternating current could transmit electricity hundreds of miles."

"Thus, Tesla won," Faust purrs.

"Yes, but Onnes speculated that rotating liquid mercury could generate magnetic fields as strong as *ten Tesla*—the unit, not the man," Cassian says. "For comparison, the magnets at CERN's Large

Hadron Collider only reach *eight Tesla*. People still feared they'd create a black hole when they flipped the switch."

Cassian is teching out now big time. Sometimes he forgets he's talking to us plebs. I can remember when discovering low-power mode on my phone was exciting.

He goes on. "When electricity flows through liquid mercury in a magnetic field, it spins. This rotation comes from the Lorentz force, creating a vortex."

So that's why his giant capacitor was filled with mercury, hoping the spinning silver would supercharge his design.

Faust adds, "Liquid mercury also fills the pyramids in China. Qin Shi Huang, the first emperor, left a pool of it in the pyramid."

"*Stop*. You're telling me ..." Cassian trails off, eyes sparkling with some new idea about how pyramids function.

"Mysterious," Andromeda says.

I think of Greece. "Mercury is the Roman name for Hermes," I say.

"Hermes wasn't just any figure," Faust says. "Mercury, Hermes—names for the Egyptian god Thoth. The greatest civilization bringer of them all. They're all the same individual, a survivor of Atlantis."

Inside the pyramid's courtyard, a film crew buzzes around bright lights and cinema cameras. A sign warns that "Turismo Mexicano" might use our images for marketing.

"Picked the wrong day." Andromeda sighs, keeping her head down. Her striking folk-rocker beauty is drawing unwanted attention.

Music blares as dancers in vibrant costumes rehearse hypnotic moves. Fashion models strike poses against the ancient stones. A tarp hides a vehicle at the center of the set while production assistants hoist a colorful banner above it.

Grips and set designers hustle around the courtyard. Tourists pause their sightseeing to gawk at the flashy spectacle, and makeup artists fuss over waiting performers.

We pass a kiosk filled with Quetzalcoatl bobbleheads, their feathered serpent headdresses trembling in the morning sunlight.

"Let's get a closer look at this pyramid," Faust suggests, steering us away from the Hollywood circus.

58

WE'RE WAITING in line for the Pyramid of the Moon—Faust, Cassian, and I—when Andromeda runs up and grips my arm. The look on her face sends a jolt through me. She has an expression of horror I haven't seen since we were sprinting for our lives through the Lyceum Theatre.

"Come here," she says, her voice tight. She pulls me aside, out of earshot. Her face is hollow and ghostly pale.

"What's going on?" I ask, good vibes evaporating.

Her voice is hoarse and shaken. "I was over there by that crowd, and I heard a boy say my name—my *full name*: thick accent, local kid. I looked down, and there he was—a disheveled street urchin with tangled black hair, no older than ten. He repeated my name. I froze. Before I could react, he glanced at a photo in his hand, shoved this envelope at me, and melted into the crowd. I chased after him, but he was gone."

I stare, trying to process. Faust is over in the line, oblivious, on his phone.

"What's in the envelope?" I ask

She tears it open with trembling fingers. Out tumble three passports from the Falkland Islands—fake identities with our photos—and two thick stacks of US dollars. A slip of paper reads YOU MUST RUN. NOW. —THE WATCHER.

59

"We gotta go. *Now*." Andromeda is scanning the crowds neurotically.

"What about Faust?" I ask.

"*Now*, Tony."

"Did Frank have anyone on the inside?"

She glances over her shoulder at the bustling film set, where crew members unveil a shiny silver truck. "I don't think so."

"How could they have found us?" Cassian is blinking, trying to understand.

"They're the goddamn CIA," she hisses.

I'm suddenly aware that cameras can be anywhere. Visiting Teotihuacan was a mistake. We need to bolt—*now*. We should grab Faust and get out.

We stride back to him. Paulo is approaching, but instead of coffee, he's clutching his tablet, his face grim. Worse, a stern-looking police officer trails him, hand resting on his holstered weapon.

Paulo sidles up to Faust, whispers something, then shows him the tablet. His eyes flick to us, filled with suspicion. I suddenly get really bad vibes from Paulo.

We lean in, but Paulo puts a hand out to stop me. He cranks the volume. It's an American news broadcast. I recognize the famous anchor; I've watched him countless times.

My driver's license photo flashes on-screen over helicopter

footage of black smoke pouring from the damaged US Capitol Building.

The chyron screams CAPITOL MASSACRE.

"Dozens are dead—" The solemn journalist continues: "We continue our coverage of the horrific explosion in our nation's capital. We now have the identities of the three domestic terrorists responsible. What do we know, Lydia?"

Unflattering photos of Cassian and Andromeda join mine. A woman with perfect NPR cadence says, "Officials are calling them accelerationists. The trio posted a manifesto online hours before the attack, declaring their goal to overthrow the government and spark civil unrest. Make no mistake, this is one of the darkest hours in our nation's history."

I'm going to vomit. The ground tilts. Andromeda looks about to die physically.

Faust staggers, groaning a hellish gasp. He clutches Paulo for support. "My God! Dear God—no!" His eyes lock onto mine, filled with terror and betrayal. "What have you done?"

"Faust," I say weakly. "It's a lie. It's not true. We found the … They're—"

He stares at me as if I'm a demon. The coverage is so real that I almost believe it myself.

"*Seguridad! Arrestenlos!*" Paulo shouts. *Security—arrest them!*

"No—no, no!" Andromeda reaches for Faust. He recoils as if brushed by a leper.

"I've never even *been* to DC," Cassian mutters in a daze.

My legs wobble. The officer dumps rapid Spanish into his radio, calling for backup, hand trembling, eyes darting between us.

"Tony!" Faust's mouth sounds dry as ash. "*What have you done? This is what you're running from?*" He watches as the Mexican officer steps forward and takes hold of my arm.

In a blur of confusion, some animal instinct kicks in. My fist balls up, and I slam it hard into the officer's jaw. He drops. Andromeda grabs his wrist, snatching his sidearm, and trains it on him.

"Radio! Radio!" she barks.

His eyes widen in horror. He tugs the radio from his uniform and hands it over.

"Police!" Faust yells, frantic. Stepping back like I'm an escaped lion.

I yank her arm. "Come on!"

We bolt through the crowd. "Why would they report that?" I shout.

"*What the fuck?*" Andromeda rasps, wild hair flying. "*What the fuck!*"

We reach the courtyard and skid to a halt. The big film production has swallowed the area. No way through.

I scan for an exit. Then I see it—a gleaming Tesla Cybertruck at the center of the set. Above it, a banner reads MEXICO IS ADVENTURE: THE ANCIENT FUTURE. The silver Cybertruck has chunky tires, and its roof has an equipped rack like an overland expedition vehicle.

Cassian and I lock eyes, saying it in unison: "Tesla."

We stride up to the truck. A stylist is leaning into the driver's door.

I tap her shoulder. "We're with the production company. Where's the key?"

The confused stylist, satisfied by the confident good looks and assertive American accent, riffles through her fanny pack and hands me a credit card key.

Andromeda moves to the passenger door, and Cassian dives into the backseat. In an instant, we're inside the truck.

"How do you turn this thing on?" I growl.

"You've never driven a Tesla?" Cassian yells. "Hit the brake!"

I press the pedal. Displays light up. Doors lock with a *thunk*. Is it on?

"Shifter?" I bellow, hands up.

"Slide it to the *D*!" Cassian howls at a graphic on the display. "Slide the damn *D*!"

"Aye!" The stylist slaps an angry palm on the window. "*Bastardos!*"

Andromeda jabs the D, and I floor it. Wheels spin on gravel, and we lurch forward, tearing through the banner as models dive out of the way.

A security guard jolts awake, grabs his walkie-talkie, and yells into it. A purple-faced man, presumably the Cybertruck's owner, screams after us.

"Go, go, go!" Andromeda's knuckles are clenched and bloodless.

"This thing's got punch," I say.

"Then *punch* it!" she explodes.

I steer for the exit but swerve when I see steel bollards sealing us inside the courtyard. "There's no way out."

Another guard charges at us, howling into a whistle, signaling to stop.

"Dammit," I rage, glimpsing the crowds in the rearview. "Change of plans."

"We are royally screwed," Andromeda says, on the edge of panic.

"Like hell we are," I roar, wrenching the wheel and sending the Tesla into a power drift across the flagstones. Tourists scatter as I lean on the horn.

"Tony!" she screams.

We plow through stalls of Aztec calendars and bobbleheads. Vendors dive as their merchandise explodes around us.

"Only one option." I swerve toward the stone staircase leading to the Avenue of the Dead. The truck's suspension hammers down the steps. We burst onto the wide avenue, swerving to face the long runway.

With more open space, I gun it, weaving through pockets of startled tourists. The Cybertruck barrels down the Avenue of the Dead, hemmed in by stone walls. The motors let out a futuristic whine like a spacecraft warbling to light speed. The truck's sci-fi torque surges, zero to sixty in three face-melting seconds. The boost pins us back, and the Tesla logo on the dash pulls away.

Andromeda's fingers sink into the armrests. "This is the … We're on the—"

"I know!"

The Pyramid of the Sun rises to our left like a cosmic monolith. Red-vested guards along the iconic thoroughfare blow into their whistles, faces red, waving their arms furiously.

"The damn Atlanteans don't believe in off-ramps?" I curse.

Ahead, police form a blockade—flashing lights, armed officers taking positions. A commander turns to face us. Is he smiling?

In the rearview, more blockades are cutting off our retreat. We're boxed in.

"Tony!" Andromeda shrieks.

My words resound like a covenant. "We're committed now."

"To what?!"

Time slows. I no longer hear sounds. I see Andromeda yelling in slow motion. I feel nothing—*nothing*. But I'm not going down like this.

Audentes fortuna iuvat. Fortune favors the bold.

With an abandon bordering on deranged, I wrench the truck so hard that it nearly rolls, directly at the largest pyramid in the Western Hemisphere. The wheels pound up into its walled courtyard.

The dark pyramid fills the windshield—one path.

Andromeda screams, *"Oh my GOD—"*

I slow just enough before impact, then hit the pyramid's slope. The Tesla launches upward, and gravity shifts. We're vertical, climbing the ancient stone face.

It's unspeakable.

We're driving up the Pyramid of the Sun—in a Cybertruck.

The vehicle bucks over jagged stones. Chunky tires claw upward. Gear flies off the roof rack. I grip the wheel, wrestling it into submission.

Startled climbers gawk and swing phones in our direction. In the rearview, police stand slack-jawed, watching the glinting spacecraft make its surreal ascent like a mythological Pegasus. The vehicle defies gravity. It defies all logic, the gods themselves.

We reach a dizzying height. I dare to glance out the window, like an astronaut peeking out during a launch. The world below is a glorious expanse of triangles and geometric architecture, like primordial circuitry. The front tires leap across a small terrace notched near the top that almost sends us tumbling.

I lull the Cybertruck as we reach the peak. Its motors spin down to a low whine, and we're on flat ground again, inching over the wide summit.

"Baller move," Cassian pants, locking eyes with a stunned tourist on the summit.

"This part might be rough." I roll to a crawl as the ground falls away into oblivion. All we can see is the horizon over the broad hood. We're hundreds of feet up. No time to hop out and verify a path down. The bumper begins to dip into thin air.

"No, no, no, no," Andromeda says with a sorceress growl. Her breath hitches, and her palm flies to my chest.

Insanos mors iuvat. Death favors the dumbass.

We're gonna die.

"Brace," I say as the truck tilts forward into nothing. Seconds later, the Tesla is facedown, gripping the back slope.

"Easy," I coax. "Come on, girl." I find a tenuous line and allow the vehicle to roll down faster. Andromeda is hyperventilating, her body hanging forward on the seat belt, hair obscuring her face as she violently tosses around. The backside of the pyramid is devoid of life.

Almost down. We're gonna make it! I accelerate—just one more little bump ahead.

Aaaaaand we're crashing.

The Cybertuck flips on its side and barrel-rolls the rest of the way down. Everything's spinning. The sound is horrifying. We're screaming. The truck hits ground level and abruptly rolls right side up with a *thud*.

Stillness. Heavy breathing. We survived. The truck survived, I think. No broken glass. The monitor's fine, motors are still on. This thing's a tank.

"You all right?" I ask.

"Go!" Andromeda wails.

I gun it. A clear line of sagebrush leads off the plateau, and we plow through a flimsy chain-link fence. No pursuers in sight.

We tear across the dusty landscape until we cross into the adjacent slums, swerving onto a poorly paved road, and I open up the Cybertruck's triple motors.

60

THE CYBERTRUCK ROARS through the slums of Mexico City, and vibrant murals flash past. I have no idea where I'm going.

"Can we talk about the fact that we just blew up DC?" Cassian wails from the backseat.

"I don't get it," I say, gripping the wheel tighter. "Why would they fabricate that?"

"It's what they do," Andromeda replies, her voice tinged with nausea. "False flag. They've made us famous. Brilliant move."

It hits me powerfully—they're afraid of us.

They're really, really afraid of us.

TEN MINUTES LATER, I swerve the Cybertruck into a grimy carport hidden down a filthy alley.

Andromeda has a bloody lip from our rollover, fat like she had a bad cosmetic injection. She looks like she's seen a ghost, a really terrifying one. "I think I'm freaking out," she whispers.

"Hey, deep breaths," I say, taking her clammy hand. "Think happy things. New moons in conjunction. Crystals. Joni Mitchell."

Her eyebrows tremble as she looks from the windshield to me. There's a tiny smile.

"Come on. *Tap, tap, tap,*" I say, doing her energy thing on my chest.

She joins me, tapping her sternum rapidly, eyes closed.

I twist around to face Cassian. He looks like he's chewing glass. "Sooner or later, the whole Mexican army will be hunting us," he says. "You better have a plan, or we're gonna end up like Butch and Sundance down here."

"All we have is the notebook now," Andromeda says between ragged breaths. "We could hide it, turn ourselves in, leverage immunity."

I shake my head. "I don't love it."

"Or ..." She pulls out the mysterious envelope from her jacket. "We vanish. Fall off the grid. Go dark."

I shoot her a skeptical glance. "You trust that?"

"No, of course not." She thumbs through the passports, examining the intricate details. "But these are authentic. One for each of us. If the CIA knew where we were, we'd already be dead."

"Who the hell is the Watcher?" Cassian asks, referring to the mysterious sender.

"Hell if I know," she says. "Someone's tracking us."

"I know who they are," I say. "The Watchers are from the biblical story of the Nephilim. Angels sent down from heaven. The Sumerians called them *the Observers*."

"Not the time for history lessons, Professor." Andromeda rubs her gemstone necklace.

Cassian leans forward. "So who were they?"

"The Watchers give mankind forbidden tools and resources. Help humanity advance into further light and knowledge."

Cassian sits back. "That's a trap."

We sit in silence.

"We should try to reconnect with Faust," Cassian says. "Explain the truth."

"Not a chance," Andromeda replies. "Faust is in the wrong hands now."

"I found Plato's Atlantis trilogy," I blurt out.

They stare at me, then at each other, like I've finally lost it.

Andromeda's expression scrunches up. *"What?"*

Cassian leans into the front like a therapist. "Is this lost trilogy in the room with us?"

I glance out the window at a mangy dog rummaging through trash. "I'm ninety-eight percent sure I know where it is."

Andromeda brings her lips into a questioning O shape. "Yaxchilan ninety-eight or New Yorker ninety-eight?"

"Faust was right about Yaxchilan. The library was there," I say defensively, watching the dog. "More like one hundred percent—it's in Venice."

"*Venice?*" she scoffs. "What makes you so sure?"

I decide not to mention the reckless call I made to a colleague from a landline; she'd hand me to the cartels herself. "Venice was the esoteric capital of the world, the center of finance for a thousand years. Home to the Venetian Council of Ten, the group that replaced the Knights Templar. The elite's lion's den. It's everything you imagine when you think of secret societies."

"Knights Templar?" She laughs. "This isn't an Indiana Jones movie, Professor."

Well, actually, it kind of has been.

"And the Marciana Library is there," I continue. "It houses the world's rarest manuscripts. Like the Venetus T—Plato's oldest surviving text in original Greek."

"I'm sure it's been scrutinized six ways to Sunday," she says.

I bite my lip. "The missing trilogy isn't in the Venetus T."

"We don't have time for this," Andromeda says, glancing down the alley. "We need to decide."

"We use the passports," I say. "We go now."

"We can't stay in Mexico," Cassian says.

She's considering it. "And what does Plato's trilogy get us?"

"Another huge bargaining chip," I reply. "Maybe more. Vendôme said it reveals the location of the true Hall of Records, the big one."

She's clutching her moonstone pendant so tight her knuckles are bloodless. "Are you afraid?" I ask.

"I've been afraid my whole life," she admits softly. "Aren't you?"

"Yeah, I am." Disturbing images flash of the fake bombing, the betrayal—my dad—it all crashes over me. They did that. They killed my dad because he got too close.

And they lied about history.

I speak for my dad when I say—*it's war.*

Okay. I take a deep breath, and a new emotion surges. Rage. Pure, untethered rage.

"Yeah, the fear hasn't really gone away since New York," I say, my tone grim and murderous. "But I'm done running. I want to take the fight to them. I want to take down their whole system. And I want them to know it was me. And God help anyone who stands in my way."

Andromeda looks at me, taken aback by my sudden intensity, and a slow smile spreads across her face. "Finally."

Cassian grins, leaning back. "Venice, baby—let's go!"

61

ANDROMEDA AND CASSIAN rush back from the corner market, plastic bags swinging. We're parked in this back alley—great spot, really—but we have zero time. They dump out knockoff sunglasses, flimsy baseball caps, a patterned headscarf, and a tiny pair of scissors.

Airport disguises are kind of our trademark now.

Andromeda crouches behind the Cybertruck, shearing fistfuls of long, unruly hair. Thick locks fall at her feet, and she grimaces, trying to reach the back. Moments later, she's kneeling in a pile of her own hair. A wild, uneven crop hangs over her freckled cheekbones. She looks up at me for approval, eyes hopeful.

"Looks awesome," I lie.

Two men appear at the end of the alley. They don't look friendly. One's shirtless, tattoos plastered across his torso. A teardrop is under his eye. Oh, fantastic—we've parked in a dangerous slum.

"I did CIA work on gangs," Andromeda whispers. "Those devil horns are MS-13. The teardrop means he's killed for his gang."

The gang members saunter up to the Cybertruck. Shirtless guy pulls a machete from his waistband. *"Qué chingados tenemos aquí?"*

I raise my hands, stepping in front of Andromeda. "Easy."

His friend in the tank top smirks. "Gringos."

Shirtless man lifts the machete to my chin.

Andromeda steps forward, voice rising. "Paco 'Tigre' Martinez!"

Is she insane?

The men glance at each other, eyes like slits.

"Paco 'Tigre' Martinez," she repeats. "We work for El Tigre. We're cartel."

The machete lowers a fraction. "El Tigre?"

"*Sí. Americanos importantes* … for Tigre." Her accent is terrible.

Sly fox, this data analyst. Her gangland intel just might've saved our asses, glad someone paid attention during CIA warlord class.

Well, if we're on cartel business. "Hey. You speak English?" I ask.

"Leetle," Shirtless says, leering.

"You want to make some money?" I make the universal sign. "*Dinero.*"

He flicks his head, eyeing the silver beast.

I look at the truck. It's in remarkable shape after our rollover crash. A few dents and scratches, dangling mirrors, and the roof rack is mangled, but you'd never know it just rolled down a UNESCO heritage site.

"Cybertruck?" I say to him. "It's yours, buddy."

Crazy idea time. I reach into the truck and pull out a stack of cash from the Watcher. "Ten thousand. *Americano*. Ten more if you make a delivery for Tigre."

"O.K."

Cassian taps the navigation screen, pulling up a village two hundred kilometers northwest—Santiago de Querétaro. That'll do. Enough battery, too. He sets the route.

In the world's worst Spanish, I tell our new drug mules to pick up a package and bring it back here. After that, they keep the Tesla. I hand over the key. "Yours."

Machete Man nods, fanning the banded cash ecstatically.

"When you get to this village—" I snap my fingers. "Hey … are you listening? You want the truck or not? Tell them we're driving a shipment to Tijuana for the border crossing. Got it?"

"*Understand.*" His teardrop stretches as he grins. Never thought I'd see a killer look so pleased.

62

THE TAXI ROLLS up to the departure curb at Aeropuerto Internacional Benito Juárez. I step out alone, adjusting the cheap sunglasses and flimsy baseball hat Andromeda got me. Pull this off, and I'm one step closer to Venice—and the lost Atlantis manuscript.

Here goes nothing.

I head into the terminal and join the slow-moving security line. Head down, I try to blend into the international crowd. I look for Cassian and Andromeda, but can't see them.

My nerves fray as the line inches toward the absurdly intimidating security podiums. It's the damn waiting.

Keep it together, Tony. Act natural.

At the podium, I hand over the red British passport for the Falkland Islands to a woman officer. She studies the passport for a long moment, *too* long.

Is the sweat visible on my brow?

She leans over to another officer and whispers. Both scrutinize my passport.

Oh no. They know it's fake.

They share a laugh over something in Spanish. The first officer turns to me. "Beautiful wildlife is nice down there, *sí?*"

"Uh—*yes*. Beautiful ... *penguins* ... the Falkland ... penguins. Because it's so—*south.*"

I wince. Shut. Up.

Are there even penguins in the Falklands? Should I have used a British accent? No, my British accent sounds like Dick Van Dyke.

She hands back my passport with a smile. "Have a nice flight, Mr. Johnson."

"You too." I'm so dumb. My heart pounds as I pass through the swooshing glass gates.

On the plane, I pass a seated woman with a headscarf covering her wild, chopped hair. Her oversized sunglasses make her look like Kurt Cobain or a 1960s film star.

I avoid eye contact and take a window seat at the back. Two rows ahead, a man in a soccer hat and Jeffrey Dahmer glasses glances back at me.

What are we, the fashion brigade?

Fifteen long minutes crawl by. *Fly the damn plane already.*

Shrill Italian pours from the PA, then rapid Spanish, and finally, brief English. "The cabin doors have now been closed. Please stow any loose items."

The engines surge. I exhale as g-forces press me into the seat. Mexico City falls away. I swear, an unusual number of flashing lights are scattered throughout the metropolis below.

Plato, here I come.

63

"Tony, wake up! You're not gonna believe it!" An adamant whisper wakes me up. "The pyramid is a Tesla tower!"

"Wha—?" I mumble, squinting at the dark ceiling of a passenger jet. *Gah!* The Dahmers hover over me—talk about a jump scare.

"Tony, the pyramid is a Tesla tower!"

I groan, shifting off the armrest stabbing my neck, and the seatbelt gouging my kidney.

"Sorry! Go back to sleep," Cassian says, returning to his seat.

I peek around my seat-back. Andromeda's feet stick into the aisle like jumbled stork legs. She's fast asleep across a row.

I have no idea what Cassian just said about Tesla. I fade back into *dreamla—*

The Great Pyramid *is a Tesla tower!*

I jolt awake, eyes adjusting to the dim cabin. The plane is silent, except for a lone pool of light illuminating Cassian. He's cradling Tesla's notebook like it holds the secrets of the universe. Which, let's face it, it might.

The plane is mostly empty back here. I slide into the seat beside him, glancing at the flight map. We're over the Azores. "What time is it?" I mumble.

He smirks without looking up. "Tesla o'clock."

I peer over his shoulder. He's got the notebook open to a schematic of Wardenclyffe Tower, tunnels plunging deep into a natural aquifer.

"Atlantis had Tesla's technology," he says, riveted.

Okay, now I'm awake.

"Wardenclyffe," he continues, tapping the page. "I used these same subterranean tunnels for my replica tower. Tesla said his tower needed to grip Earth to make the whole globe quiver."

He pulls out a graphic cut-away of the Great Pyramid. Seeing it next to Wardenclyffe Tower is … Whoa.

"Faust gave me this pyramid schematic back in Machu Picchu," Cassian says. "It shows the internal workings."

Both have subterranean tunnels tapping an aquifer. "That's … spooky," I admit.

Cassian says, "I suspected a connection because of Tesla's ancient stuff, but couldn't pinpoint how, until now. A reporter in Nikola's time even called Wardenclyffe *Tesla's electromagnetic pyramid*."

"It's simple," he says. "There are two Tesla coils—a small starter coil and a larger secondary coil. Both have windings of conductive wire."

I frown. "But the pyramid doesn't have coil windings."

"Probably long gone. The coil is key. It's like a giant spool of thread, sending current in a continuous loop. Tesla's design generates a powerful alternating current, creating a magnetic field that induces the larger secondary coil."

He pauses for effect. "Like a contagion—almost like magic—the power amplifies to the bigger secondary Tesla coil."

"Wait," I say. "How does Earth transmit the power then?"

"Earth itself is like a third Tesla coil in the chain, amplifying power enough to traverse the globe."

I nod, recalling the iconic poster in Tesla's hotel room: the inventor sitting inside a massive Tesla coil, lightning arcing around him like some kind of electric god.

"The thing I don't get"—Cassian is about to crush a molar—"is how they jump-started the damn thing!"

He explains that Tesla's tower had a direct AC line from the power company. "I'm pretty sure Atlantis didn't use extension cords," he says dryly.

"And the scale," he marvels. "The pyramid's huge. Generating enough power for induction on that scale? That's some serious zappage."

"How so?"

"Wireless iPhone charging pads use magnetic induction. Energy hopping between two coils." He looks up. "Imagine your phone is the size of the pyramid."

"What about the capacitor?" I ask, proud that I remembered a fancy component.

"Yep. To be a Tesla tower, the Great Pyramid would need a massive capacitor to pulse current into the planet. That power would transduce across a worldwide grid, converting it back into usable electricity."

"Let me guess. Obelisks as local resonator relays?" I joke. "Maybe the Great Line—the former equator—was some primordial power grid. Giza sits on that line. The pyramids acting as nodes?"

He raises an eyebrow. "It's not as crazy as it sounds, Tony. Tesla's idea was to have a global network of towers. Think about how a lightning strike rings Earth's crust like a bell. Sensors can detect it on the other side of the world."

Cassian nods thoughtfully. "The tower bridges Earth and sky, completing the circuit. The atmosphere is bristling with power. There was that one Space Shuttle Columbia experiment. They unspooled a twelve-mile metal tether with a conductive satellite. It dragged the ionosphere at orbital speeds, generating so much power that the tether snapped in a ball of plasma. Almost blew up the shuttle. Lots of energy up there."

We sit contemplating.

He leans back with a sigh. "Tesla could've been the wealthiest man alive if he'd taken the easy road. He could've built a neon empire of appliances and gizmos. Instead, he died alone in poverty, ridiculed, all because he refused to abandon the one idea the world wasn't ready to understand."

"Which idea?"

"That energy and vibration move through everything," he says, then sips a Cherry Coke.

The Demiurge pops into my mind, those dark hands pulling strings. Andromeda told me how energy researchers often "disappeared." Nikola Tesla, the granddaddy of them all, was ruined and had his research buried.

Why?

A disturbing thought crosses my mind. Had Cassian's project at Wardenclyffe been sabotaged like Tesla's work? I decide not to voice that particular paranoia.

An awkward silence settles between us. Finally, he breaks it. "There's something I've been meaning to ask you."

He flips to the back of the notebook, where Tesla had scrawled: THE EMERALD TABLET IS THE KEY.

I saw that in New York. The Emerald Tablet. Hell of a reference.

It's a bizarre thing for Tesla to write. "The Emerald Tablet is the most significant text in esoteric Hermetic tradition. Known in the East as the *Tabula Smaragdina*. Nobody knows its true origin. It's full of metaphysical, alchemical abstractions—mumbo jumbo. It's a favorite among the New Age set. Andromeda would dig it. It appears in early Islamic texts, but legend says it originated in Egypt, written by Thoth himself."

"Thoth? That Egyptian civilizer Faust was nuts about?"

"Yeah. Thoth, the guy carved on the front doors of the US Library of Congress. Also known as Hermes in Greece."

I ponder it. "Alchemists tried to crack its mysteries for centuries, convinced it held the key to understanding nature and the cosmos. You've probably heard 'As above, so below.' That's from the Emerald Tablet."

Cassian taps a sketch of two snakes coiling around a pole. "What's this healthcare symbol? Was Tesla on Medicare?"

"Common misconception," I reply. "That's the caduceus—the symbol of Hermes. It represents the Hermetic idea of 'As above, so below.' A mysterious alchemy principle nobody understands."

He looks intrigued. "So why would Tesla sketch all this?"

I shrug. "An Easter egg to mess with future geophysicists?"

He smiles. "Man, I wish that were true. It's probably the daydreams of a senile old man."

Soon, we're both asleep when turbulence shakes us awake. The plane shudders; there's a storm outside.

The notebook's gone.

Panicked, Cassian rips off his buckle, searching. It's on the floor at his feet. Lightning splits the sky as he tucks Tesla's Ninth Symphony into his pocket.

His speech slurs as sleep overtakes him. "Tesla was born during an electrical storm. They said it was a bad omen ... but his mother said ... he'd be a child of light." Cassian's out cold.

Send us some light, Nikola.

64

Venice, Italy
Tony Koviak

STANDING in front of the Doge's Palace, I get it: this is an artfully crafted middle finger aimed straight at Florence. "Oh, you guys have a Renaissance? Cute. We have sea power, global banking, and ritualistic occult soirées on the weekends."

One part wedding cake, one part Game of Thrones set.

We're in Venice because I'm an insane person.

And let's be clear, the Atlantis trilogy isn't *lost*. It's misplaced. There's a difference, okay? Misplaced means it's *around here somewhere*, probably just hiding out in a box of Neoplatonist philosophy. Right? *Right?*

God, I hope I'm right.

Behind the palace, the Bridge of Sighs arches over a green canal to a former prison. They say the condemned got one last look at the lagoon through a tiny window—hence the sighs. I can relate; this trip has been one long, exhausting sigh after another.

The Doge's Palace lines one side of the Piazzetta San Marco, the main square. At its end, two iconic granite columns rise skyward: one crowned with St. Theodore slaying a dragon, the other with a winged lion gazing out to sea, the symbol of the Republic of Venice. Classical steps descend into the sparkling waters of the Adriatic at their base.

Facing the winged lion is our target: the Biblioteca Nazionale Marciana—the Marciana Library.

The Marciana was built in 1468 during the city's grand *Renovatio Urbis*, a vast renovation that transformed Venice from a medieval village into a classical forum worthy of Ancient Rome. Designed by Jacopo Sansovino, it houses the world's rarest collection of classical texts. Sure, the Vatican Library dominates pop culture, but the Marciana? It's the *true* successor to Alexandria.

As we pass the cathedral, morning light bathes the Doge's Palace in a golden glow. St. Mark's Clock Tower looms over the square with its enormous astronomical clock. A similar clock watches over the central square in Prague. It's an odd thing to see in the heart of Venice. People sure loved their zodiac back in the day. The symbols remind me of Plato's Great Year—the time Earth takes to complete one full wobble on its axis.

Focus, Tony.

We're striding through the palace's ground-level arcade. Is that freshly baked cornetti wafting from a nearby café? My stomach growls. No time. Curse you, hungry stomach!

Rounding the front corner, we pause in the shadows to survey the Piazzetta.

"The Marciana," I say, eyeing the library. "Pulled some all-nighters there during my Cambridge years. Pretty sure I developed a Pavlovian response to the smell of parchment and espresso."

Across the square, staff is swinging open the ornate entrance. Showtime.

Inside lies the oldest surviving manuscript of Plato's Atlantis trilogy—the Venetus T. I've handled it before.

Cardinal Bessarion donated over seven hundred Greek and Latin codices to Venice in the 1400s, the backbone of the Marciana's collection. Most were salvaged from the ashes of Byzantium. Thousands of rare manuscripts call this place home now.

I pull my two jet-lagged companions into the sheltered courtyard of the Doge's Palace. "Okay, here's the plan."

Cassian peers over my shoulder. "Does he look familiar?"

We whirl around, half expecting Metatron. Instead, we find a marble statue of King Atlas, hoisting an enormous globe, standing sentinel at the base of the Scala d'Oro—the Golden Staircase.

"I'll take that as a good omen," I offer. It's just stone, but man, I'd love to chat with Atlas. Hey, buddy, how's that Atlantis reboot gig working out for you?

"King of Atlantis holding up the planet?" Cassian scoffs. "Please. The rotational momentum of Earth alone would tear any biological entity apart."

I sigh. "Let's focus."

"Here." Andromeda hands me a Toblerone. "Pyramid food."

I bite off a chocolate tetrahedron and munch, annoyed to be distracted by Platonic solids—Plato's perfect forms. If only he'd known about chocolate. Who knows? Maybe Atlantis was a wonderful confectionery hotspot—

Focus, Tony!

I square up to them. "I did my doctoral research on Plato. Venetus T—Latin for *Venetian T*—is housed here. The Marciana's rare special collections are heavily secured. Gaining access won't be easy."

"What's your plan?" Cassian asks.

I grin. "I know an old Arthurian legend."

65

WE DASH across the geometric patterns of the Piazzetta, weaving through empty café tables with stowed umbrellas. The entrance of the Marciana looms ahead ... columns, Renaissance carvings, the whole nine yards.

"I still can't believe the pyramid is a Tesla tower," I say between breaths. It's like finding out King Tut invented the iPhone.

"It's been obvious for a while, guys." Andromeda heaps scorn, keeping pace.

"Really?" Cassian asks.

"Really?" I echo. Leave it to a data analyst to connect dots.

"Ice Age power," she muses. "Sounds like science fiction.

Cassian shrugs. "Advanced technology beyond our understanding is always magic. Put a caveman in an IMAX Theater and show him *Jurassic Park*."

"Maybe Atlantis had those," I say. "Be kind to the cavepeople."

We're nearly at the entrance when Cassian's expression darkens. "He's following us."

We spin around, scanning the Piazzetta.

Cassian points upward. "There!"

Above the library's arched entrance, a weathered Neptune leans out; stone muscles flexed, trident raised. The Atlantean god's eyes seem to follow us like he knows we're after his secrets.

"Atlanteans," Cassian says. "Naturally, they'd get prime balcony seating."

"Wilder," Andromeda snaps. "You're killing my chakras." Her gaze darts around the square. "I think I should wait outside."

"You sure?" I ask, sensing her unease. She's being cautious, but sticking together is kinda our thing now.

"We're more likely to be recognized as a trio," she says, eyes flitting to the growing trickle of tourists. "I've got a bad feeling. I know the CIA. I'm gonna keep watch."

"Don't wander off," I warn, stepping inside with Cassian. I quickly regret not establishing a meet-up plan if we get separated.

The library interior is eerily empty—just a guy in a fancy vest behind the ticket counter—perks of visiting in mid-March.

I smooth down my bedhead and cross the marble floor confidently. *"Buongiorno. Parla inglese?"*

"Of course," the attendant replies, setting aside his phone. "How many tickets?"

I flash a rogue's grin. "Actually, we have an appointment to access the special collections."

The Italian looks flustered. He drags open a ledger. "There are no appointments scheduled for the collections today."

"Must be a mistake," I say, trying to summon acting skills I don't have. "We've flown from London just for this. There has to be a mix-up."

He hesitates, clearly irritated, eyes darting between us. *"Un momento."* He picks up a phone, presses a button, then rattles off a wall of rapid Italian.

"Sì, signora." He hangs up, gesturing with a singsong accent. "*Prego*, you can wait in the Reading Room. The librarian is arriving presently."

We enter the vaulted Reading Room, a Renaissance masterpiece that reminds me of the grand salons of European palaces. Murals by Tintoretto and Titian adorn the ceilings. Oil paintings of philosophers watch us from every corner. Statues of Greek thinkers line the halls. The floor is intricate tessellations of geometry.

It's a stunner.

The Marciana's Reading Room has been converted into a museum. I walk to a glass case, stomach in turmoil, thinking of all the ways this could go wrong. Has this librarian seen the news out of America?

"He found us!" Cassian exclaims.

He's pointing at the ceiling, grinning devilishly. Above us, King Atlas hoists the world on his shoulders, gazing down.

"Cass," I hiss, heart flapping. "You've got to stop crying wolf. One day, he's actually gonna throw his globe at you."

Cassian is mid-thirties—older than me—but he has the heart of a kid. It's hard not to admire it. I guess being a super genius brings out the quirk.

"Okay, this is getting bizarre," I admit.

"Bizarre is our new normal," Cassian counters.

The staccato click of stilettos on marble announces someone's arrival. A woman is gliding toward us, raven hair loosely tied back with a white ribbon, dressed in high Italian fashion. Her features are soft and classical, with an exotic, intellectual quality. A lanyard with credentials hangs around her neck.

"*Buongiorno.*" She says, offering a delicate hand. "I'm Dr. Fiammetta Valenti, head librarian of Biblioteca Marciana." Her aqua eyes are assessing us. "I understand you have an appointment to visit the collections?"

"*Buongiorno,* Signora Valenti," I reply, shaking her hand. "There seems to be a mix-up. We're supposed to be in the special collections, but perhaps our department didn't submit the request. Our flight leaves this afternoon, and we're in a pinch."

She offers a tight, mournful smile. "I am so sorry. It is not possible. We have a strict reservation policy."

"I see." I pat my pockets. "Well, let me call my fellow at Cambridge Classics. You might know Orson Pellinor?"

Signora Valenti stiffens, and her eyes widen slightly at the name.

Cambridge generously endowed the Marciana, investing tens of millions over the years. Orson Pellinor, the poster child of classical studies, shares a name with the Arthurian knight famous for slaying the Questing Beast. To the Marciana's staff, Pellinor is as mythical as his namesake of legend.

"He's in the middle of a crucial fund-raising meeting," I add. "I'd hate to bother him." I fish in my jacket pockets, pretending to find a phone I don't have. "I'm sure he can explain the—"

"No, no—no need to trouble Signor Pellinor," she says quickly. Her smile warms, though her eyes remain wary. "Of course, we can accommodate you. There is no one in the library today. Shall we visit the collections?"

"Thank you." I nod. "Signora Valenti—"

"Please, call me Fiammetta."

As we walk, I glance up at the grand ceiling. "That depiction of Atlas, does he look like he's regretting his life choices, or is it just me?"

Fiammetta laughs softly. "Ah, the masterful Alessandro Varotari. The entire library is designed around Plato's philosophical ideals. Patrons are meant to ascend to higher understanding as they move through the building—at least, that's what the architect, Jacopo Sansovino, intended."

She's kidding. The whole damn library is patterned after Plato?

"Explains the massive portraits of Plato and Aristotle at the entrance," I say.

"You know your Greek philosophers," Fiammetta says.

Okay, all this symbolism is downright freaky.

It's weird enough that Atlantis mythology is strewn all over the Serene Republic of Venice. Now, it turns out that the Marciana *itself* is oriented toward Platonic ideals of finding ancient knowledge.

I wonder … *don't be foolish, Tony.*

"Bene." Fiammetta leads us across the grand room, lamenting that the library has been converted into a museum to pay the bills. She leans in with a charming snaggletooth smile, Mediterranean eyes twinkling. "You know, the manuscripts were chained to the bookcases back then so patrons could take them to a table."

As we exit the chamber, she peers sidelong at me. "Have we met before?"

My cheeks flush hot. "Perhaps on prior visits with Pellinor," I lie, then change the subject. "When was the building converted into a museum?"

"In 1904, the library was moved next door to the *Zecca*," Fiammetta explains. "*Zecca* means mint. The money was made here." She wrinkles her nose playfully. "The coins."

The library was moved to the mint—Jean Vendôme's financial location in Europe! My blood flows.

I was right! Woo-hoo! I'm allowed a moment to celebrate my awesome cleverness. *Yes!*

Fiammetta leads us down a corridor filled with artwork. We pass through a no-access area into dim rooms lined with thousands of dusty, leather-bound volumes. The scent of aged parchment fills the air.

"When Rome fell, classical literature was almost lost," Fiammetta explains. "Venice led a heroic effort to recover these texts after Constantinople fell to the Ottoman Turks in 1453. They scoured the Mediterranean. The Renaissance began here, in these very halls."

We stop at an imposing metal door with a blinking sensor pad. She swipes her credentials, and the door clicks open with a rush of air.

Inside, the special collections room feels like a spaceship—bright lights, rows of stainless steel cabinets trimmed with frosted glass, and white examination tables. The air is thin and dry, the way these rooms always feel with their monitored climates. Ceiling vents quietly suck carbon dioxide with a soothing hum.

Fiammetta hands us each a pair of white gloves. "Which manuscripts are you interested in?"

"Where are your Proclus manuscripts?" I say, slipping on the gloves.

Cassian shoots me a puzzled look. "Aren't we here for Plato, Professor?"

I shake my head. "We're looking for the Neoplatonists."

66

I STROLL along a row of high-tech cabinets, squinting at the labels on each wide steel drawer. Fiammetta has retreated to her office—visible through a window—glued to her computer screen.

A soft hiss catches my attention. Cassian has opened a drawer behind me, the glass lid lifting with precision control. He picks up a thick Latin manuscript from its velvet bed, edged with metallic medieval illustrations. "I've heard of this one," he says.

I glance at the label. *Dante, Divina Commedia.* Dante's original *Inferno* text. "Put that back," I growl.

"Greek starts here," I say, scanning the labels.

"Venetus! Found Plato," Cassian announces, opening another drawer.

My adrenaline spikes as I read the label: VENETUS A: Codex Marcianus Graecus 454—Iliad, Homer. Cassian holds up a crumbling rolled parchment.

I stifle a shriek. "That's the Venetus A, the original Iliad in Greek. Put that down, or I will personally summon Helen of Troy to smite you, *philistine!*"

He grimaces and carefully slides Homer back into place.

"Venetus T," I declare, opening a silver space drawer. Gently, I lift out a delicate Greek manuscript and set it on the examination table. I raise a warning finger to Cassian's face. "Do not touch Plato's original, unfinished Atlantis trilogy," I say, then resume my search for the Proclus documents.

"Got it," I say, pressing the button. The drawer slides out, frosted glass lifting. Inside rests a flat, square wooden box with ornate decorations.

"An ancient pizza?" Cassian quips.

I examine the workmanship. "The markings are Byzantine. Someone from Constantinople curated this." The old hinges creak as I open the delicate doors. Inside lie the original Proclus commentaries. Familiar territory, I've pored over digitized versions countless times.

"Proclus is often overlooked," I tell Cassian. "Minor figure from late antiquity, but a die-hard Neoplatonist and Plato's fanatic disciple. Proclus swore Plato had finished his Atlantis trilogy and claimed to have seen it. Legend says it was never translated because the destruction of Atlantis was too disturbing."

I pause, thinking of pole shifts and planets tipping over. Heart pounding, I look at Cassian. My voice resounds like legend. "I think Plato's full trilogy is concealed inside this box—hidden to avoid capture by the Turks when they smuggled it out of Byzantium."

Cassian's jaw tightens. He glances at Fiammetta through the window, still engrossed in her computer. He removes the Proclus documents and sets them on the table. *What's he doing?* He just lifted the empty box from its white cushion, hovering it inside the big drawer.

"What are you doing?" I whisper urgently.

"Cough real loud, on three."

"What?"

"One ... two ..."

"No. *Wait—*"

Crack! The ancient box shatters in his hands as we both erupt into loud, fake coughs.

Fiammetta glances up, then returns to her screen.

Amid the splintered shards, a corner of parchment peeks out between broken pieces.

"There's a false back!" I exclaim.

Stiletto footsteps echo—Fiammetta is heading our way. Cassian jabs the drawer's button, and we fumble with nearby documents, pretending to study them intently.

She arrives just as the horrendous drawer clicks shut. "Did you find it?" she asks in that polite Italian intonation that lets you know you're being judged for stupidity.

"Oh, we found it," I say, gesturing to the Proclus document on the table. "We're developing a new theory on Proclus's hierarchical cosmos and emanation processes, aiming to understand their influence on Neoplatonism and their lasting effect on Western intellectual traditions."

"Ah, that's … revelatory. Astounding." She gives a tight smile and returns to her office.

We lunge for the drawer. The crime scene lid lifts, revealing the wreckage. I give a wincing grunt. Carefully, we extract the fragile parchment, breaking off stubborn bits of wood. I lift the freed pages like a surgeon handling a heart transplant, blow off the debris, and lay them out. Four sheets, incredibly aged. My eyes might just pop from their sockets.

The first page is emblazoned with the Greek word for Timaeus —Book One! The margins are adorned with intricate drawings of Plato's five elemental solids—the tetrahedron, hexahedron, octahedron, dodecahedron, and icosahedron.

Original Greek, in Plato's own hand! I'm holding Plato's actual writing in my hands! No big deal, just one of the greatest men in history. Relax, no pressure. *Oh God, don't sneeze.*

I spread out the manuscripts: Timaeus, Critias, and—drumroll— Hermocrates! Plato's complete Atlantis trilogy, all three books. Now would be a terrible time for the heart attack I feel coming on.

Wait. The Hermocrates is misspelled as *Hermeskratos.*

The fourth page isn't even Greek. It's just an illustration. It's medieval, an obscure artwork I've seen in the Siena Cathedral. For some reason, the curators included it with Plato's trilogy. I'll look at that in a moment.

I snap back to the trilogy. "Plato wrote his dialogues as conversations," I murmur. "It's like reading a screenplay." I place a magnifying disk over the tiny Greek letters of the lost third dialogue, translating on the fly:

SOCRATES: One, Two, Three; our gatherings conclude, a little while hence, with our third and final dialogue. I deliver up the argument to Hermes, for his turn has come, according to our anticipation.

HERMES: Friend Socrates, let me conclude with the tale which, though strange, is certainly true, having been attested by the wisest of the seven sages. The true power of Atlantis was a vast power which the god settled in the lost island. It is true, without lying, that as above, so below—

I gasp, eyes wide. "The Emerald Tablet."
Cassian frowns. "The emerald what, now?"
I spring to my feet, raking fingers through my hair. "The Emerald Tablet! The cornerstone of alchemy in esoteric, Hermetic tradition." I glance nervously at the security cameras dotting the ceiling. Yeah, this is all being recorded.
Cassian's eyes light up. "Hey, that was in Tesla's notebook," he says, fishing it out. "He scribbled that exact phrase—'As above, so below.' He called the Emerald Tablet the key, but … the key to *what?*"
I sit back down, retaking the document. "Why would Plato conclude his history of Atlantis with a bunch of granola alchemy? That's not his style." I gnaw the cap off a pen and grab a notepad. I hastily transcribe Plato's enigmatic text. The Emerald Tablet is short—just a few stanzas.

> As above, so below
> To do the miracle
> The Sun is its father
> The Earth is its nurse
> All things are born by its adaptation
> Its power is perfect if it is converted into Earth
> It ascends from Earth to Heaven, then descends again to
>   Earth
> And receives the power
> Thus, you will have the brightness of the whole world

And all darkness will flee from you
Its force is above all force
And penetrates every solid thing
What I have said about the operation of
The Sun is accomplished and ended

Plato's describing a vast power the gods placed in Atlantis, its true power.

What does that even mean?

And why did Tesla mention it in his Magnum Opus?

I toss the pen aside, leaning back. "There's an old tale about Apollonius of Tyana," I say. "He claimed to have found the Emerald Tablet—a green book made of unknown materials, written in an unknown language with bizarre symbols."

I think of the strange symbols I saw in the Yaxchilan Hall of Records. The ones that look like the logo for a Roman space program.

"He found it in a cave beneath a statue of Hermes in Tyana," I continue, "near Göbekli Tepe. Supposedly, he discovered the corpse of Hermes Trismegistus himself—Hermes the Thrice Majestic—clutching a tablet of green stone."

Cassian chortles. "You believe that?"

I shrug. "He lived around the time of Christ. Histories get more reliable at that time. Legend says he gave the tablet to Emperor Hadrian, who hid it in Rome. Others say it was lost in Alexandria. The Emerald Tablet has quite a history. *Wait a minute—*"

I hunch over the manuscript, eyes shifting. "Hermocrates isn't about the Greek general, as scholars think. It's a mistranslation. It's Hermes *himself* speaking!"

I slide the magnifier to the Greek title and translate for Cassian. "Hermeskratos. The suffix *kratos* means "power." I stab a gloved finger at the word. "*Hermes—kratos*. The power of Hermes."

Hermes's power.

"So it's about some power Hermes wielded?" Cassian asks. "Maybe his caduceus intertwined snakes thing, like the other electric gods?"

I chew my thumb, eyes narrowing. "There's someone else who

was *obsessed* with the Emerald Tablet. Someone you definitely know. His English translation of it is at King's College Library in Cambridge."

"Faust?"

I snort. "Isaac Newton."

67

Isaac Newton translated *the Emerald Tablet*.

A memory flickers.

One morning, I was hurrying to class at Cambridge. I passed the legendary apple tree beneath Newton's old lab window at Trinity College, the very tree that supposedly inspired his theory of gravity. Usually, I breezed by without a second glance.

But that day, a wild-haired physics professor in Harris tweed was holding class on the sidewalk, lecturing passionately to his students. Something he said snagged my attention, and I stopped alongside a cluster of curious tourists.

"It was quite the embarrassment for the scientific community!" he proclaimed in crisp Queen's English. "Sir Isaac was a secret alchemist! Imagine *that*!"

He gestured dramatically toward Newton's window above the tree. "In 1936, a chest of his unpublished works was discovered. Physicists were agog with rapt anticipation. But, inside, there were *no* celestial mechanics, *no* new mathematics. Instead, over a million words of alchemical ramblings! Oh *yes*! Newton spent his final years obsessed with esoteric speculation."

He shook his head, eyes gleaming with scandalous delight. "The grisly trove even revealed his fascination with the Great Pyramid of Egypt. He tried to use it as an analog for Earth's measurements—ledgers filled with the pyramid's dimensions! *Why*? God only knows."

I stepped closer, enraptured at the mention of the pyramid.

"Harry Potter fans may recall the fabled philosopher's stone!" the professor boomed, to the delight of the tourists. "Newton was quite taken with it. He wasted *years* translating the so-called Emerald Tablet, turning his back on revolutionary science to unlock the alchemical energies of the universe. His translation sits in the King's College Library, just over there." He smirked. "It is ... *confounding*."

I thought of an artwork I'd seen in the science halls—a painting of Newton with a beam of light streaming through a triangular prism and breaking apart into a spectrum of colors—the same imagery Pink Floyd had borrowed for their iconic album cover.

The agitated physicist's voice dropped conspiratorially. "And when Newton became Master of the Royal Mint, he devised new coins with serrated edges to prevent shaving by unscrupulous flimflammery. Gold flowed into England from all over Europe to be pressed into his innovative design." The professor's eyebrows lifted into a flying V. "One wonders if Sir Isaac's true intention was the alchemy of *so much gold*."

68

HERE I SIT, back in the Special Collections Room of the Marciana Library—once the Venetian Mint. I peer down at Plato's lost masterpiece.

Newton and Tesla both went down this rabbit hole in their final years. The two greatest scientific minds of all time were obsessed with the *same thing*.

What had these visionaries discovered? What had moved them?

The Emerald Tablet—the Bible for Illuminati-style secret societies like the Rosicrucians and Freemasons. Not really my thing, but it was a formative part of these shadowy groups. Are the veil people part of this?

Newton's translation has extensive commentary on an element he called "quicksilver," also known as liquid mercury.

The alchemical symbol for the philosopher's stone is a triangle inside a circle. A pyramid coupled with Earth! Wait a minute ... that's precisely what Tesla sketched in his strange 3-6-9 diagram on page one of his notebook.

Energy alchemy.

The original Emerald Tablet is even shaped like a pyramid with *fire* shooting from the top!

Lord, have mercy, it's all connecting.

"It's Tesla," Cassian blurts.

I blink. *Did he just read my mind?* "How did you know I was—"

"It's *Tesla*." He points at my translation, practically vibrating.

"The Emerald Tablet isn't some mystical woo-woo abstraction. It's describing the geophysics of Tesla's wireless power."

I chuckle. "Yeah, that's not possible."

"Oh, pardon me, Your Highness of History, it's not like I'm a Caltech geophysicist or anything." He adjusts his glasses, pouting.

I narrow my eyes. "How so?"

Cassian sighs, flips open Tesla's black notebook to a schematic of his world wireless system, and sets it beside my scribbled translation.

"Hermes's power is *Tesla* power," he says. "Energy transmission via the natural medium."

"No. It's not."

"Think about it," Cassian presses. "It's literally Tesla's planetary circuit: ionosphere above, Earth below, making a big loop of solar-fed energy—his tower bridging the two."

I shake my head emphatically. "Nope."

"Look." He runs a finger over my translation. "'As above, so below, to do the miracle.... The *sun* is its father, the *Earth* is its nurse. All things are born by its adaptation.... Its power is perfect if it is *converted* into Earth.'"

Converted into Earth. Tesla wanted to send current through the Earth.

He reads the following line. "'It ascends from Earth to Heaven, then descends again to Earth, and receives the power—'"

Receives the power. Sounds like Tesla's planetary circuit to me.

"'Thus, you will have the *brightness* of the whole world,'" Cassian continues.

Electricity. Light. Power. Tesla's global wireless system.

He keeps reading. "'And all darkness will flee from you. Its force is above all force and penetrates every solid thing. I am Hermes Trismegistus. What I have said about the operation of *The Sun* is accomplished and ended.'"

Solar energy is the driver.

Now, listen ... I've seen things I can't explain. I've had my fair share of *ah-ha* moments.

This was not on my felony fugitive bingo card.

"Tesla's global power," Cassian declares triumphantly.

I sit there, dumbfounded, trying to absorb it. He's right. The world's most enigmatic hippie poem is actually an IKEA instruction manual.

"Tesla, you clever son of a bitch," Cassian says. "Plato just described his Wardenclyffe Tower."

Bloody hell. The Emerald Tablet encodes the energy technology of Atlantis, the same science Tesla discovered.

Tesla and the pyramid.

Come to think of it, in Egypt, the Cosmic Ocean—the heavenly medium—was symbolized with wavy lines, like transmissions.

I slide my magnifier to the bottom of the Hermeskratos page. Plato added a sentence, a line that's not in other versions.

I read Plato's Greek scrawl. "'The remnant of Atlantis, now removed to a safer underworld, awaits anastasis'—that means *resurrection*—'beyond the horizon from Troy in the Lower Land of Crocodiles.'"

I look up, mystified. "Oh wow. This is it! The road map to the Hall of Records, where all the Atlantis knowledge is hidden!"

"So, the Hall of Records is in Troy?" Cassian asks.

"I doubt it," I say. "Sumer and Anatolia called Egypt the Lower Land over the horizon. Crocodiles are a dead giveaway." I exhale. "I have no idea why it mentions Troy."

So, the trilogy doesn't wrap up the tale of Atlantis, after all. Plato never wrote the ending!

Because he doesn't need to.

His clue points to where we'll find all the answers: the true Hall of Records.

A profound thought strikes Cassian. "Atlantis didn't have coal plants or power lines. They went a different route. They discovered what Tesla discovered: pure, natural energy. They might not have even known about combustion engines."

He continues, "Tesla's notebook is full of references to the aether, the fifth element he was crucified for believing in. It talks about plasma, vortex math, all that three, six, nine high strangeness. He observed scalar waves in Colorado but didn't know what they were. I think Atlantis used power we don't understand."

Cassian's getting excited. "That's the *true* philosopher's stone, Tony—what Newton and Tesla were after: transmutation of natural forces. The real alchemy is a Tesla tower using the natural medium to transmit energy. The pyramid *itself* is the philosopher's stone! The fire in the middle!"

"The sun and Earth," I whisper. "Tesla literally illustrated the Emerald Tablet on his hotel room ceiling."

"What?"

An icy chill grips me. They've been hunting this since 1943, classifying Tesla's work to keep it hidden. Is this why the all-seeing eye endures among secret societies—a pyramid and a circle, the secret of Atlantis, the philosopher's stone? The pyramid is even on the back of the one-dollar bill, with rays of energy shooting from its peak and "Novus Ordo Seclorum" below it—*new order of the ages*—their world government after the reset. That symbol was added to the bill while Tesla was living in the hotel.

It's the Eye of Sauron, searching for the One Ring. What they're trying to reclaim: Tesla's tech.

That's why they want the notebook so desperately. It's Tolkien's ring! Andromeda said they show their symbols in plain view for karmic reasons.

I turn to Cassian, my face grim. "The people after us ... they know the truth. We're dealing with something very powerful, very dark, and maybe very ancient."

We need to tell Andromeda.

"What about the artwork on the fourth page?" Cassian reminds.

I take the last page and study its medieval illustration. Yeah, this is in the Siena Cathedral here in Italy. The caption reads HERMES MERCURIUS TRISMEGISTUS. It shows Hermes beside the Emerald Tablet, supported by two winged lion sphinxes, their tails intertwining into a caduceus.

Two back-to-back lions. Like the Egyptian god Ruti, guardian of the underworld. The *same* carving we saw in Yaxchilan: two cats over an underground labyrinth. I remember … one of the cats was staring at the constellation Leo.

Suddenly, the sharp sound of urgent high heels approaches. Fiammetta is racing toward us, looking upset.

I huff a horrified grunt. I quickly fold Plato's lost manuscript —*ouch*, it's the most unforgivable thing I've ever done—and mash it into my jacket just as Fiammetta arrives.

"Is everything all right?" she asks, eyeing our table suspiciously. Thank goodness we closed the drawer of carnage. "I'm sorry to interrupt, but your colleague outside says it's urgent. You must come immediately."

Andromeda.

69

THE TICKET LINE for the Marciana Library has grown. Andromeda is hiding inside the grand portico, nervously watching tourists flow over the Piazzetta. Cassian and I rush over.

"What's going on?" I whisper.

"Bad vibes. Very, very bad vibes," she replies, genuine fear in her eyes. "They're here. By the cathedral."

"You sure?" I ask, remembering Venice is an island, not exactly escape-friendly.

"Trust me. They're intelligence." She flicks her head at the library. "Find anything?"

"Oh, you know, just casually carrying Plato's lost Atlantis trilogy in my pocket. No biggie."

Her eyes widen. "You're messing with me."

I grin, flashing the pages tucked in my jacket. "See for yourself."

She squeals softly. "Yes!" Then her face hardens. "We need to go."

We head to the entrance. Outside, the smaller Piazzetta looks clear—no agents in sight. But when I glance past the Campanile Tower toward St. Mark's, I spot them. Agents in bespoke suits, scanning the square.

Dammit. Yeah, they're here for us.

Then I see her. Walking through St. Mark's Square is an elegantly dressed woman with hair braided into a medieval crown.

A tattoo snakes up her neck. Her designer sunglasses sweep the crowds, and agents fan out around her.

"This way." I lower my head as we slip out.

We weave through café tables, dodging tourists sipping espresso, and make our way down the Piazzetta toward the waterfront.

The twin columns of Venice rise ahead, slender and majestic, each crowned with a statue—the one on the left bears the winged lion of St. Mark.

Andromeda leads us toward the Doge's Palace, but I can't take my eyes off that winged lion. Sunlight glints off its graceful curves. Its wings are unfurled, ready for an imminent ascent to the heavens.

A winged lion.

Wait a second.... Waaaait a second....

I stop dead in my tracks, eyes glued to the statue.

Andromeda spins around, panic flaring in her eyes. "Tony, we can't stop here," she hisses, grabbing my arm. Her gaze darts back to St. Mark's. "We have to go—now."

Can it be that simple? She yanks me forward, but my mind is racing. "A winged lion," I mumble, pointing.

"That's nice. Let's *go*," she snaps.

They're not cats—they're lions!

Double lions, seated back-to-back as guardians over an underworld, gazing at Leo. It's the Yaxchilan labyrinth carving—the same symbol as the twin winged sphinxes on the illustration I saw minutes ago in the Marciana. The one now in my pocket.

Forgetting all else, I pull out Plato's manuscript on the open square, hands trembling. The winged sphinxes confirm it: lions.

"What are you *doing?*" Andromeda snatches the pages, crumpling them as she shoves them back into my jacket. My attention snaps to her. Her sapphire eyes burn like blue Hades beneath a wild sweep of hair. She's dragging me off the Piazzetta, causing a scene.

Ancient symbols whirl in my head. Lions symbolize power across history—England's lion and unicorn, Sweden's coat of arms, Spain's flag. Lions grace Mesopotamia's Ishtar Gate in Babylon, Persia has twin guardian lions, and of course, the Lion of Judah.

The lion is the marker.

Leo.

A signpost to the former world. A symbol pointing to the hidden records.

"Leo," I whisper, awestruck. "Atlantis was in the Age of Leo. The Ice Age."

"That's *fascinating*. Move!" she orders through gritted teeth.

"Uh, we might wanna go," Cassian says, glancing across the square. The woman with the tattooed neck is glaring right at us. She lifts a radio to her ruby lips.

"Yeah," I say as we break into a sprint. But my mind is spinning.

I know where the Hall of Records is.

70

We sprint past the gothic facade of the Doge's Palace. Blending in? Not an option anymore.

"Are you trying to get us killed, Tony?" Andromeda snaps, her anger slicing through the chaos.

We dash by the palace's grand entrance, and I catch a glimpse of the small courtyard. I skid to a halt, throwing up a hand. At the far end, beside King Atlas hoisting his globe, stands Metatron in a sleek black blazer—the same man from Faust's security footage. Dark hair tousled around a porcelain face. His aviators swing in our direction.

How did he—

The world goes silent. The bustling crowd fades away as I lock eyes, paralyzed.

Metatron turns toward us with machinelike fluidity. I can't tear my gaze from the cube of sacred geometry emblazoned on his chest. A barely perceptible smirk creases his stern face. In a flash, his weapon is drawn.

"Go!" Andromeda yelps.

Three gunshots crack through the air, splintering the stone archway inches from Cassian's head. Tourists scream and scatter.

We bolt down the waterfront pavement, flying over a canal beside the palace.

I glance up at the Bridge of Sighs arching high above the water.

Metatron's silhouette moves over its white rooftop in the four-legged gait of an animal.

What the ...?

It's a horrifying sight. My legs pump harder, fueled by a newfound will to live.

I slam into a narrow passage, shoulder scraping against a pastel wall. Looking back, I see Metatron perched atop the corner of a building like a shadowy gargoyle, watching where we'll go.

"You saw that, right!" My voice shakes with disbelief. I shove them into the alley, panic surging.

The backstreets of Venice are a maze of narrow paths. We fly over bridges and through tunnels that spill into miniature piazzas. I steal glances behind us—no sign of Metatron. We dive deeper into the medieval city. Note to self: study escape routes alongside history next time.

"Keep moving!" Andromeda shouts.

We race through the labyrinth, hearts pounding. A crash of tumbling roof tiles makes me look up—I trip over my feet.

A dark shadow moves above. Metatron is leaping between rooftops five stories up, zigzagging impossibly. He skids to a stop at the roof's edge, weapon raised. But he doesn't fire. He's toying with us. Somehow, that's infinitely scarier than being shot at.

"In there!" I dive into an arched doorway.

We burst into a dim, abandoned building, stumbling over dusty furniture. Pigeons scatter in a frenzy of feathers.

"Well, this place could use a remodel," Cassian deadpans.

We barrel through another door and emerge at the edge of a green canal. A gondola rocks gently in the water. Without thinking, I leap onto it, making it sway wildly. The startled gondolier yells in Italian, nearly falling overboard.

"*Scusa!* Move it!" I shout, pushing past him as he tumbles onto the checkered floor. We vault off the gondola onto solid ground, disappearing back into the terracotta labyrinth.

Finally, we burst into a secluded square, the scent of fresh herbs mingling with the salty brine. High-walled houses enclose us.

Ahead stands a dreamlike Renaissance building with a ground-level door. A sign mounted on the brick reads Palazzo Contarini del Bovolo. The ornate entrance is locked.

Attached to the palazzo is a five-story spiral staircase, as if someone twisted the Leaning Tower of Pisa into a winding helix and glued it to the front of the architecture. We rush up it, and through the arched columns, I spot a black figure crawling headfirst down a building across the square with insectlike fluidity.

Is this guy freaking Dracula? Levels of fear manifest I never knew I had.

At the top, a belvedere veranda overlooks Venice. In the distance, the Campanile Tower rises from the Marciana above a sea of red tile roofs. An open door leads into a stately corridor. We slip inside, hurrying down a hallway filled with Renaissance opulence.

A door to a salon is ajar—a possible hiding place. A photograph of Orson Welles dressed as Othello hangs beside it, depicting this very doorway.

It's dark and windowless, with a high-domed ceiling. A massive Murano glass chandelier hangs in the center. Antique mirrors cover every inch of the walls. Standing mirrors of all shapes and sizes clutter the room, part of a historical furniture exhibit.

Outside on the spiral staircase, there's a clatter.

Andromeda shoves us into the hall of mirrors. The room smells of musty fabric, remnants of centuries-old debauchery. We crouch behind a monster freestanding mirror at the back.

Shit. Our hiding spot is visible in all the mirrors. It's no hiding place at all.

My mind flashes to the lore of Metatron—the Voice of God. The biblical Enoch transformed into an angel, given three sets of wings to protect the cosmic order. Metatron, the Angel of the Veil, the only one who knows what's beyond. His cube embodies all of Plato's geometric solids, the fundamental forms of creation.

And he reports to the Demiurge, a figure from Plato's Atlantis trilogy, bent on creating a new order using intelligence, like the CIA, or even artificial intelligence.

My skin crawls at the sound by the door.

Metatron enters, moving among the mirrors. His dark form multiplies, an army of reflections. His head moves in short sweeps, like a bird's, as his aviators scan the space. He pauses to peer into mirrors. The eyewear has some kind of technology because he doesn't remove them in the darkness.

My blood runs cold. He's going to see us.

He steps closer to a tarnished mirror angled right at us.

I brace myself. Metatron takes another step toward the glass. His hollow face is a statue framed by loose hair.

He clearly sees us! Looking right at us!

A loud Italian voice echoes from another part of the palazzo. Metatron spins and bolts out of the salon.

I exhale shakily. *"Holy—"*

"He couldn't see us," Andromeda whispers, eyes wide. "You still think they're not hunting us?"

We escape outside and resume our mad dash, weaving through passageways for what feels like forever.

"Gimme a sec," Cassian gasps, collapsing against a wall. "Who … is that freak?"

"Metatron," Andromeda pants. "The Demiurge's attack dog. He runs Targeting Division." She scowls at me, clutching a cramp in her side. "What were you doing back there in the piazza? You nearly got us captured."

I hold up a finger, gulping air. "I found something," I wheeze. "I'll tell you when we're safe."

She shakes her head, shoulders slumping. "It's only a matter of time before they have every satellite over Europe tracking us. We're officially screwed."

I glance around. "There's only one bridge out of Venice."

"We need a boat," Andromeda says, pacing. "And a distraction. Anything to throw them off our scent."

Cassian is looking up at something perched high on a rooftop, a quirky Venetian flourish on one of the buildings. He smirks like a kid about to steal his dad's Ferrari. "Oh, I have a terrible idea."

71

WE FOLLOW CASSIAN OVER A CANAL, where a poorly camouflaged cell tower sticks out on a rooftop. His eyes trace a metal conduit running down to a small utility box at street level.

"Cass, we've gotta move," Andromeda urges, her eyes scanning the alley.

"One sec," Cassian says, prying a heavy cobblestone loose. He smashes it against the utility box's padlock. The lock holds, but the thin metal latch snaps. The panel swings open, revealing a nest of wires and blinking LEDs.

Cassian pulls out some tape from his backpack, his hands melting into the cables. His fingers work quickly. "Caltech engineers are known to have a little fun with Pasadena's cell towers."

"Get my laptop," he mumbles around the tape in his mouth. Andromeda retrieves a beat-up laptop adorned with a Taylor Swift sticker.

"Swiftie?" she asks dryly.

He rolls his eyes. "Long story."

She gasps, a freckled cheek pulling up with the hint of a smile. "Girlfriend?"

"Why, hoping I'm available?"

She folds her arms. "Oh, you'd like that, wouldn't you?"

He sighs. "My ex decided she only dates guys with Wikipedia pages."

"Ticktock," I warn, watching the rooflines for bioengineered ninjas.

Cassian opens his laptop and starts muttering to himself. It's fascinating—and a bit terrifying—to hear him narrate whatever he's doing.

"Running Linux—because Windows is malware with a user interface—then plugging into the tower's Ethernet port. Now to access the backhaul network and tap into the control systems."

There's a password firewall. But Cassian says he expected that.

Ah—clearly!

"I'll run Wireshark to pinpoint the router managing the tower's internet connection and exploit its vulnerabilities to bypass the firewall. Now the easy part—*for Caltech standards*." He winks at Andromeda. "We gain admin access and locate the IMS core—the brain handling all mobile communications, including texts. *Man, I hope this works*." He winces.

"Cass?" Andromeda is biting her nails.

I peer over his shoulder. "How does a geophysicist know so much about hacking?"

"Double major—computer engineering."

Andromeda scoffs. "Meticulous. Annoyingly systematic. Oh, you're a Virgo, all right."

He pauses his work to stare at her. "That is … remarkable. How do you—"

She's smug. "I have a talent for—"

"Not a Virgo, sweetheart."

Her expression falls. "Huh." Her lip twists, sensibilities offended.

He scripts a command for something called a rogue SMPP, instructing the network to blast any text he wants to all devices connected to the emergency government channel.

Well, I'm glad I chose anthropology.

"We're online." Cassian types furiously, then swivels the laptop toward us. "Check it out."

"*Wonderful,*" Andromeda says, her eyes still scanning for enemies. "Maybe you can do some Christmas shopping while we're waiting here *to die*."

"Have a look." He grins. "Tell me this isn't awesome."

The screen displays an emergency alert in Italian: *Sistema Emergenza Veneziano—IT-Alert*.

"An emergency alert?" I ask.

"Yep," Cassian says. "This text will ping every phone in Venice."

"You hacked a cell tower?" Andromeda frowns.

"Babycakes, I hacked *all* the towers."

"Is it gonna play 'Shake It Off'?"

"They keep a dedicated channel for government alerts." He shows us the English original:

> EARTHQUAKE!—IMMEDIATE EVACUATION MANDATORY. This is NOT a test. Catastrophic flood imminent. Ocean tsunami at 12 m (40 ft). ALL OF VENICE WILL BE SUBMERGED. May God help us.

"You can't send that!" Andromeda hisses.

"Got a better plan?" Cassian says. "I programmed the towers to shut down after it sends. They'll be offline for a bit."

"Bellissima." I kiss my fingers.

Andromeda hesitates, wrestling with the ethics. She glances down the alley for Metatron, eyes like haunted orbs. "Okay ... yeah —send it."

Cassian presses ENTER. "Time for a new flood myth."

A chorus of shrill emergency alerts screams from open windows all down the alley.

72

I LEAP into the motorboat from the dilapidated dock, grabbing the weathered red-and-white spiral posts, Venice's iconic mooring poles. I reach out to Andromeda. "Come on!"

It's wild how something crazy like "Hey, let's escape Venice with a cabal assassination division on our heels" has become just another Tuesday. *Are we getting good at this? Is this a new skill set?*

Andromeda jumps from the creaking planks, and I help her aboard.

The boat's a vintage Venetian water taxi with a lacquered stern and a tiny Republic of Venice flag fluttering at the back. The captain, a grizzled old man with a hooked nose puffing on a cigar, glares at us. He's wearing a turtleneck and sports coat, grunting his displeasure. I think he's off-duty.

Andromeda shoves a wad of euros into his hand. For a second, I think he'll kick us out. But he grunts again and pockets the cash.

He doesn't seem to have a cell phone, or he's unaware of the turmoil about to hit his watery city. *"Aeroporto Marco Polo?"* he asks, squinting through smoky eyes.

I nod. "Yes." We obviously can't fly now, but we have to get to the mainland.

He swings the boat into the Grand Canal, joining the others heading out to sea.

Chaos is erupting around us. People are running along the walkways. Gondoliers shove their poles into the water with jackknifing gusto, their alarmed shouts like opera. Tourists in their boats puzzle over Italian alerts on their phones.

Our stoic captain is unfazed, eyes locked on the weaving traffic. He glances at the pandemonium, but Andromeda distracts him with a melodramatic question—saving our butts yet again.

People are gathering on the rooftops of palatial buildings along the Grand Canal, weeping as they await their doom.

Our taxi speeds into the open lagoon. The magnificent Marciana Library drifts past, facing the pastel Doge's Palace. Think of all the history they've witnessed—add our chapter to the list.

The twin columns stand like sentinels, and the winged lion comes into view, mouth agape. My heart rate spikes—that lion might've just become the most significant clue in history.

Andromeda notices my stare. *"What?"* She mouths, pointing to the column.

I turn back to the mayhem. The Piazzetta is pure madness, citizens and tourists racing along the waterfront like passengers on the Titanic. I half-expect to see a quartet start playing "Nearer, My God, to Thee."

Out in the choppy waters, the boatman throws the lever to max, the bow lifting with sprays of water.

Cassian suddenly lurches forward, nearly becoming fish food. "No, *not* the airport," he's saying, thrusting his arm down the coast. "*Porto* industrial. That way!"

What's Cassian up to? Doesn't matter, as long as it's away from here.

The salty boatman huffs mightily, puffing his cigar, gray hairs whipping in the wind. He veers toward the industrial shipping port with a grunt.

As the boat roars ahead, my mind races to the most famous Leo in the world—from the primordial time of Zep Tepi in Egypt. The time of Atlantean refugees. In the Lower Land of crocodiles. Some place connected to Troy.

The actual Hall of Records.

73

THE CAPTAIN'S cigar is a smoky stub when our water taxi slams into the ferry dock with a jarring *thud*. A sign reads PORTO MARGHERA.

I step onto the pavement, catching a strong whiff of Toscano tobacco. Ahead sprawls an industrial shipping port, a gritty metropolis of colorful containers stacked sky-high like LEGO blocks. Giant cranes service herculean vessels bound for all corners of the globe.

So, this is Cassian's plan: stow away on a cargo ship?

A chain-link fence topped with barbed wire encases the main industrial area. Cassian rattles it, searching for a weak spot. "We can infiltrate one of these freighters," he says. "I heard a podcast about maritime life. Crew turnover is high, and security is lax. No nation has jurisdiction on the high seas. I doubt these sailors watch the news. It's a calculated risk, but our best shot at invisibility."

"A *podcast?*" Andromeda arches an eyebrow. "This isn't hobos hopping boxcars, Cassian. Don't they monitor crew?"

"You'd rather waltz through Italy with Interpol on our asses?" Cassian shoots back. "I'll take my chances with the merchant marines."

She chews her lip, watching a crane lift a yellow container onto the biggest ocean-bound piece of engineering I've ever seen.

Weeks at sea as a stowaway? This is gonna suck harder than arguing with a Columbia undergrad over a lousy grade.

"We find one heading to South America. Ride the waves, sweetheart," Cassian says, yanking at a wobbly flap in the chain link. "Like I always say, if you can't find an official entrance, make one."

"You always say that?" Andromeda asks flatly.

"Not South America," I insist. "Egypt."

Cassian stops mid-struggle, face scrunched. "Egypt? It's not Pan Am, my guy. What's in Egypt?"

"I know where it is," I say. "The Hall of Records is in Giza."

They both stare at me like I've sprouted a second head. Andromeda lets out a disbelieving laugh. "We gave it our best shot, Professor. We need to *survive* now."

There's only one way out of this nightmare. We can't hide from these guys. It's not like I have a life to go back to anyway. I'm still angry—about everything. It's probably gonna get me killed, but I know where it is! How can I not go!

I'll go alone if I have to.

"Egypt sounds like a genu-wine suicide mission," Cassian says.

"*The* Hall of Records?" Andromeda asks.

"We can slip into Africa or Asia if I'm wrong," I insist. "Giza is the center of the world's landmass, remember? We can't run from these guys."

Police sirens wail from the highway a hundred yards away. We duck as a parade of emergency vehicles blitzes down the autostrada toward Venice.

"Tony's right," Cassian says, wiggling through the peeled-up fence. "There's nowhere they won't find us. If the good professor thinks he knows where it is, I say double or nothing. He's been on point so far."

I give an exaggerated bow. "Thank you, Cassian."

"What makes you so sure?" Andromeda asks, squeezing through the fence.

"It's inside the Sphinx."

Andromeda chirps a laugh. "The *Great* Sphinx? The most visited tourist attraction on the planet? That's the dumbest shit you've ever—"

"The back-to-back cats from Yaxchilan are Ruti, the Egyptian guardian lions of the underworld." I pull out Plato's manuscript from my jacket. Seeing the intact Atlantis trilogy makes my heart race. Note to self: make copies ASAP. "These winged sphinxes are back-to-back, see?"

"How is the Sphinx a cat?" she asks.

"It has a lion's body. Faces due east at sunrise on the spring equinox, directly at the constellation Leo. But not where Leo is today—where it was twelve thousand years ago. It's an archaeoastronomical timestamp."

"Nice word." Cassian grunts as his jacket snags on the fence.

"Jaguars, lions, sphinxes—the cat thing is a marker for Leo, the time of Atlantis," I explain.

"Opposite side of the zodiac wheel from us today," Andromeda nods. I sense she knows a lot about astrology. "Leo and Aquarius, the eras when Earth passes through the galactic current sheet and we get whacked with cataclysms."

Cassian grimaces. "Ah, yes, the impending pole flip. Thanks for that uplifting reminder."

We sprint across a dry field toward the massive ships looming on the horizon. "In Egypt, the Inventory Stela of Khufu says they only *restored* the Sphinx, not built it," I say between breaths. "Left Egyptologists scratching their heads when they translated it.

"It makes sense," I go on. "There are accounts scholars dismiss as fantasy. Iamblichus, a fourth-century Syrian, said there's an entrance between the Sphinx's front paws—a bronze gate only the Magi could open. Below, a library was carved out. People wrote it off as a fairy tale.

"A Sumerian cylinder seal mentions the knowledge of the Anunnaki—Atlantis—left in an underworld hidden by sands beneath a creature with the face of a lion," I say. Dots are connecting. "That means the Great Pyramid is the overworld marker from Vendôme's riddle. *Of course!*"

"Haven't archaeologists followed up on this?" Cassian asks.

"Strangely, no. The Egyptian government, under US influence, has blocked all attempts to explore inside the Sphinx."

"That checks out," Andromeda says, dripping with sarcasm.

"In 1987," I add, "scientists from Tokyo's Waseda University did ground-penetrating surveys. They found numerous cavities below the Sphinx. A second seismic survey in 1993 confirmed it."

"That'd be the biggest find of the century," Cassian says. "Why haven't they gone in?"

"No one's allowed to dig," I reply. "Even after NBC aired *The Mystery of the Sphinx* to millions, they memory-holed it. Just like the huge Void detected inside the Great Pyramid. 'Nothing to see here—move along.' Another account tells—"

"You had me at Japanese survey," Cassian cuts me off.

As we near the docks, we reach pavement and turn onto a walkway between massive piers. The signs are in Italian.

"Wasn't there some riddle of the Sphinx?" Andromeda asks as we speed-walk.

"In Greek tradition," I reply. "The Sphinx asks: What has one voice, then becomes four-footed, two-footed, then three-footed? Answer wrong, and she devours you. Any guesses?"

"That's hot," Cassian grins. "So she's the Bridgekeeper from Monty Python."

Andromeda plays along, finger in the air. "'Answer me these questions three!'"

"Oedipus solved it—it's man," I say. "Crawls as a baby, walks on two feet, then uses a cane in old age."

"And what does the Hall of Records get us again?" Cassian asks.

I laugh. "Are you serious? Everything these jokers are hiding. Frank's Nephilim files times a million, straight from the source. It'd be lights out."

Andromeda nods thoughtfully. "Then we need a name for this mission," she declares. "CIA rules."

Cassian is pursing his lips in concentration. "Hmm. Well, it would have to convey vengeance, vigilante justice, and total fiery retribution—"

"Operation RoboCop," she blurts.

I scoff, then I see Cassian is seriously considering it, brow furrowed. "Dated," he notes. "But peak '80s revenge narrative. A bit of the ultra-violence. I like it. Regular dude ... done dirty ... exposing secret overlords and torching their—"

"I'm gonna stop you right there," I interrupt. "We're not calling this Operation *RoboCop*."

"Says the killjoy," Andromeda snorts defensively, then mimics my deep voice. "Mr. 'Atlantis is a morality tale blabbity blah blah'."

Overruled. Looks like this thing we're attempting—that I'm destroying my life for—is going to be part of the *RoboCop* multiverse.

I'm no psychologist, but I'm guessing these little bursts of playful banter are some primal coping thing, a desperate attempt to feel *normal* in this insane situation. Humanity clinging on for dear life with dad jokes and sci-fi references while reality falls apart around us.

Morale is at rock bottom.

Or my companions are actual geeks. Honestly, it's probably both.

"I have an idea to get us aboard one of those freighters," Andromeda says, getting back to business.

We cut the chatter as we approach clusters of dockworkers huddled together, peering at phones and speaking in hushed voices. The cell towers here are functioning; they have no idea what's unfolding across the lagoon.

We slip into a grimy workers' lounge. Steam from communal showers fills the air, mingling with the scent of grease and coconut oil. Lockers line one wall; few have locks.

Andromeda digs through piles of filthy workwear and swipes three identification badges.

I shake my head. "You're a klepto, Wildflower."

We clip the stolen badges to our jackets and make a beeline for the central administration buildings. The sun beats down; the air is thick with the metallic tang of the seaport. Gulls circle overhead, screaming for food scraps.

After weaving past another colossal ship, we reach a large info board displaying docking assignments. We scan the rows of listings like looking for a flight departure gate; each vessel has its final destination, including all ports of call.

"There," I point to a placard: TERMINAL VECON— MARSEILLE MÆRSK, a French-flagged ship heading to Shanghai with layovers in Alexandria, Mumbai, and Manila.

Andromeda nods toward a Panama-bound ship. "Last chance."

I know the risks. Egypt is madness. But it's not even a choice. Into the fire we go.

Cassian begins rearranging the old-school magnetic placards on the board.

Andromeda gapes in disapproval like he just kicked a priest. "As a data girl, this is a war crime. You're a little hellion."

"Chaos is king."

"Ehi! Stai facendo!" a lanky guard with a face like a snout is shouting in Italian. Annnd … he's coming over to us.

Well, this is less than ideal.

We should probably run, but the unhappy Italiano is already here. His security name badge reads ANDRE ROSSELLINI.

He has one of those permanent sour expressions as if he's resentful of the world and his place in it. He demands to see our badges. I hand mine over, which features a photo of a balding Nigerian named Babajide Okeke. Maybe I can claim to be part of an international diversity exchange program.

The guard's mouth drops open. He glances at Andromeda's badge—she's apparently a Chinese national now. His face contorts in confusion.

Cassian quickly flashes his Norwegian ID, and, in a blur, his other fist connects with the guard's jaw. The soft man drops like a sack of potatoes, out cold.

"I finally got to punch one," Cassian says, conflicted, shaking out his hand as we bolt. "Violence is just entropy made visible. Shame it had to be his face, though."

Andromeda races ahead. "You boys have all the fun."

74

The Egyptian coast is a faint gray line against the endless aqua-blue Mediterranean. We're aboard a steel behemoth of a freighter, steadily chugging toward Alexandria. The sea churns around us, a constant, soothing backdrop hiss. Andromeda Dey leans over the rusted railing of our little hidden deck beneath the massive bow, inhaling the salty air like it's the first fresh breath she's ever taken.

We're on the run again. I have to work on my life choices.

The world's freakiest assassin is on our heels.

Then there's that mysterious Watcher person somehow tracking our every move. That's not creepy at all.

Getting aboard the gigantic *Marseille Mærsk* was too easy. The guard barely looked up from his phone, scrolling for the latest news about some tidal wave on its way to kill everyone in Venice.

There's no TSA on the industrial high seas.

Once inside, we tucked our badges away and hunted for a good hiding spot for the short crossing. Long gray corridors, low ceilings, like a battleship. We passed an empty crew lounge with a TV blaring an English news channel. An attractive anchor with a German accent was at the news desk.

"A chaotic scene today in Venice after the entire city was evacuated due to a faulty emergency alert. Italian authorities are blaming cyberhackers for what's being called a text hoax. No fatalities have been reported."

Cassian exhaled. "Well, I've officially hit the big leagues, Dey. I'm now an international cyber villain."

The anchor continued. "In other news, the US government has shut down—you heard that correctly—over a political stalemate, with both parties failing to negotiate a budget for the upcoming year. The American president has not been reached for comment during her diplomatic visit to Prague. Keeping with the United States, the three suspects in this week's bombing in the American capital have yet to be apprehended after an incident in Mexico City."

Great. We made both of the top stories.

Back on our secluded observation deck, the ocean breeze whips through my hair. The sea air is bracing, and for a second, I feel a bit of hope. Maybe this plan will actually work.

I'm seated on a metal bench with Tesla's notebook on my lap. "Check this out," I say, pointing at the spidery handwriting. "'If you want to find the secrets of the universe, think in terms of energy, frequency, and vibration.'"

I picture Tesla waving a wand and shouting, *"Expecto patronum!"*

Cassian leans against the railing. "Tesla's vision. Everything is interconnected at a fundamental level. Atoms, solar systems—arguably the same structure at different scales, all held together by frequency and vibration."

"Wireless electricity," I say, still trying to wrap my head around it.

"It's not electricity flying through the air," he explains. "It's resonance—setting up standing waves within Earth itself."

Cassian has explained the science before, but it's still tough to comprehend. "Like how an opera singer shatters a glass by hitting the right note?" I ask.

"Exactly!" Cassian exclaims. "If two things resonate at the same frequency, they can exchange energy. That's how a Tesla coil works. He'd start a small coil, and its power would hop over to a bigger coil, amplifying like magic. The increase comes from nature—free energy."

He taps the steel hull with a clang. "This ship is made of atoms vibrating at certain frequencies. If we *amplified* that—"

"The ship would shake apart like a wineglass," I finish.

"*Præcis.*" Cassian mimics Faust. "Now imagine this on a global scale. Tesla dreamed of providing wireless energy worldwide, piggybacking on Earth's natural frequency. He claimed he could topple the Empire State Building with just five pounds of air pressure. Just little nudges, like pushing a swing higher."

Cassian recounts the story of Mark Twain, a frequent visitor to Tesla's New York City lab. Tesla rigged up a vibrating platform where he and his associates would stand to have the living daylights jiggled out of their guts. It always resulted in a mad dash to the bathroom. Tesla swore it aided his good health.

"Mark Twain wanted to try Tesla's gizmo," he says. "Ten seconds in, and he's knocking down the bathroom door. Ah, vibration … the true physical mover."

Andromeda quiets. "What's this energy tech mean to you, Cassian?"

He gazes out at the sea. "Independence. Not being at the mercy of the grid or government. No energy crisis. That's why J. P. Morgan pulled the plug on Tesla. Tesla's ideas would've toppled the titans of industry and banking. It's every person's birthright—connection to Earth."

Heavy footsteps clang on the metal stairs leading up to our little hideaway.

"Someone's coming," I whisper.

75

"*Oooh, la belle femme!*" booms a gravelly voice from the stairs. A burly sailor with a ruddy face strides toward us, a dirty cigarette dangling from his lips. His salt-crusted hair is tucked into a cap.

So much for hiding.

"*Tu as volé mon endroit secret!*" he exclaims, joyfully clapping me on the shoulder. He sets down a half-empty bottle of port beside a portable speaker. My French is rusty. I think he said we've stolen his hideaway.

With a swipe on his device, a jaunty 1960s French pop song fills the air. The sailor saunters up to Andromeda, flashing a sly grin as he offers his hand. "*Je m'appelle Serge. Danse avec moi, mademoiselle?*" I'm Serge. Care to dance?

She eyes his greasy hand warily. But Serge's joie de vivre is downright contagious. He waggles his eyebrows, jutting out a hip with an impish grin. The grit of his job hasn't broken the man's spirit.

"No, thank you," she says, trying to demur, but a giggle escapes as Serge continues his peacocking.

"*Mais oui, oui!*" He insists. He breaks into a flamboyant flamenco, swinging his muscular arms like nautical ropes, then extends his rough hand with a boot stomp.

With a shrug, she takes his hand, then whoops as he twirls her around. She wrinkles her nose at me; I shake my head. Cassian looks on like he's just had an epiphany about the laws of physics in the middle of a dance party.

Her laughter rings out as Serge spins and dips her like a ballroom champion. It's good to see her smile after all we've been through. For a moment, we're just three weary travelers dancing with a joyful French sailor on a ship to nowhere.

Serge passes her off to me with an encouraging wink, then slaps me hard on the ass and disappears into the corridor, muttering French obscenities. His radio keeps playing at our feet.

"My mom loved this song," Andromeda says wistfully.

"High desert commune must've been a riot," I say.

Soon, we're dancing like maniacs. No idea why. Not to be outdone, Cassian joins in, busting out his best '80s discotheque moves.

In her weary euphoria, blood filled with endorphins, Andromeda leans against the railing, throws her arms to the sky, and screams into the wind, "We're coming, Hermes!"

We both collapse to the deck in a fit of uncontrolled laughter because it's the dorkiest thing any human's ever said. I think she's going to have a seizure from laughing so hard on my shoulder. Wait, is she crying? I think something's wrong. Her outburst has given way to sobs that rack her body. Tears stream down her face as if the weight of everything has crashed down all at once.

"Hey," I murmur, turning to her, unsure what brought this on. I wrap my arms around her, trying to soothe her, holding her as she bawls. I was never good with emotional situations. She clings to me like a life preserver, sobbing into my chest.

"I'm sorry …," she chokes out between cries. "It's all my fault.… I shouldn't have—"

I hold her tighter, rocking gently, letting her cry it out.

"Uh … we have a problem," Cassian says sharply. He's peering over the railing, eyes fixed on a fast-approaching line of desert sand. "We've entered the Suez Canal. This ship's headed to India."

76

Porto Marghera, Italy
Andre Rossellini

ACROSS THE LAGOON FROM VENICE, in the desolate sprawl of Porto Marghera, Andre Rossellini—port security guard—stands on weedy asphalt. The shipping port stretches out before him like a forgotten wasteland. Above, an outdoor information board displays docking assignments for dozens of cargo ships near the administration buildings. Malicious pranksters had rearranged all the placards.

Who does that? he fumes.

It took him hours to fix the mess. His jaw still aches from the punch that knocked him out when they fled.

I can't believe I let my guard down. If I ever get my hands on them ...

But now, Andre faces a bigger problem. A tall, gaunt figure in a black blazer has detained him. The sea wind whips the stranger's long hair. Andre notices the man's jacket flapping open, revealing a tactical vest emblazoned with a three-dimensional cube. Just beyond stand two rows of well-dressed agents at attention.

Is this about the altercation? Am I in trouble? I did the right thing!

Since their arrival, these strangers haven't answered a single question.

They don't speak!

Their commander steps closer, his space-black aviator

sunglasses reflecting Andre's anxious face. Strange metallic chirps emanate as two strong agents force him to his knees on the cracked pavement, all in eerie silence. The solemnity of their actions reminds him of a Catholic Mass in his hometown.

Who are these people? They're not Italian.

He scans for help, but the grounds are deserted. Everyone's been sent home for some reason.

The hollow-faced man reaches into his blazer and pulls out a matte-black crown ringed with technological nodes that gleam in the Venetian sunlight. Andre can only watch, transfixed, as the strange ringlet is placed upon his head. He hears strange thoughts.

You are loved, Andre. Let go. Tell me everything.

77

Suez Canal
Tony Koviak

WE BARREL down the ship's narrow corridors and nearly collide with Serge, the French sailor we met earlier. My French is ... not great, but I give it a shot.

"*Le ... navire ne s'arrête ... pas* Alexandria?" I manage to get out.

"*Alexandrie?*" Serge's weathered face falls with suspicion. "*Non, il y a une grève des dockers. Annulé.*" He crosses his thick arms into a giant X.

"There's a dockworker strike," I mutter.

The Frenchman's high spirits evaporate as he strides to his comrades. A severe conversation erupts in rapid, ugly French, complete with wild hand gestures. The rough mariners glare at us.

"Time to go," Cassian singsongs.

"Where?" Andromeda whispers hoarsely.

I lead them through the maze of low hallways and up a flight of metal stairs. We emerge onto the main cargo deck beneath a towering crane. Containers loom over us like skyscrapers.

We're deep in the Suez Canal. The desert shoreline is sweeping past just thirty yards beyond the railing.

Cassian dashes along the deck, his floppy hair tossing in the wind. He reaches the stern, eyes darting between the barren landscape and the churning water. Then he spins around, and his wild eyes are jewels behind the glasses.

"We jump," he says.

"Are you *crazy?*" Andromeda cranes over the railing. Off the back of the ship, dark water roils in the massive wake with a loud hiss of mist.

"Always," he replies.

"That's a hundred feet down," I say. "If the impact doesn't kill us, the suction will."

"*Arrêtez!*" a deep voice booms behind us from the middeck. *Stop!*

A mob of angry sailors is fast approaching. At their head is a skeletal man wearing a tilted captain's hat and sporting angular red lips. Oh, and he's holding a shotgun.

"*Arrêtez!*"

"We jump. *Now,*" Cassian yells.

"We have the rarest documents in history in our pockets," I shout.

The mob closes in. I can see the yellow grime of their menacing eyes, an international execution squad. This is it.

Cassian and I are already climbing over the railing. Andromeda is frozen, her fear of heights kicking in. "I can't do this! You go."

"Hey." I twist around and grab her face, trying to project calm I definitely don't feel. "We're staying together. Everything you want is on the other side of this jump. You're Wildflower fuckin' Dey—go get it."

Her face is ashen, breaths coming fast and short as she climbs over the wet railing and stands in the mist between two insane people. Wind slashes our bodies like a butcher. The deafening vibrations from the hull make me grip the railing until I can't feel my fingers. The wake is sickeningly far down.

"No. No. No. No." Andromeda is chanting.

"*ARRÊTEZ!*" A shotgun blast cracks the air. We flinch.

"The turbulence will be deadly," I shout. "Jump as far as you can, feet first, and kick hard for the surface!"

"On three!" Cassian yells. "One … Two …"

I leap from the railing with an Olympian's thrust, and time slows.

The fall is an eternity. I flail above the churning death and pull my body rigid as my feet cut the whitewater with a ripping slap. A throbbing, muted roar fills my head. My body tumbles. I'm entombed in the thrashing effervescence. There's no up or down. I kick hard for nowhere and open my eyes to a rage-sting of blinding seawater.

The current rakes at me as I cartwheel. My breath is running out. The wake is too powerful. I know I'm going to die then. My limbs claw against the magnetic forces of the turbulence. *Fight. Fight.*

At last, my head breaks the surface, and I take a mighty breath. Relief floods my body.

Andromeda is already swimming hard toward shore—no sign of Cassian.

I spin around, scanning the water. Nothing but white foam. Panic surges. I swim for the bank, dragging myself onto the sand. My limbs feel like jelly.

"Cassian..." I sputter saltwater, ready to dive back in.

Then I hear splashing to my left. Cassian hauls himself out, glasses clutched in his hand. He slips them on like nothing happened.

"You held on to the Dahmers," Andromeda says, half laughing, half groaning.

He plops down on the sand. "You know you love 'em."

I fall back, staring at the orange sunset through stinging eyes.

High above us on the sandy embankment, a group of Bedouin women in black robes peer down, faces covered. It's like a scene out of *Lawrence of Arabia*.

We're in Egypt.

PART III
EVERYTHING IS THE LIGHT

78

New Yorker Hotel, 1935

A SIZZLING FLASHBULB pops as Nikola Tesla stands at the podium, tall and gaunt. The famed Serbian inventor gazes out over the buzzing Grand Ballroom of the New Yorker Hotel, filled with reporters, dignitaries, and scientists. They're gathered for another of his annual birthday press conferences. Off to the side, a table displays Tesla's own culinary creations.

Two more magnesium bulbs explode with searing white light, forcing Tesla to squint.

"Happy birthday, Nikola!" a young reporter calls from the back. "Dick May—*the Times*. What's your take on Einstein's new cosmology?"

Tesla grips the oak podium, his knuckles whitening. A playful smile tugs at his lips, and his light eyes sparkle like solar flares. Yet his voice remains gentle.

"Relativity is a beggar wrapped in purple whom ignorant people take for a king," he says. "I have measured the speed of scalar waves at one and a half times the speed of light. My dynamic theory of gravity opposes Einstein's model and is complete. Soon, I will release it to the world, along with my breakthrough in wireless power transmission."

A murmur ripples through the crowd. In the front row, several notable physicists—Tesla's former colleagues—grimace and shift uncomfortably. One even stands, ready to challenge him.

Tesla presses on. "Last year, Mr. Zwicky coined 'dark matter' to explain how galaxies hold together because gravity alone cannot. According to Einstein, galaxies should spin apart. Something binds them into spirals. Zwicky's solution was to invent a mythical dark matter. What he must consider is the aether."

Groans and whispers of "nonsense" sweep through the assembly.

"So astounding are the facts"—Tesla continues over the dissent—"that it seems the Creator Himself electrically designed this planet."

"Mel Brown from the *London Daily*," a voice booms. "Isn't your latest invention just another fantasy, Mr. Tesla?"

A twinkle lights up Tesla's eyes. "You may think me a dreamer, far gone if I told you I've found a way to produce direct current by wireless induction." He falters midsentence, gripping the podium with a grimace. "I've harnessed the elemental energy of frequency and vibration. My oscillator could bring down the Empire State Building with five pounds of air pressure." His tone turns wistful. "I once created an earthquake in my Houston Street lab. This energy can be pumped into the ground and reach any point on Earth. I call it telegeodynamics."

"Jane Carrington—*American Scientific*. Could you elaborate on *wireless* power, sir?"

"Hello, Jane. Thank you for coming to my birthday party." Tesla's voice softens. "I mean that Earth itself can replace wires. Power transmitted without wires to homes and aeroplanes. When this is achieved, you can go anywhere—in the mountains or the Arctic—and have power. We shall communicate instantly across thousands of miles. Devices will be amazingly simple compared to our telephones today. A man will carry one in his vest pocket."

He pauses, his eyes distant. "The people near Wardenclyffe, had they been awake, would have seen even stranger things. Someday—but not now—I will announce something I never dreamed of. The world isn't prepared for it."

"It is"—Tesla hesitates, a spark in his eye—"too far ahead of its time. But the same laws will prevail and make it a triumphal success."

New Yorker Hotel, seven years later, 1942

What does Mr. Tesla want to show me?

Tesla's protégé guides the frail inventor to room 3327 on the thirty-third floor, step by slow step.

Tesla should see a doctor.

"I'm so weary," Tesla sighs. "Perhaps I'll put in my full three hours of sleep."

The protégé knows about Tesla's baffling sleep habits. The man never stops working—no friends, no diversions.

He helps Tesla into the room. "Rest, Mr. Tesla. You need to rest."

"My black notebook, please." A long finger points to the desk beneath the window overlooking the Empire State Building.

"Why did you ask me here, sir?"

Tesla hesitates, his eyes sharp and blue. "The government is after my research. You must protect it."

What is he saying!

"Listen." Tesla coughs, struggling upright. "They'll come for it all when I'm gone. I can't say more." He glances at the telephone, hinting that the room is bugged.

"I've compiled my most important work *here*." He holds up the little black notebook. "Writing it down is risky. Keep it safe. Give it to the world, my work is complete."

Merciful heavens.

"You've worked out wireless transmission?"

"Much more." Tesla lies back, wincing. "Just a few ... unconventional experiments left." He taps the notebook.

His eyes drift to the lamp above. *What visions whirl in his mind?*

"In the coming weeks, return to collect my notebook when I've finished." He looks troubled. "And if ..."

A white pigeon lands on the open windowsill, and Tesla lights up.

"Sir?"

"And if something should happen to me before …" Nikola lowers his voice to a whisper. "Remember our conversation last Sunday about my secret lab, and you'll know where to find the notebook." He winks, a conspiratorial gleam in his eye.

The protégé can hardly believe what he's witnessed. Tesla has secretly continued his wireless experiments *here at the hotel*, under everyone's noses. With zero funding, he's continued his work here—using the hotel's steel frame anchored in Manhattan bedrock and a metal tower rising from the roof.

He recalls Tesla's backup plan for hiding his notebook. It doesn't make sense. His gentle mentor has been so cryptic these past months. *Something has spooked the poor devil.*

79

Cairo, Egypt
Tony Koviak

The sunrise lights up Cairo like a golden-age cinema projection. It'll be a scorcher, but the morning's still pleasant. Palm trees line a canal across from crumbling buildings. Women are already opening carts packed with papyrus paintings, and a guy at a sugarcane stand presses fresh stalks into silky juice. Kids loiter along the road, looking for the devil's work to do.

I'm jammed in the front seat of yet another taxi, Egyptian tea in one hand and a *feteer meshaltet*—an Egyptian breakfast pastry—in the other. The driver plays Arabic pop as we zip through the streets. He eyes Andromeda in the mirror with her wild tangle of cropped hair. She's wearing the cheap Kurt Cobain sunglasses from Mexico.

We're three groggy Americans soaking in the culture shock through the windows. I fix my sight line on the horizon, where three monolithic triangles jut from the western desert.

I'm home, Dad—under very different circumstances.

Would he approve of what I'm doing? Seeing the pyramids reminds me why I'm here. Not just "Oh yeah, let's stop an evil cabal from hiding our past," but to find the mythical Hall of Records and share it with the world. Walk in the park.

Getting to Cairo was … fun. We jumped into the Suez Canal,

got soaked, and ended up stranded in the middle of nowhere at dusk, in one of the most dangerous regions on the planet. By midnight, we'd found a run-down inn on the dark side of Cairo.

This morning, I discovered our rare texts were badly crinkled. Plato's Atlantis trilogy, Tesla's notebook—water-damaged and smeared. Unforgivable. I might've cursed like a sailor for several full minutes. But they survived.

Luckily, Tesla wrote the whole thing in thick pencil. Plato's handwriting didn't fare so well. But Greek parchment and ink seem tough. It's perfectly legible.

Now comes the easy part: breaking into the Great Sphinx.

If there's one thing studying ancient civilizations has taught me, it's that sometimes everything hinges on one absolutely bonkers move. Just ask Odysseus about that crazy wooden horse idea.

But *this* move? The Oracle at Delphi herself would cringe and ask, "You sure about this, buddy?"

"I just can't figure it out," Cassian says, pulling me from my thoughts. He's hunched over Tesla's black notebook, the warped pages leaving him flummoxed. He and that thing are practically married.

"Why, Tesla, *why!*" He shakes his fist, slams the notebook shut, and rolls his head back. "It's maddening!"

Andromeda and I exchange terse glances, waiting for the follow up. A minute later, it comes.

"It's all scalar physics and aether!" he exclaims. "Why did Tesla include all this exotic cosmology?"

"His science isn't clear?" I ask.

"Oh, I understand the science," Cassian replies. "I just don't see how it connects to his tower. The tower is an *Earth* circuit—geophysics, not astrophysics. I'm starting to think he just stuffed his hobbies in here, after all."

Well, that's disappointing. Maybe it *is* just the ramblings of a senile genius.

"Isn't scalar physics part of Tesla's radical vision?" Andromeda asks. "Surely, it plays a role in whatever he discovered."

"Yeah, but his tower is an *Earth circuit!*" Cassian repeats. "The aether—the higher-dimensional source code for our spacetime—

can't transmit electricity. That's *Star Trek*–level crazy. It's like finding black hole equations in a toaster manual."

We look on helplessly. Hey, I'm just the Sphinx heist guy.

"His ancient research was relevant, right?" I pipe up, offering encouragement. "He knew the pyramids were Tesla towers. The weird physics must matter. Tesla doesn't strike me as the arbitrary type."

Andromeda swivels to him. "Explain it to us, Cass. Maybe something will click."

He sighs, nibbling a fingernail. "Scalar waves use the aether as a highway. Tesla was nuts about them. That's higher-dimensional space. And they're not zipping around, they're forming standing waves at certain spots. *Stay with me.*" He seems to be talking to himself as much as to us. "That's where zero-point energy gets concentrated. Vortices form—cosmic whirlpools—sucking in all this space power."

He checks to ensure we're tracking.

"Okay, and these energy whirlpools start spinning … we're talking *multidimensional* spin. All that energy drops into our 3-D space from the aether like a tornado funnel dropping out of a Kansas cloud. Poof. We've got subatomic particles popping into existence."

Whoa. I catch a startling glimpse of the mechanism for all creation.

He grins rapaciously. "And depending on how these vortices are configured, you get different particles—electrons, quarks, you name it. It's a 3-D spacetime printer, but instead of *Warhammer* figurines, we're getting the building blocks of the universe."

"Okay." Andromeda's eyes dance with consideration. "So there must be an interface point where energy exchanges between realms."

"Exactly—Yes!" Cassian nods vigorously. "And time plays a role. Energy becomes matter in our three-dimensional spacetime when the illusion of time is added. In the aether—five-dimensional space—time doesn't exist. Time organizes things down here."

Lucky us. Thanks, universe, for dropping me into the dimension with deadlines.

"Wait," Cassian says, Dahmers locking in. "Yeah. There must be a phase horizon where energy passes between the aether and our reality—a very different medium. The boundary where matter crystallizes from nodes of vacuum resonance." He stares at the notebook, deep in thought. We just lost Cassian.

He's back! "Oh! This explains quantum entanglement. Einstein's 'spooky action at a distance' isn't spooky when everything is connected *up there*. Spacetime distance is no longer meaningful. Remember that trippy scene in *Interstellar* with Matthew McConaughey floating around in the space library?"

"I cried," Andromeda admits with a moan.

"Yeah, he shoulda stayed with his kid. But the aether is like that, a timeless library of everything that's ever happened, or will happen."

Huh. Cassian's space library sounds like the Akashic records from esoteric lore, a cosmic database of all knowledge and experiences. When I get home, I'll have to get new business cards: Dr. Tony Koviak, Interdimensional Anthropologist.

"And here's the kicker," Cassian says conspiratorially. "Theoretically, we could use scalar waves to send messages to other *times*. Imagine the sci-fi potential!"

There's a long lull in the taxi as Cairo whizzes past.

Andromeda breathes in deeply. "This is my favorite thing you've told us, Cassian," she says matter-of-factly, a New Age magnificence in her expression. "You make aether sound like the goddam Force."

He bows. "May the vibes be with you."

She beams. "A higher energy, all around us—from which reality flows. Fantastic." Her brows knit together in thought. "Maybe consciousness itself is rooted up there. What if our thoughts interact with the aether, influencing reality? Maybe our brains are limiters, reducing our raw higher-dimensional consciousness from a fire hose to a more manageable home faucet of awareness."

"A bit woo for my taste," Cassian replies. "But that's exactly how electricity works. High-voltage transmission lines are stepped down through transformers to provide usable household current."

Andromeda's eyes get big. "And when we die, we go back to the fire hose. What if we're in a projected hologram of some designer?" Andromeda waxes philosophical as we roll into Giza. "What if our lower spacetime is a learning construct, and everything—events, thoughts, emotions—is encoded in the timeless lattice of the aether? True immortality."

"Damn," Cassian whispers. "That's cool. And scary."

"Heads up," I interrupt the granola fest. We've arrived at the pyramids.

80

THE TAXI DROPS us into a sea of tour groups at the pyramids' bus lot. Armed guards lounge around, more interested in posing for tourist photos than watching for Ice Age treasure hunters like us.

I pay the admission, and we join the crowd ascending to the overlook of the Sphinx enclosure. Selfie sticks wave like antennas as tourists snap shots with the iconic monument. One travel influencer does a strange birdlike dance for her phone; another pretends to kiss the Sphinx. Both have cameraman boyfriends.

Do they know Atlantis is behind that duck face?

A VIP group has gained access down below, right by the Sphinx. That's where we need to be.

I walk along the overlook to get a better angle on the massive leonine body. Its enormous haunches are tucked under, front paws stretched out. The ethereal Dream Stele stands between them, an upright stone slab with inscriptions.

The doorway.

Something about the Sphinx's profile bugs me. I squint. *What's off here?* Then it hits me—the head doesn't match the body. Weird, right? I've seen this thing a million times, but I'm just noticing it now. It reminds me of how Faust could spot architectural mismatches from a mile away.

"Is it just me, or does the head seem out of proportion with the body?" I ask.

Cassian studies it. "The head's cartoonishly small and less

weathered than the body. Look at the crisp lines on the headdress compared to the eroded body."

"Right! I bet it originally had a lion's head. Atlantis was in the Age of Leo. The human head must be a dynastic renovation." I peer into the enclosure. "They say sand covered it up to the neck for millennia."

Cassian nods. "But if the head was exposed all that time, it should be *more* weathered, not less. The enclosure walls show intense water erosion. I'd estimate tens of thousands of years' worth in a desert climate. No way it was buried in sand for millennia."

Ah, so that's what Faust hinted at in Machu Picchu about the Sphinx's weathering.

Lions—a marker for Leo, twelve thousand years ago. Humanity's symbols shift with the zodiac. Back in Taurus and Aries, it was all bulls and rams. You see that stuff everywhere in old cultures. Then Christianity embraced the fish when Pisces began two millennia ago. The ancients were dialed into the stars. It blew my mind that some New Yorkers have never seen a constellation.

"The Sphinx faces due east on the spring equinox," I say. "Twelve thousand years ago, Mufasa here greeted the rising constellation of Leo."

"Tomorrow is the spring equinox," Andromeda says in a mythic tone.

I watch the VIP group milling below. "We need to check out that stele. Access to the enclosure is by special arrangement only."

Cassian is formulating an illegal plan. "We could slip down unnoticed."

I put on my criminal game face. I'll break any laws now. "Yeah, we could hop that chain and shimmy over those—" Wait, where's Andromeda?

She's already chatting up a guard by the stairs leading down. Flashing a bright smile and a wad of bills, she points to the group below. "We're with them—got separated."

The guard sighs, rolls his eyes, and pockets her grease money. He waves us down with a grumble.

Yeah, that's easier.

I go straight for the enormous paws. They've been patched up over the years. Nestled between them is the six-foot Dream Stele. What I see knocks the breath out of me.

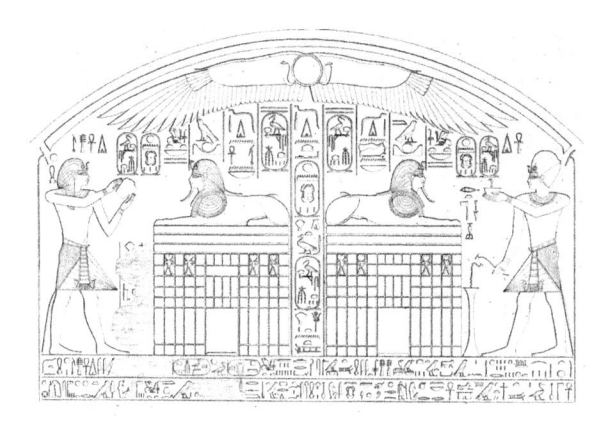

Holy smokes! Two guardian sphinx-lions sit back-to-back over a labyrinth of underground rooms. The same as the Yaxchilan cats guarding the underworld. The same motif in the Hermes illustration included with Plato's text. It's the global symbol for the Hall of Records! How did Egyptology miss this? The sign has been right here, under the Sphinx's missing nose, all along!

I skim the inscription. It's dynastic, like the recarved head. They call it the Dream Stele because a prince supposedly napped here and dreamed about restoring the Sphinx. Talk about a power nap!

I remember playing here as a kid, building sandcastles between the Sphinx's paws. The sand always vanished into cracks between the stones. Omar, my dad's Egyptian colleague, once watched me pour sand over a crack. Pile after pile disappeared like an hourglass. His eyes were watery pools of memory when he told me his father showed him the same trick—a trick his family knew for centuries: the cracks around the Sphinx never fill up.

What's down there?

Cassian climbs up to inspect the back of the slab. "This granite weighs several tons. You sure there's a doorway behind this?"

"What the legends say," I reply.

"Can we even move it?" Andromeda asks.

He examines the lion's chest, engineer gears churning. "The

mortar's crumbling." He reaches behind the stele to gauge the gap. "Huh."

Andromeda cranes to see. "What's huh?"

Cassian has the face of Hades. "I have an obscene idea."

A sharp whistle cuts through the air. A guard shouts, "Get down!" and charges toward us. My heart jolts. Cassian flashes an apologetic smile, and we make a hasty exit as he whispers his plan to get inside the Sphinx.

Well, that's certainly one *way.*

The Great Pyramid towers over us as we emerge—Plato's tetrahedron, one of his perfect forms. The overworld marker!

Cassian suddenly stops in our path, adjusting his glasses as he stares at the colossal structure. "Before we end up in prison," he says, "I have to see what's inside *there*."

81

MARCH IS shoulder season in Egypt. Fewer tourists, shorter lines. Perfect.

A small queue waits at the base of the Great Pyramid. Yes, we're going inside, are you kidding?

"Do we have time for this?" Andromeda huffs beside me.

Cassian grins. "How am I supposed to finish my book from the prison block if I don't see what's going on in there?"

"Three pyramids." I gesture ahead. "Each with three smaller satellite pyramids."

"Multiples of three, six, and nine," Cassian says. "Tesla numbers."

I point to the massive ramps leading from the pyramids into the desert. "The Nile used to flow right up here during the Ice Age."

An obvious front door, sealed with a chevron roof, looms above us, higher up on the pyramid.

Cassian squints up, "Isn't that the main entrance? Why are people going through that crude hole below it?"

"The wonders of ancient renovations. The pyramids had smooth white casing stones hiding that door. In 820 AD, Caliph al-Ma'mun hacked his way in searching for treasure—that's the hole tourists use now. They say the original entrance had a prism-shaped swivel door. Twenty tons of stone balanced so perfectly you could open it with a finger."

"Fancy," Cassian muses.

"The casing stones are mostly gone now. Oddly enough, the builders used two types of limestone. Giza limestone for the core, and Tura limestone for the casing."

"You don't say?" Cassian studies it. "Limestone's magnesium content makes it a conductor. But Tura limestone acts like an insulator, a giant insulating blanket around the structure."

"That must be why each corner is anchored into the bedrock," I say. "Like a plug in a massive Earth outlet."

"Giza is a giant circuit board." Cassian begins mumbling. "The pyramid is conductive … Wait a sec—"

Suddenly, he bolts from the queue toward the pyramid.

"Hey!" I shout, going after him.

He stops at the first row of blocks at eye level, staring up the endless slope. "Could it be … Nah, that's insane."

"What's insane?" Andromeda asks.

He walks slowly backward. "Tesla's system has two Tesla coils—a small jump-starter and a larger one to step up the power. Both need big coil windings, like …"

He blanches. "Hold up. What if the pyramid *itself*—the courses of blocks themselves—is a gigantic coil winding?

He scrambles onto a block, clambering toward the sealed entrance. I look around nervously for guards. I guess we're illegally climbing the pyramid now.

I exchange a look with Andromeda. "You think he's always like this, or only when he's inspecting Atlantean power grids?"

"Yes."

Cassian is animated, gesturing wildly. "It's Tesla's magnifying transmitter on a cosmic scale! A monstrous Tesla coil! Inside, there must be a smaller Tesla coil to kick-start the energy via resonant induction. Hell, if the pyramid matches the Schumann resonance—Earth's natural frequency—then …" He trails off, eyes gleaming. "The whole thing would couple with the planet."

We hurry after him up the stone path to the original door with its enormous chevron lintel. If there was ever a prism-shaped swivel door here, it's walled up now.

Cassian examines the blocks. "I don't get how Atlantis generated enough power to jump-start this. Look at it! You'd need Niagara Falls next door."

A carving catches my eye above the doorway. It's the only original symbol ever found on the pyramid, in an Egypt known for slapping hieroglyphs like tattoos on bikers.

Four simple characters.

$$\vee \ominus \equiv ⊕$$

I stare at it. A language that doesn't fit any known models—not Egyptian, not anything. Modern Egyptology ignores it because no one knows what the hell it means. Even my dad ignored it. Little is written about it. Yet here it is, the pyramid's welcome sign.

Why am I suddenly reminded of Mexico—

It hits me. I've seen these characters recently—*very recently*. On the triangle-shaped tablet fragment from Yaxchilan, the one that looked like a logo for the Roman Empire space program.

Yes, I saw these *exact* symbols carved in stone in the empty Hall of Records in the Americas. Is this the language of Atlantis? Mercy me, what does it say? Could the circle with the equator symbolize the Great Line, a global power grid?

Hold on. I've seen these somewhere else—in my dad's last field journal. He came to me one day, agitated and on edge. I didn't understand it then. He was onto something.

And they took him out to cover it up.

Andromeda taps my shoulder, snapping me back. "Come on," she says. "The pyramid's open."

82

I GRUNT a curse as I squeeze through the unforgiving four-foot-square upward shaft inside the Great Pyramid. These dimensions are a real pain in the neck. We're entering with the tourists.

Ahead of me, Andromeda blows her messy bangs out of her eyes, contorting her tall frame into a hunched squat-shuffle. "This was *not* made for people," she scolds the claustrophobic stone.

Cassian crabwalks up the boxy tunnel with a surprising rhythm. "I'm going with machine," he says.

We finally spill into the Grand Gallery. It's breathtaking. Towering, corbeled walls rise above us; each massive rose granite block stacked slightly narrower than the last. It's like a stone cathedral with that "ancient-future" vibe I've been seeing around. The long gallery slopes upward, like a science fiction ramp to the stars.

The precision is astounding.

Andromeda is testing the acoustics, belting out a Vashti Bunyan folk song. The gallery throbs with an ocean of harmonic overtones. Whoa. Note to self: pyramid acoustics are top-notch. Prehistoric sound engineers weren't kidding around.

"Reverb is good on you!" Cassian shouts. "You've got some serious pipes, girl!" He turns to me with a grumble, "Man, I wish I had my gear to measure magnetic fields and resonant frequencies. It's somewhere in the Suez Canal."

At the top of the Grand Gallery, we squeeze through a

bottleneck and tumble into the King's Chamber—end of the line. The room's dimensions form two perfect cubes joined together. Granite walls shine like mirrors.

I know that hidden above us, there's a stack of five mysterious lofts. Why would they need all those spaces just above? A small air shaft on the wall ascends to the exterior—the star shaft.

I approach the granite coffer. "They say this was Khufu's resting place."

Andromeda climbs into the box, folding her long legs against her chest. She shakes her head. "Nope. Only a Hobbit could fit in here."

"Napoleon slept in this chamber," I say.

"Spooky." She wiggles out. "We should get Faust in here for a sleepover. Tell ghost stories. Have pillow fights."

"Legend says this box held great power," I say, touching the chocolate granite and noticing a missing corner. "Funny thing: the sacred stone shards in Mecca's Kaaba cube match this missing piece. Locals claim they took it from here to replicate the pyramid's power."

"I know what this box held," Cassian says, patting the rim. "The capacitor."

"Like a *flux* capacitor?" Andromeda arches a pretty eyebrow. "They weren't going back in time, were they, Doc?"

"No DeLorean necessary."

I recall how we almost got zapped at Tesla's lab on Long Island. "That was the box filled with liquid mercury you were working on."

"Yep," he replies. "That capacitor is a total asshole. Two discharge plates are on top—one positive, one negative—to hammer immense energy pulses deep into the planet. If Tesla's tower is a body, the capacitor is the heartbeat."

Cassian runs his hand along the granite walls. "There's quartz all over. See these flecks? Something made this place vibrate like crazy. But what? A capacitor *collects* power; it doesn't generate it. There had to be a jump-start."

I scratch my head. "Cassian, I still don't get it. How does a big pile of rocks create electricity?"

"Quartz is piezoelectric," he explains. "It generates an electrical charge under pressure." He taps the rose granite with its crystal matrix.

A strange fact springs to mind.

"This granite was hauled from a quarry in Aswan," I tell them. "Five hundred miles up the Nile."

Cassian is floored. *"Five hundred miles?* That's like Detroit to New York. If this is a tomb, why not just use local stone?"

"They needed this exact material," Andromeda replies. "How does quartz create electricity?"

"Never owned a quartz watch?" Cassian grins. "Quartz crystals are piezoelectric; you power the watch by simply shaking it. Mechanical agitation is key. Same with BBQ lighters. Pull the trigger, and a quartz crystal sparks the ignition."

He tells us how he witnessed "earthquake lights" as a kid in San Diego—lights caused by tectonic plates squeezing and releasing electrons from rocks.

"Mountains are batteries," he says, eyes alight. "Earth is full of electrons. The pyramid sucks them up from below. We experimented at Caltech: squeezed one end of a huge granite slab in a hydraulic press, and the free end rippled with white lightning. Pressure and vibration free the electrons.

"Come to think of it"—his eyes are dancing—"the ancients *must've* known about electricity. They saw lightning, felt static shocks, and watched hair stand on end. Benjamin Franklin nearly blew himself up experimenting with a kite and Leyden jars—primitive capacitors."

A booming chant halts our discussion. A tourist group is singing bad opera in the Grand Gallery. Their voices roar into our chamber, amplifying off the smooth walls. My teeth rattle as the reverberating tones vibrate through my chest.

Andromeda covers her ears. *"Let's go!"* she mouths. The crushing bass drowns her out.

We dash for the exit.

It's time to break into the Great Sphinx.

83

THE PYRAMID FLOODLIGHTS ARE OFF. It's the dead of night, and Cairo sleeps. A storm front from the Libyan Desert whips the site into a howling wilderness.

The granite Dream Stele stands in shadow between the lion's enormous paws. I gaze up at the dark face of the Great Sphinx. Spookier in the moonlight. Over its shoulder, two black triangles slice into the starry sky like voids carved from the cosmos. Orion rises along the Milky Way, bright and clear, the way stars shine in the predawn chill.

Andromeda stares serenely at the Pleiades star cluster, probably thinking of her six sisters. Meanwhile, our cash from the Watcher is nearly gone. We blew it all on supplies and a small video camera to document everything. Another Watcher trust fund would be nice right about now.

Turns out, Giza night patrols have a pattern. Security circles the plateau in a loop, with a ten-minute window between each lone watchman. A Land Cruiser sweeps the area randomly—fingers crossed we don't run into that. Thanks to some daredevil influencers climbing the pyramids, Egypt has stepped up patrols.

Luckily, the Sphinx enclosure isn't a security priority. We slip down undetected, lugging Cassian's high school engineering project, a device that will hopefully break us into the Sphinx. This thing weighs a ton.

A patrolman with a military rifle just passed above us. Showtime. We're on the clock.

Nearly throwing out our backs, we hoist a heavy vehicle jack up behind the stele. We bartered this big sucker from a local mechanic. Getting it here was ... interesting. The taxi driver gave us some looks. I'm used to lifting dusty books, not industrial car jacks, but desperate times call for, well, car jacks.

Andromeda perches behind the stele so the jack won't backslide. Cassian and I scramble up and position the jack horizontally against the Sphinx's breast. I pump the handle, snugging the post against the slab. Sweat trickles as the stele groans a curse, angry to be disturbed after millennia of slumber.

Oh man—my Columbia lectures are going to be legendary.

Andromeda watches as the Dream Stele begins to lean forward. It creaks and moans. It's almost ready to topple, but I'm out of jack. Note to self: join a gym and stick with it this time.

"That's all she's got," I say.

A flashlight bobs over the Sphinx. The others dive behind a paw. Me? I'm plastered against Leo's chest, praying I'm invisible. *Nothing to see here, just an American terrorist changing a flat on the Sphinx.*

The guard whistles a tune, flashlight swaying like a lazy pendulum. It sweeps inches from my face. I can't breathe. Thank goodness the jack is black and not the neon yellow one at the place where I get my oil changed. Finally, the patrolman moves on.

Cassian snags a chunky signpost near the stairs and climbs back up, engineering our troubles away.

"Okay," Andromeda announces to Cassian. "Resourceful. Unpredictable. You're *definitely* an Aquarius."

"Damn." He pauses, deeply impressed. "You're really in tune with—"

"It's a gift—"

"That's not my sign, though."

She halts mid-step, mouth open like her entire worldview has been rebuked.

I deflate the jack, and he wedges the thick post. Andromeda clambers up and it hisses as she pumps it snugly, still frowning over horoscopes. She attacks the lever until she's spent, panting heavily. Then Cassian takes over. We're out of jack again! The stele is on its tippy toes. Breathing on it might tip it over. Andromeda braces against the lion's mane and kicks hard on the stele. Cassian and I join in, straining our quads like we're on a leg press in Leonidas's gym, veins bulging. *This is Sparta!*

In slow motion, the Dream Stele of Thutmose IV topples and crashes to the ground with a thundering impact. We hold our breath. Where the slab once stood, there's now a gaping black hole. Dust swirls, and the chasm seems to exhale—like a throat opening into the Earth.

84

The Red Sea
Metatron

You will not survive the passing of the age among the elect.
Ocean winds batter Serge's twisted face as the atomic voice fills his skull. On the moonlit deck of the gargantuan *Marseille Mærsk* cargo freighter, Metatron removes the circlet from the mariner's head, obliterating his mind. His eyes drift apart to the corners as two targeting agents lift his lifeless limbs without a word.

They heave his body over the railing. Serge plunges into the dark waters of the Red Sea, vanishing beneath the waves.

Under starlight, the agents board a Sikorsky King Stallion transport helicopter. The rotor blades churn to life. The aircraft ascends from the ship, banking westward over the black water.

The world's most elite hunting force is en route to Cairo.

In a dimly lit stateroom in Prague, the chandelier casts long shadows across baroque walls. The Demiurge's gaunt face emerges from a haze of cigarette smoke; thin lips curled around the filter. A vintage rotary phone is pressed to his ear.

This failure is intolerable.

"I can't understand," he says to Metatron, his voice calm and ordinary. The Voice of God listens silently on the other end. "We've poured untold resources into your mission and even accelerated timelines for you. And yet you let a simple professor and a flower child data analyst outmaneuver you."

A pause. Then, chirps accompany Metatron's acknowledgment. There's always a particular clicking cadence when he's displeased.

"We're facing new threats—on multiple fronts," the Demiurge continues, his tone steady through the swirling smoke. "They're emerging from England and even within the CIA. Humanity hangs in the balance as it hasn't for centuries. And now, the greatest threat of all looms—mass disclosure—should Andromeda Dey prevail. I don't need to remind you what that means."

He takes a long drag from his cigarette, the ember glowing hot. The silence on the line is heavy and oppressive.

"I'm willing to overlook this embarrassment," the Demiurge says softly. "You were chosen and called up above all others. If you fail, I'm afraid the consequences will be dire. The enhancements that grant you power could end—erasing your consciousness. Another would take your place as Angel of the Veil."

A series of hot, coded chirps bleep steadily over the helicopter noise from Metatron. *It shall be done.*

The Demiurge admonishes him to remember what the future holds, whispering the sacred Sumerian words:

𒀭 𒁹 𒄑 𒂗 𒄑

He flicks ash into a crystal tray and hangs up the receiver.

The veiled mothers raised Metatron from childhood to ascend to humanity's next state: godlike biological singularity—the AI transformation that awaits all who survive the cataclysm. All knowledge and truth, not buried in a hall of records this time but fused with their own minds.

The future. When we emerge from the AI cities. Soon, it will be time to go into them. Into the Arks. Robotics are developing just in time, too.

It may even be luxurious.

But only if this threat is shut down.

85

The Great Sphinx, Egypt
Tony Koviak

THE SPHINX HAS A FRONT DOOR. Why not? Next thing you know, it'll have a doorbell and a welcome mat that says: "No anthropologists."

The crashing stele reverberated like an earthquake. If someone heard that, we're toast. The plateau looks deserted, but guards could be anywhere. We need to hustle underground before company arrives.

I click on my flashlight and step into the gaping hole. The air is ancient and clammy—this passage has been untouched for millennia.

"If I see one damn spider," Cassian grumbles behind me.

"Baby," Andromeda coos.

We descend a rough bedrock tunnel that drops twenty feet, then levels off into a trapezoidal hallway of polished granite. My flashlight beam dances off walls so precisely crafted they look—say it with me—futuristic. The joints are seamless.

The surreal hallway opens into a magnificent chamber with vaulted ceilings. My beam can't reach the back. Stone boxes and shelving fill the space.

Also—it's empty.

There's *nothing* left inside. It's all gone. Not a single artifact.

Fuck.

I panic, racing around the chamber like a feral lunatic, flashlight darting. There's infrastructure for what must've been an enormous collection, but everything has been removed—no other chambers—just one massive, empty room.

Oh, it was here. They left endless shelving, storage boxes, even rows of inscriptions in that bizarre Atlantean language we saw on the Great Pyramid's front door. This place is *really* old, probably Ice Age old.

I was right. This was the Hall of Records. Except the records are gone. What a kick in the nuts. It's Yaxchilan all over again, but *so* much worse.

"Tony," Cassian says weakly, shuffling in circles. "I'm having Mexico PTSD, buddy. Where's our Atlantis Blockbuster Video, my guy?"

I'm too nauseous to reply. My throat tightens; I taste blood. I'm biting through my lip. I really thought this was our way out. I rummage through vacant bins and stone cabinets, flying through scraps of prehistoric ephemera, searching for anything. Whatever was here was cleared out in a hurry.

Andromeda's voice cuts through my despair from the far end. "Does this mean anything to you?"

Consumed by dread, I cross the long hall. She's standing near the entrance, her light angled up on a deep carving, dust motes swirling in the beam. It's a perfect depiction of Orion the Hunter aiming his bow at the Pleiades.

Faust showed us that pyramids worldwide align with Orion's three belt stars. I grasp for meaning. Come on—*think!*

"Orion comes from the Akkadian *Uru-anna*—light of heaven," I say. Sounds a lot like the Great Pyramid's name, the glorious light. In Chinese astronomy, Orion is *Shen*, meaning "three," referring to his belt stars. That's interesting since China has pyramids aligned to those stars too.

Next to Orion is a familiar primordial trident, fashioned with runic minimalism. We saw the same carving in Mexico. I think this might be the symbol of the Atlantean diaspora: Poseidon's trident.

Ψ

And there's another symbol—a maze.

Impossible.
This isn't just any old maze. It's one of the most mysterious icons from the classical world, enduring well into medieval Europe.

A Troy town.

Magic England has a folk tradition of Troy towns. The countryside is littered with them, like fairy playgrounds—ancient turf mazes. In the twelfth century, Geoffrey of Monmouth rekindled interest in them with his *Historia Regum Britanniae*, claiming Britons descended from Trojans.

I recall dating a bookish Yorkshire lass at Cambridge. She took me to her family's cottage near Haworth. One morning, we trekked the moors in search of a Troy town maze. She challenged me to walk it blindfolded for good luck. I managed one dirt path before tripping into her arms, laughing.

We sat overlooking Brontë country. She explained that the grass maze symbolized Troy's walls. Virgil called them a maze in the *Aeneid*. Invaders feared entering Troy lest they never find their way out. She told me Glastonbury Tor, a primeval mound in Southern England, resembles a Troy town from above.

My literary girlfriend said even Shakespeare mentioned them in *A Midsummer Night's Dream*, with Tatiana whispering about the "quaint mazes of the wonton green where the Morris dances were filled with mud." Was that a Great Flood reference, some antediluvian memory?

Why are Troy towns a thing in England?

Back at Cambridge, I asked Faust. My Danish mentor said hundreds of Troy town mazes, called *Trojaborg*, scatter across Scandinavia.

He unfolded the Trojan motif's history. Etruscan clay jars bore the same maze pattern with the word *Truia*—Troy. Romans held a horsemanship challenge called the Troy game, racing through a maze. He speculated it all traced back to a Proto-Indo-European city on the Eurasian steppe called Arkaim, built in concentric rings.

A year later, at Chartres Cathedral in France, I saw a vast Troy town etched into the medieval floor, with pilgrims walking its paths in reverence.

Now, standing here in the empty womb of the Sphinx, covered in dust and sick to my stomach, I puzzle at the Troy town maze carved into the Hall of Records of Atlantis's eastern colony. Is it a clue?

Plato described Atlantis as a city of concentric rings, like Troy—like a maze. *Is it connected?* Symbols don't endure for millennia without a reason.

I slump against the cold wall, defeated. Atlantis is gone again, and our future with it. Days of evading intelligence kill squads. Lives ruined. All for a forty-foot box of nothing. A torrent of emotions grips me. Part of me wants to turn myself in and end this foolish game. There's no way back. Nowhere to run where they won't find us.

In my despair, a thought sparkles deep in my mind. I sit up, wiping tears from my eyes—yeah, I'm emotional and sleep-deprived, okay? I fumble for the water-damaged Plato manuscript in my jacket. Holding the flashlight under my chin, I read the final line of his Atlantis trilogy in Greek:

The remnant of Atlantis, now *removed* to a safer underworld, awaits resurrection beyond the horizon from *Troy* in the Lower Land of Crocodiles.

Troy.

Troy towns.

That can't be a coincidence. It's Plato's clue!

The sphinx lion is obsolete.

The flashlight slips from my chin, clattering to the floor. *Seriously?* The Troy clue in Plato's manuscript was *literal?* It referenced Troy town mazes. That's why this symbol is carved here. It's basically a sign on a closed business saying: "Visit us at our new location."

I've got to be the world's worst anthropologist.

Curse my obliviousness! I was right, the Sphinx is the place. The pyramid is the overworld marker; the Sphinx is the underworld, guarded by twin lions on the Dream Stele. The Hall of Records *was* here.

They just moved it.

To someplace with a labyrinth or maze.

Yaxchilan jaguar cats, Dream Stele lions, Troy towns—they all feature mazes.

That's why Troy towns have endured, as an encoded message from deep prehistory. Mazes are the new marker!

I want to scream in frustration.

"You okay, Tony?" Andromeda asks, her freckled face colorless and clammy.

"It was moved to some maze place." I wave the Atlantis trilogy at her and point to the Troy town. My companions aren't jazzed about this twist. But I'm dazzled. It's a huge clue.

Plato is clear: the Atlantean Hall of Records was moved from the Sphinx to somewhere *better*. I should be punching walls, but I'm an archaeology detective, dammit.

I just have to locate the "Lower Land of Crocodiles"—a place with some kind of maze. How hard can it be?

86

Prague, Czech Republic
The Demiurge

STORM CLOUDS GATHER over Prague's Old Town Square, and raindrops dot the cobblestones, casting a gray pall over the city. Inside Kinský Palace, the embers of the Demiurge's cigarette flare brighter as he scrutinizes the damning photographs from Venice's Marciana Library.

His fingers tap impatiently on the ancient desk. The crime scene images reveal a shattered wooden box that houses the writings of Proclus, a Neoplatonist philosopher. What's more unsettling is the attached analysis from a scholar at Germany's Universität München. The security footage is clear. The academic speculates that the box concealed a hidden manuscript, likely Plato's elusive Atlantis trilogy.

They're still hunting for the former world, the Demiurge thinks, amazed at their persistence. *What secrets does Plato reveal?* Records and knowledge within the veil barely reach that far back. Much was lost. This new threat vector is unimaginable after so many millennia.

Knowledge of Atlantis has been zealously guarded within the veil since the sun last rose in the west. The last time humanity got too close to the truth, the great library of Alexandria had to be burned. The Demiurge hopes such drastic measures won't be necessary again.

Today, the library has migrated to the internet, where unchecked speech threatens to upend the new order. Armies of moderators and managers are now needed, monitoring content day and night just to nip anything in the bud. Algorithms are the new high priests of the sanctuary.

Information is a wildfire.

A chill rakes his spine. Why did Professor Koviak bolt to Egypt right after discovering Plato's manuscript?

The Columbia professor has found something.

No risks can be taken this close to the reset. The world can't afford an awakening—not now. It would be like a sedated patient jolting upright during surgery.

They don't grasp that we're the guardians of the light, the protectors, the healers—stewards of civilization's flame. Without guidance, without order, there is no future. Everything would vanish in the coming pole shift. Without the mothers—and those burdened with carrying the world on their backs—humanity would forget everything and become like little children, starting over in the Garden of Eden.

With no one to give them the fruit of knowledge.

The harsh galactic truths aren't etched on megalithic calendars anymore. The cosmic cycle is no longer tracked with stone. Mankind must remain unaware of what's coming. It's too perilous. Disclosure would destabilize everything. Brother would turn against brother.

We are humanity's saviors.

Yes, many in this generation will perish, but it's for the greater good.

Our posterity will honor us.

The Demiurge lifts an antique telephone and dials with a slender finger. The undersecretary-general for Peace Operations at the United Nations answers promptly.

"Sir?" The undersecretary's gruff voice carries a weight of expectation. "Do you have a directive?" He waits as the Demiurge exhales a plume of smoke.

"Mr. Undersecretary," the Demiurge says, his American accent plain and unremarkable. "We have an urgent situation in Egypt requiring immediate intervention. Authorize the deployment of UN forces to support local Egyptian units."

The undersecretary hesitates. "Sir, the Egyptians refuse to cooperate with—"

"We are invoking Imperium Majus," the Demiurge interrupts. "You know the protocol."

A long pause. "Imperium Majus?"

"Yes."

Another hesitation. "It's been centuries."

"Yes." The cigarette sparkles with a hissing flare. "Chaos breeds the most beautiful order."

"It shall be done."

The Demiurge replaces the receiver, smoke curling from his nostrils like a dragon. He picks up a badge photo of CIA data analyst Andromeda Dey.

PRAGUE'S HIDDEN GEM, the Speculum Alchemiae—the mirror of alchemy—is packed with tourists eager to explore. Discovered in 2002 after floods collapsed the cobblestones above, this underground workshop was a shocking time capsule from centuries past.

A cheerful tour guide gathers her group, reaching for a mythical figurine on a bookshelf—a secret lever. With a theatrical twist, the bookcase slides aside, revealing a spiral staircase that descends into the alchemist's lair. The newly installed entrance never fails to enchant visitors.

Suddenly, the front door bursts open. Prague police swarm in, ordering everyone to evacuate.

"Please! You can't just barge in!" the flustered manager protests in Czech from behind the gift shop counter. "This is a UNESCO heritage site—under UN protection!"

The Demiurge steps in from the rain, shaking his umbrella. His Czech is flawless. "*I am the UN.*"

Below ground, the Demiurge stands alone in the stale air, surrounded by dried herbs, colorful liquids, and shelves laden with elemental curiosities, all artfully arranged for the tourists. Candles cast dancing shadows over ancient ledgers. He pictures a wild-eyed alchemist from the 1500s, hunched over the stained workbench, measuring shimmering powders.

Tourists wander right on top of humanity's greatest secret.

He peers down a dark stone tunnel leading to Prague Castle, a secret passage commissioned by Rudolf II, the alchemist emperor of Bohemia. Rudolf was one of the few permitted to see beyond the veil in his era, chosen by the mothers themselves.

Prague's mystique as the world's alchemical capital wasn't mere legend. In the sixteenth century, Rudolf II had summoned the finest astrologers and alchemists to unlock the enigma of the philosopher's stone. Among them was Michael Sendivogius, who allegedly transmuted liquid mercury before the emperor's eyes. Mercury, long the obsession of alchemists, was believed to harbor untapped potential.

The secret of Atlantean alchemy was never unlocked. Their technology remains lost.

The Demiurge reflects on the lost science of Atlantis, the greatest casualty of the cataclysm. Survivors from twelve thousand years ago couldn't preserve their secrets. The previous pole shift had been horrendous.

We lost the energy science of Atlantis—some force.

The Demiurge is one of the few people alive who knows that the Emerald Tablet—the alchemical bible of Atlantis—is the oldest recorded text. It's now garbled in abstraction and twisted into esoteric hippie mantras. Its loss is immeasurable.

Disturbing intelligence from the CIA has drawn the Demiurge to the Speculum Alchemiae. Field reports hint at a disconcerting alchemical thread in Professor Koviak's pursuits. Could Koviak and his associates have stumbled upon the answers after all these years? Did Plato's trilogy record clues?

Those beyond the veil once researched in this very lab. Alchemical answers were abandoned centuries ago. This forgotten lair is a testament to that failure.

Then, Nikola Tesla emerged with his revolutionary ideas, reigniting hope that we might recover the lost Ice Age tech. Silencing the stubborn inventor had been easy, with the levers of finance and academia, but Tesla hid his work well. His missing notebook remained an enigma. It was no coincidence that the CIA formed shortly after his death. The agency was created to find the notebook. Those idiots couldn't find their own feet.

Tesla should've allied with us. We could've done great things—fearsome things.

The inventor had approached the wonder and terror of Atlantis, but he selfishly took his work to the grave.

The Demiurge turns his thoughts back to Professor Koviak. *What's his endgame?* He's not merely chasing the fabled Hall of Records. Lighting another cigarette, the Demiurge exhales thoughtfully through the medieval jars and furnaces. He retraces recent events: the NSA data breach, their rampage in Tesla's hotel, and the strange involvement of Dr. Cassian Wilder, a geophysicist and Tesla disciple.

He contemplates in the silent candlelight. Alchemy. Atlantis. Myths. Tesla's room …

His pulse quickens. He throws the cigarette to the floor and whirls to the exit.

My God. They have the notebook.

They're not merely trying to expose the truth; they're after the ultimate power. The philosopher's stone. The energy technology of Atlantis.

87

Giza Plateau, Egypt
Tony Koviak

OPERATION *"ROBOCOP"* isn't exactly a ringing success.

We just bolted from the Sphinx, empty-handed and exposed with dawn breaking. Patrols haven't spotted the gaping hole we left—yet.

Cairo lies to the east, but a roving Land Cruiser is heading our way. We veer west, up the causeway—not ideal. Skirting the massive pyramids, it's soon clear they've discovered our handiwork. Chaos erupts behind us. Guards sprint up the causeway, and distant sirens wail to life.

We scamper over a chain-link fence and run like hell.

Oh shit. Police are converging from every neighborhood, already forming checkpoints on each road leading down into Cairo to our right. They'll see us up here. The only immediate cover is the Grand Egyptian Museum—the GEM—to our left. It's not even a choice; we have to hide. *Now.*

The GEM finally opened in 2024 after decades of delays. Budget issues and Arab Spring turmoil slowed the billion-dollar project, but now it's the world's largest archaeological museum. And it's open. We'll have to hide here until the coast is clear.

The museum's facade is a mosaic of triangles, echoing Egypt's monumental wonders. The Hanging Obelisk hovers in the plaza, a cracked beauty from Tanis's apocalyptic ruins, suspended so visitors can walk beneath it.

Dodging the long line, we slip under a pyramid-shaped canopy into a bright atrium. While the attendants are distracted, we sneak to a second-floor wing and collapse onto a bench, gasping for air. Just a quick rest. Andromeda's face is smudged with dirt, her hair wild under the sunglasses. I probably look worse.

The mood is bleak. We're tired. No one speaks, but we need a plan. I stare at the polished floor, wondering if just napping is a bad idea. That maze symbol, or labyrinth—the Troy town—spins in my mind. Was the Hall of Records moved to a place with a maze? My foggy brain can't think of anywhere with a maze.

Hiding here might've been a bad call. We're sort of trapped. We're exhausted and not thinking clearly. With our faces plastered all over the news, it's only a matter of time before someone recognizes us in this crowd. I shove the thought away.

Plato mentioned a "land of crocodiles." That must be Egypt, right?

Andromeda looks on the verge of a breakdown. We never had a chance of pulling this off. Little people like us can't challenge the system. I stare vacantly at a row of glass cabinets displaying ancient stone vases. A sign says the collection is from the University of Cairo. Thoth—AKA Hermes—graces the school's logo.

One of my Columbia students did a project on these Egyptian vases—the oldest in Egypt. She scanned them and found they were made of corundum, a nine on the Mohs hardness scale. Diamond is a ten.

Her conclusion irked me. She claimed these predynastic potters must've used five-axis CNC machines to achieve such "precision, consistency, and proportions." Then she joked they were from Atlantis, carved with orichalcum, the mythical red metal Plato described.

At the time, I was not amused. I gave the cheeky paper a poor grade.

My eyes drift to another case of later dynastic vases. They're crudely made from clay, downright primitive by comparison. *The oldest work is the most advanced, just like Faust's walls in Machu Picchu.*

History is a lie.

Perfect. That knowledge will keep me warm in federal prison.

"We melt into Asia," Cassian is saying. "Fall off the grid."

"Further into Africa," Andromeda counters.

He chuckles darkly. "Sure, because nothing says 'low profile' like ending up on a Somali pirate's Instagram."

She pouts. "You'd prefer Pakistan over the border with Iran?"

"We could head back to the Americas," I suggest. "Catch a cargo ship from Alexandria."

"We're out of money," Andromeda says flatly. "And they'll be watching ports now."

"Then ... what?" Cassian throws up his hands. "Burn off our fingerprints and move to Mongolia?"

A museum guard saunters toward us, eying our disheveled state. "We need to get out of Cairo," Andromeda whispers urgently. "We're going into *Africa*."

Another guard approaches. We duck into the GEM's Children's Museum across the way. Inside, kids run amok with state-of-the-art interactive exhibits and hands-on challenges. Parents attempt to herd them with limited success.

We find an empty bench in the back corner, hidden from view, and hunker down amid the chaos.

"What's your plan for Africa?" I ask her.

"Plan?" Andromeda snorts. "We're making this up as we go, Professor."

Beside us, a row of brightly colored computers is full of kids smashing away at keyboards. They're playing archaeology video games.

Cassian sighs. "Maybe we just sit here and play games until they haul us away." He eyes a young Portuguese girl navigating a pixelated maze on her screen. "I call dibs on—" He squints at the game's title. "*The Egypt Labyrinth*. Nothing says 'game over' like getting eaten by a virtual Minotaur."

The labyrinth.

My blood turns to ice. I bolt upright, suddenly wide awake. "What did you say?"

Andromeda rolls her eyes at me. She snaps her fingers in front of my face. "Earth to Professor! Did you miss the part where we're headed to the firing squad?"

I barely hear her. My gaze is locked on the kid's maze game screen.

She waves a hand in front of my face. "Ground Control to Major Koviak."

"Okay, he really wants my game," Cassian says defiantly, pushing up the Dahmers. "No, sir—I called dibs."

I point at the video game like a numbskull. Ancient visions tumble and whirl: myths and legends and lore and—

"*Professor*," Andromeda snaps. She mumbles, "He's doing that Venice thing again."

"The labyrinth," I murmur. "The fable." My words are a battle cry. "I need the internet."

88

CIA Headquarters, Langley, Virginia,
President of the United States

THE COMMAND CENTER falls silent as a live feed from Egypt fills the screens. The American president stands at the center, her auburn hair pulled into a tight bun, eyes fixed on the shaky footage.

Well, this can't be good. She marvels.

On the monitor, a gaping cavity yawns in the chest of the Great Sphinx. Egyptian investigators are emerging from its depths. The president's expression hardens. She braces for the inevitable repercussions from Prague.

Targeting Division failed to neutralize the threat.

The Demiurge will take matters into his own hands—the old way.

Around her, wasted CIA analysts exchange uneasy glances, fingers attacking keyboards as they scramble to process the flood of updates.

"Why is the CIA standing down?" the lead analyst demands. "This is our op."

The director of national intelligence strides into the room, coming to an abrupt halt beside the president. His voice is loud for the whole room to hear. "Brussels is running point with the UN and Egypt."

"The Egyptians?" an agent says from the shadows. The director ignores him.

A communications officer turns to the director. "The meeting is ready, sir."

The president's nerves ratchet up. She exits the Command Center, following behind the national intelligence chief.

"This should be fun," he says under his breath as they descend a hallway.

The president clears her throat. "I know you intelligence boys run this country, but don't get in my way on this one."

"Nothing is off the table, Madam President."

They arrive at a green door leading to a room that doesn't exist. Two guards salute as they approach. One opens the door for them with a key swipe. Inside is a sophisticated conference room. Monitors surround the space, flickering to life as they take their seats.

One by one, foreign participants join a virtual meeting on the central screen: prime ministers of Australia, Japan, and India; presidents of South Africa and Brazil, and several other heads of state. At the center is the president of the European Commission, presiding from Brussels. The leaders straighten as the thin face of the Demiurge appears from Prague.

"Where's the United Kingdom?" the US president asks.

The European president hesitates, then responds in her husky French accent. "The situation in the UK is dire. We've lost contact with our people there."

Unease ripples through the virtual gathering. The European president takes a deep breath. "That's partly why we are issuing a new directive—"

"We are invoking Imperium Majus," the Demiurge declares.

There's a moment of stunned silence, then chaos erupts on the grid of faces as voices overlap. One participant stands abruptly, knocking over a coffee mug. An older leader leans so close to his camera that only one giant eye is visible, blinking rapidly in disbelief.

"Settle down!" The Demiurge commands. Silence.

The American president bites back her fury. This is the Rubicon.

Madness. The world just shifted from puppet republics to an outright imperium fit for Caesar. Under Majus, freedoms will be stripped away on a massive scale.

This is profoundly reckless. We've already taken steps to ensure disclosure won't happen.

Social media is dangerous, it's true.

But in Europe, the Digital Services Act was rushed into law in 2022—a bulwark against such threats. With oversight from the European Commission for Very Large Online Platforms, the DSA granted Brussels new tools to suppress information. Necessary, though she had warned that the name sounded too Orwellian.

No one cares about optics anymore.

In the US, similar laws have rolled out in recent years, met with surprisingly little resistance.

Prague is overreacting. We have this under control. He's a paranoid, old-fashioned fool.

"We're past political theater," the Demiurge says, stubbing out his cigarette. "If they succeed in disclosure, unrest will engulf us. We must wield power while we can. This was always the plan."

"But not so soon!" the Japanese head of state protests. "It's too soon!"

"This will lead to loss of control," the Australian prime minister says, his brow clouding. "You've got to help us understand. What are we doing here? And don't feed us some bullshit about the greater good."

"That's *precisely* what this is about." The Demiurge fires back. "Humanity has been at this point before—*many* times. We had this conversation twelve thousand years ago. And a million years before that. Always the same conversation. Don't forget that even the darkest threads have purpose in the great fabric of history."

The meeting falls silent with a somber heaviness.

The Australian prime minister leans forward, eyes blazing. "You're not a monarch. We've always been a guild of common interest, like the Greek oligarchies of old. Your megalomania will destroy us!"

"Sir, I must agree," the US president says firmly. "We can't risk a revolution in America. If we impose such draconian measures, there will be militias in the streets by morning—"

"We *are* the revolutions," the Demiurge snaps with uncharacteristic viciousness. The president steps back, hand to her throat.

"Politics has been our greatest vector of illusion," he continues softly. "But we face an existential threat. The time for soft power is over."

89

Grand Egyptian Museum, Cairo, Egypt
Tony Koviak

THE LABYRINTH of Egypt is a fable. It's not real!

Can it be real?

I pace behind the row of kids glued to their video games, nerves jangling like live wires. Cassian and Andromeda watch me, eyes wide, as if I'm about to pull a rabbit out of a hat.

Operation RoboCop lives!

I turn to the Caltech scientist. "Cassian, can you get me online?"

He snorts. Turns out Cassian has a geeky engineer's version of Andromeda's *"Look."*

Every computer is occupied. Andromeda kneels beside a little girl engrossed in her game. "Hey, sweetie, mind if we borrow this for a second?" The girl frowns, clutching the mouse like a teddy bear. Her mother eyes us suspiciously.

"Let the kid have her moment of glory," I say. Just then, the girl spots a better attraction—a pharaoh dress-up booth—and scurries off. Cassian slides into the vacated seat.

Andromeda glows. "I love it when my guys work together like the A-Team to save the world."

Cassian is typing furiously. His glasses reflect streams of code, like data waterfalls. In seconds, the kiddie game morphs into a desktop, then a browser.

"Search engine's nerfed," he reports. Moments later, he's bypassed the firewall, accessing the internet *in the United States.* "Might've hitched a ride on a Chinese nuclear sub. Untraceable. You want the Vatican Archive—what?"

"Not bad, Cass," Andromeda says, her spark returning. "But we need to escape. Now."

Cassian stands, offering me the tiny golden chair shaped like a scarab beetle. "Professor."

Andromeda folds her arms. "So, you gonna tell us what's up?"

I squeeze into the pint-sized seat. "The Labyrinth of Egypt ... it's an old legend. Most scholars don't believe it exists. *I*—don't believe it exists. No one's seriously researched it in over a century. Kind of lost to history, like Atlantis."

How did I miss this?

I need caffeine.

I'm not exaggerating when I say no modern scholars take this legend for real. It's forgotten. No one even goes out there. I can be forgiven for not making this connection sooner, because it's insane.

I type: "The Labyrinth of Egypt."

"A real labyrinth? Seriously?" Cassian leans in. "Where?"

"Tradition says it's in Hawara, at the entrance to the Faiyum Oasis, about sixty miles south. There's a lone pyramid out there, endless sand. In 450 BC, Herodotus called the Labyrinth *beyond words*, more impressive than the Great Pyramid."

I try to imagine a labyrinth so spectacular it makes the Great Pyramid seem lame. Herodotus—Father of History—wasn't allowed inside but heard tales of endless underground halls designed to confuse and disorient. "He said the Labyrinth of Egypt contains 'memorials of the Homeland.'"

"Another lost-homeland myth." Andromeda hugs her torso. "But you said nothing's out there."

I consider it. I've only been there once. "In 1889, Petrie—the British Egyptologist—found what he thought was the Labyrinth's *floor* at Hawara." My voice drops. "What if he found the roof?"

A thought strikes me. "It's well-known that Daedalus designed his famous Minotaur labyrinth after a visit to the Labyrinth of Egypt. Cretan coins even had the Troy town maze symbol, the one carved in the Sphinx." That's a really big clue.

Yaxchilan had a labyrinth.

The Dream Stele had a labyrinth.

Troy towns *are* a labyrinth.

I'll be damned. Troy towns are markers for the Labyrinth of Egypt!

Yeah, I'm pretty sure this is the—

Another memory flashes.

Dad kept a picture of Hawara in his office. *Think, Tony—what was it? Something about Paris* ... I can see it now, pinned on his wall of Egyptology. The Versailles drawing! Of course—a sketch of the Labyrinth of Egypt by Paul Lucas, a French explorer King Louis XIV sent to Egypt in 1714. He illustrated his adventures, and the publication was a sensation across Europe. I need to search for—

Wait.

Oh my God. It can't be.

Breathless and stunned, I pull the wallet from my pocket and retrieve the photo of my dad. Dread sweeps me as I stare at the large photograph on the wall behind him. It's the Versailles drawing of Hawara.

This can't be a coincidence.

My dad gave me this photo for a reason.

I flip it over to the solar system model on the back—the one that led us to Tesla's hotel room—and my heart goes haywire.

The ringed orbital positions of the planets form a rudimentary Troy town. My hand flies over my mouth.

It hits me all at once: my dad knew where the Hall of Records was.

And they killed him.

They killed him because he wouldn't reveal the location.

My hands begin to shake. A cruel numbness settles over me. A dark savagery. I want to murder all of them now. I want to kill them all. I'm filled with blinding fury.

No time for that. *Focus, Tony. Breathe.*

I wipe my eyes and return to the search results. They're fringe and amateur. I click the top link: the Mataha Expedition—Arabic for *labyrinth*. In 2008, they did ground-penetrating radar over Hawara with Egypt's blessing. The findings? A granite grid thirty feet underground, held up by columns. Then, the authorities shut it down and memory-holed the findings.

No wonder I've never heard of this.

I open another link, a 2015 satellite scan done over Hawara using spaceborne synthetic aperture radar (SAR). It revealed an underground network on multiple levels, the size of eighty football fields. Five chambers as big as Olympic swimming pools. One could fit a Boeing 747 jetliner.

Holy. Shit.

I leap up. *Eighty football fields.* Are you kidding me? That discovery was buried, too. What is going on in archaeology!

Andromeda points to a line deep in the article. She reads it aloud. "The Labyrinth of Egypt is located in an ancient area the Egyptians called Crocodilopolis—"

Plato's Lower Land of Crocodiles.

Don't panic—we just found the location of the actual Hall of Records.

90

It's a simple decision, right? Just choose A or B.

Go to a fabled labyrinth, or vanish into safety.

And Option C? Oh wait, *there is no Option C*, unless you enjoy ancient occult gulags. Excellent. *Moving on.*

Before we can even think about that, we need to pull a disappearing act from Giza.

As we hurry from the children's exhibit, Andromeda pats her jacket, checking to ensure Tesla's notebook is still snug inside. We consider stashing our growing collection of rare artifacts somewhere in Cairo in case we get nabbed, but it's too risky.

Loud Arabic shouting just erupted from the museum's main entrance. Don't love the sound of that.

We should've left sooner. I got greedy with the Labyrinth.

We dash to the balcony, sunlight streaming through the glass atrium above. Below, in the great hall, Egyptian soldiers are herding tourists out, fanning around the ticket lines. Well, this escalated quickly. Very, very *bad*.

A cluster of guys in fashionable suits is striding in, eyes scanning the cavernous hall. A woman is with them—wheat-blond hair in braids, tattoo on her neck. She looks up, and our eyes lock.

Sure, let's hide in the museum, brilliant plan. We're trapped like rats.

"Targeting Division." Andromeda almost faints.

Oh, even better.

We rush down the upper wing. "That woman was in Venice!" Andromeda shouts.

"Find a back door!" Cassian yells.

I shove them into the King Tut Experience, elbowing past tourists glued to an animated show. A guard in maroon spots us, eyes wide as he grabs his radio. Not that way.

"This way!" I shout, skidding into a hall filled with mummies, then bursting onto the top of the Grand Staircase. Soldiers are swarming the atrium below. So much for the front door.

I spin. The Great Pyramid looms through a glass wall. Statues dot the staircase like an Egyptian slalom course. Targeting agents are running up, pistols drawn, weaving through granite pharaohs and sphinxes.

"Nope," Cassian says, bolting.

We rip down another wing through cases of jewelry. Behind the bejeweled mannequins, a line of soldiers is raising rifles, shouting at us. Tourists scream and dive to the floor.

We're cornered.

I shove Andromeda and Cassian into a side gallery. More soldiers converge from that direction.

"We're boxed in!" Andromeda cries.

Trapped, we fly back to the Grand Staircase, only to find ourselves surrounded by agents and military personnel. Game over.

The braided woman steps forward. Her gray eyes glimmer preternaturally—soft British accent.

"My, my," she purrs. "What a delightful game of cat and mouse."

91

The Great Sphinx
Captain of the Egyptian National Police

UNDER THE LOOMING presence of the opened Sphinx, the stout Egyptian police captain watches as foreign intelligence agents swarm his crime scene.

Just what I need, he thinks, *foreign oversight of our investigation.*

A tall, lean man emerges from the gaping hole in the Sphinx's chest. Dust clings to his black blazer. His aviators reflect the searing Egyptian sun, and his long hair drifts in the dry wind, like a pale specter risen from the tomb.

The police step back instinctively to make way, warily observing as the mute agents scour their national landmark. A mysterious pulse swarm of electronic bleeps echoes against the weathered stones, and the agents halt in unison, then file out behind their commander without a word.

These guys are something else.

One blond agent in a dark, fitted suit lingers, aggressive clicks emanating behind his ear as he turns to the captain, speaking in flawless Cairene Arabic, "ربما تم اختراق قواتك من قبل العدو." *The enemy has infiltrated your forces.*

The captain's eyes widen at the foreigner's perfect local dialect. He nods curtly at the clean-cut youth, then watches as the bizarre entourage departs.

They never spoke a word to each other.

92

Grand Egyptian Museum, Cairo, Egypt
Tony Koviak

Welp—it was a good run.

We're captured on the Grand Staircase of Egypt's fancy new museum, surrounded by Egyptian forces with long guns and European agents wielding pistols. There's enough firepower aimed at us to mow down Napoleon's Grande Armée.

The woman with the tattoos and braids raises a hand like she's giving an execution order. Gunmetal shifts, and they take aim. I'm cringing for instant death. *They're just going to shoot us?*

Then, with a twirl of her fingers, her agents spin and aim their weapons at the Egyptian soldiers instead, shouting at them to drop their guns. Their British accents are sharp and commanding. The Egyptians blink in confusion as their rifles clatter to the polished cement floor.

"Confiscate their radios and mobiles," the Englishwoman commands. "Detain them somewhere secure."

She turns to us. "Your little maneuver at the Sphinx really poked the tiger. The CIA is on the warpath, and the Demiurge is losing his mind."

She knows about the Demiurge. It's freaky having confirmation that someone spooky like that is real.

"Victoria Bennet." She extends a hand with the poise of a

ballerina. "You know me by another name—"

"The Watcher," Andromeda says. "Who are you?"

"British intelligence," she replies. Andromeda's eyes just left their sockets.

"No time, love," Victoria says, heading down the stairs. "I'll explain during extraction."

"Extraction? To where?" Andromeda demands.

"I'll explain later."

Andromeda blocks her path. "Explain now."

Victoria sighs, offering a weary smile. "We're on your side."

"*Our* side?" Andromeda snaps. "We don't have a side."

"Oh yes, you do, love." Victoria's eyes sparkle. "Did you think you were the only ones in this fight? We've been planning a coup for years alongside a rogue faction in your CIA. Project Nephilim isn't just CIA, it's ultranational—beyond any one nation. Your data heist with Agent Vergazza caught everyone off guard, damn you for that. It's ignited the revolution. How the devil did you find Project Nephilim? We've been hunting it for years."

She studies Andromeda with awe. "Have you actually seen its contents? I'd give anything to see it."

"Frank traced it to an NSA data center," Andromeda says. "They fragment across organizations so no one sees the full agenda."

"Silos." Victoria nods. "NSA is beyond our reach."

Andromeda looks saddened. "It was all Frank. How did you find us—"

"Fabian Faust."

I choke. "Excuse me?"

"Cambridge. He's a UK citizen, dear. When your name popped up, it was an easy match for Scotland Yard. The CIA was slow to connect the dots. We've been watching you since Peru."

"That man we saw in the jungle at Yaxchilan …"

Victoria smiles. "Our asset. He'll be sacked by morning."

I ask, "So the UK is working *against* the US?"

She pauses. "Unofficially? Yes. British intelligence has declared war on the US, but it's more complex than that. Nations aren't what they used to be. We have to move quickly." She descends the stairs, her voice dropping. "There's a civil war within your CIA. The rogue faction allied with us tried an open revolt. I'm afraid they were rather badly done over, but it's bought us time. The CIA—the primary tool of Veil Society—is distracted."

Veil Society. That's a Bond villain name if I've ever heard one.

"You can't be serious," Andromeda says.

Victoria keeps moving, and we follow. "The Demiurge shut down the US government. The president rushed home," she explains. "Media's saying it's political, but it's damage control—because of *you*. You've struck the fear of Jove in them, and they're overplaying their hand. That's good."

Victoria's demeanor turns cryptic. There's a depth of wisdom in her eyes. "Had you succeeded … They have *severe* contingencies. Let's pray it doesn't come to that." Her face fills with sorrow. "What's unfolding now is the culmination of the life's work of some brave souls who gave their lives to uncover the truth. We need them to fear. They've been strangling us so gradually that we haven't noticed we're in a dystopia. We need to force their hand."

"Whose side is Egypt on?" Andromeda asks the relevant question.

Victoria's lips tighten. "I'm not going to sugarcoat it, we're in a bad way. The Demiurge has nearly complete control here. They've invoked radical proxy control over almost the entire world. They're taking the wheel for the first time."

"Can they do that?" Cassian asks.

"Oh yes," Victoria says. "They've been building their shadow government for centuries. They prefer the shadows but will step into the light when necessary. They're resorting to hard power."

"So we're trapped," I say.

She arches an elegant eyebrow. "I said *nearly* complete control."

I glance at Andromeda, desperate for someone to explain what the hell is happening. These veil guys seem to control America, Europe, and the UN. Metatron could crash through the door any second. What chance do we have?

Victoria notices my hesitation. She stops and flashes a coy smile. "Darling, I'm the chief of the Secret Intelligence Service for the United Kingdom. I know some people." She winks and continues down.

I'm not sure what her title means. It *sounds* nice.

Andromeda's eyes widen. "You're the director of MI6? I thought that was Milo Baker?"

"Milo's … indisposed." Victoria is triumphant. Her mouth forms a petite smile. "The prime minister is gone too. Wanker. *Our* coup succeeded. Fortunately, His Majesty is on the side of right. It's unthinkable, but Parliament has temporarily suspended its authority and reinstated absolute monarchy to streamline our response and unify the British people. I've been given carte blanche to secure the Realm and its allies."

She faces us directly. "What do you require?"

I'm floored. Andromeda can only manage incoherent noises.

Victoria smiles warmly. "You lit the fuse, love. We've got resources in Egypt. They can get us out, but we must reach our extraction point within the hour." She strides through the sunlit atrium. Not a soul remains in the vast museum.

I lag behind, thoughts whirling. Go to England? The Hall of Records is sixty miles away! Did she just say the king reclaimed power?

"Director Bennet …" I stammer. "We need to get to Hawara."

She eyes me dubiously. "Hawara? Where the devil is that?"

"There's something there," I insist. "It could change everything."

"Not possible, love. Egypt is collapsing around us. We must get out."

———

I STEP out of the restroom, water dripping from my face, the sun glaring through the atrium glass. Cassian and Andromeda are waiting. The idea of Hawara is gnawing at me, but my survival instinct screams otherwise. I sigh. "It's good we're getting to safety."

Andromeda's eyes lock onto mine. "Since when do you play it safe?"

Her challenge catches me off guard. "It's not about safety," I mope. "It's about staying alive."

She sets her jaw, giving me that familiar look that says I'm making the wrong choice. "Britain can't stand alone, Tony. The

Demiurge will trigger World War Three if he must. Disclosure is still our best shot. Metatron's after *us*, not MI6. It's obvious what they fear."

She's got a point. It feels like we've been hovering over some forbidden target for a while now.

Cassian looks incredulous. "It's a suicide mission, honey."

Her eyes flash. "We can take down their whole empire. Reveal the Hall of Records to the world. Those assholes would never recover."

Cassian's laugh is hollow. "So that's it? We're just gonna throw our lives away on a hunch?" He turns to me, pleading. "Tony, talk some sense into her."

I avoid her gaze, shame creeping in. Turns out, I really don't want to die. MI6 can get us out, *right now*.

Andromeda offers me a soft, melancholy smile. The freckled face is miserable and magnificent, ravaged and filthy. I've never seen her look so beautiful, so overcome. Luna's moonstone is back between her fingers.

"These people won't stop, Tony," she whispers. "They will have to *be* stopped. They'll keep everyone in the dark, living like cattle awaiting slaughter. They're close to it. They're positioning to be the *next* civilization bringers. Billions will die, and no one will even know the pole flip is coming."

That hits hard. Cassian shifts uneasily.

An obscure fact pops into my head: *Apocalypse* didn't mean "cataclysm" in ancient times. In Greek, *apokalypsis* means "uncovering" or "revelation." These people have been waiting for the apocalypse to unveil their new world order. It'd be a shame if three nobodies from New York derailed their Ice Age agenda.

"What hope do we have?" I say quietly, watching MI6 exit the museum. I can't believe she thinks we can do this.

"You can't despair like that when you don't know the outcome yet," she chides gently. "We don't know how this ends."

"What about Metatron?"

Her lip trembles softly. "I'm not afraid of what they'll do to me, Tony. I want my conscience to be clean at the end. There is *nothing* but the truth."

My dad died for this, why am I hesitating? I see him at the Great Pyramid, steadfast and resolute. He's speaking:

Calm your mind, son. Think about what you need to do. Trust your instincts.

He launched his career by taking an impossible risk that almost landed him in jail, but it changed archaeology forever. "Sometimes you just have to jump," he'd say.

Right. Some things can only be achieved in the storm.

At least the eulogy will be interesting.

I look back at Andromeda. "Then, we have to try."

Her big eyes are glowing. She hugs me tightly, infusing me with her courage. My hands awkwardly pat her long torso.

"*Ughh.*" Cassian exhales. "You're both certifiable. Fine, I'm in. Honestly, I kind of need to know what this labyrinth says about Tesla pyramids."

We huddle together, a trio of misfits with a death wish.

A minute later, beneath the Hanging Obelisk outside the museum, a squad of elite MI6 agents in designer sunglasses and tailored suits watches us emerge like a ragtag biker gang. Our strides are determined, faces grim, full of glory—

Okay, fine, we look like hell. *And we're definitely about to die.*

Victoria squints at us, her braids tipping back with displeasure. "Why do I feel you're about to ruin my day?"

93

THE HANGING OBELISK towers over the plaza of the Grand Egyptian Museum, and tourists mill about, hoping to get back inside the evacuated building. Nearby, a line of MI6 Land Cruisers waits, agents piling in.

I just laid out our degenerate plan for Victoria, trying to convey its magnitude, but the poised MI6 director isn't having it. She's almost amused, hand on hip, holding a door open for us. "That's your plan? Operation ..." She looks away with an irritated sneer. "I'm not calling it that—"

"*RoboCop*," Andromeda mouths.

"Absolutely reckless. Not happening," Victoria says.

"Fine." Andromeda crosses her arms. "Then we'll be on our way."

Victoria turns to her. "Is this the part where three tourists work out the solution to humanity's greatest threat with a suicide run?"

"This is the part where we say goodbye."

"Agent Dey." Victoria gives a tired sigh. "Get in the damn vehicle."

We start to protest, but it's clear MI6 isn't about to let us wander off in search of a mythical labyrinth. And honestly, she's right, we can't stand here in Giza debating. Half the world's hunting us, and they're closing in fast.

Sirens scream from the direction of the Sphinx. Andromeda and

I exchange a reluctant glance, then climb into the armored cruiser with Cassian.

I'm actually ashamed of how quickly our resolve just crumbled. Curse my survival instincts!

AN HOUR LATER, we're holed up in an MI6 safe house on Cairo's outskirts, near the extraction point. In twenty-five minutes, helicopters will whisk us to a bona fide aircraft carrier off the coast. From there, fighter jets to England.

I lean on the rooftop terrace railing, looking at a killer view of Cairo. The pyramids rise to the west, bathed in morning light. Man, I can only imagine the mayhem unfolding over there. It's like we kicked an ancient anthill and ran.

Victoria and some of her agents are up here on the roof, sipping Stella beers and smoking cigarettes, counting down to departure. She's on an intense call with London. I catch the word "labyrinth" at least twice. Interesting.

On the drive here, Victoria suddenly took a keen interest in labyrinths. So, I went over the details again. Her questions had a troubled edge. She had me compile everything to send to the Ministry of Defence in London for further analysis.

Now, exhausted, I lean against the wall and close my eyes—too beat to care anymore. I'm eager to have Victoria take it from here.

"Incoming video call for Professor Tony Koviak!" A fresh-faced Brit strides up, thrusting a satellite tablet at me. Victoria abruptly ends her call, looking apprehensive.

I have a call? Here? I tap ACCEPT, and my nerves jolt. I can't believe who's on the screen.

I'M face-to-face with the king of England. Yeah. King Henry IX just video-chatted me. I compose myself, sounding like a teenager. "Hello?"

"Your Majesty," Victoria whispers with a poke in my ribs.

"Your Majesty."

Henry IX—the ninth monarch with that name—is middle-aged and regal, with a handsome face. The young king was coronated following the unexpected death of his father, King Edward, last year. He's severe, studying me for an eternity. I feel like I should curtsy or something.

"Professor Koviak," he says at last. "We face a grave hour. Director Bennet has informed me of your bold strategy. I must ask, are you certain what you seek is there?"

I fumble. It's the king! "Yes. One hundred percent," I reply, hoping I don't look as wasted as I feel.

Another long moment of scrutiny, like he's carefully assessing my character. "Every historian in Britain agrees with you. We've shared your information with our top academics. They're … rather stunned." He pauses. "Your countrymen at the CIA have gone silent. We presume they are captured or dead. America is lost to us."

I resist the urge to point out he's not the first king to say that. Not the time for levity. I picture Frank Vergazza's dying face. The news out of America is awful.

The monarch continues. "The vipers in Prague have set their gaze upon these isles. Britain stands ready, but we cannot hope to fight both Washington and Brussels. After much counsel, I'm placing the fate of our world in your capable hands. We're throwing everything we've got at your plan for disclosure."

"*What?*" Victoria explodes. "Majesty." She recovers. "With all due respect, pinning all hope on a mythical Atlantean library is … wildly speculative. We're trusting in myth—"

"It's no myth," I interrupt. "The halls are real."

The king nods. "Yes, when something frightens the adversary this completely, you can be sure there is good cause. Even Dr. Faust agrees with your analysis, Koviak."

"Faust?" I straighten up.

"Yes. He's told us everything—says he's terribly sorry about Mexico. He's here with Orson Pellinor. Both insist you are indeed correct about the labyrinth."

I fist-pump—aaaand then I remember I'm on vid-chat with the king of England. It's the most surreal moment of my life, and I've had a few whoppers contend for that title recently. I wish my Columbia students could see this.

"We'll escort you, Professor," the king says. "You shall have the full might of the United Kingdom and our allies."

Okay—*what*? I gawk at the screen.

"Majesty!" Victoria protests.

"We're following these three hooligans?" A gruff MI6 agent grumbles. "They haven't even got clearance to manage a McDonald's." There's a slight chuckle from some.

"Damn the clearances," the king snaps, sobering the ranks. "We're fighting for survival, not filling out bloody forms." He looks away, trouble clouding his brow, takes a deep breath, then addresses MI6. "I'm going to level with you—it's difficult to hear, and you are not to speak this to *anyone*. Do you understand? Here is the truth, unvarnished: I've just been to a three-hour meeting with our top military minds. The belief among them all is that we shall be invaded and overrun within a week. We have no chance of resisting."

The oxygen sucks out of the group. The gravity sinks in. I become acutely aware of Cairo's distant sounds. No one's breathing. Whatever intel they have, it's bad enough to risk it all on a Hail Mary pass to find the Hall of Records. The king explains that such a revelation could awaken the masses around the world, our best hope against the global nature of this enemy.

So … Operation *RoboCop*.

The monarch's eyes sparkle at me. "Actually, I believe you shall have your authority. Right, no time for proper investiture. You three —kneel."

Victoria gasps sharply. "Oh my God."

I blink at her. Did he just say—*kneel*? I don't know a thing about royal protocol. Victoria's eyes are all whites. She encourages me in astonishment.

Unsure, I awkwardly bend the knee alongside Andromeda and Cassian. Is he about to give royal orders?

The king speaks through the tablet like a lion. "For bravery and decisive action in the face of certain death and against the dark apparatus of evil now arrayed before us, I bestow knighthood upon you. You are hereby Knight Commanders of the Order of the British Empire."

Oh.

Okay, *this* is the most surreal moment of my life. I get up.

A few tough agents are grinning approval through cigarette drags, watching us rise. Cassian asks, "Are we …? Did we just get knighted via FaceTime?" Andromeda is smiling wider than the Cheshire Cat, all swollen cheekbones.

"There, you have your clearance." The king's eyes twinkle. "Godspeed."

"Righty, then." Victoria's lips curl into a sardonic smile. "Seems you've taken the world upon your shoulders. We'll be lucky to see sunset, but if His Majesty wishes it, we'll move heaven and Earth to see you at Hawara."

"What's that, Faust?" The king leans off-screen. "Listen, Koviak—your man Faust has a message. He's hounding on about … *Venice.*" The king frowns as he relays Faust's words. "He says, 'It was in the Proclus box, wasn't it? You son of a bitch.'"

Faust just figured out where Plato's trilogy was hidden.

94

THE AFTERNOON SUN paints Egypt in a golden haze as our caravan of MI6 Land Cruisers tears south down the Giza-Luxor Highway. Egyptian military convoys blur past us, rushing toward the pyramids.

Victoria rides shotgun, her braids bouncing around on her slender, tattooed neck. She swivels to us. "This could get messy. If we encounter trouble, keep your heads down and do whatever Lord Mark here says."

"Lord Who?" I ask.

The driver looks at me in the rearview mirror.

Those eyes ...

He's a beast of a man, a rough face with three days of stubble and a scar slashing down one cheek. He's got a sporty undercut. Here we are in this wasteland, and he's wearing a three-piece fawn-colored suit.

"Lord Mark is head of special ops," Victoria says. "Best in the field."

"Did she say, *Lord*?" Cassian glances up, eyebrows raised.

"Aristocrat?" Andromeda asks.

"Northern working class." Lord Mark rumbles. He gestures to his weapon. "License to kill, all that crap."

Victoria smirks. "He never misses a shot, love. He's the Lord Mark."

Andromeda peers at him. "I saw you in Venice. That was you who chased off Metatron."

Lord Mark tips his head. "At your service."

"What can you tell us about Metatron?" I ask Victoria.

She's quiet, then says, "One man is always called up to be Demiurge, another to be Metatron. It goes back to the Ice Age. Metatron is made into a destroying angel—a protector of their order. But, as you know, the mothers hold the true power."

"Excuse me?" Andromeda cuts in. "The *mothers?*"

"Oh, you don't know?"

"Who are the mothers?" I ask uneasily.

"The Mothers of Darkness," Victoria replies.

Cassian screws up his face. "How come all these guys sound like '80s metal bands?"

"Mothers of Darkness?" Andromeda asks with a shudder. "Like … *evil mothers?*"

"No," I reply. "In ancient times, 'darkness' meant hidden or occulted."

The Mothers of Darkness? Yeah, they're real. Part of occult lore and Illuminati-style secret societies—women with veiled faces—removed from the world. Legend says this cult performs secret rites out of a castle in Belgium. All sorts of dark tales swirl among conspiracy types. Some of them are downright scary.

Cassian pushes up his Dahmers. "You guys, uh … have any extra guns?"

Lord Mark reaches under the dash and hands back a pistol like he's passing the salt.

"That one." Cassian points to an Uzi.

Lord Mark passes it back. Cassian laughs softly.

Victoria eyes him. "Should we worry about that one?"

"Yes," Andromeda says flatly. "He's a mad scientist, and we're gonna die."

Victoria continues. "The Demiurge isn't the top of Veil Society. He creates the order, organizing things, but he answers to the mothers. Occult tradition holds they exist in the aether, in the realm of Plato's fundamental forms."

Whoa. Plato *again*.

Wait a hot minute—

These dark mothers sound a *lot* like the Fates from ancient Greece—an unseen group of women controlling humanity from the shadows. They represent the inescapable fate of man and *cosmic forces*, as if NASA's pole shift were a person. I see where this is going.

Plato records that the Fates sing of mankind's past and future.

Harbingers of our fate. Mothers of Darkness.

Were the Fates the same people—ancient mothers with hidden knowledge of the apocalypse? Veil Society goes back to the Ice Age, after all.

Andromeda is awestruck. "Women run the world?"

"Wonder if they're single," Cassian quips.

She frowns. "You'd ditch us for a bunch of veiled bunker-mamas?"

"Nah, I'm sticking with you, Earth Mama."

A few miles later, Andromeda is gnawing her lip, crystal necklace twirling in her fingers. I flash her a "What's up?" look.

She leans close to my ear. "We've tried this twice already. What if it's not there?"

I look out at the endless dunes. She's right. It's stupid risky. "Third time's the charm," I offer with a grin. "You know, as a kid, I dreamed of making a discovery that would rewrite history. Be careful what you wish for, I guess."

Andromeda is a real paradox.

I'm learning to trust her New Age instincts. The freaky part isn't the crystals and planetary alignments, it's how often she turns out to be right. Like when she said we needed to take that random left turn in Venice because the "flow felt stronger." Five minutes later? We stumble onto our destination, right where she said it'd be.

Trust the vibes.

There's a magical quality.

Director Bennet hands me a titanium briefcase. "Computer, as requested."

I pop it open. The spring-loaded lid reveals a satellite laptop embedded inside.

Victoria's knuckles whiten around her satphone. "Control, this is Watcher. Rendezvous at Hawara Pyramid, seventy-four miles due south of Cairo, grid Delta-Five-Tango. ETA 18:14 hours. Activate all local assets. Set up perimeter and prepare for extraction. Coordinate air strikes at Egyptian bases to the south. Let's throw everything we've got at crippling these guys. Manifest wish list inbound—stand by." Her voice has a tremor. She's preparing for war.

"London," she adds. "We'll need a full documentary team down here. Send the very best. Over."

She turns to me. "Give me your wish list. What do you require?"

Wonder washes over me. This is happening. I think of the Greek myth of Ariadne, who gave her lover, Theseus, a ball of string to find his way out of the labyrinth after defeating the Minotaur. The word *clue* means ball of yarn—*clew*, named for the labyrinth myth.

"String," I joke. "*Lots* of string."

Victoria is perplexed and then raises her chin. "I'll get you one better than Theseus's thread, doll. MI6 has better toys."

She lifts the satphone again. "London, one more thing—bring Medusa. Watcher out."

Medusa? I mouth the word to Andromeda. This just keeps getting better.

95

THE HAWARA PYRAMID sits like a lone sentinel on the edge of the Sahara. It marks the entrance to the Faiyum Oasis, an emerald dreamland of lakes and waterfalls in a fertile basin flooded by the Nile. It has a mystical quality, and it's where Paulo Coelho set his legendary book, *The Alchemist*.

Unlike the megalithic Giza pyramids, Hawara is a crumbling mud-brick structure from Pharaoh Amenemhat III's Twelfth Dynasty. Just a pile of bricks jutting from a sea of sand. Another overworld marker with an underworld at its base. Atlantis is nothing if not consistent.

Our MI6 caravan pulls up to the forgotten pyramid in the mid-afternoon—no signs of life out here. The green of Faiyum shimmers in the distance. The emptiness churns my stomach. It's way emptier than I remember. *Sure, we'll just roll up and magically find the entrance to the legendary Labyrinth of Egypt. What could possibly go wrong?*

I push down the rising anxiety. I need six months, five million dollars, and an archaeological team. Maybe a miracle.

Cassian ambles over, dumping sand from his shoe. "Hey, I hear some Columbia professor thinks this big sandbox hides a lost maze. You know him?"

"Zip it, Cass," I say. Doubts are clawing at me. *What am I doing? I'm just a teacher.* Yeah, don't panic—just the entire fate of human knowledge riding on a three-hundred-year-old sketch—piece of cake. I really don't want to call King Henry IX and tell him I'm a fraud and a loser.

On my laptop screen is a baroque illustration I found in an online archive. A 1670 sketch of the Labyrinth by Athanasius Kircher—the Father of Egyptology, no less. He based it on Herodotus's detailed description. The Labyrinth features a central maze surrounded by twelve outer courts with complex room patterns. I still can't believe Herodotus was being literal. Academics think the Labyrinth is a myth, but he claimed to have seen it.

I pull up more historical data. The best info comes from Petrie, the British Egyptologist. His Victorian notebooks include detailed maps of the site, showing where the Labyrinth once stood, right at the foot of Hawara Pyramid. He found a stone foundation and thought the structure was destroyed. Whatever he saw is long buried under the desert.

It's just sand now.

Petrie even made his own speculative map. None of it helps as I gaze out at pure desolation. How do you unearth a twelve-thousand-year-old labyrinth? I'm sweating. We should've headed to the extraction point. I've put everyone in danger. Sleep deprivation makes me stupid—note to self: get more sleep. It would take months of excavation with heavy machinery to find anything here, assuming we even know where to dig. My shoulders sag.

Andromeda strolls up, looking parched. "At least Tatooine had a cantina. I'd endure a wretched hive of scum and villainy for a cold one."

My dad always had ice chests full of drinks on his digs. That would be—

Dad.

I tear the wallet from my pocket and slide out the photo, the one with the sketch of Hawara on his wall. "I need a magnifying glass!" I call out.

An MI6 agent runs up holding a phone with a magnifying app. I place it over the photo of my dad and the Versailles drawing by Paul Lucas. The drawing shows a classical entrance structure in the Ptolemaic style, the Macedonian Greek period of Egypt, famous for Cleopatra. It's a mausoleum-style doorway partially sticking out of the sand. It was still here in 1714!

I stare at the carvings on the entrance.

Andromeda peers down. "Looks like a mythical stargate to wherever Conan the Barbarian and Red Sonja live."

"Don't say that again," I say, studying the picture.

Lucas labeled the sketch: *Plan et dessein du Labyrinthe d'Egypte dans l'état qu'il est aujourd'hui.* "Plan and design of the Labyrinth of Egypt in its current state." Thank you, high school French.

Whatever Paul Lucas saw has vanished—*or has it?*

My dad gave me this for a reason.

Pinning humanity's hopes on Lucas's eighteenth-century TikTok post, I focus all my archaeological prowess on the French illustration.

Hang on. What's this scrawled writing underneath? I move the magnifier and increase the zoom. My dad wrote a message: TONY, USE THE LANDSCAPE.

My head flies up, and my breathing quickens. It doesn't say that. The landscape? *What landscape?*

The landscape.

I go back to the sketch. It's easy to make out the details. Lucas recorded features of the area:

Hills.

Pyramid.

Nile.

Oasis.
Ridgeline.
Palms.
Rocks … *Rocks*.

I hold the photo up to the horizon, trying to match the sketch's perspective. The illustration mirrors the scenery.

Okay. I can work with this.

A rocky outcrop on the plateau's edge doesn't align with the one in the sketch. I slog forty yards to my left through deep sand, holding up the photograph like a holy relic.

Still wrong. I exhale and trudge thirty more yards, holding up the magnifier again. Better, but the hills are still wrong. Twenty yards ahead. Finally, it's a match. Lucas, you clever rapscallion.

Paul Lucas stood on this spot in 1714.

My dad stood here.

Where Lucas drew the Hellenistic doorway, there's an irregular dune. It's *big*. The desert has swallowed something—my heart pounds. I stride forward, drag my heel to mark an X in the sand, and punch the air three times.

The entrance.

96

THE WIND KICKS up the Hawara sand into tiny tornadoes as the Osprey's rotors churn the desert into a storm of grit and dust. The airplane's wings are swiveled into helicopter mode—because why be just a plane or a helicopter when you can be both?

British commandos leap out with equipment boxes. Cassian points at the plane-turned-chopper. "You know, Tesla had a patent for this sort of thing back in the day. Man's gotta get his royalties."

"He should add it to his LinkedIn," I shout, already bounding toward the commotion.

For the past three hours, Victoria has been marshaling a small army—intelligence assets, locals, and even a few farm tractors. It's all very hush-hush. The aircraft raced in from the Royal Air Force base in Akrotiri, Cyprus, a British Overseas Territory in the Mediterranean.

Victoria is briefing her men as we approach. "We've set up strategic decoys off Dover, Gibraltar, and Malta. Straight out of the D-Day playbook—fake invasion forces to keep the enemy guessing."

Andromeda lifts an eyebrow. "Impressive. But isn't that the military's job? Why is MI6 running point?"

"His Majesty has put me in charge of our strategic response," Victoria replies over the thwapping rotors.

"Don't let her modesty fool ya, mate," Lord Mark says. "Victoria here runs *everything*. The king made her Lady Protector."

I choke on my water bottle. "I thought the title of Lord Protector was only used once when Oliver Cromwell wielded monarchical power during a crisis."

"Exactly. The king's a history buff. He's revived it—for her." Lord Mark shakes his head with a teasing smirk. "God help us, all."

So, Victoria Bennet is essentially the Queen. Good to know. She hands Andromeda a small satphone. "Document everything you see down there, love."

Andromeda frowns. "Oh, I'm not good with cameras."

"That's quite all right. We have a documentary team joining us," Victoria says, giving a sharp whistle.

A man and woman are stumbling off the Osprey, overloaded with gear, looking like aging rock stars. The man is lean and mid-forties, wearing jeans and a black T-shirt, and his hair is a tousled mess. The woman sports a fashionable jumpsuit with chunky boots, her dark waves perfectly disheveled under stylish bangs. Cameras dangle from them like technicolor Christmas ornaments. Behind designer sunglasses, they seem a bit dazed.

Wait a minute. I know these two. I saw a piece on them back in New York, some NYU film symposium.

Victoria gestures as they arrive. "May I present Wynn and Lola Jones, Britain's finest filmmakers—or at least the only ones we could kidnap on short notice."

Wynn offers a lopsided frown. "I believe it's 'Britain's hell-raising husband-and-wife power couple.' The tabloids would never lie."

"You're married?" Andromeda says, noticing the rings.

Lola shrugs, voice dripping with dry sarcasm. "Allows us to bundle our arguments into a sorta package deal. Hot marriage tip."

Wynn nods. "It's why I'm always going around like: 'Sweetheart, did you mean to overwrite my footage with shots of the cat?' And 'is there a reason my director's chair is on fire?'"

"Please," Lola drawls, casting a critical eye over the expanse of sand. "If I wanted to get rid of you, I'd just let you screen your director's cut."

I extend a hand, heading off a blossoming divorce. "Wynn, Lola —great to have you aboard. Hopefully, we don't throw too many curveballs your way."

Victoria is amused. "Don't let their appearance deceive you,

Professor. These two were mentored under Stanley Kubrick. Who knows? Might even make you three look sexy."

"I was referring to not dying," I say.

Lola tips her head back, surveying us through tinted Stella McCartney frames. "Kubrick was a riot. Sadly, he passed unexpectedly a few days after delivering his extended cut of *Eyes Wide Shut*—studio had to trim it back."

"What was in his longer cut?" Cassian asks.

Victoria blanches. "We don't talk about that."

Cassian says, "I'm gonna need my agent to sign off on any personal brand makeovers."

Lola angles her sunglasses down to asses him, dark eyes flicking up and down. "I left production on *Jane Eyre* ... for *this*?"

"Promise you won't regret it, darling," Victoria assures.

Wynn sighs. "Our government's still putting out fires with gasoline, I see." He and Lola lug their packs away to prep for the trek.

Andromeda slips Victoria's satphone into her wildflower pouch and eyes the workers. "There's no way we're keeping this secret with so many people."

I had the same thought. All it takes is one person for a leak. "Just say it's survey work for a new highway, with military running logistics. Locals have been clamoring for a better connector road for years."

Victoria considers it. Without a word, she retrieves her phone and then tells me I'm a genius, nothing like an attaboy from the Lady Protector of Britain.

The tractors dig away, and it doesn't take long to hit the upper lintel of the forgotten doorway and trace out its edges, what little remains. We feign surprise at the discovery. *Oh, would you look at that? Ancient history just lying around. Who would've guessed?*

Since Paul Lucas's 1714 sketch, much has been looted and quarried off. By sunset, enough sand has been clawed away to reveal the outline of a gigantic doorway that leads down like a portal into a sandblasted realm.

Lord Mark tells me, "You just cost me fifty quid."

"Why?"

"He wagered you wouldn't find it," Victoria says, folding the cash into her pocket with satisfaction.

"Et tu, Lord Mark?" I give him an exaggerated look of mock hurt.

"This is interesting, Tony." Andromeda is holding the MI6 laptop. "Petrie's survey shows the Labyrinth doesn't align with the Hawara Pyramid," she says, squinting at the screen. "Look. I plotted its cardinal meridian on Google Earth." Her eyes hold wonder. "Guess where the Labyrinth aligns to?"

Cassian lights up. "A former North Pole?"

"The *Alaska* Pole," she says.

I furrow my brow. "The one from the Ice Age?"

"No." Her sapphire eyes are fiery gems in her skull. "Alaska was the North Pole when the Great Line was the equator, *four* pole shifts ago. That means whatever's down here is unbelievably archaic."

"We have a problem!" One of the Egyptian assets is yelling from inside the excavated doorway.

We rush over and peer into the dark passage. The sand inside looks strangely fluid, like—

Aaand, it's flooded.

I groan. Can I get a break—just once—in my life? Whatever's down there is soaked. Through a translator, a local farmer tells us the Ministry of Irrigation sliced a canal through the plateau a few years ago. Must've nicked the Labyrinth. I step into the vibrant green water; the cold murk envelops my knees.

"Guess it's a beach day." Cassian wades into the lurid water.

With a flurry of intelligence-speak, Victoria circles the MI6 wagons and stations a rear guard outside under Lord Mark. She follows us into the dark passage. An elite team of agents in tactical gear brings up the rear. Twenty-three of us on this expedition to Atlantis. Yeah, it's just cooler saying it that way.

Strong lights click on, piercing the dank gloom. A musty, stagnant smell fills the air, reminding me of algae-choked lakes from my childhood. Wynn and Lola are with us, cameras rolling expectantly with furry microphones attached.

Andromeda trails a hand on the limestone as she wades. Her voice is low and husky. "How doth the little crocodile improve his shining tail, and pour the waters of the Nile on every golden scale?"

"Nerd alert," Cassian says, sloshing through the stagnant water.

"Alice," she insists, "in the Pool of Tears, when she's about to enter Wonderland."

Victoria's face sparkles with reflected Nile water. Her English becomes Shakespearean. "'How cheerfully he seems to grin, how neatly spreads his claws, and welcomes little fishes in, with gently smiling jaws'—I was in literature at Warwick before I made the profoundly regrettable decision to become a spy. That poem lands darker down here."

We trudge down the passage. I say, "Diodorus of Sicily—a librarian at Alexandria—wrote that the Egyptians were strangers who came from a homeland in the west. America, according to Professor Faust."

An MI6 guy shoots me a bemused glance. "That's some high-grade wonkery."

"Oh, there's a higher grade of wonkery," Cassian says.

Part of me wishes Faust were here despite everything. No one knows myths like Fabian Faust. Can I blame him for falling for an exquisite government psyop?

We're submerged to our waists now, and the faint glow from the entrance vanishes as we round a corner. Panic creeps in. Thirty yards farther, we reach a disappointing dead end where a limestone wall blocks the passage.

"Tell me that's not it," Victoria grumbles.

I study the slab. "They sealed this up pretty hastily. Someone didn't want visitors, like Mexico."

"Please don't be like Mexico," Cassian says.

Andromeda's brow pinches. "The spiders or the empty library?"

"Yes."

"Reza!" Victoria calls.

A Persian commando steps forward, wielding what looks like the world's first flamethrower-turned-jackhammer. The metal nozzle has a blunt, wide tip like a mini shovel. A braided cable runs from it into his heavy backpack.

"Atlantean leaf blower?" Cassian asks.

"MI6 Proton Pack," Andromeda says, slapping Cassian on the

back with a smile. Those two really do come from the same planet. They'd probably be a good match back in the real world.

"Ultrasonic drill," Reza says with a silky Farsi purr. "Allows me to scoop away the masonry"—he gives Andromeda an eyebrow waggle—"as if it were lemon sorbet."

Cassian whistles. "Unreal. Say, you don't have MI6 jet packs, do you?" He watches Reza set up. "If only the ancients had tech to scoop away stone."

"Maybe they did," I reply.

Cassian leans in like a curious engineer, retro frames tilted up.

Reza explains, "Ultrasonic vibrations in the diamond-tipped horn induce microfractures in the stone. It disaggregates the material at the molecular level."

Home Depot would make a killing.

Victoria elaborates. "It's designed for silently creating entry points into fortified structures instead of using explosives."

I direct Reza as the scoop shaves away the masonry. Disaggregated grains fall in piles at our feet, shaken apart at some structural level that I find unsettling. All this technology—

We wait twenty long minutes in the cramped tunnel with cold water up to our hips. Finally, Reza has outlined a rectangle clear through the stone. An uncut tab holds the door in place. Fortunately, it's softer limestone, not granite—a thin block installed as a hasty plug.

"Stand back," Reza warns, then dissolves the limestone tab. It snaps free, falling into the dark water beyond with a thunderous splash.

Good God!

97

BEHIND THE OPENING, long marble steps rise from the acrid water like a luxury swimming pool, opening into a breathtaking, pristine courtyard. The water hasn't reached that high. Thank the stars.

"Abandon all hope, ye who enter here." Victoria quotes Dante as we ascend the steps. "Let's get to it."

Industrial floodlights click to life, bathing the underground courtyard in illumination. It's Classical Greek—a perfectly square room lined with colonnades. A high ceiling is painted with sky and clouds, its surface scorched by firelight. Haunting statues fill the space. The craftsmanship is remarkable. Dozens of marble figures peer at us, wondering who these human visitors are.

Familiar myths adorn the mosaic floors. Everything is preserved—I mean *perfectly*. This single courtyard would be the most remarkable archaeological find of a lifetime.

Our crew is stunned. Even the most skeptical among them begin to grasp what's unfolding.

We haven't even started.

As we move through the courtyard, I can't shake the feeling that the statues are watching us. "Does anyone else think these things might come to life and try to kill us?" I half-joke.

Cassian chuckles uncomfortably. "Don't even say that, man."

"Is somebody keeping track of our way back?" Andromeda calls out.

"We could spend days getting lost down here," I warn. "Pomponius Mela, the first Roman geographer, wrote that the Labyrinth of Egypt has endless paths that will leave you panicked because of winding porticos, which reverse direction."

"At least we'll get our steps in," Lola deadpans, deftly hovering her camera over a row of female statues with veils covering their faces.

I peer at the ancient women. "The Fates—"

"Mothers of Darkness," Andromeda says quickly. "They were here."

Nothing spooky about that in a place like this. The current mothers don't know this labyrinth exists. They must have lost the knowledge at some point. Interesting.

Lola abruptly lowers her camera, shudders, and does an agitated pirouette. "Something's wriggling in my boot!"

"What's the plan for getting back out?" an MI6 agent asks me, sounding worried.

I want to tell him we've been getting by on sarcasm and reckless abandon, but Victoria has us covered.

"Percy, it's your big moment, doll," she says, calling up her man.

"Mum." A bruiser named Percy strides forward and sets down a hefty backpack. He pulls out a strange sphere and then straps a control plate to his forearm.

"Percy here will keep us on the straight and narrow," Victoria says.

"Right." Percy's accent is a rough South London tenor. He taps his arm plate, and long tendrils push out of the sphere. "This here's our Advanced 3-D Mappin' System, Medusa. It combines LIDAR, infrared, and ground-penetrating radar. We can scan the space in all directions, creating a three-dimensional map—in *these*." He holds up horn-rimmed glasses. "This ugly girl can also predict structural instabilities."

Oh. I get it now. Medusa. Because of snake hair thingies. It's fantastic that MI6 has a device referencing Greek myth. Compliments to the secret spy inventor team.

"Can we look, or will we turn to stone?" Andromeda asks.

The drones leave the sphere, quietly hovering above us. It's mesmerizing. What'll they think of next?

"Medusa here," Percy explains, "uses bladeless filament drones that look like flagellatin' nope-ropes when airborne. That's where the nickname comes in. Your boy Nikola laid the groundwork for this propulsion tech. Electric fields ionize and manipulate air for movement. Near silent. Ideal for surveillance and reconnaissance. It's got sensors for temperature, humidity, gas composition, radon, and radiation levels. We'll know if we're about to walk into a shit show."

Cassian mumbles, "What else is the military hiding?"

"More than you know," Andromeda replies.

"Obviously. That's ... kind of the point."

"You mean MI6," Victoria says. "Never seen a Bond film?"

Andromeda smirks, amused. "Try anti-gravitics and sentient plasmas. If you're wondering how the government-UFO-orb-things work, it's vibrating oscillations, not rotational spin. Whatever that means."

"No one likes a math geek, Agent Dey." Cassian sighs. "So ... Tesla was right *again*. Man, I hate that guy."

Percy puts on the thick-rimmed glasses. "The drones have an intelligent navigation assistant, an AI-driven guidance system that works with Medusa." His hard eyes dart around behind some augmented reality.

"You could call it Gorgon Vision," I say. For some reason, I just made a Medusa dad joke, and Percy is giving me a mean eyebrow.

"*Medusa ... scan!*" He says it like he's asking a smart speaker to play dinner music. The snaky drones fly off in all directions, disappearing into the dark mysteries beyond.

He double-taps his smart glasses and slides a finger on his forearm screen, manipulating his view. "The AI will track our route in real time and even calculate the quickest exit."

"Ariadne just wept in her grave," I say, thinking of the string she gave Theseus to find his way out of the labyrinth. "Cassian, I think you've met your match, buddy."

"Venice disagrees," Andromeda says.

Thirty minutes pass while we wait for the drones to complete their scan. I use the time to explore the courtyard, examining artifacts. According to Percy, who has scanned the catacombs of

Paris and the Colosseum's basements, the Labyrinth is vast—*really* vast.

"Incredible." Percy sighs and hands me the AR glasses.

I put them on and stagger. The detailed contours of the multilevel labyrinth materialize in a sprawling hologram that fills my view. It's gargantuan—an underground metropolis. Our location is a teeny red dot on the edge. I stumble through the 3-D schematic, drawn to a sizable central section on the lowest level where data is missing, like a hole punched out of the hologram. "What's this down here?"

"The drones can't access that area. Must be sealed." Percy pinches and rotates two fingers on his armband map; my hologram zooms in. Feeling motion sickness, I remove the glasses.

Percy's voice is gravel. "Only one path leads down there, mate."

"Yeah—that's the Hall of Records," I say.

98

CIA Headquarters, Langley, Virginia
Director of National Intelligence

THE COMMAND CENTER IS A HELLSCAPE. The director of national intelligence stands amid the chaos, frowning, studying the satellite imagery.

"What else can go wrong?" he mutters.

"We've lost them," the lead analyst barks, pacing between rows of technicians. "Cairo's a ghost. Someone's pulling strings. Come on, people—talk to me!"

The director rubs his temples. Two days without sleep are catching up to him. He points sharply at the geospatial intelligence team. "Pull up the latest imagery over Egypt."

The chief of satellite reconnaissance rises from her console, a confident woman in a floral blouse, headset dangling off one ear. "NROL-87 only passes over Egypt every twenty-four hours."

"You're kidding me." The director stares at her. "When's the next pass?"

She flinches, jaw tight. "Six and a half hours, sir."

"Six *hours?*"

She steadies herself, an exhausted edge to her voice. "NROL-87 is in sun-synchronous orbit, pole to pole. It's a lazy sweeper."

"Don't we have better recon on Egypt?" His tone is accusatory.

She meets his gaze defiantly, sleep deprivation evident in her eyes. "It's not Iran, sir. We were told to make Egypt a low priority." She cocks her head, words biting. "Budget cuts. Take it up with Congress."

A vein throbs in his temple. "Reposition the satellites. *Now.*"

She scoffs, pulling off her headset entirely. Thirty-two hours on duty have frayed her patience. "We can't just reroute a satellite orbiting at seventeen thousand miles per hour. It's not Uber, sir."

He lets out a short, incredulous laugh. "Get me the damn imagery!" he shouts, storming out with his phone pressed to his ear. "I want a list of every asset within five hundred miles of Cairo!"

99

Prague, Czech Republic
The Demiurge

Dark thunderclouds hang over Prague, casting the city in a brooding gloom. Inside the ornate chamber of Kinský Palace, the Demiurge pours himself three fingers of scotch. He downs it in one burning gulp, but the amber liquid does nothing to steady his nerves. The walls feel like they're closing in.

The antique phone on his desk rings. He's been waiting for this call from the president of the European Commission.

Finally.

He lifts the receiver. "Report."

A husky woman's voice comes through, thick with a French accent and tinged with astonishment. "The United Kingdom has launched an unexpected blitz. Military airfields in Egypt have been hit. The strikes were surgical."

The Demiurge rises to his feet, aghast.

"When?"

"Ten minutes ago."

The news is as mystifying as it is alarming. If he's not careful, this could spiral out of control.

"There's more," she continues. "Offensives are mounting from Gibraltar and Malta, and a fleet of British warships has amassed in the English Channel. We have no idea why."

He stares out the window, dumbfounded. *What is this treachery? It's unspeakable. Are they invading Europe? Damn the British.*

"They must have an objective," he says evenly, masking his concern.

"We don't know, sir. I thought the new king was brought within the veil."

"No. But we have ways of ensuring cooperation. It appears the young monarch has chosen to defy us."

"Might this strike be connected to the rogue elements from the CIA?" she asks.

The British are assisting Agent Dey and Professor Koviak. Why?

His eyes narrow, deep creases forming on his face. His heart pounds. *Is this subterfuge?* There's nothing in Egypt or Malta—unless ...

"Sir? We need a firm response. Egyptian airfields are destroyed, but UN fighters stand ready in Greece, Italy, and Israel—"

"Do not escalate," he snaps. "Convene an emergency council. Within the veil."

"It shall be done."

He hangs up and moves to the window. Across the medieval square, Prague's famous astronomical clock stares back at him, the zodiac wheel turning slowly. The figure of Death flips his hourglass.

The pole shift is here. Too much is at stake to falter now.

100

The Labyrinth of Egypt
Tony Koviak

PERCY LEADS US DEEPER UNDERGROUND, following Medusa's route through a maze of Hellenistic courtyards. The architecture is so pristine that it looks like a Hollywood set. I've only ever seen this stuff in ruins. Each chamber we enter has Greek treasures scattered everywhere. It's a time capsule, an anthropologist's wildest dream.

Every step is a "look at that!" moment. But there's no time. A more profound mystery awaits in the primordial levels below. So, we press on, like characters in a Jules Verne novel heading to the center of the Earth.

I peek into colossal branching doorways leading in every direction. These black openings are death traps. We could so easily get lost down here. My stomach knots at the thought of our gear failing, slowly starving to death as we roam in endless—

Nope. Bad thought.

Note to self: next time, hit up Ariadne for a big-ass ball of old-fashioned string. I grip my flashlight tighter.

An MI6 agent reports walking almost two miles when we reach a grand staircase. We descend and—boom—Old Kingdom Egypt. The rooms shift to warmer tones, plastered with deep hieroglyphs. Cool, damp air wraps around us like we're in the Valley of the

Kings. It's like traveling back in time, with newer structures protecting the older. Just like Machu Picchu. Man, this place is wild!

The Egyptian tunnels twist endlessly—an actual maze—the OG Troy town. I no longer have any sense of direction. Percy's faith in Medusa's navigation is unshakable. He follows the holo-route like a delivery driver glued to his GPS. I'm used to tight spots and buried ruins, but this labyrinth pushes my claustrophobia to the limit.

My mind plays tricks. I stare down a dark passage and imagine a minotaur rushing from the black. My skin crawls. Still better than Metatron.

Back in college, my girlfriend squeezed my arm so tight in a haunted house that I almost lost feeling. That's nothing compared to how Andromeda is gripping me now. Her eyes dart at every shadow. "It's so spooky down here!" she whispers, voice trembling. "I keep expecting something to jump out."

"Don't worry," Cassian says with a wink. "If anything does, I'll act like mainstream academics and scientifically prove it doesn't exist."

We descend a sloping tunnel and cross into yet another era. The masonry is smooth, megalithic granite now. Each block must be five hundred tons. Joints are invisible. I recognize the futuristic aesthetic from the Osirion and Serapeum, or the trapezoidal passages of Mesoamerica. Cool as hell.

The walls are bare, no hieroglyphs or Greek designs. We're back in the former world—Zep Tepi—The world of the electric gods.

The sleek passages wrap a few more turns, but it's no longer a maze. We're on a straight shot. Percy says the obscured region is dead ahead. The path narrows until it ends at a monstrous block of … solid granite.

Blocking our way is one of the biggest megaliths I've ever seen, a trek-stopper for sure.

On one edge of the granite slab, a familiar symbol is carved with machinelike precision: a runic trident—the symbol of Atlantis.

Ψ

"How do we get through *this?*" Andromeda rakes a hand through her messy crop.

"Reza?" Victoria calls for the scoop drill.

Reza, the Persian drill operator, examines the stone, face grim. "Granite is problem. This block—very thick. Scooping will take …" He counts on all fingers. "Two days."

"We haven't got two days," Victoria says.

A tense argument ensues, quickly devolving into a shouting match.

"We're wasting precious time!"

"Scan for another entrance—"

"Well, you're all sat there, not helping!"

"We shouldn't have come—"

"We've got enough evidence. We must evacuate!"

While the team argues, I return to the trident symbol. Why is this lone carving offset to the edge? The placement is odd. I study it, puzzled. Everything at this stratum of time has been precise—each minimalist carving executed like the layout of a modern graphic designer.

The placement bugs me. I stare at it, irritated.

"Jumper," Victoria shouts down the passage. "Let's blow it."

The agent they call Jumper weaves to the front and opens his pack. He pulls out bricks of C-4, then digs deeper into his bag. He fishes more ardently, freezes, and closes his eyes like he's been given a terminal diagnosis. "The switch is …" He gulps. "… topside, mum."

"*What?*" Victoria is magnificent in her wrath.

"We left in such haste," he stammers. "I—I'm sorry. It's in the cruiser."

"Sod it, Jumper." The MI6 director sighs. "No choice. Back up we go."

"Can't we radio someone to bring it down?" an agent asks.

"Unaccompanied?" Percy responds in his Cockney. "They'd be toast in minutes."

"Blast," Victoria curses. "Percy, take Jumper and run for the switch. He's buying pints tonight."

A senior agent grabs her arm. "Vic, we haven't got time." He glances at me. His expression makes me think MI6 is withholding something. They start a hushed discussion.

Lola Jones is circling the drama with catlike steps, camera in the nook of her elbow, capturing our failure for all time.

I return to the offset trident. Why is it on the edge? Why would a marking on a sealed doorway be off to one side?

That's deliberate.

A thought hits me: a wild piece of fringe Egyptian lore, a legend about the original door to the Great Pyramid.

It's ridiculous. But don't all doors have …?

Wynn aims his lens over my shoulder at the rune symbol. Those two don't miss a thing.

I place my palm on the cold trident, almost laughing at myself. I press, and the megalith shifts with a groan as if the Earth itself is moving. Cold, stale air rushes out. I jump back.

Everyone turns in silence. All lights are on my dusty hand. Lola swings her camera toward me, eyes blazing.

I push more, and the megalith begins to swivel weightlessly with a low grinding sound. We're talking five hundred tons, moving under my palm. It rotates to reveal a gem-cut prism door balanced on a single point, like a ballerina's toe.

The Great Pyramid's front door mechanism from legend!

I step through the black threshold. Darkness envelops me like walking into the void. My echoing footsteps are the only sound, telling me I've entered a vast space. I swing my light up.

Atlantis.

101

Grand Egyptian Museum, Cairo, Egypt
Museum Administrator

THE HEAD of the Grand Egyptian Museum seethes with frustration. *We've only been open a month—now this!*

Foreign intelligence agents have swarmed his museum, disrupting exhibits with their intrusive searches. He watches helplessly as artifacts are jostled and displaced.

"This will knock us offline for a *week*," he says under his breath, but they don't seem to care.

The soft beeping of their strange metal ear devices irritates him. He's a curator of the classics. He despises their gaudy technology.

They move like ants. Like jackals. Abominations.

As they sweep a basement hallway, an agent tugs at a locked storage room door in the dim corridor. He turns to the administrator. "Open it," he demands curtly.

The administrator sighs heavily. "That room is off-limits. It contains sensitive—"

"Open it," the agent repeats, unyielding.

Reluctantly, he swipes his key card. The door clicks open.

Inside, a group of Egyptian military prisoners huddle together, bound to a railing, mouths gagged. One soldier—a disheveled officer with a bloodied lip and torn uniform—mumbles frantically in Arabic about British MI6 treachery.

The agent's metallic implants pulse aggressively. Some kind of LED light is going berserk behind his ear.

A different kind of agent steps in. His presence is commanding, and his long, witch-like hair reminds the administrator of dark spirits and jinn from Islamic folklore his mother told him about as a boy. He feels a chill.

His eyes fix on the symbol emblazoned on the man's chest—sacred geometry, ancient and powerful—the mark of *Mīṭaṭrūn*, Islamic Angel of the Veil.

Why does this dark captain wear Metatron's Cube?

102

The Hall of Records
Tony Koviak

MY FLASHLIGHT BEAM fades into the abyss of the Hall of Records. It's endless. It's filled with—*everything*.
All of it.
I can't move. Overwhelmed doesn't begin to cover it. Andromeda and Cassian are beside me. We're laughing, and crying, and hollering. Our shouts echo through the colossal space.
MI6 agents glide past, eyes wide, mouths ajar. Even the real skeptics are in a total stupor. Wynn and Lola lower their cameras, utterly spellbound.
The ceiling soars thirty feet overhead, supported by endless granite columns. Stone boxes line every partition, and the vast central area is crammed with storage structures.
Cassian leans in. "Millennial house flippers will eventually turn this into an Airbnb. You know that, right?"
"Don't ruin this moment, Wilder," I say, noticing Lola tracking us in close up.
I swing my light to the wall on the right, revealing towering murals—masterpieces of Atlantis. Exotic scenes from unknown mythologies. New history!
The memorials of the Homeland. Herodotus told the truth. They were here!

"Holy smokes," I whisper. "Look at this." Majestic murals of celestial alignments, cosmic cycles... It's Stonehenge on steroids. "These people weren't just scientists or artists. They were ..."

"Dreamers," Andromeda finishes, gazing upward.

I follow the narrative depicted on the expansive panels—tales of creation and destruction, civilizations rising and falling, and a heroic legacy of diasporas, mass extinctions, and the will to endure. Then I see an unmistakable veil marking Earth's passage through cataclysm, tied to cosmic dynamics. Symbols for Leo and Aquarius at each end indicate the ages when Earth suffers a geomagnetic excursion event like a pendulum swinging eternally.

The veil symbology goes beyond the Ice Age, maybe back hundreds of thousands of years. They knew about the apocalyptic cycle—Plato's Great Year.

The murals show them finding refuge among primitive tribes after the disaster, sharing their architecture, language, laws, and science, just like the myths—Faust's civilization bringers.

I'm fascinated to recognize Göbekli Tepe's layout. It was their first attempt to reboot civilization at the dawn of the Holocene, right after the last reset.

I stare in awe. Every myth ever told is here, in its pure form. The puzzle pieces I've chased my whole life suddenly fit. This is humanity's source code, the root of all stories. Our mother history, in high resolution, filling gaps eroded by time.

This is who we are. We've had amnesia, all these years.

And there's so much more.

Andromeda and I step into an alcove filled with metal plates engraved with writings meant to stand the test of time. "These aren't just records of Atlantis," I murmur. "They've preserved histories of tens—no, *hundreds* of thousands of years of prior civilizations."

Across the way, Cassian is running his fingers over star charts etched into granite slabs. "I think this is climate data," he calls out. "Ancient beyond belief. My geology buddies at Caltech are gonna flip. It confirms the cycle. They recorded everything."

A shelf grabs my attention. I gingerly lift a parchment, fragile and paper-thin. I start to unroll it, then think better of it. *Breathe, Tony.* It's global migration data—maps—with continents oriented to a *different* north! Look at these landmasses above water in Southeast Asia that rewrite everything we thought about human origins.

Andromeda leans over a broad tablet, squinting at an unfamiliar script. "I don't know this language," she says.

"Nobody knows that language," I reply, scanning for patterns. Bits of Proto-Indo-European, archaic Egyptian, Proto-Chinese, and even rongorongo symbols from Polynesia. It's the mother tongue that birthed them all.

We wander into a high-vaulted room filled with exotic weaponry. Damn, this is one hell of a cool armory. Andromeda moves like a dancer among the artifacts, stopping at a slender, tri-bladed dagger mounted on the wall. It resembles a trident with a long central blade, gleaming with a reddish sparkle.

Reddish metals ... Wait, that rings a bell. Could it be?

I lift the dagger. *It is!* Orichalcum—the mythical alloy Plato described. Second only to gold. He said the high walls of the citadel in Atlantis flashed with the red light of orichalcum.

Andromeda takes it, fingers caressing the smooth hilt fashioned from stones in the colors of Atlantis: white, black, and red, like the flag of Egypt. She grins mischievously and slips it into her wildflower pouch.

I frown. "Hey, no looting."

"Just this one." She bites her lip, nose wrinkling playfully.

Another opening leads to a shadowy chamber filled with storage units cataloged scientifically. Is this a seed bank? An ark? The Labyrinth is a prepper's bunker. I imagine Atlanteans desperately saving what they could before the cataclysm. Could unknown species be preserved down here?

"Hang on," Andromeda says, realization dawning. "That's why governments built the Svalbard Arctic seed bank. They're making new Halls of Records."

Interesting. *Are Veil Society the good guys?*

No. Not after what I've seen. Maybe long ago.

It's an intriguing thought. According to Cassian's pole flip and crustal shift projections, Svalbard—the northernmost settlement—will be near the equator by mid-century.

I force it aside and hurry back. Best not to get lost in a mammoth hall of records. There'll be time to explore later.

Andromeda is gawking at something. "Check this out," she says, pointing to engraved brass pages. "These look like blueprints for urban development." She gestures to a city layout. Instead of our familiar grid system, it shows hexagonal city blocks with three-way intersections.

"That's so efficient it makes me angry," Cassian says.

Lola tracks in on Andromeda and her discovery, documenting everything.

"Biophilic designs from nature," Andromeda says.

"How so?" I ask.

"Hexagons." She smiles, capturing a clip with her satphone. "They sure were buzzy bees!"

Groans all around.

"And there goes my Oscar," Lola sighs.

On a shelf, something resembling a primitive photograph—etched on silver, like a Victorian daguerreotype—catches my eye. It shows seven Atlantean heroes. The Seven Sages from myth! Three of them are women.

They had photographic technology! The image is so clear, like it was taken yesterday.

Their clothing is similar to ours, in an ancient-future way. They're just regular folks, smiling, good-natured, like they've returned from a National Geographic expedition. Not mythical gods, just people like us, fighting to save their world from oblivion in the wake of the unimaginable.

They look like characters from a post-apocalyptic movie.

Noah. Quetzalcoatl. Hermes.

Faust's haunting words echo: *"They tried to reboot civilization—they failed."* And humanity plunged into twelve thousand years of darkness.

We're here now, at last.

At the dawning of Aquarius, at the turning of the great arc. Are we ready for this revelation? We have a chance to break the cycle, to save ourselves. Time is short, but we can warn people. We can prepare.

"Holy ... guys!" Cassian's voice cracks like a teenager's. "You've gotta see this!"

We rush over. Oh boy, he found the jackpot.

103

CASSIAN IS FIXATED on an enormous stone slab—more like a wall—angled up and away and smooth as glass. Intricate carvings cover it, reminding me of the symbols on the *Voyager* spacecraft's Golden Record—universal symbology to communicate across time.
In the center is a monumental triangle outline.
Well, look at that.
It's a schematic of the Great Pyramid.
Cassian pushes up his glasses and swallows hard. He steps forward like the Cowardly Lion before the Great Oz. "It shows the pyramid as an analog to Earth's dimensions, just like Tesla and Newton obsessed over. Every chamber is a different ratio, matching Earth's harmonic frequencies. This thing couples with Earth not as a single unit, like Tesla's tower, but as an array of chambers, each tuned to a complementary harmonic up and down the spectrum. Russian dolls. It's a goddamn musical instrument."
He cranes up at the interior layouts. "Acoustics play a big role somehow."
"You mean sound?" Andromeda's face is scrunched up. "How?"
"No idea."
The schematic has chambers I've never seen—*hidden* chambers. The big Void is on there too. *I knew it!*
"Look." Cassian points to a large box etched inside the Void, bolts shooting from it. A grin spreads across his face. "See? That's

gotta be the capacitor. The pulse generator," he says. "It's Tesla!" He's about to weep with joy.

"A global grid." Andromeda points to a network of pyramids at the bottom.

"Is that a tuning fork?" I ask.

Beside the capacitor symbol, a tuning fork is carved inside the Void. A memory strikes. "There was a tuning fork—"

"In Tesla's hotel room," Andromeda says. "Tuned to F sharp, at 369 hertz. With a steel ball."

"Oh, for crying out loud!" Cassian says, exasperated. "And you never told me this?"

Andromeda's expression hardens. "Must've slipped my mind when we were trying not to fall off the New Yorker Hotel."

"Tesla called Earth a steel ball," Cassian says. "It's conductive like one. F sharp is Earth's native frequency. Several octaves lower than we can hear, but the background hum—the Schumann resonance—is an F sharp chord. Tesla measured it in Colorado Springs when lightning rang the crust like a bell."

F sharp. The foundational note of our world.

Cassian is amused. "Anyone with a Mac knows F sharp. Steve Jobs was so mystified by it that he made it chime every time a Mac boots up."

He suddenly grabs Andromeda's shoulders, eyes blazing. "The *shape* is the key! The pyramid is a scalar wave funnel!"

Andromeda shoots me a concerned look.

"I know why Tesla's notebook fixated on scalar physics!" Cassian declares. "The Great Pyramid is wildly coherent—its geometry gathers and organizes electromagnetic energy, converting it to scalar waves. Everything converges at the top, forming a vortex in the aether, the way atoms are spun up. It's the interface point."

Understanding dawns on Andromeda's face. "The fingertip of God," she whispers. "The top of the pyramid is the gateway."

The shape *is the key?* Platonic forms swirl in my mind. Plato's tetrahedron—a pyramid—is sacred geometry. It incorporates pi and the golden ratio. Are Plato's forms connected to the fabric of spacetime?

Damn. Atlantis was way cooler than us.

I remember Faust's rope trick at Machu Picchu, showing how

civilizations might've risen and fallen for ages. Could this technology predate even Atlantis, back to earlier people, some golden age of explosive innovation? I shiver. It's a hell of a thought.

"Oh man," I say. "Not many people know this, but the pyramid has eight sides."

They stare at me like I'm mental.

I clarify, "Each face is slightly angled in." I make a V with my hands. It's mind-blowing engineering on an already complex structure. Egyptologists can't figure out why they did it.

"You're serious right now, Koviak?" Cassian says. "Don't toy with my fragile heart."

"Aerial photos show it clearly. Eight sides."

I watch Cassian's gears turn. He's pacing before the slab, palm pressed to his forehead. "Scalar waveguides! That's what that is. Parabolic faces collect energy like a dish."

He turns to me. "You said there's a huge unopened void, right?"

"The Void," I confirm. "Scans show an unopened chamber high up in the pyramid. It's depicted here on this slab."

He strokes his chin like Archimedes. "Huh."

"Hold the phone," Andromeda says, making a nuclear explosion at her temples, voice raspy and urgent. "The Emerald Tablet isn't describing an electrical circuit of Earth, Cassian. It's scalar waves moving through the aether."

Cassian narrows his eyes. "Go on."

She holds out her hand to me. "Let me see Plato's manuscript."

Sure, let's just casually wave around Plato's *lost freaking Atlantis trilogy* like it's a flyer for poetry night at the coffee shop. I sigh and remove the crinkled masterpiece from 348 BC. It's like carrying the Mona Lisa in my pocket.

She reads the translation of the Emerald Tablet:

As above, so below
To do the miracle
The Sun is its father
The Earth is its nurse
All things are born by its adaptation
Its power is perfect if it is converted into Earth
It ascends from Earth to Heaven,

Then descends again to Earth
And receives the power
Thus, you will have the brightness of the whole world
And all darkness will flee from you
Its force is above all force
And penetrates every solid thing

There's a hippie majesty on her face. "The Emerald Tablet says this force 'ascends to heaven.' It's not the ionosphere, Cassian. It's the aether—*literal* heaven—the crystalline lattice of the fifth dimension," she says, excitement building. "'As above, so below' describes the interface where aetheric energy becomes matter in our spacetime. The pyramid taps that same alchemy."

Cassian looks dazed. "You sublime, moonlit flower child." He grabs the page and finds the line about receiving power. "Receives the power ... Receives the power," he mumbles, lost in thought. "The pyramid doesn't *generate* power; it taps the ultimate power: zero-point energy from the quantum vacuum. Like a bridge between worlds."

He's dumbfounded. "Just send our Nobels to prison block B, please."

"You should totally get the Nobel," Andromeda says, winking. "I'd vote for you."

Cassian turns to me. "Tesla talked about this in 1891 at Columbia, your old stomping ground. He said, 'Nature has stored up in the universe infinite energy. The eternal recipient and transmitter of this infinite energy is the aether ...'"

"Prophetic," Andromeda says quietly.

My brow wrinkles. "How does the pyramid tap the aether?"

Cassian has a rogue's grin. "Zero-point energy is energy in a quantum system at absolute zero. Space isn't empty. Theoretically, we can harness this endless space energy. The aether, or 'quantum vacuum,' is the fabric of energy, matter, and spacetime itself."

He leans against the Atlantean slab. "Conventional generators mechanically force a dipole imbalance in a capacitor. But the aetheric model is superior. It keeps the dipole imbalance open perpetually, like a faucet that never stops running, drawing energy from the quantum vacuum."

My eyes glaze over, but *hey*, if this helps him work it out.

He continues, "According to Tesla's notebook, this is achieved with exotic vacuum objects—like ball lightning—plasma structures stabilized by magnetic fields. They bridge with the aether to maintain a continuous energy flow. Once set in motion, this system could pull energy endlessly ... a perpetual source with no mechanical input."

I'm lost. My head throbs. "That's too much for my humanities degree brain, buddy."

"Okay." He searches for a simpler way. "Imagine using an old-timey hand pump to get water from a well. You stop pumping, the water stops. That's your standard generator. Now imagine tapping a natural spring. Water gushes continuously, *no pumping*. That's zero-point energy. You just need to set the flow in motion."

"An energy wellspring." Andromeda is nodding. "Where do I sign up?"

I have to remind myself this is the same Emerald Tablet Isaac Newton spent much of his life trying to decipher.

One line stands out. "'Its force is *above* all force.' In this context, 'above' means higher-dimensional space. Hermes writes that this force 'penetrates every solid thing' because aether flows through everything—the literal *Star Wars* Force. Plato's forms are the language of the aether. Tesla spoke that language."

"Its power is perfect if it's *converted into Earth*," Andromeda says, sounding like a fortune-teller. She laughs—one sharp bark—then clamps a hand over her mouth. When she lowers it, her face is blank except for the supernova detonating behind her eyes. Her voice drops to a low, hoarse rasp. "Cassian ... it's not talking about sending electricity through the planet. It's talking about converting frequencies of aether into solid elements."

She drifts, as if on a cosmic journey, still unpacking her epiphany. "'All things are born by its *adaptation*,'" she whispers. "Because all physical reality in our lower spacetime is born by adapting eternal energy into new forms over the phase horizon."

Cassian looks like he's glimpsed some exotic future. "I finally understand Tesla. Reality is waveform energy that can be manipulated via specific geometries. We can write and erase local base code. With advanced understanding, you could change matter. Real *Matrix* spoon stuff."

Andromeda shimmers. "Real alchemy."

Plato was right. His fundamental geometric forms are *the key to creation.*

So that's why the Egyptians depicted the cosmic ocean as wavy lines. It's not transmissions. It's the waveforms.

Cassian returns to the slab. "That leaves one big riddle."

"What riddle?" she asks.

"How did they turn the damn thing on?"

Victoria's distant shouts, shrill and panicked, echo through the Hall of Records. My pulse quickens. "Everyone back! Now!" She's screaming. The dread in her voice makes my legs tremble as we sprint back.

At the prism door, Victoria is barking orders. One agent radios the surface. Percy wears Medusa's horn-rimmed glasses, punching up our return route. His snaky filament drones shoot into the darkness with techno-warbles, verifying the way back.

"Have we got sufficient documentation?" Victoria asks, watching Wynn and Lola capture wide shots.

Wynn just stares, a decadent smile spreading.

"Oh, darling," Lola coos. "Have we got it."

"What's going on?" I ask, a knot forming in my gut.

Victoria yells into her radio. "Stand by for extraction. Get ready to roll out." Her eyes flick to me, cold and resolute.

"Metatron is on his way."

104

DUNES RISE and fall like golden waves along the highway as our MI6 convoy barrels north to Cairo. I stare out the window, watching the green Nile snake back into view. The Hall of Records haunts my thoughts. What we saw down there—it consumes me. I just want to go back, but that's not an option.

We're racing to reach the extraction point before Targeting Division intercepts us. It's going to be close.

Our ranks have swelled with fresh reinforcements. Victoria Bennet pulled every MI6 asset in Egypt, and a supply plane dropped off a military escort. Our caravan is like an armada rolling through the desert on a *Mad Max* road run.

A British invasion force landed at Alexandria, but they're too far to help. We're on our own.

Beside me, Andromeda fiddles with her moonstone necklace like she's trying to conjure good vibes. The mood is grim, but I can't wipe the perma-grin off my face. *We found it!* Safeguarding our discovery is now priority number one. The thought of it being memory-holed again is appalling.

Victoria left a team in Hawara to backfill the Labyrinth entrance. Their orders are to create as much misdirection as possible, then slip across the border and rendezvous in London. They are to hide the archaeological find at all costs.

I lean forward. "Victoria, if looters find it—"

"Jumper's blowing the entrance to smithereens," she replies calmly. "It'll take months to dig back down."

I relax—a little.

Victoria sits in the passenger seat behind designer sunglasses, calm as a summer's morning. I see why she's the Lady Protector.

In the back, Wynn Jones is hunched over his laptop, transferring footage from the Labyrinth.

"Keep it safe," I say.

"Making backups now." He holds up a fistful of rugged SD cards.

"How is it, Wynn?" Victoria asks.

"First video is live on socials across all royal channels. Views are past sixty million. Comments and shares are breaking the Internet. Biggest site in the States just deplatformed it. Circumventing now."

My pulse quickens. This is history's most significant moment, the unveiling of our true past. Before posting Wynn and Lola's footage, the king himself went live, prepping the masses. The announcement was a global sensation. Controlled media tried a blackout, but the internet is too widespread. Lola says everyone is waiting for the Labyrinth videos to drop. MI6 reports Manchester, Bristol, and other cities have come to a standstill—but it's not just the UK.

I think of my students and colleagues. I hope they're seeing this.

But something else is brewing. Something alarming.

London is reporting widespread revolts across Europe and America. Veil Society has issued some kind of draconian measures. No other details, but unrest is spreading. We might be in for a rocky road ahead. Interesting times indeed. *Is this World War Three?*

We have a more pressing problem: getting out of Egypt alive.

London's war rooms are feeding us satellite surveillance in real time. The UN sniffed out our location and called up Egyptian ground forces from the south, cutting off escape routes. We have to punch through Cairo.

"What's Metatron's position?" Victoria asks softly.

Lord Mark squints at the bleached landscape over the steering wheel. "Four kliks."

"Too close. We're not gonna make it." Victoria says. "That's it. I'm calling in air support."

Lord Mark shouts from the driver's seat. "Any combat experience?"

"Does dodging arguments with my ex count?" Cassian says, attempting to lighten the mood.

"This isn't a joke." Lord Mark scans the horizon. "Listen carefully. This will get ugly. Keep your heads down and stay on the floor. Do not leave the vehicle under *any* circumstance. Copy?"

Silence. I lock eyes with Lola. Her bangs sweep over her brow; dread is written all over her face.

"Can't we avoid a confrontation?" Andromeda wrings her hands. "Make an end run?"

"Negative." Victoria's texting London. Her voice is clear and calming, like the pure tone of a bell. "It's all desert out here, love. Egyptian forces are closing in from the south and east. CIA's tracking us from space. Our Osprey had to bug out—UN fighters inbound. No one's coming to save us. We've got to deal with these targeting nutters, or we'll never get out."

"Combat box-breathe," Lord Mark commands. "Inhale for four seconds, hold four, exhale four, hold four. Start now. Keeps your mind sharp."

Andromeda closes her eyes and obeys. We all do. She's clutching the orichalcum trident dagger.

Minutes later, white dots appear on the horizon—Targeting Division.

Lord Mark's voice cracks like a whip over the comms. "Listen up, ya pricks. They're in standard UN peacekeeping patrol vehicles. *Twats.* We'll establish defensive positions and take them out. We've got the numbers."

Our cruiser swerves to a stop with the rest of the convoy, creating a roadblock thirty yards from Targeting Division. "Babysittin' you bastards has been my greatest honor," Lord Mark says. "Make 'em pay for this, lads."

Cassian drums his fingers on the loaded SMG in his lap. The cabin fills with the smell of gun oil as everyone racks in rounds. Targeting Division forms a blockade opposite us.

I fixate on the weapons. Andromeda is box-breathing harder, her serene, freckled face looking like a woodland druid.

Lord Mark turns to her. "Did you receive firearm training at Langley?"

Her eyes remain closed. "Yes." She stows the Ice Age weapon in her pouch and tucks the gemstone into her blouse.

"Take up an overwatch position from here. Aim for noggins." He hands Andromeda a bolt-action sniper rifle with a wink. "Try not to hit us."

105

Traffic grinds to a halt, turning the highway into a parking lot. Egyptian motorists lift from their windows to see if there's been an accident.

Cassian is studying the enemy's UN cruisers. His legs bounce, eyes darting. Is he having a panic attack? If so, it's bad timing.

"What is it?" I ask.

"Those are just regular UN peacekeeping trucks, right?"

"Affirmative," Victoria confirms.

"I have a Caltech-y idea," he blurts. "Victoria, I need your satellite laptop—right now!"

Without taking her eyes off the terrifying blockade, Victoria hands it back. Targeting Division pours out like agile locusts. My God, they're charging us. She holds the phone to her ear; her breath ragged over the opening gunfire. "London, we need that air support. Talk to me. Over." There's only static.

Cassian's fingers are mauling the laptop. I recognize now when the Dahmers are in abject insanity mode. Man, I hope he's got another Venice up his sleeve.

Lord Mark unbuttons his three-piece suit with casual ease, slings a Benelli semiauto shotgun over his back, and yanks two tactical pistols from his hips.

"No AR?" Andromeda asks.

"I prefer my girls," he says, racking chambers with a satisfying snap. "Fast as a Merseyside lass."

The first shots pepper our armored vehicle with metallic pings. Metatron's agents move like a pack of wolves in unison.

Lord Mark's voice blares over the comms. "Steady, lads ... Hold!"

"SURRENDER," an unnatural voice booms from our speakers. Targeting Division has somehow hijacked our stereo. *"Surrender, and we will spare your lives."*

Victoria lunges for the hands-free button. A chime indicates the console is listening for speech. She leans to the mic in the ceiling. "I always thought we'd clash with the best one day. But you're not the best, are you, Metatron? You're just a sad little man." She fires a bullet into the stereo. Sparks fly.

Andromeda is in a Zen state, eyes still closed, lips speaking a silent affirmation, fingers clutching her rifle.

A targeting agent in aviators—who wears sunglasses in a gunfight?—is almost at our door. He swaps a spent mag and lunges to fire.

"Victory!" Lord Mark kicks open his door, disarms the young agent, and shoots him through the chin with his own gun. He crouches, twin pistols barking death in the harsh sunlight. With a battle cry, MI6 charges. Enemy ranks jerk as body armor absorbs hits, but they keep coming.

Behind them, Metatron watches like a gothic archangel, desert wind sweeping his black hair.

"I'm not in range of their networks!" Cassian yells. "Get us closer!"

"*Closer?*" Victoria ducks as shots spiderweb the bulletproof glass.

"Yeah," Cassian hollers. "To their trucks!"

"Are you out of your goddamn mind?"

"Just *do it*!"

She chuffs, then starts the engine, easing us forward into the hail of bullets. She yells into the comms, "We're getting Cassian in range. Cover us!"

Lord Mark looks back in disbelief, then unleashes fury. His movements are brutal—a knee to a solar plexus here, a bullet to a temple there—each duck and roll executed with lethal precision.

He's landing headshots from twenty yards, midroll, shell casings cascading.

Agents are engaged in hand-to-hand combat everywhere. It's mayhem.

Two targeting agents rush Lord Mark, neural chirps blaring. He pivots, pistol-whips one in the face, and pops two rounds into his chest. The other approaches from behind. Lord Mark drops, sweeps his legs, and drills a round through his skull from the hip before he hits the ground.

Andromeda's still meditating, cradling her rifle. "Agent Dey," Victoria yells. "You planning to join this fight?"

The eyes open with unholy resolve. That face means business.

"The CIA gun range was my therapy," she says, stepping outside.

She posts up behind her door, creeping along as we roll forward, one eye shut, squeezing off ace headshots like it's 1917.

The enemy swarms. Their coordination is surreal, like some AI deity is choreographing. The British have greater numbers, but they're being rapidly slaughtered by the inhuman fighting skills of Targeting Division.

I unload bursts of SMG spitfire whenever a targeting agent gets too close. I don't dare aim into our guys. My hands shake, but hey, I'm not wetting myself—yet. Small victories.

Wynn and Lola crouch behind a cruiser with a death wish, cameras swinging as bullets fly around them. Are they nuts?

Return fire pelts our armor, shattering windows. We cower as Andromeda dives into a pool of glass chips on the seat. The gunfire is deafening.

On the periphery, targeting agents overpower a young British commando. They don't kill him. They pin him down and drive a silver crescent onto his scalp. He screams, then goes limp. What did I just witness? I watch him for a long while, but he's motionless.

The British fight with grit and start gaining the upper hand. Lord Mark slices through, spinning, diving, rolling, unleashing holy hell.

"Cassian!" Victoria inches us closer, her voice raw.

"I'm in range!" Cassian is abusing the poor laptop and mumbling technical jargon: WPA2, CAN bus, ECU, corrupted firmware, sysconfig wipe. Sounds intense. With a smirk, he says, "One enemy vehicle down!"

"Down?" I echo, confused, glancing back at the lifeless commando with the device hugging his scalp.

"I hacked their computer modules. Disabling their trucks remotely."

"*Seriously?*" Victoria is stunned. "Metatron can override whatever you've done."

Cassian grins wickedly. "I lobotomized their ECUs, babe. So we can escape. Trust me, they're bricked."

Damn, remind me never to get on Cassian's naughty list.

I look over again at the downed British commando, disturbed by what I saw done to him. He's still lifeless—no, wait … he's rising, mouth agape, eyes rolling back, face hollow and vacant, and now—I kid you not—he's just standing there staring at the sky, catatonic. Like he's linking with something above. It's the most nightmarish thing I've ever seen.

Andromeda told me their biotech is decades ahead. My blood runs cold. Is this how *Terminator* begins?

The air around us sizzles. A beam of concentrated light tears into a British truck, which explodes into flames. Bodies eject like rag dolls.

"No," Victoria whispers.

"Directed energy weapon!" someone is screaming over comms. "They've got a bloody railgun!"

I peek out. A sleek barrel mounted on a UN vehicle glows red hot.

"Mark, we've got to take that out," Victoria says.

Seconds later, Metatron raises his arm. Another blue flash engulfs the battlefield, and a British army truck erupts in fire. I shield my eyes, feeling the heat even from here. I'm sick thinking of the men in those trucks.

All right, you coward. Get up.

I grab a pistol, exhale twice, then dash to Andromeda's position. Teeth gritted, I aim at the enemy near the cannon, squeezing off rounds that only dink the truck. I hit a targeting agent in the leg; he dives for cover.

Overhead, the sky erupts in a screeching roar. A UN fighter jet screams past with a British plane in hot pursuit. Machine-gun fire sprays from the UK jet in orange streaks. There's an honest-to-God dogfight above us.

The UN jet rolls, trying to shake the British pilot. A missile fires, and the UN jet explodes in a fireball. The British plane banks hard through the debris.

"Yes!" Victoria cries out.

We stop firing when Lord Mark, like violent poetry, vaults atop the weaponized UN truck, Benelli in hand, blasting away at the agents operating the railgun. Heavy shotgun thumps echo as bodies are flung back. He disables the cannon, then reenters the fray with fresh mags.

Lifeless bodies litter the highway. Metatron fires into Lord Mark's chest armor with sickening *thunks*. He stumbles back, gasping like he's been hit by a freight train. For a split second, he looks like he's going down.

He returns fire, and Metatron executes an unnatural lateral slide like some phantom. What the hell is that guy? A bullet rips his shoulder sleeve. Blood trickles, and he glares at the MI6 commander.

Cassian huffs. "I can't reach the networks of the last two UN trucks."

"That's as close as you're going to get," Victoria hisses, then yells a strike command into her radio.

Moments later, a British pilot is on comms. "Target acquired."

A deafening engine streaks overhead. I look up just in time to see missiles raining down. The entire fleet of UN vehicles explodes into twisted metal. Metatron and his agents leap for cover amid smoldering wrecks. Black smoke fills the air.

Cheers erupt from our guys. Lord Mark raises a fist. Enemy vehicles are disabled. Targeting Division is stranded.

"Yeah, that's easier," Cassian admits with a sigh.

"Return to vehicles! *Now!*" Victoria barks over comms.

We peel out, fishtailing past the enemy, knocking a bumper off. The other MI6 vehicles follow. Lord Mark is driving one.

The last thing I see is Metatron standing motionless on the road in his aviators, watching me through black smoke.

106

I'M STILL ALIVE. We're racing toward the extraction point with the other MI6 Land Cruisers. The air inside feels heavy. We lost good people, and I can't shake the guilt. Hawara was my idea. I glance at Andromeda, her face is chalk-white, eyes distant. She feels it, too.

I've never killed before.

So, this is ... well ... I'm trying not to think about what I just had to do. I know they were targeting agents. I know they represent the ultimate threat to humanity and all. But still—

Back in Hawara, Wynn and Lola uploaded the first Labyrinth video to the internet, unedited and raw. The British government amplified it across all channels. It went viral instantly. Before our clash with Targeting Division, Wynn had been shouting view counts like an excited auctioneer. The numbers became staggering.

Five more videos have gone up since. The cabal keeps taking them down, playing a global game of Whac-A-Mole, but they're spreading like wildfire. Mirrors are popping up worldwide. The cat's out of the bag. I'm almost giddy thinking about what this means.

I think we just won.

From the jump seat behind me, Wynn's excited chatter fades. Frustration laces his voice. "Hey, Vic," he says. "I can't access our videos anymore. My internet's offline."

Victoria flips open her satphone. "London, this is Watcher. We can't access the internet. Is the satellite down?" She listens, frowning at the static.

A broken reply crackles through. "We have no internet."

"Well, route us through a node of the Theta-12 Relay," she says, impatience edging her tone.

"There is no internet."

She pauses. "There is no internet?"

"There's no internet, ma'am. It's offline." More static.

"Our servers are offline, you say?"

"The internet is offline, ma'am."

She stares ahead. "The *internet* is offline?"

"Yes, ma'am, that's what I'm trying to tell you. It's down."

"Route us through our dark web relays, for God's sake."

"Ma'am, there is no web—dark or otherwise."

Victoria exhales sharply. "Damn your eyes, man. Route us through Elon Musk's Martian villa if you must. We need bloody internet—on the double."

"It doesn't *exist*, ma'am. The internet's gone." Static hisses. "They flipped the kill switch."

Her eyes widen. "What did you say?" She grips the radio tightly. "Gone? You did say the whole internet is—*gone*?"

He sighs heavily. "*Bloody time.* Yes, ma'am."

"Worldwide?"

"Universe-wide. No longer exists, ma'am—in *any* form."

The radio slips from Victoria's hand into her lap. Her voice drops to a whisper. "Those bastards actually did it."

"Did he just say they derezzed the net?" Cassian's jaw hangs open.

"You're joking," Lola grumbles from the backseat.

Silence settles over us. Only the noise of the highway. That's impossible. The reality sinks in. We can't get our message out. It's like it's 1989. What are we supposed to do, print basement newsletters and mail them like Reagan-era conspiracy theorists? Beg for a daytime slot on Donahue?

"All digital currency was just wiped out then," Victoria adds. "I'll leave it to you to imagine what that means."

"No!" Andromeda cries, fists clenched. "They can't do this!"

"Oh, honey," Victoria says softly. "They can."

107

Our convoy limps into a rundown gas station fifteen miles outside Cairo. The fuel gauge flashes orange—perfect timing. A group of Egyptian men squatting on the dusty curb halt their animated conversation. Their eyes widen as our bullet-riddled vehicles roll up to the pumps. Nearby, a pack of mischievous boys have hands full of penny candies.

The late afternoon sun sinks low. It's the spring equinox. Fitting backdrop for a botched Sphinx heist. Was that really just last night? Time's gone stretchy on me.

Veil Society just nuked the internet—and Operation RoboCop with it.

The pumps are slower than finals week. Cassian, Lola, and I dash into the minimart in search of caffeine. We grab tamarind-date flavored energy drinks to pep us up. Flies swarm everything. We crack open the sweet, cold drinks and stretch under the awning. Shell casings clatter from Cassian's jacket as he takes a swig.

Andromeda and Victoria are hunched over the truck's hood, plotting our next move. I clink cans with Cassian and take a sip.

To our left, the boys blow into half-empty Arabic Coke bottles, coaxing out musical notes. Each bottle plays a different pitch, depending on how full it is. I grin. Kids everywhere discover the same tricks. Soon, they've formed an impromptu Egyptian pipe organ.

Cassian suddenly staggers. *Whoa.* Is he about to keel over? I steady his arm.

"*Bottles ...*" he gasps, pointing at the kids. "*Ba ... Bahh ...*" His eyes are wild behind cosmic Dahmers.

Heatstroke? No, some physics epiphany has seized him. He grabs my lapels like I killed his dog.

He grits out, "*It can't be this elegant, Koviak.*"

108

Prague, Czech Republic
The Demiurge

PRAGUE SHIVERS under a cold March drizzle. The medieval buildings, once bursting with color, have been robbed of their whimsy beneath the gray sky. A handful of tourists shuffle along, unwilling to surrender their holidays to the miserable weather.

The Demiurge stands alone under a black umbrella on the ancient Charles Bridge, flanked by baroque statues. The Gothic Old Town Bridge Tower looms above, rain streaming down its face like tears. His trench coat flutters in the Bohemian wind as he takes a slow drag from his cigarette, the smoke disintegrating in the gale.

He contemplates the bridge's history. Built in 1357 and aligned with the stars and sun, symbols of alchemy and transformation. This is the heart of the world's alchemy capital. The bridge leads to Prague's Golden Lane, Alchemist's Alley, winding toward the castle. Suns, moons, aether—the path is littered with signs of transmutation. The lion, emblem of the Age of Leo, reigns supreme among them.

Illuminati? Freemasons? Templars? Hell, even the Lizard People... Over the years, many names have been invented as misdirection to protect the true order.

People are gullible.

From the bridge, he watches an American news broadcast on his satphone, the signal beamed from space. Across the US, citizens—already shaken by revelations of an ancient, advanced civilization and a hidden international power structure—cling to analog TV updates about the crippling internet outage.

Their bank cards no longer work.

Imperium Majus has been deployed—under the guise of maintaining order during the outage—and martial law has been declared in every nation under his control. Revolts have ignited even in the most tranquil corners of the world.

They should've revolted decades ago. Now, we're too powerful. Camps are already preparing to receive dissenters.

His lips move in sync with the newscaster. He knows the script. He wrote it.

The anchor's expression is grave. "The Egyptian labyrinth video has been confirmed as a hoax. Forensic experts at the FBI are calling it a 'deepfake.' Internet outages persist due to recent X-class solar flares. Service is expected to resume this weekend. The recent auroral displays are nothing to worry about. Looks like we have nothing to fear." She offers a reassuring smile.

A blatant lie.

The endgame has been triggered prematurely. The Demiurge knows the internet is gone forever, an essential step as humanity enters the pole shift. Before the internet, the regime controlled all messaging. News programs, sitcoms—everything aligned with the new order's goals. The internet was an unforeseen wrinkle. It became a powerful tool but also a liability.

The internet was always going to be taken out.

He flips to a rival network where the anchor parrots the same script verbatim. It won't be enough. The world is spiraling into chaos.

The viral labyrinth videos had streamed everywhere.

We blew up the internet, but it's too late.

The order has had two objectives since the Ice Age: to track the cosmic cycle and prevent humanity from knowing about the resets. It's the only way to sustain civilization.

If humanity knew, they'd destroy themselves in panic.

Now, everything could unravel for the first time in millennia—the preparations, the perfect future—gone. Mankind will revert to children with amnesia unless order is restored. *We are the saviors, the keepers.*

He scrolls through reports of mob violence. Even he is startled by the rapid escalation. People have flooded the streets and stormed government halls. The internet outage has only stoked their suspicions. A grave miscalculation. He scolds himself for not sticking to traditional misinformation tactics. America and Europe are openly revolting.

I've taken away their drug: their screens. The real conspiracy was always to hijack their attention.

Rain hammers his umbrella. He fumes at this disastrous turn.

The labyrinth video was catastrophic. Victoria Bennet's testimony was damning, especially in the British Isles. Worse, the new king *himself* went on air to confirm its truth. That royal traitor, exposing long-guarded secrets, he'll be first against the wall. The blackmail will be released, and it will ruin him.

Britain is lost. It must be quarantined. Even lesser nations openly defy Imperium Majus.

He switches to an Arabic channel airing stunning footage of the lost labyrinth, just like Chinese networks.

Bastards.

No—destroying the internet won't stop this. There's only one option left, a terrible one. The Demiurge feels a rush of adrenaline. It's too soon to play that card. But it must be done quickly.

He places the call.

The line connects to orbit. A voice answers.

"Initiate Starlight Protocol," the Demiurge says.

He takes a drag in the howling wind. The cigarette flares and his neurotic expression briefly flashes.

"Starlight Protocol?" The voice on the line repeats the words with extreme precision.

"Yes."

Silence ... only the soft clicks of the satellite relay and the faint exhale of smoke.

"Confirming—you want to engage *Starlight* Protocol?"

He gazes into the gloom. Soon, the entire world will look so bleak. He hadn't planned to do this until the 2030s or until Earth's weakening magnetic field did it for him. But everything has changed. The timeline has accelerated because of three insignificant nobodies.

The uprising must be crushed.

He flicks his cigarette into the river and watches it blow skyward.

"Yes. It's time," the Demiurge replies, hollow and unmoved. "Prepare the counternarrative for street teams. Invert everything."

"It shall be done."

109

Twenty miles south of Cairo, Egypt
Tony Koviak

THE SUN IS DROPPING FAST as we wait at a dusty gas station south of Cairo. Victoria slams the pump back with a metallic *thunk*. "Let's roll!" she commands.

"Uh-oh," Andromeda smirks. Cassian is ambling over, hands waving, grunting like a nerdy Moses descending from Sinai. He's figured out something big.

"You all right, buddy?" I ask.

"Is he having a stroke?" Victoria purrs.

Andromeda knits her brows at me, circling her finger near her temple.

"I know how Atlantis turned on the pyramid," Cassian blurts. "I know what the jump-start mechanism was: acoustics!"

Okay, not a medical emergency, just having a thunderstrike moment. Been there.

"Acoustics?" Andromeda folds her arms. "If we're talking Nirvana's Unplugged album? *Pfff*—overrated."

"*Electro*-acoustics," Cassian grits through his teeth.

She nods solemnly. "Ah, more of a Depeche Mode guy."

Victoria slides behind the wheel. "Looks like someone nicked a little Ice Age DMT from the labby," she says.

Cassian grins, wagging a finger at her, laughing in slow grunts, eyes like Willy Wonka's behind the glass.

We peel out of the gas station. Minutes later, we're crossing the Nile, racing toward the extraction point. Wynn and Lola are in a different MI6 cruiser.

"All right. Spill your beans," Andromeda demands.

Cassian blinks like he's just noticed us, and his voice steadies. "Everything we do is electromechanical. We rely on crude explosions and mechanical force, right?"

He mimes an explosion with his hands. "Big boom—car move."

His eyes gleam. "But Atlantis, they had a more elegant solution. Imagine harnessing the very fabric of the universe. A power source drawn from Earth's resonance, vibrations that shape reality itself. The music of the spheres, man! Tesla and Newton got it—the force that manifests atoms from the quantum vacuum: energy, frequency, vibration!"

He exhales sharply. "Tesla knew it all those years ago. The old dog cracked the code!"

Cassian's geeking out hard, recounting some lab demo from the University of Florida. They did this thing with cymatics, how sound frequencies create physical patterns. Researchers sprinkled sand on this metal plate, hit it with powerful tones, and boom, the sand snapped into geometric shapes. Changing the tone formed new shapes.

"They took it further," he continues. "By focusing sound energy, they suspended water droplets—sonic levitation. Manipulated them in three dimensions by adjusting amplitude and frequency. YouTube is full of videos showing this."

"Was full of videos," Andromeda corrects.

As we speed toward the extraction point, his voice drops. "The pyramid … I know how they turned it on."

110

Cassian thinks the Great Pyramid is activated with ... *sound*. That's a new one. Give me three-thousand-year-old pottery shards any day ... at least those don't have motherboards.

Victoria's GPS says we're nineteen minutes from the airfield on Cairo's east side. Fingers crossed that the UN isn't waiting with handcuffs.

Cassian's sonic theory baffles me. I'm trying to overlay my knowledge of the ancient world. Egyptology whirls in my brain, and a weird tale springs to mind.

"Hey, there was this odd report a while back," I say. "Caused quite a stir in Egyptology circles. Some Americans got lost in the Cairo Museum's basement and stumbled on a room with hundreds of tuning forks, some nine feet tall. Could those have been inside the pyramid, like the labyrinth schematic shows?"

"You believe that story?" Victoria glances at her sat-nav, eyebrows raised.

I shrug. "I don't know what's real anymore. But it's a weird thing to make up."

I recall one of my favorite Egyptian sculptures at the Met in New York: Isis and Wepwawet. Two tuning forks are carved between them, connected by wavy lines like they're resonating.

Cassian leans back. "It's the same physics behind Tesla's resonant global electricity grid. Music is resonance."

Victoria, who's been silent, nearly swerves off the road as she turns to us. "Have you been talking this way since New York?"

"Nonstop," Andromeda says, blowing a stray hair from her face.

Cassian deadpans, "You haven't lived until Faust tells you Merlin is a refugee from Atlantis."

Victoria huffs. "Right—I'm angry I missed all that."

"Oh, there'll probably be a book," I say.

Silence settles over us. The desert sweeps past the windows, and the sun is setting. I break the quiet with my curiosity: "But how can mere sound waves jump-start the pyramid?"

Cassian curls a finger at Andromeda. "Gimme notebook."

"*Please* ... give me the notebook," she chides.

"Please gimme notebook."

She hands it over. Cassian flips to a page with Tesla's quote: "If you want to find the secrets of the universe, think in terms of energy, frequency, and vibration."

"Remember when we explored the Great Pyramid?" he asks. "How those chambers throbbed with sound?"

"Nearly shook my teeth out," I say.

"I felt it vibrate through my whole body," Andromeda adds. "Remarkable energy."

He nods. "It's like an opera singer shattering a wineglass or a trampoline jumper sending another flying if their jumps align just right."

"Oh, I have PTSD from that," Andromeda groans. "My sisters nearly broke my neck."

Cassian's voice softens. "Think of two Tesla coils. The Void is the first jumper, sending the pyramid—the second jumper—rocking with induction. Earth is a third trampoline jumper, and that's when things get wild. Once the pyramid couples with the planet—boom."

Andromeda stares out the window. "So Tesla's three, six, nine diagram *is* the philosopher's stone—triangle and circle—pyramid coupled with Earth."

"Yep. The pyramid is just where the energy is focused. Earth is the muscle."

I picture the chambers. The Void remains sealed. An astonishing possibility presents itself: "Cassian, the Great Pyramid ... Do you think it still—"

"The Void," he says immediately. "It's in the Void, Tony. The pyramid still works."

"That thing's operational!" Andromeda says. "It's a crumbling ruin. There's nothing inside. How can it work without parts?"

"The best part is no parts," Cassian replies. "It's solid-state tech. The architecture *is* the technology, like a flute. No engines, just an instrument tuned to the planet. The jump-start is sonic vibration. Each chamber is a bigger domino. It triggers a piezoelectric effect in the quartz crystals. I'll bet it's all tuned to F sharp, Earth's frequency. It's all on the slab down in the Labyrinth."

Unreal. This is *my* Great Pyramid we're talking about—the one I grew up around. "But what generates the sound?" I ask.

"Some amplifier or generator in the big Void," Cassian says. "A mechanism to start the whole sequence. Bet my life on it."

"Maybe they used energy crystals," Andromeda jokes with a coy smile—at least, I think she's joking.

"Now you're diving into Sumerian fairy tales," I say. "Ninurta, the Mesopotamian god, entered the Great Pyramid and called it a 'radiant' place, similar to the Egyptian name, *the glorious light*. Inside, he found powerful crystals."

Cassian laughs, shaking his head. "I promise there are no renfaire stalls selling magic crystals up there. Sorry, sweetie."

"I was joking," Andromeda says. "Sheesh, it's not that deep."

"If Tesla was right—and Tesla was always right," Cassian says, "the Void is where the magic happens."

"What magic?" Andromeda asks, still puzzled.

I know what magic. "*Pyr-amid.*"

Cassian grins. "Fire in the middle."

111

WE'RE STILL REELING from the loss of the internet when Victoria drops the mother of all bombs.

It's only eight miles to the extraction point, a deserted airstrip east of Cairo. It's looking like we'll at least be able to escape Egypt.

"Metatron's heading for Alexandria," Victoria informs us. "Our invasion force has them spooked, but he won't be fooled for long. We're not out of the woods."

Minutes later, she starts acting ... off. She's texting furiously on her satphone, eyes wide, making strange little grunts and uttering bizarre exclamations. I've never seen her unhinged like this. *What now?*

"We've got a real problem," she says finally, voice cracking. Her eyes are glassy. Has the extraction been canceled? Did England sink into the sea? What?

"What is it?" Andromeda asks.

Victoria looks back at us, haunted. "I can't believe what I've just been told. All global power grids are now offline."

That takes a moment to process.

"*Offline?*" Cassian growls.

She nods, regaining a bit of composure. "They've severed all power grids. There's no electricity anywhere. Look outside."

I scan in all directions.

It occurs to me that it's been dark out there for some time. The Cairo sprawl is gone, like it's been covered in black paint.

Twenty minutes ago, it shimmered in the sunset. Now, only headlights and bonfires punctuate the haze. Dread pools in my gut.

"Can they do that?" Andromeda whispers.

"It's a grid. They could shut it down in minutes," Victoria says, staring at her satphone. "Reports say isolated grids are still up in Asia and Latin America, but most of the world—including Egypt—is back in the 1800s."

"Just to clarify," I say, jaw tightening. "We're talking about Cairo, right?"

"Professor, I'm talking about the whole world."

"Holy shit," Cassian says. "Why nuke global power grids?"

Andromeda's fingers fly to her lips. "Imagine the chaos."

"It's a known protocol—a panic button," Victoria explains, still texting via satellite. "Your operation worked better than we imagined. Millions of influencers amplified it. Our videos became the most-viewed in history—*in one hour*. Word spread fast.

"That's not all," she adds. "We secretly created an exposé video a year ago, revealing everything about Veil Society. The king livestreamed it himself, with commentary. They had to step in. But it was too widespread to contain. So they nuked the internet. Which only fueled more suspicion and outrage. Unrest has been intensifying all over the West."

Silence fills the cabin. My nerves are fried.

"So they *shut off* the power grids?" Cassian shakes his head. "We're three missed meals away from the collapse of civilization."

"Info triage," Andromeda says. "Diabolical."

"Starlight Protocol," Victoria says. "This was always their plan. Their endgame tactic. Out of the chaos, they'll form a one-world government with no resistance. It's how they plan to transition power before the pole shift."

She gazes ahead, eyes searching. "They're playing it too soon. It means they're afraid. They'll never let themselves lose power."

"How can society unravel this fast?" Andromeda asks.

"Permanent loss of the power grid is catastrophic," Victoria replies. "Civilization won't stand a chance. In the murk of their planned demolition of society, people will comply with whatever martial law they invoke just to feel a sense of security. They'll have full control. In the agency, there's a saying: when the collapse happens, it'll be overnight and global."

She's right. I'm a student of history. That's the thing about revolutions: they happen slowly, then all at once. Add multipliers like loss of internet and power, and we're talking hours. The Demiurge knows exactly what he's doing.

I've been chewing my lower lip without realizing it. We went from uncovering the world's most profound discovery to crushing defeat in a single day. Society is unraveling. There's a real chance we'll be killed, and everything will be memory-holed.

What hope is there now?

I stare out the window, numb. I just want to go home. Is that too much to ask?

"ETA for extraction: five minutes," an agent says. "Plane standing by."

"Get me to England." Victoria sighs, laying her braids back.

The pyramids loom westward, dark alien teeth against the blazing sunset. We're racing east, away from them. We speed past an English sign—the turn-off for the pyramids is one kilometer ahead. The Nile is a dark snake in the gathering gloom.

No power. No light. The end of the world as we know it. The Demiurge isn't planning to turn it back on. They're letting the world fall apart before the pole shift. Then, they'll usher in their utopia.

Hell on Earth starts tonight.

Cassian is watching me with an almost agitated expression—a Mona Lisa smile—eyes darting between me and the pyramids. It takes me a second, but suddenly, I know exactly what he's thinking. Oh, man. Talk about a *crazy* idea. My heart races. There's no way.

Andromeda is eyeing the pyramids, too. The moonstone twirls between her fingers. Her gaze meets mine, it's fatalistic and resolute. She knows what Cassian is thinking.

We're all thinking it.

My heart is about to leave my chest.

The Mothers of Darkness.

The Demiurge.

A new world.

Yeah, their utopia doesn't include any of us riffraff.

Or …

My words are a sonnet, as I quote from the Emerald Tablet. "'Thus, you will have the brightness of the whole world—'"

"'And all darkness will flee from you,'" Andromeda whispers, completing the line.

"Cassian?" My voice rises. "Do you think we can—"

"I thought you'd never ask. I thought you'd never ask."

"Turn! Turn—*here!*" I shout, reaching over Victoria and grabbing the wheel as headlights illuminate the turnoff for Giza.

She slams the brakes. The vehicle swerves off the highway. "What in blazes—"

"Exit!"

Our Land Cruiser screeches down the off-ramp and halts on the shoulder. The other vehicles nearly rear-end us. MI6 agents leap out, guns drawn.

"As *God* is my witness—" Victoria rages.

"Change of plans," I say firmly because, apparently, I've lost all sense of self-preservation. "We're going to Giza."

It's the first time I've seen the unflappable Lady Protector lose her shit altogether. She blinks at me, face malfunctioning with shock and confusion.

"No time to explain," I urge. "Floor it to the pyramids—*now!*"

"Mr. Koviak." Her knuckles whiten on the steering wheel. "Professor, I need a *damn* good reason to divert from our extraction."

Okay. Yeah, she needs an explanation.

"We can do it, Vic," Cassian says from behind me, his voice carrying that familiar mix of brilliance and insanity.

"Do I want to know what?" The edge in Victoria's voice could cut diamond.

I take a breath. *Focus.* "Look around. No power. Anywhere. Hospitals are running on generators that will fail in hours. The internet is … well, not *interneting.* Air traffic control is gone. To say nothing of the violence about to erupt." I lean forward, meeting her eyes in the rearview mirror. "They played this card because it's their ace. England won't survive now, you know that."

"There's nowhere to run," Andromeda says quietly. "Not this time."

Victoria is searching for words. "I have no idea what you are—"

Cassian cuts in. "I believe we can activate an ancient power grid. Pyramids worldwide are solid state tech; all resonant structures will respond globally."

Victoria's laugh is sharp, brittle. "An ancient *power grid*? That's your plan?"

"Believe in miracles, Vic," Cassian says.

"This is the *actual* kill shot," Andromeda says, voice rising. "Irrefutable proof of prehistoric tech. Instant global awakening."

Damn, that is the ultimate disclosure.

I watch Victoria's face in the mirror. The same calculations I've been running are playing across her features. Chance of success: maybe ten percent. Chance of survival if we do nothing: zero.

Her voice softens. "Can it really be done?"

I sigh. "Well, I didn't wake up today expecting to jump-start an ancient desert triangle, but when Dr. Wilder has a batshit-crazy idea, you go with it. Maybe we can hijack the Demiurge's endgame."

The silence stretches. Beyond our headlights, Cairo is a sea of darkness. Somewhere in that black, the oldest machines on Earth are waiting.

"Unfathomably reckless," Victoria whispers.

Lord Mark knocks on the window, peering in. "Is this a private mental breakdown, or can anyone join?"

The director of MI6 studies us wide-eyed, enthralled, awash with trembling and heavy breathing. Then, with a decisive vibe shift, she gulps a breath and speaks into her satphone:

"London, this is Watcher. Stand by for a new directive. Immediate tasking: mobilize *all* combat-ready units within a thousand-mile radius of Giza. Repeat: *Giza*. Prioritize rapid deployment, full-force engagement—repeat, full-force engagement. This is an all-or-nothing operation. Execute. Over."

She exhales in terror, her face bone-white as she lowers the phone. She grips the wheel and the Cruiser roars forward, veering west into the sunset.

I shoot Andromeda a grin, recalling her tattoo. "Per aspera, ad astra," I say. *Through hardship to the stars.*

112

What we're attempting is criminally reckless. It's funny how that's like our theme now. Insanity seems to be the realm of breakthroughs. We set fire to our comfort zone long ago. Might as well dance on the ashes.

Victoria scattered the remaining vehicles in all directions—decoys to buy us time.

She arranged for an Egyptian contact to meet us in Giza with the gear Cassian needs in exchange for evacuating his family to England. Cairo's a mess since the power went out.

Cassian gave her his wish list: PA loudspeakers, high-powered amps, signal processors, generators—the works. He plans to flood the Void with a wall of sound. Or maybe he secretly aspires to be an ancient DJ.

Victoria squints into the darkness. "I can't see a damn thing up ahead. Give me the GPS coordinates for the Great Pyramid," she says.

An agent pulls up military maps and types on the navigation screen. "Latitude 29.9792458 degrees north—"

"Wait, *what!*" Cassian spills his water bottle.

"The Great Pyramid's latitude," the agent repeats, annoyed.

Cassian leans back, Dahmers down his nose. He speaks like an apostle. "The speed of light is exactly 299,792,458 meters per second. Exactly. Same number."

I explode, "What the—"

"The speed of light is a limitation in *our* spacetime." Cassian rolls over me with excitement. "Latitude is degrees on a sphere—zero at the equator, ninety degrees at the poles—a universal language of geometry. The standardized *meter* is derived from a unit of measurement for the speed of light, a fundamental constant of nature. This location is a message: Here is where the rules of our spacetime end, and we break on through to the aetheric dimension."

"Man, I love you guys." Andromeda beams. "If we survive, can we never end this trip?"

WE MEET Lord Mark at the foot of the pyramid. An Egyptian audio engineer with greying hair is with him, lugging Cassian's requested gear.

I marvel at how they could do that, given the situation. Victoria reminds me that the full might of the United Kingdom is at our disposal. They'll move heaven and Earth to help us.

That's ... daunting.

Driving right up to the pyramid was easy; the plateau's deserted. It seems everyone fled after the blackout.

When a lone guard asked about the bullet holes that turned our Cruiser into Swiss cheese, Victoria flashed her badge and deadpanned, "Land pirates. Somalia." He nodded slowly, with huge eyes, and waved us in.

Cassian outlined his plan earlier. *Acoustics?* I'm still fuzzy on how we're going to activate a giant stone triangle. But hey, Tesla did wonders with a metal one. I have faith in Nikola Tesla, and Cassian knows his stuff.

"Have you any idea, Dr. Wilder," Victoria snaps, "how fabulously hard it is to find a sound engineer in Cairo—in the dark—with the world in shambles?" She thrusts a canvas bag at Cassian. "Inside, you'll find *most* of the silly little components you require."

Cassian frowns. "No PA speaker?"

Lord Mark adjusts his three-piece, looking sheepish. "Well, we managed—*this*."

The Egyptian man steps forward with a beat-up electric guitar and a portable, battery-powered amp shredded to ribbons. His accent is thick. "My son is garage band ... he is skater."

"You're joking." Cassian scowls. "Where's my scientific sound gear, Vic?" He throws up his hands. "You brought me an Arabic Fender knockoff?"

"It's a madhouse out there, lad," Lord Mark says, glancing at the flashing police lights in the city. "At least it's keeping the authorities busy."

Andromeda holds up the guitar, face reverent. "So, a Zeppelin guy?"

Cassian pushes up his glasses. "No, it was Nirvana all along."

"Ah. Angsty."

"Helps me focus."

Victoria turns to Andromeda. "Have you still got the satphone I gave you, love?"

She nods.

"Good. Document everything." She faces me. "How will you get in?"

I squint up at the vast geometry with its sealed chevron entrance. "Through the front door, of course."

"All right," Victoria says, handing me the ultrasonic drill. "Reza, my masonry expert, is running decoy to Alexandria. You'll have to drill yourselves. We'll be on comms, covering your rear."

She shares a tense glance with Lord Mark. "We have intel that Metatron is returning to Cairo. He'll find us long before our forces arrive. Whatever you March hares are going to do, you'd better do it fast."

113

It's dusk, and the first stars shine brighter without Cairo's usual light pollution, just like in classical times. A crescent moon rises over the amber sunset. Andromeda, Cassian, and I scramble up the massive stone blocks of the Great Pyramid.

We're climbing without lights, which makes footing treacherous. Can't draw attention. The winds have picked up. I'm lugging the portable high-frequency generator Cassian needs for his magic show—heavy bugger—like a supersized power bank.

Cassian grunts as he hauls himself up another gigantic block, hoisting the amp. "Wait, I almost forgot," he says. "There are *three* pyramids here. It's an array. Each one acts like a giant Tesla coil. If we get one going, the others will resonate sympathetically."

"Tuning forks," I say.

"Bingo."

I scramble up to him. "Your sonic theory reminds me of Plato. He talked about music representing order and balance—vibrating harmonics holding everything together. Inspired by Pythagoras and his 'music of the spheres.'"

Cassian's out of breath. "Ancient string theory. I dig it."

"Pythagoras studied here in Egypt. Like Jesus did as a youth." My fingertips grip the scratchy limestone, trying not to look down as dust blows into my eyes. "In his Atlantis trilogy, Plato says the Demiurge brings harmony from chaos with math and music. Using perfect ratios: octaves, fifths, fourths."

I shudder, thinking about the inverted connection to the actual Demiurge, a hidden hand who believes he's creating a new order from chaos. The literal Dark Side of the Force. A twisted subversion of Plato's philosophy.

Cassian slings the heavy equipment bag over a shoulder, grunting as he lifts the guitar amp. Whatever MI6 scrounged up weighs a ton.

Andromeda reaches for a foothold, guitar over her back like a hippie hitchhiker. "They changed instrument tuning to 440 hertz back in the '50s," she says. "It's harsher than the original 432 hertz. Some claim it was to make us angrier. There's a push to return to 432 tuning, considered by many to be the frequency of God."

"That's when rock and roll started," Cassian notes.

"Explains the '60s," I jest.

A chilling howl echoes from the darkening Cairo slums. Things are unraveling in the city. We need to hustle. The blacked-out view is disturbing from up here—just a sea of darkness with occasional pops of light.

And the screams.

"Reminds me of Kepler's planetary motion," Cassian says between breaths. "He called the orbits 'one continuous song.' Kepler was a weird dude. He lived in Prague under Rudolf the Second—the Alchemy King of Bohemia—right when all that secret alchemy was happening. Wild times."

Interesting. Tesla drew the solar system on his circuit diagram. The music of the spheres. My dad sketched the same thing on the photo in my wallet. Frequency and vibration. Is Plato describing Tesla's aetheric base code of creation? Can it really all be down to music?

Andromeda slips on debris behind us, nearly dying. She squeals, recovers, then says, "For centuries, they tried to work out what you discovered, Cass. The philosopher's stone. The energy secrets of Atlantis."

"What *we* discovered," he corrects.

I consider how music was tuned to 432 hertz. Four thirty-two … 432 … Why does that number feel so familiar?

Come on, brain—work!

Oh, hey, the Great Pyramid's ratio to Planet Earth is 1:43,200.

The number that encodes Earth's axial wobble—the zodiac arc—Plato's Great Year. I explained this to Frank at the Lyceum Theatre right before he was shot. Tesla had that ratio diagrammed on his map.

It all relates to the cataclysmic cycle. The CIA's Project Holocene. Veil Society. A sinking feeling hits me. The pole shift is coming. I can't worry about that now. We have a pyramid to crank.

That's a genuinely thrilling thought. Yeah, think positively. *We're doing this!*

"Let's see ...," Cassian is mumbling, reviewing Tesla's energy schematic like a student cramming for finals. "Subterranean chamber is the bedrock tap via the aquifer, just like Wardenclyffe. The Grand Gallery is a Helmholtz resonator with corbeled walls tuned for clarity at each harmonic. AKA, the Coke bottle. The King's Chamber is the ... is the ..."

He grinds his jaw, deep in thought. "With those dimensions, it's gotta be a standing wave chamber for amplitude—"

"We still good, Cassian?" Andromeda's unease spreads to my nerves like one of Tesla's tuning forks. Sometimes, emotions are like Tesla coils—they're contagious.

He nods tersely. "If I'm wrong, we'll just—"

"If you're wrong, we're not leaving Egypt alive, and the world falls into darkness," Andromeda says.

"Well, don't sugarcoat it."

Fires burn across the city, and distant mobs shout as night falls. More bloodcurdling screams drift up from far away.

Similar scenes will play out in Paris, Sydney, Boston, LA—all over the world. Cities and towns across America will soon descend into night, and people will die in darkness.

We gotta flip this switch.

"What are the chances this works?" I wonder.

"Afraid we might fail?" Cassian replies, struggling upward.

"I'm afraid we might succeed."

114

I study the limestone wall sealing the Great Pyramid's original entrance. Over the lintel is the enigmatic inscription in the language of Atlantis. A prism swivel door once stood here.

"Sedimentary limestone should be a cakewalk," Cassian says, examining the geology. I rev up the magic molecule scooper.

Andromeda sweeps her strawberry bangs out of her freckled face. "We're already wanted for driving over a pyramid and stealing Plato's rarest manuscript. May as well go for the hat trick."

"Atta girl," Cassian growls low, pleased with her audacity.

"The trifecta was the Sphinx," I correct. "We're on to quadfecta now."

I step up with the buzzing ultrasonic drill shaking my arm silly. Fifteen minutes later, we've got an ugly, gaping hole in the stone. Reza had more finesse. A dark passage yawns beyond.

"I knew it," I hiss, worming through the opening like a reverse birth. I can't believe Egyptologists haven't tried opening the literal front door.

Inside, I switch on my light. I'm crouched in a cramped, four-foot-square passage, like the Ascending Passage tourists use below us. Ten yards ahead, the tunnel bends sharply upward into darkness.

It's aimed directly at the Void anomaly.

Let's go!

My pulse races. I pause, savoring the moment. No one's entered this passage since the Ice Age. I'm instantly humbled. The scent of ancient stone and dust fills my nostrils. It's stuffy and humid. I exhale in the muffled stillness. There's probably nothing up here, *right?*

Who am I kidding? It's an unopened chamber the length of a Boeing 747!

I shimmy up the steep, polished slope, rising into darkness like a mechanic's crawl space. The pyramid's industrial nature—it's so obvious now—blows my mind.

Andromeda labors behind me, jackknifed over in the tight tunnel. "Looks like the passage on the Nostromo from *Alien*," she notes. "Maybe a xenomorph's gonna come flying out."

"Not the time for scary stories," I exhale through clenched teeth, staring into the horrendous black, my lizard brain believing she's right. Why am *I* going first? Great. I'm an alien snack.

I find a rhythm scooting up the weird angle, recalling Cassian's comparison of the Void's length to an NBA court. "Now would be a good time to warn us if there's anything sketchy up in this ancient basketball court, Cass."

"Should be safe enough," he says. "Remember that capacitor I mentioned? How it's the heartbeat of Tesla's design? The Void is exactly where he put it on his tower. The mother of all capacitors should be up here."

"Is that the box you tinkered with back at Wardenclyffe?" Andromeda arches an eyebrow. "The one that nearly fried us?"

"Exactly. Think of a capacitor as a supercharged battery. It sucks power from the pyramid and pulls electrons straight up from Earth's crust."

"How does it work?" I ask as we ascend.

"A capacitor has two metal plates separated by a gap," he explains. "Even tiny earbuds have them. Think positive and negative ends of a battery. In that gap, the stored energy zaps out.

"But unlike a battery, which releases power slowly, a capacitor discharges all its energy at once, like snapping a rubber band. Snap it repeatedly—that's Tesla's magnifying pulse transmitter. It pounds current into Earth, creating waves like a hand slapping water."

We scramble upward, trying to wrap our heads around it.

"The pyramid funnels electromagnetic and scalar waves to its peak, creating an 'aetheric stress zone'—a boundary between our spacetime and the aether," Cassian continues. "It triggers a self-sustaining loop that draws zero-point energy. Presto, free power."

I frown. "And you turn it on with—*sound?*"

"Yep," he affirms. "The pyramid uses acoustics to jump-start the process. Each chamber is a dimensional analog of Earth, nested like Russian dolls—oscillators within oscillators. Their dimensions are harmonics of Earth's frequency at ascending scales. It's a massive, multistage cha-cha creating an ungodly acoustic feedback loop."

"English, Wilder," Andromeda sighs.

Cassian winces at a fresh scratch, then looks amused. "Means it's designed to ring like hell's bells, lady. It's an opera cathedral."

I picture the five stacked lofts above the King's Chamber. Why did the builders smooth the bottoms of the granite beams but leave the tops rough? They were tuning them to F sharp! It's the body of a guitar. Every space needs to resonate with Earth's frequency.

My dad's last message takes on a new meaning. He'd said, "Can't go wrong with the music of the spheres, son." I recall his solar system drawing in my wallet. *The Planets* by Gustav Holst. Tesla's frequency and vibration. Plato's fundamental forms.

Andromeda drags herself through my debris waterfall, her long legs bent up like a bug's. She curses and shakes dust from her pixie hair.

Cassian presses his palms to the walls, lifting himself higher. "It's an acoustic snowball effect, stepping up the amplitude at each stage. The Void houses the sonic jump-start mechanism."

I don't love the idea of being inside a Tesla coil when it fires up. "Is it safe?"

He plants a knee, boot skidding on dust, breath whistling. "Probably best not to hang around when it gets to rippin'."

I halt and reposition. The end of the passage is in sight. We're perched high within the heart of the Great Pyramid. The cramped shaft opens into a black chamber.

"This one's for you, Dad," I whisper, dragging myself to the threshold. I cast my beam into the otherworldly Void.

HOLY MOTHER OF—

115

OKAY, the Void is officially surreal.

I'm an anthropologist, and I'm telling you—this shouldn't exist.

My flashlight barely cuts through the darkness, but what I can see is mind-blowing. The chamber is level, as tall as the Grand Gallery but wider. The walls are precision-cut rose granite flecked with quartz. And here's the kicker: they're wrapped in gold circuitry.

Yep. Gold circuitry.

Two-inch bands of shiny gold spiral around the room, separated by five inches of exposed granite. The effect is a psychedelic stripey look.

But that's not even the weirdest part.

Stretching back into the shadows is a forest of tall quartz crystals. Some stand eight feet high and are too thick to hug—not that I'd try. Interspersed among these crystal monoliths are gigantic metal tuning forks with U-shaped prongs jutting up like catapult arms. The metal has a reddish sheen.

Orichalcum. The mythical metal of Atlantis.

Right in front of me, a stunning crystal stands on a base. Gold cords wind up around it like vines.

"Magic crystals," I mutter, shaking my head.

Andromeda's smile could power the planet. Her freckles dance in the flashlight glow. "Told you so."

"Fine, I admit it. Crystals are officially badass."

She beams with glee.

Cassian strolls up, unfazed. "What? Am I the only one who owned a quartz watch as a kid?" He shines his light through the crystal, and prismatic colors scatter around us. His eyes radiate behind the Dahmers. "I just see piezoelectric inductive resonance energy transducers—with optional mini Tesla coil expansion packs."

We stare at him.

"Ancient batteries," he clarifies, nudging up his glasses. "Archaic Energizer Bunnies."

Andromeda's voice is a hoarse whisper. "You're telling me we're in a giant Casio?"

Cassian arches a brow. "Oh, I had one of those watches ... digital face with the calculator buttons. Made me feel like a little Avenger in grade school.

"You know"—Cassian's loving this—"Tesla said crystals have a life force ... like they're alive. I think he was referring to their structure. The aether itself could be similar."

I run my hand along the crystal's smooth surface. "These don't look natural. Almost like they were—"

"Grown," Cassian says. "Or cut to match a resonant frequency."

Andromeda cocks her head. "F sharp?"

"Or harmonics," he agrees. "Maybe a fifth, strengthening the sound, like adding rebar to concrete."

She closes her eyes, taking a deep breath. "The energy in here is really good," she says.

"Glad to hear it," I say. "Let's get to work."

Cassian digs into his bag and pulls out a handheld spectrum analyzer. "Let's see what kind of disco we've got in here."

He sets the device on the floor and starts clapping like a demented seal. Echoes reverberate around us. The acoustics are ... well, exquisite doesn't cover it. We watch as the meter spasms, then settles on F sharp.

Andromeda whistles, and the sound ricochets mercilessly.

Cassian scans the golden coils on the walls. "Coil windings. We're inside the primary Tesla coil."

"The first trampoline jumper," Andromeda notes.

"Faraday's law says that when this coil creates a magnetic field, it'll supercharge the voltage in the bigger secondary coil—the pyramid itself. It's a giant Wardenclyffe Tower!"

I consider the Void's size compared to the pyramid. A Tesla coil *within* a Tesla coil. Earth is the ultimate Tesla coil in the system, the third trampoline jumper launching us into the aether.

Wireless transmission of energy via the natural medium. Tesla would approve.

I circle one of the crystals, eyeing the golden ropes curling up around it. "These gold wraps form a double helix."

Andromeda steps closer. "Hey, that looks like … a caduceus."

Click.

"The symbol of Hermes!" I exclaim, adrenaline surging. "The caduceus isn't just some symbol, it's a *schematic!*"

The gold coils wrap up the crystal pillars like entwined serpents. At the top, two bulbs—like snake heads—face each other with a slight gap. I can see how this design morphed into the snake symbol over time. They do look kind of snaky.

"The Power of Hermes—*Hermes-Kratos,*" I recall, thinking of Plato's lost book title. The caduceus was more than a cool design; it was a blueprint for … whatever *this* thing is.

We weave through the crystal forest, dozens of them towering over us with their golden caducei wraps. Then I spot it.

"Guys, over here!"

I crouch down to a small rectangular vent cut neatly into the wall. Shining my light inside, I see it angles down to the King's Chamber.

Cassian peers in. "Is this the shaft from the King's Chamber?"

"Yes, so it must continue over here." I dash to the opposite wall, where a twin opening angles upward to an exit high on the pyramid's exterior. The star shaft bisects the Void! *Why?*

"Where does it open in the King's Chamber?" Cassian asks.

"I dunno—toward one end?"

"A quarter down the wall?"

I nod.

His face lights up. "Right where a standing wave hits its peak in a resonant cavity. This shaft acts like an old gramophone, amplifying the signal. The King's Chamber is the next stage—

world's first subwoofer! The ancient version of 'turn it up to eleven'."

"Why does the shaft extend outside?" I wonder.

"My guess?" Andromeda says. "It acts like the embouchure hole on a flute. Wind blows across the pyramid's face—like blowing over a bottle—and boosts the resonance."

I venture deeper into the crystal wood, feeling like I'm in an Ice Age fairy tale. I round a sparkling quartz tower and stop dead.

Set in the center of the Void is an oversized granite box, the color of chocolate, like the one in the King's Chamber, but bigger. The rim is chest-high.

And it's not empty.

I know what's inside it.

Not possible. Not possible. Not possible.

Andromeda steps up beside me, her voice barely audible. "Does that look like—"

"The Ark of the Covenant."

116

THE ARK of the Covenant on steroids. Here, *in the Void!* Because, of course, it is.

I baby-step toward the hulking installation, eyes wide with uneasy wonder. The dark granite box glitters with a million quartz flecks, like stars trapped in stone.

A solid gold rectangle sits inside—*the Ark!* No familiar symbols or mythologies here. It's minimalist, almost futuristic. Purely functional.

Two large gold wings stretch inward over the box, facing each other but not touching. They're not the cherubim wings from the paintings. These are plain, tapered, trapezoidal plates—like golden swords about to cross.

But ... this doesn't make any sense. Why would ...?

Cassian grins knowingly, tongue firmly in cheek, waiting for me to catch up. He reaches up to the brilliant metal, stroking it like a prized racehorse. The gold's luster hasn't faded after all these millennia.

I flail for a rational explanation. "Moses. Israelites. Exodus. Plagues. Most people know the Ark from *Indiana Jones*—by the way, *do not* open it."

Cassian withdraws his hand with a mortal grimace.

The granite box reminds me of the mysterious boxes in the Serapeum under Saqqara. The same gem-cut angle on the bevel—

the one I'd seen on the prism door to the Labyrinth—and, over in the Americas, the aesthetic of Atlantis.

"Lift me up!" Cassian says, grabbing the thick rim. Before I know it, he's stepping onto my laced palms. He hoists himself up and balances his butt on the corner of the granite. His face turns mystical. "My God, it's full of stars."

"Stop it." Andromeda laughs, swatting his leg. "Perfect meme, Cass."

I crane my neck. "What do you see?"

He gazes into the Ark, oversized lenses reflecting a golden universe. "There's no lid. It's filled with ... liquid mercury."

I sigh. "No more joking."

"I'm not joking."

He dips a fingertip and holds up a silvery digit. Sniffs it. Winces hard. Then, a low gurgle bubbles from his throat. He looks ill. He grabs his wrist, and his body begins convulsing, head whipping back in agony, veins protruding from his neck. He shrieks violently. *"The elixir of Thoth is upon me!"*

He hops down with a chuckle and wipes twelve-thousand-year-old mercury on his pants.

Andromeda and I just had twin aneurysms. She's clutching her blouse, chest heaving.

I'm dealing with infants—got it.

Cassian gloats. "Found the capacitor. The Tesla pulse generator. Just like the one atop Wardenclyffe Tower. These golden 'Ark wings' form a spark gap where pulses are released, powering up the Tesla coil we're standing in."

He gestures to the coiled circuitry on the walls. "The electromagnetic field then jumps via induction to the massive secondary Tesla coil formed by the winding blocks of the pyramid's core masonry. Then it boogies on down to the planet like dominoes."

Hang on.

The Ark of the Covenant is a Tesla capacitor?

Stick a fork in me.

"The Ark functions as both a capacitor *and* an oscillator," Cassian explains. "It generates high-frequency currents and emits electromagnetic waves. The oscillator bit is like a swing—small pushes eventually get the swing real high. Tesla claimed he could bring down the Empire State Building by starting with only five pounds of air. The pulsed waves radiate through the aether and can be tapped anywhere on Earth by matching the frequency and reversing the energy conversion. Free energy, baby."

"Oh, they'll find a way to slap a meter on it," Andromeda says.

"Mercury," Cassian mumbles. "Wasn't that another name for Hermes?"

"In Rome, yes," I reply.

"Rotating liquid mercury can generate magnetic fields as strong as *ten Tesla*. Electric current causes it to spin, creating a vortex. *Ten Tesla* is stronger than the Large Hadron Collider at CERN. Such force could produce exotic vacuum objects, like ball lightning." He gulps.

No idea what those are, but they sound … painful.

Andromeda is shaking her head in confusion. "So does this mean the empty box in the King's Chamber once held another, smaller Ark?"

"Wait." I stagger back, dots connecting. "Wow—oh *wow*."

I know the lore. Everything about the Ark of the Covenant is energetic. The stories are all electrical in nature.

"Moses was Egyptian elite," I say. "He would have known everything, including the truth about a legacy power source within the pyramid."

The Ark threw people back when they got too close. One guy tried to steady it and was electrocuted. They even had laws keeping it covered and far from camp. Was that a safety protocol?

Great. Now we're standing beside its big brother.

"In the wilderness," I continue, "the Israelites saw lightning shoot from the mercy seat—that's what they called the two wings. They carried it into battle. At Jericho, the Ark was brought forth, and when the priests blew their acoustic horns—making a great sound—the walls came down as if from an earthquake."

"Tesla's earthquake machine," Andromeda says. "Acoustic resonance?"

I'm thunderstruck. I'm buzzing now. "Moses demanded precise building dimensions for the Tabernacle that housed the Ark. Was he attempting to recreate the pyramid's architecture?"

I lower my voice. "But they couldn't control it. The Philistines captured the Ark, and it wreaked havoc. They shipped it back on a wagon, begging the Israelites to take it off their hands."

A shiver runs down my spine. What if we're meddling with something deadly? In the Book of Leviticus, Moses's grandsons burned incense near the Ark. Fire came out and consumed them. Those handling the Ark were even required to wear protective clothing.

"*The vestments!*" I exclaim. "The high priest of Israel wore a special breastplate over a protective tunic embedded with twelve *crystal* gemstones. Gold cords fastened it, like the caduceus wrappings in here. They had to wear them when approaching the Ark."

I look around at the towering crystals. Were they trying to replicate the functionality of this chamber? Is the tradition of placing crown jewels on royalty another echo of wielding Ice Age Tesla technology? Ambitious people LARPing a lost power?

"Huh," Cassian muses. "Tesla wrote an article in 1915 called 'The Wonder World to Be Created by Electricity.' He calls Moses a skillful electrician far ahead of his time and claims the Bible describes machines for generating electricity."

"Moses was an electrician?" Andromeda looks skeptical.

Good Lord.

"Think about it," I say. "He went up alone into the mountains of Sinai. The oldest legends say the children of Israel saw smoke and lightning on the mountain. What if Moses was attempting to restore the Ark? He saw a burning bush, and when he returned, his face shone."

Andromeda recoils. "You're telling me *Raiders* is a documentary?"

Cassian wrinkles his brow. "I don't know about faces melting off, but it'd be one hell of a show. There's a famous photo of Tesla sitting in a Tesla coil with lightning arcing around him."

"We saw that picture in his hotel room," Andromeda says, shaking her head. "Let me get this straight. The Hebrews stole an Atlantis capacitor from the King's Chamber and ran, and when they tried to operate it, it started taking people out?"

Cassian freezes mid-step, eyes on the Mercy Seat. "No—hold

up. This is an *asymmetrical* capacitor—like a lopsided seesaw in the world of electrical components. Capacitor plates are usually the same size," he continues. "One of these is bigger, see? It creates a mismatch. The electric field between them gets ... weird."

Can't say I like the sound of that. "Weird how?" I ask.

"Spooky weird." He studies the larger plate. "A broken symmetry in the local spacetime fabric. Some theorists think this imbalance acts as a gateway for zero-point energy, drawing from the aether to feed the system via the Casimir effect. The pairing is always off-balance, and energy keeps flowing in, trying to equalize. Except it never does, thanks to the aether constantly delivering more."

"An energy wellspring," Andromeda whispers. "The Ark is a gateway to heaven. The fifth-dimensional ocean of raw energy."

"Wait a minute." Cassian turns to the gold caduceus ropes winding up the crystals, solemn as a bishop. "These caduceus coils form a double helix, wound in *opposite* directions. Möbius topology. When you run current through them, their magnetic fields cancel out, creating scalar waves."

"Scalar waves are the aether ones, right?" Andromeda asks.

"Down here, they're longitudinal compression waves, like sound waves. But in the aether, they're ..." He trails off, then refocuses. "It forces counter-rotating supercurrents onto intersecting geodesics, creating topologically protected phase coherence. These caducei work *with* the Ark, tapping into the fabric of the universe. The snakey spark gaps ..."—he's out of breath—"generate a negative energy Casimir effect."

Cassian is in outer space. Andromeda and I can only stare, spellbound.

"See how they're placed around the chamber?" he continues. "Their scalar emissions form an interference lattice ... a 3D standing wave, a coherent scalar field. If it manages to create exotic vacuum objects ... *dear God*, we may be looking at an array of microwormhole throat stabilizers."

"No wonder Pharaoh pursued them," I say in a daze. "They nicked his symbol of power. This Void has been sealed since Atlantis. Not even the Egyptians knew this was up here."

I recall Andromeda's insight about Excalibur as a lost

technology myth. "We're about to pull the sword from the stone, the forgotten power locked in the megaliths. That's where the Arthur myth originates."

"Like Tesla's electric gods," Andromeda says. "Zeus, Thor, and Indra—wielders of Atlantean energy."

Cassian exhales. "Let's see if humanity is finally worthy to pull the sword."

117

"Giant piezoelectric crystals," Cassian says, eyes wide. "Didn't see that coming."

He's been staring at the crystals for five minutes, motionless.

"What do you mean?" Andromeda asks.

He runs a hand through his hair. "I thought we'd find ancient drums or a prehistoric air raid siren to kick-start some sonic cascade."

"Will it work without the smaller Ark from the King's Chamber?" she asks.

"Hope so." He's already pulling gadgets from his bag like a retro Mary Poppins.

She squats beside him. "What's the plan, MacGyver?"

He pauses. "Ah, you know—fire up an extinct society's longitudinal wave emitter, topple a secret society, and make it home for the Padres' season opener."

Cassian strides into the crystal woodland, stopping before a tuning fork taller than him. "We're gonna bring down the pyramid with five pounds of air pressure."

He flips open a beat-up laptop and connects it to the shredded guitar amp at the base of a tuning fork. He loads a synth module and plays an F sharp above middle C. The note rings out like a synthpop pad through the stone hall.

He tweaks dials, fattening the sound with digital processors. Satisfied, he hands us earplugs. "You'll need these."

He cranks up the volume. The tone blares. It hurts. We shove in the earplugs.

Nothing happens—no Neanderthal feedback loops.

He frowns and adds an overtone an octave below. The sound vibrates through me. Did an iMac just boot up in heaven? Still nothing.

He kills the tone. The tuning forks ring softly.

"Uh, guys." Andromeda holds up a walkie. "Hate to break up the science fair, but Metatron's inbound from the north. He found us."

Well, that's not good.

Her face is a mask of concern. "How can we help?"

"What did the builders know?" Cassian's eyes dart around. "It's an acoustic system. Look at these tuning forks!"

I feel useless. Egyptology isn't helping here.

"It's not strong enough," he says, pacing.

A loud ping breaks the tension. Andromeda's satphone just died, powering down. She shrugs. "So much for documenting."

Cassian freezes, eyes boring into her, disoriented. "Vibration," he announces, then mutters under his breath, "trust the vibes …"

She steps forward. "Cassian?"

"Andromeda Dey, you're a wild genius."

She points to herself in confusion.

"Idiot!" He smacks his forehead. "It's not *volume*—it's resonance. *Vibration!*"

He points at a giant crystal wrapped in a golden caduceus helix. "What if the caduceus … what if exciting the crystals *is* the jump start? They're not batteries! They're loudspeakers! We need to *reverse* the piezoelectric effect."

"Speakers? They're rocks," I protest.

He grins wildly. "Ever heard a bell? It's not a speaker. Don't you see? We're inside the world's largest vibraphone."

Andromeda sighs. "Less cryptic, please."

"You can't just blast a Skid Row concert in here. We need to agitate the crystals."

"How?"

Cassian points at her pouch. "Your phone uses piezoelectric

speakers, crystals that vibrate when electric current passes through them. This tech is in everyone's pocket."

Andromeda blinks. "You're saying my phone is Atlantean tech?"

He nods eagerly. "This much quartz could produce sound louder than a rock show."

Cassian rummages through his backpack and pulls out a compact, high-voltage function generator. "This little guy can output precise frequencies with enough voltage to excite the crystals."

He unspools a roll of copper wire. "Help me connect these to the caducei on the largest crystals. The gold wraps will serve as electrodes, allowing us to apply the electric field directly across the quartz."

We get to work, carefully attaching the wires to the gold coils with tape. I feel like Dr. Frankenstein wiring up inanimate life forms, waiting for the spark of life.

As she connects the last wire, Andromeda asks, "Do we have enough power?"

Cassian nods. "It's only a jump start. Nature will take over."

He moves to his equipment. "Now, we'll set the generator to output an alternating current at a specific frequency—I'm betting on F sharp. If I'm wrong—well—we'll have crystal confetti."

"An opera singer breaking a glass," Andromeda says. "Sounds safe."

He looks at us. "Ready?"

We cover our soft tissue the best we can.

He flips the switch.

118

I DON'T HEAR ANYTHING. *Did it work?*

"Oh, there's tone, all right," Cassian assures. "Feel that? It's below our hearing range."

A low, barely perceptible buzz fills the air. I feel a tingling sensation as if the room is vibrating. The resonance grows in my chest, filling the chamber. Other crystals start vibrating in unison. The entire quartz forest is coming alive. The tuning forks are joining in. I feel it in my bones. I remember the tuning fork back in Tesla's hotel room. Its sound was haunting. But *this*? These gigantic forks are making a wall of sonic magnificence I never knew existed. It's kind of terrifying.

Glittering dust is falling at the dark end of the Void, shaking loose from the ceiling.

"We can boost the resonance." Cassian is reaching for the guitar.

"How?" Andromeda asks.

"*We* can boost it!" he repeats, eyes shining as he cranks the volume on the amp.

Cassian slashes a painful power chord. A dissonant blast rips through the Void, making us wince.

"That's F minor," Andromeda yells over the cacophony. "You gotta barre the second fret!"

"You play guitar?" I blurt out.

She blushes. "Bangles cover band. Kids back at the commune weren't allowed on social media."

Cassian's jaw drops. "You were Susannah Hoffs?"

She nods, looking sheepish.

"Be still, my teenage heart," Cassian says.

He lifts the guitar and plays a proper F sharp. The sound thickens, and the tuning forks rumble louder.

"More!" Cassian shouts. "We gotta boost it! We gotta sing!" He belts out an off-key warble.

He's wailing like a drunken pirate, chest out like Pavarotti, searching for the resonant match.

I stare at him like he's lost his marbles.

But when he hits the elusive note, it's obvious. The whole chamber vibrates. He mauls the strings like he's in a metal band, and the Void rocks. The resonance pummels my body as Andromeda joins in, throwing her alto one octave higher, nose scrunching up in a primordial yell.

The air becomes electric. Her hair begins to lift. Every crystal is visibly buzzing. The giant tuning forks are getting *intense*, a low-pitch howling. Suddenly, the floor trembles. Dust rains down from above.

Cassian raises a hand. "Keep singing!"

What is he, the damn Phantom of the Opera?

Great. The fate of the world rests on my ability to carry a pitch. Nature has a twisted sense of humor. We bellow as the guitar rages.

We hold the note in sustained resonance as Cassian cranks the EQ knob. The tone sears down the chamber like hellfire. The crystals are shaking, almost blurry, ringing out with a deafening throb.

Farther down, in the dark end of the chamber, something's happening. Oh, wait. I was wrong. It's not falling dust. It's ripples of white lightning in the granite—glittering flecks of electricity in the pitch-blackness!

The quartz is responding ... in the granite and the crystals.

White plasma filaments are zapping between the caduceus heads down through the crystal forest like gods chattering in Morse code. An eerie glow reveals the cavernous Void.

"Hit the harmonic!" Cassian shrieks at Andromeda over the crushing amplitude, pointing up. "Hit the fifth!"

She understands instantly. Music is math. With a screwed-up face, she arcs up her pitch, a vocal explosion with the force of a thousand myths.

A powerful grip locks her jaw, and we sway at the sudden escalation. The crystals blare. A soft, golden light is filling the chamber. The Ark is awakening.

I'm transfixed.

Runaway resonance spills down the star shaft like a nuclear explosion, ripping into the upper acoustic lofts above the King's Chamber like a sonic tidal wave. The bass wobbles and groans in deep, rhythmic pulses that I feel more than hear.

Then it goes truly berserk.

It blasts down the Grand Gallery below us like a train horn, cascading and amplifying out of control at each nested oscillator, kicked up at every stage, defying all proportion and logic. The pyramid shakes as the ungodly resonance spreads to the subterranean chamber, gripping the bedrock, where the miracle occurs—the handshake with the planet itself.

I'm certain the whole pyramid will collapse.

Then, without warning, a massive surge courses through the system. The crystals emit a blinding shriek, and a sonic shockwave blasts through the chamber, knocking us off our feet. Our flashlights and electronics explode with sparks, and we're plunged into complete darkness.

All is silent.

A whooshing sound sucks below us like the Earth inhaling a titanic breath. I can't see anything. We freeze. Has it stopped? The Void is dimming, the rippling quartz ebbing back into total darkness. The pyramid still trembles with a low rumbling. The air is full of dust. I only hear our heavy breathing in the blackness.

Have we failed?

BOOM!

Like a bolt from Zeus, a violent plasma arc snaps between the Ark's wings with a deafening clap. Liquid mercury lifts above the rim. A lightning bolt rips overhead, slapping the gold windings on the granite wall with a shattering *crack*. White sparks shower us, and we cower in terror.

"Time to go," I curse, shoving them toward the exit. "Go. Go. Go!"

We sprint through the crackling caducei of the crystal trees, now ringing louder than ever, each a mini plasma arc. Behind us, the mercy seat pulses lightning arcs with loud pops, strobing light illuminating the square opening at the far end. Adrenaline surges. We scramble through the turmoil, slipping on polished stone as bolts of white-hot plasma leap from the Ark in all directions, accompanied by a staccato chorus of sizzling snaps.

Nikola Tesla's fire.

"Don't touch the walls!" Cassian roars.

He slides feetfirst into the descending passage like a baseball player going for home and disappears down the slick stone, picking up speed in the darkness. Andromeda follows, vanishing swiftly out of sight.

I'm the last to exit the Void. A massive bolt zaps the gold-striped wall a few feet from my head, and plasma explodes. I dive headfirst into the passage through a curtain of white sparks.

"Yeehaw!" Cassian whoops as he cowboys down the smooth granite.

We actually did it.

119

Giza Plateau, Egypt

SAND TREMBLES beneath an Egyptian guard's feet. *"Earthquake!"* he shouts in Arabic, panic strangling his voice. He stands at a makeshift security checkpoint on the far edge of the Giza Plateau.

A Targeting Division agent braces beside him, feeling the tremors. He gazes at the distant Great Pyramid, slipping on his black sunglasses in the twilight. His neural implant chirps behind his ear. In fluent Cairene Arabic, he addresses the cowering guard. *"There's intense electromagnetic activity coming off the pyramid. Who's inside?"*

A deep, otherworldly thrum pulses from the monument, intensifying. The guard's face twists with fear. *"The old gods have returned!"* he cries out, then bolts.

Across the plateau, staff recoil in terror, then scatter, fleeing into the dangerous blackout of Cairo.

Every agent in the division receives a new telepathic command to converge on Giza. Metatron's clarion voice pierces their minds like the horns of the Rapture:

THEY ARE INSIDE THE PYRAMID.

120

The Great Pyramid
Tony Koviak

GUNSHOTS ECHO like thunder into the limestone passage from outside as I stumble toward the Great Pyramid's exit.
This is bad. Really bad. Why is there shooting?
I worm through the gaping hole and step into the gathering dusk. Andromeda and Cassian exited before me; now they're nowhere in sight.
At the base of the pyramid, bodies lie motionless in a heap, their outlines barely visible in the dim light. Egyptian guards. MI6 agents. My friends are dead down there.
Please. Not this way.
Adrenaline surges, and I lurch forward, desperately scanning the grim scene for a woman with cropped hair.
One of the bodies groans and rolls over, blood streaming from his face. It's Lord Mark. He fires into the darkness.
"*Run!*" Lord Mark shouts, squeezing off three more shots toward Cairo.
I follow his line of sight. Targeting agents are charging from two hundred yards away, emerging from the shadowy slums. Leading them is Metatron in a full sprint.
"Up here!" a woman shrieks above me.

I whirl around. Andromeda and Cassian are scrambling up the pyramid's north face like frightened mountain goats.

"Not up!" I shout. "We'll be trapped!"

"We're already trapped!" Andromeda points frantically as agents close in from every direction.

A gunshot rings out, and a chunk of limestone explodes inches from me. *Whoa!* Another bullet whizzes over my shoulder.

Okay—up it is.

I leap and grab the jagged stone, my hands scraping raw as I claw for holds. *Come on, Tony, move!*

In frantic bounds, I catch up to Andromeda. *Crack!* Another gunshot ricochets. Cassian climbs to our side. "Don't look down!" he yells. "Climb!"

We're scaling the sheer face, and seeing anything is difficult. The ledges are narrow and crumbling. One slip, and we're history. Yeah, I'm trying not to think about the thousands of people who've died climbing the pyramid, *under ideal conditions.*

Us? We're recklessly flying up.

Halfway to the top, I dare a glance back. Cairo is a black sea of bonfires and headlights, filled with the distant roar of mob shouting. The western sky glows purple and amber.

Then I see him—Metatron reaches the pyramid's base at full speed. With a single leap, he clears a six-foot block and starts an animalistic climb, keeping perfect eye contact with me through his aviators. A chill grips me.

"We gotta move," I say.

Andromeda looks down. Her eyes bulge, the color draining from her freckled cheeks. Not sure if it's the heights or the assassin galloping up with eye contact.

We scramble upward, hands bleeding. The summit looms against the sky. The gunshots have stopped; I think they're corralling us. Andromeda's foot slips, and she teeters on the edge. I grab her.

A memory flashes—me as a kid in Giza, Dad coaxing me up this same slope. "One step at a time, Tony. The view from the top is always worth it."

I take a breath and find my footing.

Exhausted and sputtering, we haul ourselves onto the flat

summit—a fifteen-foot-square platform. The weathered blocks are rough and uneven, with deep gaps between them. Not ideal for a showdown with an elite killer.

Atop the pyramid, I scan all four faces, desperate for a way down. Targeting agents are climbing up all of them, closing in like a noose.

"He's going to kill us!" Andromeda cries with terror.

I grip her shoulders and look at Cassian. The hair on my arms is standing up, tingling with static. "Remember how Allied pilots wouldn't fly over the pyramids because their instruments went haywire?"

Cassian's eyes ignite. "The tip of the scalar funnel. We're in the aetheric stress zone."

If I'm going out, it won't be on my knees. "When he gets up here, we need to be ready."

121

METATRON'S FOOTSTEPS echo twenty feet away. My stomach is in my throat.

From our hidden spot, a couple of blocks down one corner, I glimpse his arm swing a pistol up into thin air. He moves silently across the empty platform, then drops to a knee with a violent head shake. Something's happening with his tech. He's pressing his temples and pounding his scalp like he's in agony. There's a lot of technological chirping.

Andromeda puts her hand on my shoulder to steady herself, and I get a big shock. Energy is flowing up here.

Metatron peers over the far edge, his back to us, hunting. He sees something below and crouches, gazing down.

Now or never.

With catlike steps, I pad over behind him. Summoning all my strength, I unleash the mother of all kicks. He spins just as my foot sweeps the pistol from his grasp, sending it flying into the abyss.

He pulls back his stinging arm and looks up at me as my second kick lands on his temple. The aviators vanish into the night sky.

I draw back in terror. Where his eyes should be, there's only a thin curve of silver metal anchored deeply into grotesque empty sockets—some sensor array implanted directly into his brain.

What the *fuck?*

In my fright, I hesitate, then attempt another kick. He catches my heel, yanking me down onto the hard stones. Pain jolts through me.

Cassian rushes him, pistol drawn, firing deafening gunshots. Metatron dodges with superhuman agility, then lunges, knocking the gun from Cassian's hands and locking him in a grapple.

Cassian slams a small device into Metatron's neck and shouts, "Have a Red Bull, Darth!"

There's a flash of light—a jolt of electricity tears through Metatron.

Enraged, he slaps a nylon patch onto Cassian's neck. The mesh glows neon. Cassian collapses, paralysis overtaking him. Foam is bubbling from his lips as veins bulge on his forehead.

Metatron turns to me.

I glance around the uneven terrain. In the dusk, I hear running footsteps. Andromeda is charging with a warrior's cry.

Metatron twists, catching her arm, hurling her over the edge like a rag doll. Her scream fades into the twilight.

She's gone.

I cry out, grabbing Metatron in a chokehold. But I'm no match for the world's most elite operative, even with his enhancements faltering.

In an instant, I'm slammed to the ground. I try to stand, but Metatron brutally kicks me down, looming over me, his eyeless face a horror in the low light. He straddles me, unleashing a flurry of hateful blows. Fists hammer into flesh and bone—ribs, face, shoulders.

I'm a bloody, sputtering mess under his assault.

He stands, pressing a boot onto my face, grinding my cheek into the stone. I can't breathe.

Now, I'm being forced to kneel. God, it hurts to move. Something's placed on my head, a thin black crown with glistening nodules. Am I being tortured? Made into a targeting agent? What? The Angel of the Veil lowers his hollow sockets to my battered face.

Triumphant chirping emanates from the back of his skull. I gasp for breath, hot blood trickling from my lips. I'm numb. My scalp tingles as powerful euphoria sweeps through me like a drug.

His neural implants are reaching into my mind like tendrils of ice. I feel them all. A rabid presence. Like staring into madness, and it's staring back. Thousands of intelligences—fractalized, malevolent, and all-seeing. Hungry and methodical. *Alien.* I'm naked before them.

I'm not being interrogated. They're here to tear my mind apart.

I try to get up, flailing for survival, but the galaxy of AIs flares like the sun, forcing me down.

When Metatron speaks aloud, his real voice is unnaturally deep and layered with bizarre, artificial overtones. "Your father looked beyond the veil."

He lowers his chin, witchy hair brushing my face, voice like mockery, "You cannot even comprehend the Nephilim."

"Nephilim this." Andromeda drives her orichalcum dagger through Metatron's back, straight into his heart.

His head jerks up with a distorted exhale of oscillating tones. His body scorpions, arms flung wide like a scarecrow. The metal sensor trembles at the red roots of his eye sockets. Fluid drains down his cheeks. He staggers, and his windswept hair reveals six frenzied neural chips embedded in his skull, like three sets of wings. They overload and spark, bursting into flames.

The AIs are screaming in my head. Existential. Frantic. *They're sentient.*

I see everything.

I can see the ultrasensory vision of the dark horizon rising as Metatron goes over the edge into the abyss.

He calls out in ancient Sumerian, "AN-ME-EN-NE-EN."

We are The Gods.

His facial bones hit the limestone with a sickening crush of metal and blood, feet arcing over him. *I feel it all.* The Voice of God —the violent rip of his dislocating limbs and screaming oscillations as he cartwheels down the slope of the Great Pyramid.

Howls erupt from down below. Targeting agents are wailing some collective torment directly into my brain.

122

The Void

IN THE MADNESS of the Void, the chamber reeks of sulfur and heat. Plasma discharges shoot from the Ark in all directions, like the jagged lightning legs of a colossal spider.

A senior Archangel agent stands mesmerized. *How can this be possible?*

He twists toward his junior Archon partner, who is reaching up to the Ark. They recoil, realizing their peril, and turn to flee as the acoustic crush envelops them. It compresses their chests, sucking the breath away. The pressure in their heads is unspeakable. AI chips rip from their scalps in flashes of red circuitry, dragging their minds away. Their faces glow. Eardrums burst as they collapse onto the cold granite.

Streams of liquid mercury spin up from the Ark, forming impossibly fast toroidal vortices that trace invisible magnetic fields, threading the glowing spark gaps above each caduceus. Within the blur of these silver orbits, points of plasma ball lightning crackle into existence, growing into a constellation of miniature stars that blind the agents. The fabric of spacetime tears above them.

Within this giant atom of white-hot energy, their bodies snap up into suspended levitation. Limbs shatter at unnatural angles along unseen cymatic pathways as if held aloft by incomprehensible forces.

They shake apart.

123

The Top of the Great Pyramid
Tony Koviak

I FEEL EARTH BENEATH ME, the sky flowing through me.

A harmonic pulse rises up from the planet, surging through the pyramid. It's alive with the song of Earth.

"Tony!" Andromeda falls to my side and yanks the circlet off my head. The visions evaporate. My scalp burns.

I taste blood pooled under my cheek. I must look bad; she's trying to hide her concern. *Am I dying?* Talking hurts, but I manage. "I saw you go over. How did you—"

"I don't know," she says, breathless. "Hit an outcrop below—just enough to break my fall. Lanky limbs." She lets out a shaky laugh.

I wince. "The agents. We have to get down." Then I see Cassian—he's seizing violently, face purple. I reach out. "Cassian, hang on, buddy."

Andromeda shrieks when she sees him. She rushes over and rips the patch from his neck. Cassian exhales, his face sweaty and turning pale. She cradles his head for a moment, then hurries to the edge, peering down. Her face falls. "Tony! There's a lot of them!"

I close my eyes, accepting the end. My body is too battered to resist. These might be my last moments. Any second now, they'll crest the summit. Doesn't matter anymore. Andromeda is back at Cassian's side, weeping softly. Joy or sorrow? Maybe she loves him.

It's okay to die, right?

My dad's here with me now.

Something dazzling catches my eye—Andromeda is waving her hand. A faint trail of golden sparks drops from it like fairy dust.

Beneath me, the vibration intensifies. In the distance, a low earthquake rumbles, and the other two pyramids emit shock waves with a bottomless drone. Dust billows off their slopes; the sand ripples.

Tesla coils. Tuning forks.

Andromeda is holding her sparkling hand before her face, spellbound. Time stands still. She brings her fingertips together, then opens them with a burst of sparks, like a Fourth of July sparkler. They're soft and delicate. I watch as they fall on Cassian, enthralled by strings of soft energy pulling between her fingers like electric taffy.

Cassian stands up. "Look."

To the east, a slow-motion wave of city lights illuminates buildings across Cairo. The leading edge travels outward, powering everything in its wake, like a shimmering ripple in an ink-black pond.

I smile through the pain and force myself up on shaky legs, breathless at the sight of Cairo unveiling itself in a tidal wave of light. I'm not missing this, even if it kills me.

Andromeda's wildflower pouch is buzzing. A tear falls as she pulls out the dead satphone. The home screen is booting up, the battery symbol glowing neon green. A short, fatalistic laugh escapes her. She stands on the trembling stones, and the phone clatters away.

Cassian's face is a symphony of emotions as he gazes into the last violet haze.

My skin stings—not painful, just ... odd. A weird, burnt-metallic taste fills my mouth. Not blood. It tastes like how astronauts describe the smell of space.

Suddenly, I see ... *something*. A distortion in the air, like a rivulet of water—there, then gone. I rub my eyes. Hallucination?

"Please tell me I'm not the only one seeing this," Cassian says.

Reality glitches again. Okay, that one was real.

And—oh, wow—that can't be good.

The space around me is warping, like looking through a slowly cracking mirror, the cracks shifting and moving. Can't say I like the look of that. Like heatwave distortions, but structured. The air twists into a gridlike pattern, constantly reassembling.

What in the actual—

I squeeze my eyes shut.

Open.

Shut.

Still there!

The wind just picked up. Hard gusts are blowing around us. The temperature has dropped, and my breaths are visible.

Colors bleed into my vision, hues I've never experienced like prisms breaking apart. It's mesmerizing and disorienting. *Whoa.* Tiny sparks of light are popping in and out around us, like fireflies. Then they're gone.

The pyramid shakes underfoot, and I realize we're at the apex of the interface, the focal point of the pyramid's scalar wave pulses.

The fabric of spacetime is being cut to ribbons.

Time feels ... wrong. My stomach drops. Moments stretch like elastic, then snap back. I sway. Oh, this is trippy. Andromeda is several feet away, moving toward me unnaturally—her motion a stilted judder, looping like a bad video feed. Her mouth moves, but the words are delayed. I shut my eyes and gasp, terrified out of my skull. When I open them, she's normal again, but her face is brighter, flashing with colors, peering into a rift filled with blinding waveforms, her voice dreamlike.

"Everything is the light."

I understand then—I don't know how—more intuition than knowledge.

Time isn't real.

For a split second, I see ... shapes that shouldn't exist, forms that defy all logic. They're there and gone so fast I can't be sure, but it leaves me with overwhelming ... awe.

They begin to materialize more coherently. A small sphere appears and grows into some kind of hypercube, angles rotating and twisting through dimensions my mind can't grasp. It morphs again—tetrahedrons folding into dodecahedrons, spheres warping into toroids. Some very *real* thing is passing through our lower space—real because I'm looking right at it.

The object is both approaching and receding as if distance has lost all meaning. Light bends around it, and colors refract unpredictably. I don't think this is from around here.

And then ... *holy smokes*. There's intelligence here—primordial. Others. I don't know how I know that—figures blurred across time, just an instant—gone.

Scalar physics. Aetheric dimension. A vision of higher realms? Whatever it is, the phenomenon subsides, reducing to occasional blips of high strangeness. Not fast enough, though. More shapes spill through, like weird higher-dimensional debris—objects collapsing and twisting into Möbius strips, then just vanishing.

Cassian dares to reach into the darkest black imaginable, and his arm points back at him from an impossible vector. He grunts and yanks it back so hard he almost falls over. He's flexing his hand.

"Can you see it, too?" Andromeda asks, the wind carrying trails of golden fairy sparkles from her fingertips. The three of us huddle together, trying to anchor ourselves to reality.

It's gone.

Cassian's tone is holy. "We're coupled with the aether. It's in the ionosphere," he says, turning skyward.

An aurora ripples from the heavens, folds over itself, and then spreads over Cairo like a billowing shawl.

―――

VICTORIA STANDS at the base of the Great Pyramid, staring up at its illuminated face. Floodlights bathe the ancient stones in a harsh glow, and her gray eyes mirror the swirling auroras overhead.

Halfway up the slope, Targeting Division agents are immobilized on the limestone blocks. They seem to convulse in agony. Some stare at the undulating plasma sheets above, weapons slipping from their grasp and clattering down the steps.

Her forces have secured the Giza Plateau. British troops are scaling the pyramid.

124

IF A HORRIBLE DEATH IS IMMINENT, I suppose that's a decent thing to witness before I go.

Shouldn't the targeting agents be up here by now?

"They're here!" Andromeda shouts, oddly excited as she looks over the edge. Wait, she's happy about this? "They're here!"

Curiosity beats exhaustion, and I hobble over to look down. Below, Victoria's forces are apprehending the targeting agents—they're spasming, blood streaming down their necks, expressions vacant. Medics climb toward us. In the distance, a fleet of Chinook helicopters with Union Jacks hover over the Sphinx, rotors thwapping away. British infantry swarms the Giza Plateau.

I don't believe it. We're saved.

I blink. *We're saved.* I really didn't want to die today. Overcome with emotion, we collapse onto our backs beneath the peaceful auroras.

Andromeda's ruddy face glows with the dancing light. She smiles wistfully. "We're hanging out on a Tesla tower."

Cassian laughs, half disbelief, half joy. "Yeah—yes, we are."

"The philosopher's stone, Cass," Andromeda notes. "Tesla, Newton, Hermes—energy alchemy. That was a hell of a jump start you pulled off in there."

After a long moment, she seems to consider something else. "Audacious. Practical. Dangerously committed. *Capricorn*—you're a Capricorn, Cassian Wilder."

"Took you long enough."

A freckled cheek pulls up with delight. "Huh."

Cassian studies the majesty overhead. "Guess we're gonna need reverse light switches. Everything's just *on* now."

125

Prague, Czech Republic
The Demiurge

THE DEMIURGE STANDS at his tall window in the Kinský Palace, watching celebrations consume the square below. Lights are coming on everywhere. The city has gone mad.

Naive. We're saving your civilization. We're the keepers of the flame. Without us, you're—

A phone rings on his wooden desk. He lifts the receiver to hear a frantic American woman.

"Hello? Are you there? What's the plan? We need to act *now!*"

He lights a cigarette, exhaling slowly as he turns to the astronomical clock across the square with its zodiacal dial. Death's hourglass has run out.

After a long pause, he replies in a bland, detached voice. "We measure our designs in millennia. Subversion is only one means to an end. They aren't prepared for what's coming. Disappear and wait a while. A new age is upon us—they'll be reset, forgetting everything as before. We'll usher in a golden paradise when—"

His satphone buzzes in his coat pocket. The caller ID reads METATRON.

He hangs up the receiver and answers the satphone. "I watched you die," he hisses, disbelief edging his tone.

A familiar voice responds—MI6 director Victoria Bennet.

AT THE BASE of the Great Pyramid, Victoria Bennet stands over the twisted body. Lord Mark looks on beside her, clothing torn, face grim and smeared with blood. At their feet lies Metatron's crumpled corpse, a gash in the back of his skull where a neural chip has been ripped away.

She holds up the bloodstained AI hardware, its LEDs flickering angrily. Her eyes harden.

"We're going to show them your hidden hand—everything you've kept from them. We're taking back this world."

A heavy silence settles. From Metatron's lifeless lips comes a guttural sound—a soft, eerie crackle, like a cigarette flaring in his throat. The Demiurge's voice emanates as harmonic oscillations gurgling from the dead man's blue-tinged mouth.

"We are everywhere."

She places the blinking chip on the pyramid's limestone and crushes it under her heel.

EPILOGUE

Journal entry, six months later
Tony Koviak

TIME FLIES when you're rewriting history.

Dad always said the job of an anthropologist is to understand our past to help shape our future. I never quite understood that until now.

Everything has changed.

Where do I even start?

Pyramids are a good place. Our Giza stunt worked better than we imagined. Around the globe, ancient pyramidal structures shook to life. Forgotten mounds in the remotest hinterlands of Africa, America, and Asia woke up, to everyone's shock.

The new MIT pyramid gang tells me a planetary network of megalithic receivers—obelisks and ancient mountaintops—was tuned to receive the long-awaited resonance. Zero-point energy surged, converting into pure electricity.

Limitless power flooded the planet.

They nearly fainted when they discovered Tesla's scalar physics could create actual wormholes, and that there's more energy in a teacup than in our star. They say teleportation is now a possibility, that we can create matter at will, straight from the zero-point field. It's all waves and resonant frequencies. They tell us the aether engineers will need to think like musicians.

Gravity is optional.

I'm picking up the science quickly—two hours a day now.

The paint hasn't even dried on the prismatic resonance labs, and we already have prototypes that use geometry to manipulate aetheric waveforms: *harmonic lattice projectors … reality forge fabricators … scalar resonant crystals.* Some are even handheld, allowing folks to slide standing-wave nodes through the lattice on the go, as if painting their desired reality.

Lose your keys? Simply tap your phase-pen to recollimate their standing wave signature and—*zing*—they're back in your hand from wherever they wandered off to … under the couch … or in the Pleiades. Distance is meaningless in the waveforms.

Now, don't get me wrong: surfing the aether is great, but can someone please tell me how to resonate a decent pizza? What, no scalar physics culinary division? Fine. Just mute the laws of thermodynamics until five p.m. and we'll call it even.

Oh, and the ancients were right. We think consciousness lives forever there, too. We may never really die, which is exhilarating. And terrifying.

Then there are the scalar interferometric telescopes for the *big* stuff. For serious deep spacetime perturbations. Those … scare me.

But they'll play a critical role in the very near future.

International scalar accords have capped local lattice displacement to five percent of the natural node positioning to avoid systemic phase horizon cascades. After the Shanghai incident, all systems now include reservoirs—graphene-boron honeycomb matrices that absorb runaway scalar energy resonance. Last thing we need is another asteroid belt where Earth once was. Yeah … we should probably talk about that asteroid belt sometime.

According to the eggheads, this means we technically qualify as a Type IV civilization on the Kardashev scale, some classification system. I guess leap-frogging the first three types is a big deal or something. Fifth-dimensional aether juice is no joke. Still have no idea what that means.

When they began using big-brain MIT phrases like "we're about to sorta become the *Star Wars* galaxy"—yeah, let's just say Andromeda Dey went full-tilt. The John Williams score was stuck in my head for days after all her celebrating.

It is pretty exciting.

Back home, we thought we'd have to take America back, revolution-style. We braced ourselves for apocalyptic chaos: wars, famines, a lost generation. But we underestimated the power of, well, truth. Once people learned about the Veil Society, they were shaken, then furious. So, they did the logical thing: they cleaned house.

All those puppet politicians found themselves abruptly de-puppeted. The CIA, FBI, IRS, and every other Big Brother agency? Dissolved.

The Demiurge was never found.

The Mothers of Darkness were never found.

For the past three months, I've been cataloging the Labyrinth of Egypt. We uncovered something deep inside that will melt people's minds. I could tell you, but what's the use? You'd never believe me.

And, oh yeah, those big triangles? Our best scientists and engineers are now custodians of our shiny new—er, old—power grid, trying to figure out how to run it. It's a fixer-upper, but seriously robust. After millennia, it's still going. We're even building new pyramids based on ancient designs. There'll be one in Texas, another in Ohio, and one up on the mountain where the NSA's Utah Data Center used to sit. Several more are going up across Europe and Asia. Australia has already nicknamed their future tetrahedron the Shockodile Dundee. Latin America has so many damn operational legacy pyramids, they don't even *need* new ones.

These are the most significant public works projects in history —*our* history, anyway. That's why Dr. Cassian Wilder is heading up the whole thing: Project Tesla.

He's making sure they're cataclysm-proof.

For once, it feels like humanity is stepping forward without tripping over its own feet.

And yet, here I am, scribbling in a diary like some teenager pondering his place in all this. Maybe it's because I still can't fully grasp that we pulled it off, that we yanked humanity back from the brink and set it on a path of literal enlightenment. Yeah, we did that. Feels good, man.

But there's serious work ahead. All this tech development is being rushed for a reason. We've got an impending pole shift, and we don't intend to be Atlantis 2.0—or is it 20.0? Faust was right. Who knows how long this has been happening? We can't afford twelve thousand more years of amnesia.

But that's another story.

Bryant Park, New York City
Tony Koviak

Manhattan is crisp on this chilly fall morning. It's the October equinox.

I stroll into the quiet nook of Bryant Park known as Tesla Corner. A statue of Nikola Tesla stands where he once fed pigeons daily—the bronze glints in dappled sunlight. Two blocks east, the New Yorker Hotel looms.

Andromeda and Cassian are here, all dressed up, holding hands and exchanging smiles that only they seem to understand. They're engaged now. Blows my mind. A lot can happen in six months. I suspected they had a thing. Their chemistry was, dare I say, electric—a perfectly nerdy match.

"Ready?" Andromeda asks, her big eyes sparkling. She pulls an old tin box and a tuning fork from her wildflower pouch. Of course, it's tuned to F sharp. She places it inside the box.

"I owe you a replacement, Mr. Tesla," she says, glancing up at his statue with a smile.

Cassian steps forward, holding a chip of Giza limestone. He looks at it thoughtfully before adding it to the tin. "A bit of the 'ol natural medium for you, Nicky."

My turn.

I reach into my coat pocket and pull out a small quartzite ankh my dad always kept on his desk. It feels heavy—not in weight but in significance. "Seems fitting," I say, placing it alongside the other items.

"Tesla's electric oscillator, cool," Cassian muses, giving me a sailor's grin.

I roll my eyes. "Ankh."

Together, we kneel and claw into the soil beneath Tesla's statue. Andromeda sets the box deep, and we bury it.

She pats the dirt. I notice her engagement ring—a smooth band with a reddish patina, an "ancient-future" aesthetic. *Wait*—I recognize it. I saw a bunch just like it down in the Labyrinth of Egypt.

Her ring is orichalcum—and it's twelve thousand years old.

"Klepto," I mutter, shaking my head.

She shrugs, freckles upturned, nose crinkled.

"You better name your first kid after me," I tease.

"I was thinking, Fabian," Cassian says, steepling his fingers. "Fabian Wilder."

"Stop," she laughs, slugging his arm.

A thought strikes me. "Might want to brush up on Greek myths. Andromeda's kid has an electrifying name." I fist-bump Cassian and tousle her folk-rock hair.

We stand under Tesla's watchful gaze. It feels like we've come full circle.

I have a plane to catch back to Cambridge. I'd hate to miss it.

As I leave, I glance back. Cassian's wrapping up Andromeda, her head buried in her phone, probably Googling Greek myths. Tesla's outstretched hand seems to preside over them.

Yeah, Electryon would be a terrible name for a mere mortal. But Nikola—that's a damn fine name.

THANKS FOR READING

If you enjoyed this book, be sure to leave a review.

Your support greatly helps this first-time indie author compete with the juggernaut of the traditional publishing industry. Thanks for coming along on this adventure.

Illustration credits:

- Newton's prism experiment. *La Vie des Savants Illustres* by Louis Figuier, Nineteenth Century.
- Hermes Mercurius Trismegistus. Floor inlay in the Cathedral of Siena, 1480s.
- Dream Stele as recorded by Lepsius, 1800s—date unknown.
- Troy Town Trojeborg, a stone labyrinth from Visby, 1919.
- The Labyrinth of Egypt. *Turris Babel* by Athanasius Kircher, 1679.

ACKNOWLEDGMENTS

Thanks to Café Un Deux Trois and the Lyceum Theatre in New York City. Special thanks to the New Yorker Hotel for preserving the rich history of Tesla's time there. Yes, you can actually stay in room 3327. Just don't break any walls...

A warm thank you to Walther Sallaberger at the University of Munich and Nicole Brisch at the University of Copenhagen for their expertise in translating texts into ancient Sumerian Cuneiform. Both generously shared their knowledge, which does **not** constitute an endorsement of the speculative theories in this work of fiction.

Thanks to all of my beta readers who helped refine the story. Dan Larsen provided the initial copy edits.

And finally, a big salute to all the pioneers working in the speculative and alternative fields of history and science. *Yeah, this stuff's actually real.* I think Tesla himself would approve of your Faustian spirit. There are still more questions than answers. Let's collectively get to the bottom of these very real mysteries.

Oh, and ... Tesla knew.

ABOUT THE AUTHOR

Jenner Brown is a filmmaker and lifelong science and history nerd, still trying to convince his kids that flip phones were cool. He lives in Utah near two highly suspicious smart speakers. *Tesla And The Pyramid* is his first novel.

X x.com/jennerbrownX

Printed in Dunstable, United Kingdom